The Karma Sequence

A. O. Wagner

The characters and events portrayed in this book are fictitious. Any similarity to real persons, living or dead, is coincidental and not intended by the author.

No part of this book may be reproduced, or stored in a retrieval system, or transmitted in any form or by any means, electronic, mechanical, photocopying, recording, or otherwise, without express written permission of the publisher.

Second Edition

Copyright © 2022, 2024 by A. O. Wagner
All rights reserved.
ISBN: 9798367744941
Imprint: Independently published

**Cover design by James T. Egan
of Bookfly Design**

To my sister Lone

CONTENTS

PROLOGUE 1
ONE 4
TWO 11
THREE 22
FOUR 33
FIVE 47
SIX 58
SEVEN 69
EIGHT 82
NINE 93
TEN 106
ELEVEN 118
TWELVE 129
THIRTEEN 140
FOURTEEN 150
FIFTEEN 160
SIXTEEN 168
SEVENTEEN 179
EIGHTEEN 190
NINETEEN 200
TWENTY 212
TWENTY-ONE 223
TWENTY-TWO 234
TWENTY-THREE 247
TWENTY-FOUR 259
TWENTY-FIVE 270
TWENTY-SIX 282
TWENTY-SEVEN 295
EPILOGUE...308
AUTHOR NOTE 311

ACKNOWLEDGMENTS

There are so many people I think of with gratitude who have made it possible for me to write this book. I would especially like to thank the following: Jonna, Erling, Peter, Lone, Anne, Rikke, Iben, Simon, Michael, Berit, Kenneth, Pia, Morten, Claus, Ulla, Jørgen, Per, Tina, Jesper, Steen, Danny, Chris, Liviu, Hildegard.

PROLOGUE

On a highway heading toward Copenhagen, a man was sitting behind the wheel of his car in the early morning traffic. He was on his way to work from his home outside Køge—a town south of the Danish capital.

Traffic flowed quietly, as it normally did. Not fast, but perfectly acceptable. On a typical day, he spent the time in the car reviewing his plan for the day and the suggestions and comments he'd prepared in the evening for his various projects.

He was in his early forties and had a relatively exciting job as a project manager in a software company, which he'd advanced to through many years of working in system development. He often missed the direct participation in designing and programming the systems the company delivered—mainly to the banking sector. But with the position he'd now advanced to, he had more responsibility and was better paid.

In his private life, he'd married a sweet woman eight years younger than himself. She worked in Køge and consequently didn't have to leave as early in the morning as he did. They'd played badminton together for many years and were both in good shape. They jogged frequently and had some exercise equipment in the basement, which he mainly used. In addition, he tried to be conscious of his diet and habits, though occasionally, there had to be space to relax and enjoy himself.

Although he had much sedentary work, with meetings and planning, he still felt he was as fit as he'd been in his twenties.

Two months earlier, he'd also paid a professional firm to prepare a full report on his health and prospects—based on an extensive questionnaire and a mouth swab he had to perform on himself and submit in an envelope he'd received from the firm. Besides a series of analyses and recommendations, the report—or *document*, as the company called it— also included predictions of which risk categories one might fall into with age, and an estimate of how old one would become. It estimated his life expectancy at ninety-two years, which he was pretty happy with. Still, he reminded himself that this was a calculation with very few inputs. Being a system developer, he understood it was a simple algorithm that did the math—there was no guarantee.

But he'd noticed one small thing in the document he'd received that looked like a mistake. After the calculated expectation of how old he'd get, there was an odd number that looked entirely out of place. The number was 15,529, and there was no indication of what it meant, so a part of his analytical mind had seen it as a technical challenge and had set about finding possible explanations—besides the most likely, that it was a mistake and that the number was completely random and insignificant. But because it stood next to the field showing life expectancy, one of his first hypotheses had been that it might be the number of days in his life.

Even before he'd divided the number by 365, he could easily see that it wouldn't give ninety-two years, and as it only showed about forty-two, it confirmed his initial assessment that it must be an error with a random value. Still, part of him couldn't shake the idea, and when he added the number to his date of birth in a spreadsheet, the result showed that he'd die on May 15th, that year.

And that was today.

When he'd seen the result, he tried to push the thought away, blaming himself for taking his own far-fetched guess seriously. The number was some sort of error; it was impossible to predict how many days a person would live. He'd promised himself not to think about it anymore and never to purchase a similar analysis again, but to rely more on his own assessments of his health and habits.

But despite his rational conclusion, the stupid document had made him spot danger everywhere the past few days. And when he looked in the rearview mirror, he could see a man in a car, two positions behind him, that he thought had also been there the day before, possibly even the day before that. Even though many people went to work using the same highway every morning, he still found it strange to spot the same car at the same distance, two—maybe three—days in a row. Especially since the car had also been there when he went home from work. It was difficult to dismiss as pure coincidence.

As he squinted to see if he could get a better look at the man behind the wheel, the traffic came to a stretch of roadwork that had been going on for a while and where oncoming traffic was being diverted onto one of the lanes on the same side as the many cars heading into town.

In the mirror, it looked like the man was trying to signal to him with open mouth and wild gestures.

He shifted his focus back to the road ahead, but before he could react, he realized he'd crossed into the wrong lane, and a split second later, he collided head-on with a large truck going at high speed in the opposite direction.

ONE

Dan walked the last stretch to the almost-finished City Tower after having parked his car two hundred meters down the street. He didn't want to leave it next to the construction site, where building work was still being carried out and where a rogue brick could damage it. Before entering the area, he stood for a few minutes, looking up at the imposing structure facing the waterfront at the far end of Copenhagen's Nordhavn district. A lot had changed in this part of the city since Dan had been there on a bike ride ten years ago when he'd come to see the container port.

The building was as round as a thick silo—a seven-story cylinder with a curved glass facade. He estimated its diameter at about 40 meters, which would correspond to a circumference of about 125 meters and a floor area of 1,256 square meters—if his quick calculations in his head were correct. Most floors looked empty, waiting for companies to move in and fill the unused space with desks, cabinets, employees, and projects. On one of the lower floors, he could see two people in white coveralls who looked like they were laying cables—perhaps for power or computer networks. A yellow construction crane, which had probably been used to lift concrete elements and glass facades during construction, still stood next to the building. It was lifting a heavy machine, no longer needed at the site, onto a flatbed truck that would move it away. Three men in hard hats maneuvered the hovering machine, positioning it correctly on the trailer, while a fourth signaled with his arms to the crane operator. Before long, the crane itself would be dismantled and removed.

It was a warm Friday afternoon in early June. The sun was shining from an almost cloudless sky, and there was virtually no wind. Dan checked the clock on his phone, confirming that he was on time, and opted to take a walk around the site to view the harbor and get a look at the Sound—the strait between Denmark and Sweden.

He'd left his summer house in Liseleje—a seaside resort on the north coast of the Zealand island—a little more than an hour earlier than he needed to, but he didn't want to risk being late for the board meeting. It would be embarrassing enough without him also arriving after the meeting had begun.

It had been almost a month since he'd last been to Copenhagen—and that had only been to pick up some books from his apartment in the Østerbro district—in the city's eastern end. On that occasion, he'd considered driving to the Nordhavn district to see how far the construction had come, but had decided that it could wait for another day.

As he walked around the building, he looked out over the Sound. He caught sight of the tiny artificial islands that had been part of the city's fortifications in the old days and the twenty motionless wind turbines further out on the water.

For the last twelve months, he'd lived permanently in his small summer house and had only been in town when he had to attend meetings. On those occasions, he'd also checked that everything was okay in the apartment and if there was any mail, which there never was. From time to time, he'd spend the night in his apartment but drive straight back to the summer house the following morning: mainly because it was quieter away from the city, but probably also to keep some distance from his former life and all the bad memories.

He reflected on the past year of being isolated from everything, and how he'd had to pick up his life from the floor and start over—after the worst crisis of his life. On a lovely summer day like today, the entire process could almost feel like a dream—but not one of the good ones, and unfortunately not one of those dreams you quickly forget after waking up.

Even though he felt physically on top again, he knew there would be many situations where he would be reminded of his mistakes and the people he'd disappointed. However, the most important thing was that he'd escaped from the dark hole that he, at one point, had feared he would die in. Even though everything might not be perfect, his life was a thousand times better now than it had been when he was at his lowest point.

Today's board meeting in the Lifeline company would undoubtedly be one of those embarrassing situations he knew he would have to go through eventually. Nothing would happen by skipping it, but it was the first meeting in the new premises in the City Tower—which Dan was looking forward to seeing—and sooner or later, he would have to bite the bullet and take part again. Plus, he knew he'd feel better about himself when it was over, and he could go back to the summer house and continue his daily routine of reading, walking in the woods and by the beach, and surfing the web to get up to date on his various areas of interest.

At some later point, he would also have to plan what he wanted to do with the rest of his life, or at least with the years to come. From a financial point of view, he could easily retire now and move to a nice warm island somewhere south, if he wanted—but he estimated it would be a bit early at thirty-two. He knew he would quickly get bored to death, or even worse: that he might end up succumbing to his old addiction again, however unlikely it might be.

If that happened, he didn't doubt for a second that he would never escape the dark hole again. Eventually, it would all be over, and the hole would be filled with dirt—like the skid loader driving around outside the City Tower, leveling the area after the tracks left by the enormous machines.

What he was most nervous about at today's board meeting was seeing Michael again. It was going to feel awkward—probably for both.

It had been more than a year and a half since they'd last spoken, and the conversation had only lasted a few minutes. But he still looked forward to seeing him and hearing what he'd spent his time and energy on. Although Dan had speculated for a long time about what he wanted to say to Michael, he still didn't know exactly how to say it all—only that he needed to say he was sorry and acknowledge that Michael had been right in his reservations about selling Avaram to Ryan.

Michael hadn't been sure it was the right way to go when they agreed to sell their company four years ago. In retrospect—and with Dan's current knowledge—he would have to admit that perhaps he'd been too focused on the prospect of them both becoming multimillionaires. In contrast, Michael had been more aware of the risk of losing control over Avaram and the system they'd developed.

However, it wasn't even a given that this conversation would take place today, as Michael only attended as few board meetings as he could get away with. Still, Dan hoped Michael would be there, and he would have a chance to talk to him. Dan often missed the time at their small company—when it had been just him and Michael—where they'd tinkered on their system and coded almost around the clock. And when they hadn't been working, they'd been solving current world problems and discussing philosophical and spiritual topics—although it was probably mainly Michael who'd been interested in those things back then. It was an exciting time, and everything had been much more straightforward.

As Dan stood on the waterfront looking over the harbor, he also thought about Ryan. Unlike Michael, there was little doubt that he would attend the board meeting; after all, Ryan was Lifeline's chairman and majority shareholder, as well as the company's founder and CEO. Dan was looking forward to seeing Ryan again, too, although he was even more unsure about what to say to him than he was with Michael. But there wasn't the same risk of their meeting feeling strange, or of an awkward silence where neither of them knew what to say. Ryan was the type of person who talked all the time, and he possessed an almost aggressive optimism and drive that rubbed off on the people around him and those he worked with.

In the three years they'd known each other, Dan had always admired Ryan for his visions and ability to find opportunities and solutions; and especially his ability, and not least his determination, to implement his plans and visions—regardless of what people might think of them and him. Not that Ryan didn't think twice before he acted—he probably thought a hundred times—but he did it ten times faster than most people and then put all his resources behind turning the plan he'd come up with into reality.

Dan had often felt flattered and privileged that Ryan included him in many of his considerations and visions. And because Dan's assessments had typically influenced Ryan's plans and had, frequently, even made him change a decision or even drop an idea altogether.

Although Ryan was nineteen years older than Dan, they'd developed a friendship—also in private—after they met and after Ryan had bought Avaram. It wasn't the same friendship as Michael's and Dan's, who were the same age, had many overlapping interests, and had even known each other since high school. The best way to describe it was that Ryan had become a kind of mentor to Dan—perhaps even a role model. Dan had been inspired, and probably also a little impressed, by Ryan's panache and man-of-the-world style. But their friendship had also been an eye-opener for

Dan. He'd had to admit that he couldn't match Ryan's flamboyant lifestyle, with its frequent travel and partying—both involving disrupted circadian rhythms and lots of alcohol.

Part of the payment Dan and Michael had received for Avaram was in the form of shares in the Lifeline company. Ryan had asked them both to join the board, although Dan was usually the only one he discussed his ideas and plans with. Michael's attitude had shifted from uncertainty about whether selling Avaram was a good idea to outright dislike of Ryan, which he didn't attempt to hide from Dan.

After a few months, Michael cared even less about Ryan, which was the primary reason he only attended board meetings sporadically. And when he actually did attend, it was with a disinterested approach or—as had happened occasionally—a thinly veiled criticism of Ryan's plans and the way he was exploiting the system he'd bought from Dan and Michael.

Dan had now walked all the way around the City Tower and was back on the side where he'd started. On his way to the entrance, he passed a small group of construction workers, all wearing coveralls and hard hats with various company names and logos. They seemed to disagree about how to solve a particular task—or perhaps whether it had been done correctly. Some of them gestured and pointed around the area, exchanging suggestions and arguments in broken English, sometimes with German phrases and some words that sounded Eastern European—Polish was Dan's best bet. Dan nodded to them, and the two who saw him nodded back.

Taking a deep breath, he walked through the large glass doors that automatically opened for him and entered the empty, dark, and cool ground floor of the building. Although he was looking forward to the board meeting being over and returning to his familiar, quiet routine, he could feel that he was no longer as nervous about meeting Michael, Ryan, and the others on the board.

One last time, he reminded himself of the decision he'd made several months earlier: he didn't want to be drawn into Ryan's turbulent universe again, with all the risks that would entail.

He knew he wouldn't survive another trip down into the dark hole.

TWO

The elevator and stair shaft was a concrete silo in the center of the building, which, in combination with the steel girders around the perimeter, formed the supporting structure. The cylinder appeared to be about eight meters in diameter, and the elevator was on the side facing the entrance. As Dan walked across the empty concrete deck, he wondered what the ground level might be intended for. Perhaps there would be shops or a single big supermarket.

Above the elevator's control panel, someone had placed a sheet of A4 paper with gaffer tape. It had two words written with a thick marker pen, informing that the elevator was, unfortunately, not yet functional. Dan tried to press the button a few times before accepting that the information was correct and that he would have to bite the bullet and use the stairs. The seven floors weren't an insurmountable task either—especially now that he'd regained his former physical shape. Had it been six months ago, the very thought of struggling up the seven flights of stairs would have made him sweat and look for alternative ideas.

Dan found the door to the staircase on the opposite side of the central shaft and began the ascent. He deliberately kept a slow pace so he wouldn't appear sweaty and out of breath when he reached the top floor. When he made it to the top, a few minutes later, and opened the door to Lifeline's new offices, he felt no more exhausted than he'd felt at the bottom of the staircase.

The level had been completed with a circular inner corridor around the entire perimeter of the elevator and stair shaft. A high glass wall separated the corridor, which was approximately three meters wide, from the individual offices, and the entire space was divided into eight equally sized rooms, each with a door leading to the central corridor. Some rooms apparently had other doors connecting them directly, but if a person needed to get from one place to another, it would always be possible via the central corridor.

Although there were no people in the corridor at the moment, it looked as if it was also intended to have a social function, where people could meet and chat, perhaps over a cup of water from one of the water coolers. There were also vending machines for hot and soft drinks—but none of them had been switched on yet, and the cold drinks machine hadn't been filled.

Dan walked to the right in the corridor, searching for a room where he could sit and wait and where there might be a good view of the city and the harbor. Of the four rooms he passed, only one was in use, with fourteen people sitting at their computers. Most of their desks were positioned so the persons sitting there could enjoy the beautiful vista and avoid glare on the screens when, like today, the sun was shining through the large, curved windows. Even though everyone sat with their backs to the central corridor, Dan recognized many of them from Lifeline's old office in central Copenhagen. Most were system developers, but there were also a handful of web designers. It suited Dan just fine that they didn't see him walking by in the corridor—he didn't want to be recognized by a probably well-meaning colleague who might even get up and step out into the corridor to start a conversation with him.

Halfway around the central corridor, Dan reached the room that had to be the reception. It was somewhat evident because inside the room, behind a large desk, was a stunning woman with blonde hair, dark eyes, and red pouting lips. She was exactly the type of woman Ryan would employ as his receptionist, Dan thought. Unlike the people in the office Dan had just passed, she sat facing the door, so she could see when someone entered the room, almost enticing visitors to enter.

Two low white leather couches stood facing each other between the entrance door and the desk, which was placed at the far end, close to the curved panoramic windows facing the harbor. Dan recognized the couches from the old premises where they'd been used in a small, cozy meeting room. Now their function was obviously for guests to sit there—waiting to meet with Ryan or other Lifeline employees—while admiring the magnificent view of the harbor; and probably the view of the beautiful receptionist, too. Both views were likely deliberately intended to give an overwhelming, perhaps even intimidating, first impression of the company.

Something else that revealed to Dan that this must be the reception was the sheet of A4 paper taped to the glass door, which read 'Lifeline - reception' in the same handwriting as the note he'd seen next to the elevator.

Dan stepped through the door and walked toward the receptionist's large desk. Separating the reception from the two rooms on either side were only the enormous glass walls, which seemed to be the way all the rooms on the floor were separated. The room on the left—when looking counterclockwise—was empty, apart from a row of moving boxes lining the glass wall. But in the room on the right, Dan could see that Ryan had set up his personal office at the familiar large conference table he remembered from the old address. There was nothing in the room except the table and the twelve chairs around it, but at one end of the table was Ryan's laptop—the only evidence that it was anyone's workplace.

Ryan was there, too. He stood by the panoramic windows, with his back to the conference table, peering over the harbor, and was obviously in the middle of a phone call. Dan recognized the way Ryan was standing when he talked on the phone, headset in his ears, arms crossed, and giving little thoughtful nods—both when he listened and when he spoke.

When Dan reached the receptionist's desk, she looked up from her laptop and smiled at him. She looked great in her gray summer dress, her blonde hair gathered in a bun at the nape of her neck.

"Hello, Dan, and welcome to Lifeline's new premises," she said in a formal but welcoming voice that perfectly matched the rest of her appearance.

Dan was pretty sure he'd never seen her before and briefly wondered how she knew who he was. Maybe she remembered his face from the times he'd appeared in one of the colorful weekly magazines, on one of his and Ryan's many trips through the Copenhagen nightlife, or receptions and premieres Ryan had taken him to. Another possibility was that Ryan had given her a list of photos of the board members, so she could recognize them when they arrived and give them a slightly more personal welcome. That kind of detail would be typical for Ryan.

"I figured it must be you," she continued, as if she'd read his mind. "Ryan has told me a lot about you, and I was looking forward to meeting you. My name is Vibeke, but I'm always just called Vibs."

"Hi, Vibs—thanks for the welcome. Yes, it's certainly turned out nicely here," said Dan, looking appreciatively from side to side and out over the harbor behind her. "Have you been with the company for long?"

"Only this week," she replied. "I started a week after the first people moved out here."

She'd risen and now leaned over the desk, shaking hands with Dan. Although he kept eye contact with her, he couldn't help but notice her beautiful, slender figure. Her perfume made Dan think of Susan, whom he hadn't seen in a year and a half. He quickly stopped his thoughts in their tracks before they could upset him.

"I'm sure you'll be happy to be part of Lifeline," Dan said after she let go of his hand. "I'm here for the board meeting, but I think I'm pretty early."

He'd glanced at her elegant wristwatch, which showed that it was only 3:25 p.m. There were still thirty-five minutes until the meeting was to start.

"That's no problem," said Vibs. "If you like, you can sit over on the couch and wait. Ryan said you would probably be early and that he would want to chat with you before the board meeting. At least now he can see you've arrived."

Ryan was still in his office, talking on his phone while looking over the harbor. It didn't seem like he'd noticed Dan arrive.

"Would you like some water or a cola?" asked Vibs. "I'll get you a bottle."

"A cola would be nice," replied Dan. "But I can get it myself—you shouldn't have to trouble yourself with that. Besides, I don't think there's anything in the vending machines out in the corridor—at least not the one I saw?"

"No, that's true," she replied. "It won't be filled until sometime next week. But we've got a little fridge inside Ryan's office, so he doesn't have to move too much to get his cola. Two seconds."

Dan looked at her as she got to her feet and walked toward the door between the two rooms. She looked sporty and elegant in her white sneakers and dress, which Dan could now see only went to just above her knees. As she opened the door, Ryan turned his head to look at her and simultaneously caught sight of Dan on the white couch. He smiled in surprise and winked at Dan before he turned back to the view, continuing his phone conversation.

Once again, Dan wondered about the effect Ryan had on him. With just that one smile, it was as if the last vestige of Dan's nervousness about their meeting had vanished, and he instantly felt more relaxed.

While Vibs walked over to a small fridge placed under the large conference table, Dan saw Ryan turn a few degrees to follow her with his eyes—especially when she squatted down and opened the door, taking out a half-liter bottle of cola. It didn't surprise Dan that Ryan was looking at her the way he was—nor that he was utterly unaffected by Dan seeing it. He knew Ryan and that he didn't give a damn what anyone thought of him. As Vibs stood up and walked back to the reception, Ryan smiled again at Dan while licking his lips behind Vibs's back. Dan couldn't help but smile at this behavior, so typical of Ryan, which he'd experienced plenty of times—also because it was probably Ryan's way of signaling to Dan that everything was fine and that he didn't need to be nervous. As a bonus, Vibs saw Dan's smile and smiled back happily, but with a slightly puzzled look in her eyes. She was probably wondering if Dan's smile was because of her or the cola.

Dan got to his feet and walked toward her. He didn't want to give her the impression that he considered her some kind of servant who had to bring the cola all the way to the sofa—even if it was only three or four meters, he saved her.

"At least now Ryan knows you're here," she said with a smile as she handed him the bottle.

"Thanks a lot, Vibs—I appreciate that."

Vibs returned to her seat, where she continued what she'd been doing on her laptop, and Dan walked back to the sofa that stood against the glass wall and sat down again. He opened the bottle, took a big gulp, screwed the cap back on, and placed it on the floor. From where he sat, he could see both Vibs behind her desk and Ryan in the next room—and the giant panoramic windows also gave an excellent view of the harbor.

While he waited, he looked closer at the large company logo on the front of Vibs's desk. It was a brand-new logo, apparently made during the period Dan hadn't been on Lifeline. The logo was a stylized, horizontal DNA double helix over the outline of an open hand with fingers pointing forty-five degrees upwards. The DNA strand could either be interpreted as the lifeline in the hand's palm or as a wave, so it seemed as if the hand was reaching out for—and grasping—a lifeline. Under the hand and the strand of DNA was the company name in thin, light blue letters, simply saying "Lifeline". It was a simple but inspired company logo that could easily have cost real money to design. Alternatively, it wasn't unlikely that it was an idea Ryan had come up with on his own, quickly sketched on a napkin or something, and then fine-tuned into the current layout by one of Lifeline's web designers. The logo signaled the image of the company and conveyed a clear and optimistic message about what customers were getting for their money.

Lifeline's primary business model was to sell an analysis—called the "Lifeline document"—to customers who submitted a mouth swab in a special return envelope sent to them by mail. The customers did the mouth swab themselves, using a small foam stick to scrape the tongue and inside of the cheek to take a cell sample. Based on the DNA from the mouth swab and a range of other information—including lifestyle and habits, which the customer filled out—a document was produced and sent to the customer. The document allegedly contained an analysis of the person's genes, describing potential diseases and conditions to which they might be predisposed, and recommendations for lifestyle and dietary changes and other actions that would ensure the customer's good health and a long and happy life.

When Ryan had started Lifeline eight years earlier, however, the promise of genetic analysis had primarily been a marketing ploy to give the company and product an aura of science and high tech. Customers submitted their mouth swabs to Lifeline, but the actual data processing was done solely on the detailed information that customers provided about themselves, combined with demographic and statistical data that was freely available or bought cheaply from subcontractors—called service providers—around the world. But after the cost of gene sequencing and analysis fell drastically—as had been the case over the past decade—they'd started sending some of the customers' submitted mouth swabs to companies that specialized in sequencing a person's genome. Initially, these were the same companies who also did a few simple tests on specific markers and could identify whether the customer was predisposed to various disorders and diseases.

Concurrently, as the cost of data storage plummeted and the bandwidth of the internet increased to the degree that allowed vast amounts of data to be transferred quickly, proper analysis companies emerged, offering general and rudimentary analysis. Others began specializing in specific sequences and markers; and as the price of sequencing and analysis also fell, an increasing number of Lifeline's customers benefited from the more comprehensive and accurate examination, which was now partially based on their actual DNA—something they'd always assumed it to be.

When he looked up from the logo, Dan discovered Vibs watching him. She probably thought he'd been looking at her, and he could feel his cheeks flushing. But she just smiled at him and then continued working on her laptop.

Dan understood the reason behind the vast interest and gigantic market for genetic analysis well. The more everyone realized how many aspects of their lives were controlled by their genes, the more they concluded it would be beneficial to know what was in the cards for them. If you knew the problems and obstacles you were predisposed to encounter in advance, it would be easier to navigate them—or maybe even prevent them from occurring in the first place.

Personally, Dan had never gone through the process of acquiring a Lifeline document. In the early days—after Ryan bought Avaram, and Dan and Michael became part of

Lifeline—he knew the document was essentially a structured listing and restatement of things the customer had filled out about themselves: the typical pattern of *tell us who you are, and we will tell you who you are*. But as the document came to include more elements of actual genetic analysis and indications of what the customer might be predisposed to, Dan had contemplated creating a document himself.

His hesitation and reluctance to get a genetic test was based on a wish to keep a balance between having useful and decisive knowledge about his own future life on the one hand; and, on the other, having the freedom to experience life in the order it came—expecting he could influence it with his decisions and choices. Even if the notion of free will was probably an illusion—as Dan had gradually concluded, it was.

But perhaps knowing what might happen many years in the future—as well as what one was predisposed to—could be an advantage, even if it was only based on probabilities and not necessarily destined to evolve into a real problem.

A genetic analysis might also have warned him about his predisposition to alcohol dependency—knowledge that could have prevented him from getting caught up in the addiction that had nearly cost him his life. However, he knew himself well enough to feel sure he would have dismissed it as something he could easily control.

As the travel and partying with Ryan started taking over, Dan could easily see the pattern emerging and how he was finding it harder to finish a binge. But he kept believing he was in charge and could stay in control and slow down when he wanted to. The problem was that when he finally pulled himself together and concluded it had to stop, the addiction had taken control away from him. Even with the steeliest determination, it was only a matter of weeks—or months at best—before his willpower snapped like a dry twig, and he fell back in again.

Besides, he didn't need a gene test to find out that he was most likely predisposed to alcoholism. His biological mother, Anette, was trapped in the same dependency and had resigned herself to it, more or less giving up ever changing her habits. He knew about her addiction because he'd visited her in her apartment in the southern part of Copenhagen—on the Amager island—twice. The first time, he'd been seventeen years old and had done so because she'd written a letter to him asking if he would like to meet her. He'd never really considered contacting his biological mother—whom he'd never known. Anyway, he'd taken the train from Hillerød—a town in the northern part of Zealand, where he lived with one of the many foster families he'd grown up with—to Copenhagen Central Station and continued with the metro to Amager to visit her.

The second time was on his way home from the airport after a business trip to India with Ryan, where they'd visited a potential subcontractor for a web service they contemplated integrating with the Lifeline system. He'd already had too much to drink on the plane and was looking forward to returning to his new apartment in the Østerbro district—where he knew the drinking would continue. For some unknown reason, he'd gotten off the metro at a station on Amager and walked to Anette's apartment to see her.

Anette's apartment hadn't changed in the fourteen years between the two visits. The same two paintings hung on the walls, and the same furniture stood in the same way as the first time he'd been there. And although her home was neither messy nor dirty, Anette's alcohol dependency was evident from the many filled ashtrays and empty red wine bottles piled up on the kitchen table on both occasions. The first time, she'd talked about how sorry she felt for having placed him for adoption when he was a little boy; and explained that it was because she couldn't manage being a single mother—alone, with the responsibility for a child.

Dan couldn't remember what they talked about the second time. On both occasions, he'd been there less than fifteen minutes before politely saying goodbye, and on the way back to the metro station, he'd made up his mind not to contact her again.

Apart from those two visits, he'd never wanted to meet her, and he neither replied to the texts she sent from time to time when she was most influenced by the wine and on a sentimental trip—nor to her messages when she was briefly sober again, apologizing for the prior texts she'd written. Even when gauging his feelings, he couldn't quite determine whether he was blaming her for placing him for adoption or whether he might even hold her partly responsible for his addiction—because of the genes he'd inherited from her.

Dan couldn't remember if he ever missed having real biological parents. The foster families he'd grown up with had always been sweet and loving; understanding and accommodating to his need to be on his own and immerse himself in his books and computer programs. In retrospect, Dan didn't think he'd ever missed having neither a mother nor a father at any point in his life.

"Hi, Dan," Ryan's voice rumbled, abruptly pulling Dan out of his thoughts. He hadn't noticed that Ryan had entered the reception and was now standing right next to the couch where Dan was sitting. He quickly stood up and shook Ryan's outstretched hand.

THREE

"I'm so glad to see you, Dan," Ryan said. "You look great—completely like yourself again!"

He let go of Dan's hand and pulled him in for a big hug, patting him on the back. Dan also tried to pat Ryan on the back, but Ryan was holding him so tightly that he could barely move his arms. He'd completely forgotten how hard Ryan's hugs were—just like his handshakes. Like a good-natured bear who doesn't know his own strength.

Dan also instantly recognized the scent of the expensive aftershave Ryan always used. He knew Ryan shaved every morning after his bath: not with a razor, but with a costly Japanese scraper. And it didn't matter if he was going to the office or working from home. It was a ritual for Ryan.

Personally, Dan preferred his professional electric trimmer, which he used for both hair and beard, both of which were trimmed to a fine point every Friday evening.

"Let's sit down for a minute," said Ryan, gesturing toward the couch Dan had just gotten up from, "and have a little chat."

Ryan continued talking as he took off his jacket and sat down on the other couch opposite Dan. When he was in the office or on a business trip, he always wore one of the dark suits which he traveled to Milan every year to get measured for. This wasn't only a luxury he allowed himself, but something he considered necessary in order to get proper clothes in a size that suited him. Dan wasn't sure if the well-known brands even made clothes in Ryan's size. At six and a half feet tall and weighing what Dan had always estimated to be well over three hundred pounds, Ryan was a man who took up much space in the landscape. At home, Ryan rarely wore his formal clothes, though. When he took the occasional day off, he typically wore a coverall—at least on the days when he was working on his collection of expensive cars that he kept in his large basement.

"It's so wonderful that you're on top again," said Ryan after they sat down. "I've been looking forward to seeing you and showing you all this." Ryan spread his arms wide. "And I was convinced you would show up today. Mainly because I knew you wouldn't want to miss the first board meeting here at our new domicile."

"Yes, it's turned out fantastic," conceded Dan. "It's just as impressive as you promised it would be."

"I'm happy you think so," said Ryan enthusiastically. "I'm also very pleased myself. But getting all the people relocated out here is an extensive process. We've had to do it in stages over the last two weeks—and we still need to move a handful of the coders out here. Some of them are still sitting in their caves in the old office because they're not convinced that the network is a hundred percent up and running out here. Hang on—"

Ryan half-turned with difficulty on the couch and looked at Vibs, who'd gotten up from the desk and was heading into the conference room.

"Vibs? Could you get me a cola, please? And one for Dan, too."

"Not for me. Thanks," said Dan and shook his head. "I still have the one you got me earlier."

She nodded and smiled at them both before continuing into the other room, where she went to get a cola from the same fridge she'd used earlier.

"What do you think of Vibs?" asked Ryan in a hushed voice, smiling slyly as he laboriously turned back to face Dan. Dan had no doubt what Ryan was thinking and needed no elaboration on the question. It wasn't her language skills Ryan was inquiring about.

"She looks outstanding. Decidedly beautiful, I would say."

"Yeah, she's really hot. She's part of the gang Gitte hangs out with on the various projects she's got going."

Gitte was Ryan's young wife, to whom he'd been married for six years. She was the same age as Dan and as least as good-looking as Vibs. Gitte could easily pass for a top model, and it was always paradoxical to see her and Ryan together because they were so different in age and physical appearance. Dan also knew that many wondered how the two had fallen for each other. Some thought it must be Ryan's money, but Dan knew Gitte was not only beautiful but also very intelligent. She had a small consulting firm of her own and could easily make the money she needed by herself.

"Gitte has long insisted that I needed an assistant, and when she suggested Vibs a few weeks ago, I could hardly refuse—especially after I'd seen her. In fairness, she's also super sharp and has her finger on the pulse of many things. And on a day like today, she's also super to have sitting in the reception, as you can see."

Ryan paused as Vibs returned from the conference room and walked over to the couch, where she handed him his cola. She'd already unscrewed the cap.

"Here you go."

"Thank you, sweetie," said Ryan, looking up at her. He took a good gulp and handed the bottle back to Vibs, who screwed the cap back on, and placed the bottle on the table in front of Ryan. With another smile for both of them, she turned around and walked back to the conference room, where she began taking bottles out of the fridge and placing them on the large conference table.

"But it hasn't even been fully decided if there's going to be a permanent reception up here," continued Ryan after a deep breath. "Maybe we'll have a shared reception on the ground floor—by the entrance. That hasn't quite been determined yet. It mostly depends on who will rent the ground floor. And, of course, whether the other companies getting ready to move in also needs a reception. But it would be really spectacular to have down there; and then we'll have more space up here. I have a feeling that we'll need a lot more room soon, but I'll get into that during the meeting."

Ryan leaned forward with difficulty and took his cola, unscrewed the cap, and took another big gulp. Setting it back on the table, he glanced briefly toward Vibs's desk before he leaned back again. It seemed to Dan that he wanted to make sure they were alone. Vibs was still busy in the conference room, wheeling a cart carrying a large monitor to the end of the large conference table.

"But recently some other incredible things have happened, which I would like to discuss with you at some point—preferably as soon as possible. I'll come back to that later."

Ryan looked appreciatively up and down at Dan.

"Right now, it's just good to see you again, and great that you seem to have recovered completely from that nasty experience. As you know, I'm not religious, but I've often prayed—to God, fate, or what have you—for you to escape from that dark hole you were stuck in for so long. I can't express how happy I was when you wrote to me you'd started that treatment. From that moment on, I didn't doubt one second you would make it and beat your addiction."

Ryan paused for a second and took a deep breath before he continued. "I have to say that I blame myself for not picking up on the signals earlier and doing something about it before it was too late."

Dan could tell he was being sincere and quickly shook his head dismissively. "You definitely shouldn't blame yourself, Ryan. It's entirely my own responsibility that it evolved as severely as it did. Both Susan and Michael told me several times that they thought I was losing control, but I always shrugged it off, promising them—and myself—that I could stop when I wanted to."

For a moment, Ryan sat thoughtfully and—quite uncharacteristically—saying nothing. Dan thought back on the process and the moment when he had to admit that the alcohol had taken over and he'd lost control of his life.

It had started when he'd had to take a day out of his calendar to recover after a party—as the binges were called in the beginning—and then it had turned into a few days; because he'd continued drinking when he woke up. Later, he had to rip several days out of the calendar, and eventually, he'd thrown the whole calendar into the toilet and flushed it out—there were no longer any appointments left he could keep. "The Binge" had become a chronic condition, and he alternated between drinking and being sick. When he was finally well enough to get up again, all he thought about—and did—was to go out and get fresh supplies.

Only after Susan had broken up had it dawned on him he was no longer the same person—and that he had lost control. This was a harsh realization for a person who identified as being responsible and taking charge of his own life.

It was Ryan who broke the silence. "Well, the important thing is that you're back on your feet. I'm super excited you're here, and tonight you'll be the guest of honor at the board dinner at the usual restaurant. It'll be just like old times."

Dan thought that was precisely why he shouldn't attend the dinner. The lavish dinners after the board meetings always continued with a night out on the town, which for a hard core of board members typically turned into a genuine bender lasting till dawn. Often the hard core had consisted only of Ryan and Dan.

"If it's alright with you, Ryan, I would prefer to pass on dinner tonight," said Dan. His hesitation wasn't because he was afraid of falling in, but more to avoid exposing himself to unnecessary temptation.

"Sure, Dan," said Ryan and nodded. "It's perfectly all right. But if it's because you're afraid of drinking too much, I promise I'll make sure you don't get more than you can handle—and that we try to go home in decent time."

"Ryan, the central point in my addiction treatment is that even a single drink is more than I can handle. But that's not the only reason I would rather skip the dinner. It's because I have an important meeting at seven o'clock."

Ryan looked questioningly at Dan, as if wondering why he didn't elaborate on the important meeting. Then his face lit up in a knowing smile as he realized.

"Of course! It's not only an important meeting—it's a *vital* meeting. I'm sure the AA meetings will help you so you don't fall in again."

With an effort, Ryan rose from the couch, and Dan followed his lead. After getting up, Ryan glanced briefly at his expensive watch. Dan knew he was proud of his many watches, which he could talk about for hours—especially after he'd had a drink or two. He always wore one, except when he was working on his cars. In the basement, he took the watch off so as not to risk getting oil or scratches on them, but also because, in those situations, he disappeared into a state of mind where time didn't matter. Gitte had told Dan that Ryan sometimes came up from the basement, surprised that it had become the next day while he'd been absorbed in his own world.

This was also something Dan often experienced when he was coding and transcended into that unique flow state where tasks almost solved themselves and everything fell into place with minimal conscious effort.

"There's almost fifteen minutes until the meeting. Why don't we go for a quick tour of the new premises?"

"That sounds like a good idea," replied Dan. He would like to hear what Ryan planned to do with all the extra space. It seemed to Dan as if there were three times as much square footage as there had been at the old address.

As they headed for the door, Vibs returned from the conference room and sat down at her laptop again. While holding the door for Dan, Ryan turned and looked at her. "Dan and I are going to do a quick tour of the office. We'll be back in five minutes."

"Fine," replied Vibs. "I'll welcome the people from the board when they start arriving."

In the central circular corridor, Ryan pointed to the elevator and the note that said it wasn't working.

"I'm a little annoyed that they haven't activated the elevator yet," he said. "I would have preferred it to be ready for today when the entire board comes here for the first time—so their first impression of our new domicile won't be having to fight their way up the stairwell. Vibs has prompted the contractor for a date, but it looks like it won't be until sometime next week."

Ryan pressed the elevator button hard eight times, as if—by his insistence and sheer willpower—he could make it work, but nothing happened. The arrows above the elevator remained off, and the doors shut.

"On the other hand, I probably benefit from the daily exercise up and down the stairs. Then I can also better justify drinking my colas."

Dan nodded. He could only make a ballpark estimate of how many calories a man Ryan's size burned by walking up to the seventh floor; but it was hardly sufficient to be called adequate daily exercise. Sometimes, Dan had wondered why—on a personal level—Ryan didn't seem to care at all about the advice his company had made a business out of giving customers. He didn't know what recommendations might be in Ryan's Lifeline document, but judging by his size and difficulty getting up from a couch, it wasn't something he took seriously—or at least not something he complied with.

They walked counterclockwise along the wide corridor. The first room on the right, after the reception, was the largely empty one, with only a row of moving boxes.

"That room will be my office in the short term," said Ryan, pointing through the glass wall. "But it still needs a desk and cabinets for all my files and books." He nodded toward the many moving boxes. "So, until that's in place, the conference room functions as my office. There's direct access between each room, so it's smartest to have both my workplace and the large conference room right next to the reception. And when we need the space, we'll probably merge my office with the reception."

They continued a few steps until they stood outside the next room, where Dan had already spotted some system developers and web designers. Although the walls between all rooms were glass, this room appeared more isolated because of the many posters and charts hanging everywhere. In several places, the glass walls were covered with large mosaics of sticky notes that the various development teams used to overview the individual sub-tasks and track how their implementation was coming along.

"As you can see, we've assembled coding and networking responsibilities in one room. I also think it's practical that backend and front-end developers are so close. And though we try to prioritize full-stack developers, as you've recommended since day one, there are still a few specialists in the very low-level networking areas we could never do without, even though we don't have a single server in-house anymore."

Ryan glanced at his watch again before continuing. "Is it okay if we don't go in and say hi? I know they're busy, and our meeting starts in ten minutes."

Dan nodded and smiled—it suited him just fine.

Although he was looking forward to talking to them and hearing how the different platforms were evolving, he preferred to wait for another day.

The following two rooms were empty, except for several moving boxes and a lot of desks and office chairs still unpacked in their cardboard boxes.

"This will be the web designers' space when the last group of coders eventually decide to cross the Rubicon and move out here," explained Ryan, pointing into one of the rooms. "For now, the coders use it for their meetings, so they don't disturb their colleagues when discussing how to implement their tasks and projects."

They passed the second, empty room without Ryan explaining what it was intended for. It was the room directly opposite the stairwell door, which Dan now knew was diametrically opposite the reception.

In the next room, eleven people sat at tables positioned the same way as the developers and web designers—with their backs to the corridor and with a view of eastern and northern Copenhagen. Even from behind, Dan recognized several of them—but without being able to name anyone. He'd never been directly involved with that part of the company.

"Here we have the administration with finance and legal," said Ryan. "They were the first to move out here after we felt reasonably sure the network installation was working. And after they'd been here a week and approved everything, I decided the rest of the organization could follow. I expect we'll have completed the move and be able to close the old office one hundred percent by next Friday."

When Dan joined Lifeline, he'd wondered about the need for so many lawyers. It wasn't something he and Michael had needed at Avaram, until they sold the company to Ryan, at which point they'd a lawyer review and approve the proposal for a contract Ryan had presented to them. But afterward, Dan had observed how Lifeline's agreements with service providers had to be meticulously analyzed before any real collaboration could begin. And on his and Ryan's travels around the world to potential service providers and partners, he'd seen how Ryan regularly called the lawyers back home, either to debate a specific phrasing or to make sure Lifeline wasn't committing to something he didn't like. Dan had asked why he didn't take one of the lawyers along on the trips, but Ryan felt it wasn't necessary—the technical and substantive stuff was the critical part. The legal part was a formality he expected to be in order, but he just didn't want to take any unnecessary chances.

On one occasion, Michael had told Dan that he'd heard that Ryan had 'released' the lawyers on two of Lifeline's developers because they threatened to publish their knowledge about Lifeline's exceptional marketing as part of a negotiation for a higher salary. It was one of those occasions when Dan slowly started understanding how little Michael cared for Ryan. He'd brushed it off and concluded that Michael was exaggerating. On the same occasion, Michael had mentioned some other rumors saying that Ryan had made his first million by even more amoral methods than deceptive marketing. These supposedly included money laundering and slightly too 'creative' accounting. He hadn't wanted to elaborate on where he got that information, and Dan had presumed that he was exaggerating, and hadn't given it much thought.

While Ryan had been talking about the moving plans, the door to the stairwell had opened, and three people had entered the circular corridor, where they were now standing and taking in the scene. Two of them were older board members who'd been with the company for several years—going back to before Ryan bought Avaram. They smiled in surprise when they spotted Ryan and Dan and started walking toward them.

The third person was Michael, who remained standing at the door, looking appraisingly at Dan as if to make sure it was him. The two board members greeted Ryan and Dan warmly, and Ryan led them in the direction of the reception, gesturing as he told them about the new premises.

Dan took a deep breath, walked over to Michael, and held out his hand. Michael took it hesitantly while nodding gravely to Dan. Neither of them said anything, and Dan could tell that Michael was just as unsure of what to say as he was.

Then Michael's expression changed to a big smile. "Are you still an atheist?" he asked with a twinkle in his eye, without letting go of Dan's hand.

Dan didn't know what to answer and just smiled back.

FOUR

Every seat around the large conference table was filled with the Lifeline company's board members, except for an empty chair between Ryan and Dan. Ryan sat at the end of the table with his back to the magnificent outlook over the harbor, looking at his laptop. He hadn't removed the laptop or the stack of printouts and booklets he'd been working on earlier in the day.

Dan sat in the seat after the empty chair on Ryan's right, and directly across from him was Michael, who sat glancing demonstratively at his watch every few minutes. It was apparent that he wanted to show Ryan he was annoyed that the meeting didn't start on time. Not because Michael himself was usually exceptionally punctual, but to stress Ryan out a little.

To Ryan's left, between him and Michael, sat one of the four female board members—an older woman Dan had spoken to several times, and whom he knew had a phenomenal analytical overview. Ryan consulted extensively with her regarding finances and how to scale the business. Along the rest of the table sat six more people: two to Dan's right, two to Michael's left on the other side, and the last three at the end of the table, opposite Ryan.

Dan knew the names, ages, and areas of expertise of all the board members, as well as a great deal about their family circumstances—knowledge he'd gained involuntarily through numerous conversations at previous meetings, as well as at dinners and parties at expensive Copenhagen restaurants, and in Ryan and Gitte's home. They were all polite and likable, but it had always amazed him how much people would reveal about themselves—even personal things—especially when they'd enjoyed a glass of wine or two.

Vibs had placed bottles of water, cola, and juice in the middle of the table, and most people had already opened bottles and filled their glasses. A few were checking their phones, and the rest were looking at Ryan or the beautiful view of the harbor and the Sound.

After a few minutes, Ryan pushed his laptop away, placed both hands heavily on the large table, and cleared his throat.

"Okay, everyone. Let's get this meeting started. Gitte wrote that she'll be ten minutes late, but told me to start without her."

He looked around at all the board members before proceeding.

"I'm delighted to welcome you to this board meeting. It is—in many ways—a special meeting this time. Primarily because it's our first meeting here, at our new domicile. Some of you have already dropped by in the last couple of weeks, but for most of you, it's your first time here," he said, spreading his arms in an including gesture.

"I hope you'll be as happy to come here as I am, and that it'll be a suitable environment for all of us for many years to come."

Several board members around the table nodded, and some made short, appreciative statements to express their concurrence. Ryan paused briefly, then looked at Dan.

"But it's also a special day for a different reason," he said, without taking his eyes off Dan. "Namely because Dan is back for the first time after far, far too long an absence."

Dan could feel his cheeks getting warm, and he just wanted to look down at the table in front of him—but he forced himself to look around the table and nod briefly at everyone. All the board members nodded back smilingly, and a few winked at him or gave him the thumbs-up.

Although he was ashamed of the adversity he'd been through, at no point had he tried to keep it a secret, and he was sure everyone on the board knew the history.

"Way to go, Dan," said the older board member sitting across from him, nodding several times and glancing around at the others, causing them all to nod in agreement.

"Thank you, everyone—it means a lot to me," said Dan, looking around at them once more. Their warm expressions touched him, and it seemed as if everyone meant it with an honest heart.

"Yes, you've made a spectacular achievement, Dan," said Ryan. "I can't tell you how happy I am, that you won your fight against dependency—for the company's sake, too!"

"Thank you, Ryan," replied Dan, turning in his chair to look more directly at him—hoping to shift everyone's focus back to the agenda.

Ryan smiled and then pressed a key on his laptop—instantly producing a mirror image of its screen on the large monitor Vibs had previously rolled to the end of the table. Everyone around the table could now see the meeting's agenda on the screen above Ryan's head, while keeping up with what he was saying. At the same time, Ryan could see and control the current slide on his laptop, so he didn't have to turn around to see the points he planned to go through. Dan repressed a smile as he observed how Ryan morphed into his salesman persona, speaking to the board as if they were customers, and not the owners' representatives—just like he always did when he had to talk about his, and, consequently, the company's vision.

Dan quickly read through the seven points—it was mainly about financial status, new plans for marketing, and expectations for the coming quarter. He wasn't expecting any big surprises for himself or anyone else around the table. He had no problem keeping up and appearing attentive while privately thinking about other things.

Out of the corner of his eye, he looked over at Michael, who still seemed discontented, even though the meeting had now started. Dan knew Michael was patiently waiting for some inaccuracy or inconsistency in Ryan's presentation that he could superiorly comment on to expose Ryan—and he also knew that Ryan knew it, without it affecting him in the least.

It had been nice to meet Michael again and have a quick chat with him. After the initial awkward greeting, they'd quickly found their way back to the old banter and private humor. While maundering the corridor, Dan had repeated what Ryan had explained to him about the plans a little earlier.

Michael hadn't changed a bit, which Dan hadn't expected either. Physically, he looked the same—as muscular and fit as Dan had always known him. In all the time they'd been friends, Michael had spent most of his free time doing various forms of martial arts, strength training, and, in periods, bodybuilding. And it wasn't just for his health and looks that he did it: Dan had always known that Michael often ventured alone into the city's nightlife to seek out confrontations—that could develop into actual fights—with other people or groups of people.

They'd talked about it several times, and Michael could only explain it as a kind of rush when he was in a situation where every move was crucial, and mistakes could cause broken bones or other nasty injuries. Somehow, it was a test of whether his training and hard work with his body had made any difference.

On the mornings when Michael had shown up at their small office after one of his nightly city walks, Dan could sense it. He exuded an unusual energy, even on those occasions when it was apparent that he'd faced adamant opposition, and he had a black eye or had swellings or fresh cuts in his face. He didn't drink at all on these trips—in fact, Michael never touched alcohol—but it was as if he had an inner switch he could use to turn on and off a wild rage whenever he wanted to.

In recent years, however, Michael had tried to kick the habit and cut down on his trips, and had succeeded to some extent. This had happened as he became increasingly interested in eastern philosophy and religion. He still exercised, but now spent much of his time doing yoga and reading books on spiritual subjects. In contrast to his nightly trips, which he rarely mentioned, he often brought up his new pursuit in their conversations—clearly hoping to kindle Dan's interest in the same topics.

Dan had never thought of himself as a religious person, so Michael often referred to him—with a humorous glint in his eye—as an atheist. Dan kept explaining that he wasn't an atheist, but just wasn't as interested in the spiritual side of life as Michael was. When he reflected on it once in a while, he concluded he would probably describe himself as agnostic because there seemed to be no scientific evidence proving or disproving the existence of a higher, transcendent power.

Or at least that's how it had seemed until he'd had an extraordinary experience while at the rock bottom of his abuse.

After their chat in the corridor, they'd gone into the conference room, greeting the other board members, before everyone sat down around the table in the places they usually occupied at meetings. Dan had noticed how Michael greeted Ryan with a slightly mocking smile, as was his wont—and now that the meeting was underway, he made no secret that he found the view of the harbor more interesting than what Ryan was saying.

Ryan was laying out his plans for more aggressive marketing and ambitions to expand Lifeline to more regions worldwide, when Dan suddenly heard stiletto heels against the hard wooden floor of the reception next door. Although he was facing the other way and couldn't see the person, he had no doubt that it was Gitte making her entrance. Another sure clue was that all the board members on the opposite side of the table shifted their focus from Ryan's monologue to the new arrival. Not least Michael, who leaned marginally to the side to get as much of a view of her as possible.

The glass door opened, and Dan heard her cross the floor to the chair between him and Ryan. When she arrived, Dan turned in his chair and watched as she pulled her laptop out of her bag and placed it on the table before sitting down. She leaned forward over the table, looking around at everyone.

"Hi, everybody. I'm sorry I'm late—my apologies," she said with an apologetic smile. Everyone around the table greeted her back, signaling with their body language that everything was fine.

"It's all right, honey," said Ryan, with no hint of irritation at being interrupted. He looked at his screen for a moment before continuing, as if he hadn't been distracted. Gitte opened her laptop, but before looking at the screen, she turned briefly to Dan, winked at him, and patted him gently on the back—something he'd never seen her do before. She didn't say anything, and Dan didn't know how to react, so he just gave her a nonsensical nod before she moved her gaze to her laptop. As far as Dan could see, out of the corner of his eye, she was scrolling through a list of news items, which she skimmed briefly while glancing at Ryan every so often, to signal that she was also following what took place at the meeting.

Without looking directly at him, Dan could see that Michael's attitude had changed since Gitte's arrival. He was no longer looking primarily out over the harbor, but as much at Gitte as he could get away with, without it coming across as strange or indiscreet. And even when he looked at Ryan, he seemed to pay more attention to Gitte—at least, that's how Dan perceived it.

At no point did Gitte look at Michael. She merely shifted her gaze between her laptop and Ryan's presentation. Dan knew Michael was physically very attracted to Gitte—which, given her looks, wasn't surprising—but he'd never observed Gitte looking at Michael, or any other man, in the same interested way. Dan's best assessment was that they probably didn't have a clandestine affair; if they did, they kept it hidden well. On the other hand, neither would probably tell him if it were the case, because of his friendship with all three of them, and the risks that would entail.

As far as Dan knew, Michael had never had a steady girlfriend—at least not in the many years they'd been friends. On his nightly walks in the city, he often met women he fell in love with, but none of these relationships developed into anything long-lasting or permanent. At the beginning of a new relationship, Michael enthusiastically told Dan about it, and how he was sure it was the right one this time. But, after a short while, his enthusiasm faded, and he ended the relationship.

Dan knew Michael dreamed of meeting the one and only, and—with some luck—establishing a family with her, but he hadn't succeeded; not yet. Maybe this was how he saw Gitte—as a prospective life partner—in which case his interest wasn't only rooted in a sexual attraction. And perhaps it was also part of the reason for Michael's dislike of Ryan, on top of the other issues: Ryan had something Michael couldn't have—a committed relationship with a woman who was in every way amazing.

Dan hoped for Michael that one day he would find someone with whom he could have a committed relationship, with the promise of friendship, intimacy, and confidentiality that could bring. Personally, he'd felt that his time with Susan was the absolute highlight of his life, and not a day went by without him reflecting—voluntarily or involuntarily—on their time together, even though he tried not to get caught up in the memories. But even though he missed her, he'd accepted that it was a chapter in his life that had been definitively closed. The analytical part of his mind said he could probably meet another woman and build a similar relationship. Still, on a more emotional level, he felt convinced that it would never happen. Susan had been the one and only, and he'd ruined it by letting the addiction take control of his life.

Dan smiled to himself as he thought back on their relationship. Although he'd never had siblings in his many foster homes, or anything that could be perceived in the same way, he felt that a good relationship could be like having a twin, obviously without including the romantic and sexual aspects in the comparison: a person you could talk to about anything and who often understood your thoughts and feelings better than you did yourself—even if you didn't necessarily agree on everything. Dan and Susan had seen many things differently. For example, Susan didn't think he was very romantic, constantly analyzing and separating emotions and motives into their individual components, which she felt took away from the magic and wonder of life.

Moreover, Susan dreamed of having children, which Dan had decided long ago that he didn't want. He didn't want to take on the role of being a parent, with the risks and costs that would spark off.

But they'd both been convinced they could solve even that challenge—eventually by one of them changing their mind. This, and all their other differences, had never been a problem or something that had threatened their relationship. That had only happened with Dan's fundamental personality change, where the alcohol abuse gradually became the order of the day in his life.

However, he didn't intend to live as a monk for the rest of his life. With a bit of luck, he could meet a sweet woman with some of the same qualities as Susan. Currently, however, he had no clue who that might be or where to find her.

Suddenly, he realized Gitte was looking at him questioningly. He returned her gaze with a similarly questioning expression on his face.

Someone—probably Ryan—must have asked him about something. He looked at Ryan, who smiled indulgently at him.

"Super that you're thinking about the question," said Ryan, winking at Dan. "I was just asking if you and Michael estimate our databases to be able to handle ten times as many transactions or more when needed. Michael thought it wouldn't be a problem."

Dan could see that Ryan was aware that his mind had been somewhere else when he'd asked the question. He often disappeared into his own world of thoughts—although this usually only happened when he had to ponder over abstract and technical issues. Everyone Dan had worked with had experienced this many times, and Dan knew that most of them thought it was perfectly fine.

"I agree with Michael," said Dan, glancing over at Michael, who was looking at him with an air of reproach but with a twinkle in his eye. "Our databases aren't running inhouse, but as an external service that is scaled dynamically and in real-time by the service provider, automatically adjusting to the current load."

He glanced around the table to assess whether the answer was adequate and hadn't been too technical, as he knew his explanations sometimes were. But most of the board seemed to have understood his brief description.

"Great!" said Ryan. "Good to know we won't have to make major investments on that front. It's going to be expensive enough as it is, with the new marketing and sales initiatives."

On the large monitor, Dan saw Ryan had moved on to a new point on the agenda, with the title 'Interactive App'. He decided to pay more attention during the rest of the meeting and not let his mind wander so much.

"It's no secret—at least in this closed circle," continued Ryan, raising his arms in an inclusive gesture, "that our product has a significant element of pseudo-science about it. In addition to the completed questionnaire, we ask our customers to submit a mouth swab, to give them the impression that it's predominantly their DNA that's being used to create their individual Lifeline document. And while everything indicates we'll be able to retrieve more useful knowledge from the DNA in the future—and at a reasonable price—so far, we've essentially sold the customers a document largely built on information they've filled out about themselves."

Dan could see that Michael was about to protest, and he knew why. In recent years, they'd continually expanded the system to adjust several of the document's fields, so that they, to some extent, reflected the results received from the services performing the actual genetic analysis on selected markers. Although these services were expensive, they'd so far provided only rudimentary output, showing whether the person was genetically predisposed to the most common diseases. The primary content of the Lifeline document was still suggestions and recommendations on diet, exercise, quitting smoking—and similar generalized issues—in the form of standardized text paragraphs and charts, combined mainly based on the customer's input.

Making eye contact with Michael, Dan slowly turned his head back and forth a few millimeters—so vaguely that only Michael noticed—and he could see that Michael chose not to comment on Ryan's inaccurate generalization.

Dan wouldn't dream of contradicting Ryan at a board meeting, but he wondered if there might be a reason Ryan was trying to downplay the significance of the genetic analysis, although he couldn't figure out what that reason might be. He turned his gaze back to Ryan, who continued explaining.

"The customer is left with the impression that the document is based solely on scientific methods. This impression of formal authority motivates him to change his habits and lifestyle—if that's what the document recommends. Our product can undoubtedly be a tremendous help to the customer: either because it confirms that his lifestyle is okay, or because it gives him a solid incentive to change his habits. And as our user surveys show, it can have a huge life-improving effect on the individual's life."

Before proceeding, he paused briefly to leave no one in doubt that he saw their product as providing excellent value to the customer.

"But there's something I think our document is missing, and I know several of you have mentioned it, too," he said, without looking at anyone specifically. Dan knew Ryan well enough to know that it wasn't at all certain that a single person present had voiced this concern. This was a way for Ryan to lead each person to believe that someone else had probably brought it up—and subsequently fret that they hadn't been forward-thinking enough to consider the issue.

"We simply need more interactivity with the customer. I think we should change the static document to an online app," announced Ryan. "Something that will keep users interested and have them checking the app all the time."

He was clearly about to elaborate when Michael demonstratively straightened his back and cleared his throat.

"Why on earth would such an app have to be interactive all of a sudden, Ryan?" he asked incredulously, with a slightly condescending smile. Obviously, he was glad that an opportunity to disagree with Ryan—perhaps even to catch him in an error—had finally presented itself.

"I mean—there aren't that many fields that change value after the Lifeline document is created. Especially when, as you've just said, we imply to customers that the document is based primarily on their DNA. That doesn't change continuously, does it!?"

Ryan smiled back at Michael. Dan knew from experience that Ryan was considerably better at hiding his feelings than Michael, but he didn't doubt that Ryan was deeply annoyed by Michael's interruption. And, though it might be hard to judge, it also seemed that his jaw muscles were tighter than usual as he answered Michael's question.

"That's certainly a good point you're making, Michael," said Ryan calmly. "Most of the information we show the customer in the Lifeline document consists of static values and descriptions. But to the best of my knowledge, it would certainly be possible to add some dynamic fields that the user can update over time in an app. This could be, for example, the person's weight and other biometrics, which can change continuously based on our initial recommendations. It might also be parameters and goals that the user defines himself, allowing him to follow his progress, visualized using charts and other statistics."

Ryan kept eye contact with Michael without saying anything, putting pressure on Michael, who didn't need many seconds to formulate a response.

"There are countless apps like that," said Michael, leaning back in his chair before continuing, now addressing the entire board. "You almost can't buy a watch, a bathroom scale, a sports tracker, or XR glasses—without an app like that being included for free. Don't you think the customers who want this kind of app have it on one of their devices already?"

Dan agreed with Michael, but expected that there could be other motives behind Ryan's plan. However, it didn't surprise him that Ryan chose not to take the bait, entering into a discussion about whether his idea would solve an existing demand that users would be willing to pay for. He was far too experienced for that.

"The point is not whether there's an unknown market for this type of app," continued Ryan, as if he hadn't been interrupted. "I've no doubts that we can come up with some clever features that will make our app a fixture on the users' devices. It's more about psychology and entertainment than actual data as such. And there's another reason we should consider changing our product from a snapshot of static information at a specific point in time to an interactive app with a continuously updated and developing experience."

Ryan looked around at everyone at the table to ensure he had their attention before proceeding.

"I would like to propose a strategic change to the board. My idea—which is the last thing I'll present today, and hope you'll all take note of and consider—is that we should change the business model from a single transaction sale to an app-based subscription. I'm confident that this will increase revenues dramatically."

Ryan spent almost fifteen minutes elaborating on his idea and then ended the meeting.

"Thank you for another good board meeting," he said, smiling at everyone around the table. "I'll see you all again at the usual board dinner tonight, and please remember to reserve Friday, June 21st—two weeks from today—for the traditional summer party at Gitte's and my humble abode; if you haven't already done so."

Everyone smiled and thanked him—and expressed how much they were looking forward to both the dinner the same evening and to the party.

A few minutes later, all the board members stood scattered in the conference room, speaking in pairs or small groups. Dan could see that Michael and Gitte conversed with the older woman, though he couldn't hear what they were talking about. Standing alone by the large panoramic windows, he turned to enjoy the harbor view while thinking about Ryan's presentation. It seemed to Dan that there was general concurrence that the subscription solution with an app was an exciting way forward, but he found it hard to estimate how much the system would have to be changed and extended in order to implement Ryan's proposal; and how the Lifeline app would need to be developed for users to feel the need—or desire—to use it regularly, perhaps even daily.

In the window reflection, he saw Ryan approaching the window and stopping next to him.

"Super meeting, don't you think?" asked Ryan as they both stood looking out over the harbor.

"Absolutely," replied Dan, nodding thoughtfully. "But it's an ambitious plan you're presenting, I must say. I think the announcement surprised everyone."

Dan could see Ryan's reflection light up in a big smile, as if Dan's comment was predominantly positive, which it definitely hadn't meant to be.

"I'm glad you think so!" said Ryan. "I'm sure it'll be fantastic; and it doesn't have to be as ambitious and unmanageable as you think. We can buy most of the functions as pre-existing off-the-shelf web services from subcontractors, so we don't have to code it all from scratch ourselves."

Dan nodded. It didn't sound improbable, but he feared it might be more extensive than they imagined.

"As I mentioned earlier, there's something else I would like to talk to you about, as soon as possible," Ryan continued in a more subdued voice, turning to face Dan. Dan turned correspondingly to hear what was on Ryan's mind. He had a feeling it might be severe, judging by Ryan's worried expression.

"There have been some weird things happening lately, and I don't have the technical expertise to find out where in our system it's coming from," said Ryan. "It's not necessarily a bug—but it's certainly something I don't understand, and I would rather not involve the other coders in it, let alone Michael."

"What exactly is the problem?" asked Dan, his voice equally subdued. It wasn't like Ryan to beat around the bush as he was doing right now.

"It might not be a problem, but it's certainly something weird I don't understand," replied Ryan, glancing briefly over his shoulder to make sure no one heard him before continuing. "Our system is clever—but perhaps it's a little too clever. It looks like it can now predict which day the customer will die. Not only what day of the week, but the exact year and date on the calendar!"

FIVE

Saturday morning, Dan arrived at Ryan and Gitte's villa on a quiet street in the Strandvejen district, north of Copenhagen. He'd been there many times before—maybe fifteen to twenty times; it was impossible to say precisely, as some visits, during his period of addiction, overlapped in his memory.

The weather was as lovely as it had been the previous day. Dan parked next to Ryan's black Mercedes and Gitte's red Maserati, which were parked on the narrow strip of gravel in front of the high white wall that surrounded the large lot. After a deep breath, he got out of his car and walked to the large wrought-iron gate, where he pressed the intercom. It took three seconds before the lock buzzed and the gate swung inward.

Walking down the gravel driveway, he again reflected on what Ryan had told him after the board meeting: that the Lifeline system had started predicting when each customer would die. He looked forward to seeing Ryan's data and documentation, and felt reasonably confident that he'd be able to spot the errors or determine why the results might be ambiguous or inaccurate, or that the analysis was based primarily on an interpretation that was simply too vague to lead to the outlandish conclusion Ryan had arrived at.

But something nagged at him. Dan had always known Ryan to be a skilled analyst who examined the data and its sources carefully before attaching value to it and letting it govern his decisions. Furthermore, Dan was no longer the same person who, in the past, would have felt one hundred percent confident in his rejection of any claim that sounded even a little supernatural and couldn't be explained scientifically.

Dan looked around the beautiful and well-kept backyard. Although it hadn't rained for almost three weeks, everything looked green and fresh: the large lawn and the shrubs and trees scattered across it. He knew Ryan spared no expense in tending the garden, and that a gardener came by regularly to ensure everything looked its best. The giant lot had a slight slope, and on this side of the house, dense clusters of sycamore trees stood near each end wall. There was no access or view to the opposite side of the house—with the terrace and the large garden facing east over the Sound.

From the backyard where Dan walked, the house didn't look as grand and flashy as it did from the other side. It appeared to be just a sizeable two-story villa with a few small windows, a wide garage door at the end of the driveway, and the main entrance door next to the garage. It was impossible to guess that the entire garage was also a huge elevator, used by Ryan when he wanted to move a car in or out of the large basement, where he had his workshop and car collection.

Twenty meters before the garage door, a small tiled path connected to the driveway. The path led around a group of tall bushes to the front door, where Dan—out of habit—knocked, even though Ryan and Gitte had often told him just to enter. He waited a moment, then opened the door and stepped in.

Although the summer heat outside didn't bother him, it felt comfortable to enter the air-conditioned house. From the large entrance hall, there was access to two bathrooms and the basement staircase on the left, to the large living room in the middle, and the door on the right led into the house's vast kitchen. As always, Dan started by going into the kitchen to say hello to Gitte, who would typically spend most of her time there, when she was home. Not because she cooked or did other domestic things—they had people helping them with that, too—but because she'd made the kitchen her office. It was in the kitchen that Gitte did most of her work—with a small laptop as her only aid—and it was here that she met her colleagues and friends, those whom Ryan referred to as her *gang*. Although Ryan would sometimes cook at home in their kitchen, he'd typically eaten in town before coming home.

The kitchen was separated from the large living room by a low bar table across the width of the room, with a wide passage in the middle, and there were bar stools on either side where you could sit and eat, work, or just relax.

Gitte and Ryan's kitchen also had a special meaning for Dan because it was where he and Susan had first met.

It was at a party three years earlier, one of Ryan and Gitte's smaller get-togethers, with 'only' fourteen guests. Dan was making some special drinks that Gitte had said she would like—and which he'd immediately offered to procure. Having found the required bottles and other ingredients, he was standing by the enormous kitchen island, pouring the finished mixture into four glasses, when Susan stepped into the kitchen through the passage from the living room.

"Hi," she said, smiling at him. "The bathroom—is it this way?"

Dan returned her smile, frantically trying to think of something to say that might evolve into a conversation. He'd seen her earlier in the evening—out in the garden, talking to another guest, a short distance from where Dan was standing. He hadn't heard what they were talking about, but her voice was as charming as her looks—especially when she was laughing at something. She had been dressed plainly in light trousers and a gray shirt, and Dan had a hard time taking his eyes off her. But after a few seconds, he became aware of Gitte, standing a little further up the slope, watching him. He could feel his cheeks flushing, and quickly looked away, but noticed how Gitte was still looking at him with a little smile.

And now the beautiful woman was standing right in front of him, on the other side of the kitchen island, and he couldn't think of anything to say.

To answer her question, he pointed to the left, toward the door to the entrance hall. He was still smiling, convinced that he looked like a clown, but it was reassuring, after all, that she was still smiling at him, too. Fortunately, instead of immediately continuing to the door, she stayed and looked at the drinks he'd just finished making.

"Looking nice! Is one of those drinks for me?" she asked.

"Uh, yeah—sure," replied Dan. He didn't know if Gitte had thought of anyone special, other than herself and Dan—she'd just asked if he could make a few, and when he'd continued to look a little quizzical, she'd specified, explicitly asking him to make four.

"Great! I'll be back in a minute, and I'll help carry them out," she said and started walking toward the door. "By the way, I'm Susan," she said, glancing back at Dan before disappearing out the door—before he could tell her his own name.

When she returned, they took the glasses and walked out into the garden to find Gitte. On their way through the living room to the large panoramic doors, Dan thought he'd better introduce himself—so she would at least remember his name in case he didn't get a chance to talk to her again during the evening.

"My name is Dan. I work with Ryan at Lifeline."

"Okay, I thought it might be you. I think I saw a picture of you in one of the magazines once," said Susan.

Dan sincerely hoped it wasn't one of the many pictures where he was drunk and acting like a fool.

Out on the terrace, they looked for Gitte and finally spotted her at the far end of the garden, where she was sitting on a small garden bench talking to one of the other guests. They managed to get there without spilling too much of the contents of the glasses. When they arrived, Gitte stood up from the bench, and the man she was talking to rose right after her. Gitte accepted the two drinks from Dan and offered one of them to the other guest.

"Come, I want to show you something new up in the house," she said, leading him away from the small bench before he had a chance to start a conversation with Dan or Susan. She looked back at Dan and Susan and nodded toward the bench.

"Sit down and enjoy the view," she said. It almost sounded more like an order than a polite suggestion, so Dan and Susan hurried to sit down.

Gitte and the guest kept talking as they slowly disappeared in the direction of the house, and Dan and Susan toasted each other, tasting the drink Dan had made. It didn't taste like anything special, but Dan emptied the glass in a single gulp, anyway.

After sitting together on the bench talking for hours, without noticing that it had gotten darker—and also slightly cooler—Gitte came down and informed them that the other guests had left the party; but Dan and Susan were welcome to spend the night if they wanted. Both Dan and Susan had declined, although Dan had the impression that Susan was as close to accepting the offer as he was.

All three returned to the house and sat in the kitchen for a while, chatting with Ryan after they ordered two taxis. After saying goodnight to Gitte and Ryan, Dan and Susan walked up the driveway and waited outside the tall wall for their taxis to arrive. When the first taxi approached, Dan was about to shake Susan's hand and say goodbye when she pulled him close and kissed him briefly.

"I really want to see you again. That is, if you want to," she said softly. "Won't you please call me sometime?"

Dan smiled and nodded repeatedly, but couldn't think of anything to say. She got into the taxi, told the driver her address, and waved to Dan as the car began driving down toward the main road to the city.

Gitte was sitting on a high stool at the far end of the kitchen island. When she saw Dan, she closed her laptop and waved him over while taking a sip from her large coffee mug. She didn't get up to exchange handshakes or to hug, and Dan had never seen her shake hands with anyone—even at meetings or parties. But she smiled warmly at him as he walked through the kitchen, where he hadn't been in more than a year.

"Hi, Dan. Sit down for a moment," she said, pointing to the chair next to her own. "I just have to hear how you're doing."

"Hi, Gitte. I have an appointment with Ryan. I think he's waiting for me," tried Dan cautiously, but to no avail.

"Ryan can wait a few minutes—he's sitting in the garden, enjoying the wonderful weather."

Gitte looked thoughtfully and approvingly up and down at him as he sat down on the chair to her left.

"You seem to have recovered one hundred percent after your disease," she said after he'd settled himself on the high stool. "You can't imagine how happy I am that you came out of that in one piece."

"Thank you. That's sweet of you, Gitte," replied Dan, and though he assumed there was a significant element of polite accommodation in her statement, he couldn't help but notice that her eyes went a little moist as she said it. She briefly sipped her coffee before continuing.

"It's really impressive that you've gotten through your dependency problems—and with no help at all."

Dan nodded. "Thanks, Gitte—but it's not quite true. I couldn't have done it without the treatment and the AA meetings. The addiction would have ended up killing me." He pondered for a moment before proceeding.

"And I also had another experience that was crucial, not only for my recovery but also for my entire outlook on life and self-understanding."

Dan didn't know why he told this part of his experience to Gitte. He'd decided never to share it with anyone—not even with Michael, the person he knew most interested in spiritual things—mainly because he realized how strange it must sound. But, for some reason he couldn't put his finger on, Gitte seemed like someone who would understand. And besides, it might be good to have the courage to share with another person. He took a deep breath before continuing.

"When I was at the bottom of the hole, as I picture it, I had a strange dream, or vision is probably a better term."

He paused briefly to find the proper wording and noticed that Gitte looked interestedly at him.

"I think it's normal to have nightmares and weird dreams when your body, and consequently your mind, is so destroyed by alcohol," he continued. "Digestion stops, and your system can't absorb any energy. You also lose the ability to sleep, so you don't experience the periods of deep sleep where the brain cleans up the day's inputs and experiences. You're so destroyed in every way that it's hard to comprehend."

Dan looked around the room as he tried to articulate his experience to Gitte—and perhaps also to himself.

"There may be a scientific, neurological explanation for my particular experience, but it was so intense and unforgettable that it changed everything—not only in getting my life back on track but also in my perception of other aspects of life and existence."

He glanced at her, trying to determine if his story still had her interest. It seemed like it, so he opted to continue.

"This happened one night, when I was so down and out that I had no strength to move, and just lay on my sofa watching a bit of TV from time to time, waiting for my body to be able to sleep, just for five, ten minutes. Once when I finally slept—it sometimes took a few days before it happened—I met in my dream a being that I perceived only as a voice, coming from a black, shapeless object that filled the entire visual area of my attention."

Again he looked at Gitte, who nodded to show she understood, encouraging him to continue.

"I've never been religious, but I had no choice but to identify this voice as God or an oracle explaining things, and to whom I could ask questions."

"So, what did you ask it?" Gitte interjected with interest.

"I formulated the obvious question when such an opportunity presents itself, and asked what the meaning of life is," said Dan, smiling sheepishly.

"And what did the voice say to that?"

"In a matter-of-factly tone, it stated that life is its own purpose, that the purpose of all living things is to try to survive and reproduce."

Now Gitte was smiling too.

"Well, that's true, I guess—if you reduce the definition of life to a purely biological phenomenon."

"Exactly! As you ask, you're answered. I tried to rephrase and then asked, what's the meaning or purpose of my personal existence?"

"Good thinking," commented Gitte with a smile. "You hadn't lost your rational faculties entirely, after all."

"Thanks. Well, the strange thing was that even though my body and my thoughts were a big, broken mess, my dialogue with the voice was surprisingly clear, as if it was another—deeper—part of myself doing the talking. This wasn't something going on in my body or mind—but still something I was part of. Perhaps something that was, in fact, more *me* than my body or consciousness."

"So, what did the voice answer to the question about the meaning of your existence?" asked Gitte, now clearly even more interested.

"The voice, God, or the oracle, replied that the meaning of my existence is the same as for all humans, but that I should find out for myself what it is—that it's the reason we're here."

"Have you found the answer?" asked Gitte, without a hint of sarcasm.

"Not yet," replied Dan. "But I'm working on it; and the voice told me it wasn't too hard to figure out."

Dan referred to it as the voice, but he felt certain that it had to be God. It had referred to itself as *the Master Entity*, and told him he was very close to dying. But it said someone was shielding him and had advocated giving him one more chance.

The reason its message had made such a deep and indelible impression on him and his entire existence wasn't only the words, but the way they were spoken. He'd experienced them more clearly than if they'd been shouted into his ears with a megaphone. Not as screams—just words that struck him at a depth he hadn't known existed. In a depth where only the words existed.

It surprised him how much of his conversation with the Master Entity he'd referred to Gitte, and how uplifted he felt for having dared to share his profound experience with another human being. It would have been even better to share it with Susan, but he knew that would never happen.

On an intellectual level, he understood that the entire experience could probably be explained as hallucinations in a weakened brain—perhaps due to poor oxygen supply or some other physiological or clinical phenomenon. But this didn't for a moment shake his newfound belief that a higher, transcendent power must exist, and that he wouldn't have escaped from the dark hole without it. He was sure it was real: at least as real as the sensory experience of the physical world he had, for example, here and now in Gitte and Ryan's kitchen.

Dan could see the hint of tears in Gitte's eyes again, as she leaned forward, took one of his hands in hers, and squeezed it. It wasn't often that Dan had seen her having physical contact with another person.

"Thanks for sharing this experience with me, Dan. You've no idea how much it means to me," she said with a trembling voice, wiping her eyes with a quick movement before she continued.

"Ryan hasn't been functioning well while you've been sick. He's clearly missed you—and, what's worse, I'm sure he's made some decisions he wouldn't have made if he'd had the chance to review them with you. He needs you to brainstorm ideas and plans, and maybe take the top off the most unrealistic and wild ambitions."

Dan looked at her, puzzled—not knowing what to say. He assumed Gitte was magnifying the problems Ryan could have had during his absence. Nevertheless, he also knew Gitte as someone who was always objective and precise in her statements and who never exaggerated. He merely nodded, and after a moment, she continued.

"He discusses some things with me, but typically it's because he wants to impress me or because he simply needs to hear what the plans sound like to someone else. And to be fair—he does listen quite attentively to my feedback and sometimes takes it to heart; but certainly not to the extent that he usually listens to you."

Dan nodded, but also felt he had to stand up for Ryan. "On several occasions, Ryan has told me how much he values your opinion and judgments, Gitte," he said, which was true.

"Okay, maybe I'm not being entirely fair to him—but I guess it's probably something he told you while drunk. In any case, it's good that you're yourself again—for that reason, too."

Dan turned in his chair to leave the kitchen and join Ryan in the garden, but Gitte wouldn't let him off the hook so easily; and he already had a hunch about what she was going to bring up.

"How are you and Susan doing?" she asked, as if she'd read his mind.

It annoyed him a little that he had to be reminded of Susan again and also talk about her. He looked around the large kitchen.

"We're not together anymore," replied Dan. "My alcohol abuse and all the lies were too much for her—and I completely understand that."

"Yes, I knew you weren't together anymore. But now you're back on top and have put the terrible ordeal behind you. I think you should try to contact her again."

"I plan to talk to her before too long. But it's purely to say sorry for all the bullshit I did and for ruining our relationship." He paused briefly, thinking about what he wanted to say to Susan, before continuing.

"But I know her well enough to accept that she's moved on with her life and couldn't dream of looking back. I've no illusions that we'll get back together. She refuses to meet with me when I try to contact her. I hope one day I'll get the opportunity to meet her and apologize—to close the chapter properly—but I would rather not do it over the phone."

Gitte nodded thoughtfully. "That sounds like a good plan. Somehow, I have a feeling you'll reach her sooner or later."

She got up from the chair, walked to the fridge and took two bottles of cola and a bottle of water, and gave the colas to Dan.

"Shall we go out into the garden and see what Ryan is doing?"

SIX

From the kitchen, Gitte and Dan walked through the living room, out the large panoramic doors, and across the terrace that ran the width of the house.

They found Ryan sitting in a sofa arrangement in the upper part of the garden, one level below the terrace, and when he heard Gitte and Dan coming down the broad steps, he put aside his tablet computer and waved them over. Dan handed a cola to Ryan so he could take it without having to stand up or lean forward, and then sat down on a two-person sofa at the end of the low coffee table. Gitte chose the sofa opposite Ryan's.

"Thanks, that's just what I needed," said Ryan with a smile, obviously happy to see Dan again.

On the grass behind Ryan's sofa, Dan could see three empty cola bottles lying on the grass, and estimated that Ryan must have been sitting there for just over an hour.

Everyone unscrewed the caps of their bottles, and Ryan raised his cola in a greeting to the other two.

"It's great to sit here in the garden with you two again," he said. "It's just like old times."

Dan and Gitte nodded and smiled at each other and Ryan—and everyone drank from their bottles. Dan looked around the garden, which looked like he remembered. At the far end of the lower level, he could see the small bench where he and Susan had talked the first time they met. It felt like an eternity ago—or at least in another life.

"You've probably been up all night, thinking about our big plans—and especially about the baffling discovery I told you about yesterday?" said Ryan as he turned on the sofa to see Dan better as he spoke.

Dan smiled and shook his head a little.

"Fortunately, I don't have a problem sleeping at night anymore," he said, briefly thinking back to the period of abuse, when he'd often been unable to sleep for days at a time when it was at its worst. "But yes, of course, I've thought a lot about what you said yesterday—but I'm pretty sure there must be a good and rational explanation," he continued, glancing toward Gitte on the other sofa. She sat looking up at the house as if she were lost in her own thoughts.

"Don't worry," said Ryan. "Gitte is fully aware of what's going on. I don't have any secrets from Gitte. Do I, dear?"

Gitte moved her gaze from the house and glanced at him before answering.

"Sure, Ryan," she said with a friendly smile, though it still didn't seem entirely genuine to Dan. However, he'd often seen them tease each other for fun, and when they sometimes competed in trivia knowledge, they both spent much energy impressing each other—always in a relaxed and amicable tone. Despite the age difference, it was evident that they had many things in common and appreciated each other's company.

Ryan leaned back, closed his eyes, and smiled up at the cloudless sky. It was clear he was enjoying the warm summer day and the company of Gitte and Dan.

When Ryan and Dan traveled the world—to meet with potential partners and suppliers of web services they were considering for the Lifeline system—Gitte had always been the main reason Ryan looked forward to coming home.

Similarly, Dan was also looking forward to being with Susan again, but didn't talk about her as much as Ryan talked about Gitte.

On the plane home from one of their first trips, where they'd been in Vietnam to talk to a company about a potential collaboration, Ryan had described how he and Gitte initially met. Ryan and Dan had already had a few drinks after a successful meeting with the Vietnamese company: first at a bar in town, then in the airport lounge while waiting to board, and finally after they'd settled into their business class seats and the plane had taken off. They were both tired after a long day but in high spirits—and fast on their way to getting drunk.

"I'll never forget the first time I saw Gitte," Ryan said, unprompted. "It was after a presentation I'd given on the last day of a Glasgow conference on the crossover between IT and biotech."

Ryan smiled nostalgically as he relived the situation in his memories. "Back then, I wasn't exactly an expert in either area, but I thought it would be good publicity for the company. So, I'd put together a decent presentation, with some discreet copy-paste from various articles I'd found on the web, and exaggerated some aspects, so it all sounded a bit science fiction-like, and made me look like a visionary thinker with a clear picture of what the future would look like."

Both laughed at the description, and Dan could easily imagine the process. It was typical of Ryan to be grandstanding in all sorts of disciplines—whether or not he knew anything about them. But even though Ryan would often adorn himself with borrowed plumes, the extent of his knowledge still surprised Dan—even in Dan's own fields like AI, databases, and IT in general.

"After my presentation, Gitte came up to me to ask some follow-up questions. We left the auditorium together while we talked about various subjects—especially in the areas of biotech, genetic analysis, and that sort of thing," recounted Ryan. "It was clear that she knew what she was talking about—certainly better than I did at the time."

Ryan sipped his whisky again before he continued the story.

"She was without comparison the most beautiful woman I'd ever seen, and I was naturally wildly attracted to her; and it only got worse the more we talked. It was a special experience to be walking with her in the conference area—and see how people looked after us, that is, after her—and not after me, as I'm normally used to."

Dan recognized the description. He'd noticed how people often turned and looked, or even pointed, at Ryan because of his size, and it had always puzzled him that Ryan seemed utterly indifferent to their looks and comments. Dan often wanted to walk up to people and comment on their unsympathetic behavior, but chose not to because he didn't want to draw attention.

"After we'd walked around and talked for at least an hour, we had a cup of coffee at a small snack bar in the area, and she suggested we dine together in the evening. Naturally, I thought it was a great idea. During dinner, we continued the professional talk—but gradually, it became more casual and personal, and afterward, we wandered around the cozy streets of Glasgow, talking about all sorts of things—I no longer remember exactly what it was. And finally, she walked with me to my hotel, where we spent the night together."

Ryan paused and drank the last of his whisky in one gulp while smiling distractedly, slowly shaking his head, as if he still couldn't believe how it could all have happened.

"I was in the seventh heaven, and after we returned to Copenhagen, I was flabbergasted when she wanted to make the relationship permanent, at which point she immediately moved in with me. She's undeniably the type who can have any man she wants—not only because of her looks, but equally because of her personality and charisma."

He paused briefly as he looked around the cabin and made eye contact with a flight attendant, who immediately began walking toward their seats.

"I don't kid myself that she wants to be with me because she thinks I'm a gorgeous fella. But we can't all have Michael's looks; and apparently, I have something his type doesn't have, after all."

With a smile, Ryan handed his empty glass to the flight attendant and politely requested a refill.

"But it's quite puzzling," he continued with a contemplative expression. "I don't think I've ever seen her physically attracted to any man. Or any woman, for that matter."

Neither of them said anything until the flight attendant returned with a fresh glass of whisky, which she smilingly handed to Ryan. Ryan sipped his drink and turned his head to make sure that Dan hadn't fallen asleep.

"No doubt she's an exceptional woman—in every way," said Dan. "She must be an invaluable help to you in your work?"

"She certainly is," replied Ryan with a thoughtful look. "Come to think of it, it was actually Gitte who brought Avaram to my attention and even explained why investing in your and Michael's company—and your know-how—would be a smart move. So don't give me that old stereotype about blondes and intelligence."

"Absolutely. I would never do that," said Dan. "Not about Gitte or anyone else."

He was surprised that Lifeline's purchase of Avaram had originally been Gitte's idea, and he tried to find an explanation for how she could have known anything about his and Michael's tiny outfit.

Ryan turned in his seat to look out the small airplane window. "Sometimes she frightens me a little with her keen intelligence," he said, not addressing anyone in particular.

"And her peculiar insight into the ways people think and react," he added a few seconds later, so quietly that Dan could barely hear it, while absentmindedly watching the clouds below them as they were dyed red by the setting sun.

Dan took a sip of his cola, leaned forward, and set the bottle on the coffee table. He looked first at Ryan, who was still sitting with closed eyes and a casual smile, and then at Gitte.

Gitte looked over at Ryan and cleared her throat loudly.

"How about updating Dan on the recent events with the uncanny predictions in the Lifeline document?" She asked.

Dan had been about to suggest the same thing, but she beat him to it. He looked forward to hearing more about the problem and felt well-equipped to pinpoint the error—even if it was to be located deep within their software.

"Sure—that's a good idea," said Ryan, opening his eyes and looking first at Gitte and then at Dan before commencing.

"As I briefly mentioned to you yesterday, our system has begun predicting the customer's date of death," said Ryan, then pausing briefly—presumably to find the most accurate way to explain it, before continuing.

"The Lifeline document suddenly had an added number showing how many days the specific person's life will comprise—starting from the day they were born. The text in the field used for displaying our moderately scientific estimate of how old the person will live to be now has this unexplained number added—it happens somewhere in our system, but I'm not technical enough to pinpoint where exactly."

Ryan leaned forward to illustrate. "So, for example, where the label shows 'Life expectancy', the value '85 years' is displayed, followed by the puzzling number, without space—as part of the same string." As he explained, he showed with air quotes where the quotation marks were and how the parts of the text were joined.

"Ryan and I've started referring to the inexplicable number as the *omega value*," remarked Gitte.

Dan nodded to show he understood what they were conveying—but he couldn't help smiling a little at how absurd it would be, if the number indeed showed what Ryan and Gitte implied.

"So, for example, if the number is 30,000, and it gets divided by 365 days per year," said Dan, trying to do the math in his head. "Then it indicates the person will supposedly live around, uh, eighty years?"

"You got it," said Ryan as he picked up his tablet from the sofa and started tapping the screen with his fingers.

"More precisely, it'll be 82.19 years. Good shot, Dan!" he said, nodding approvingly at Dan. "And leap years in the given period must, of course, be factored in to find the precise date of death, calculated as days from the date of birth."

Dan bit his lower lip and gazed in front of him, not focusing on anything, as he warily shook his head. He tried to find the best point to attack the problem.

"How did you discover the extra number in the Lifeline document?" he asked. "And how long ago was that?"

"It was exactly April 3rd," replied Ryan. "One of our young, newly hired lawyers had tested the document on herself, submitted the mouth swab, and filled out the questionnaire—the normal flow that our customers follow. One morning she came into my old office and told me about the process and the Lifeline document she'd received—and said it all looked satisfactory from a legal point of view and that she thought it had been a good customer experience. She didn't think she had the prerequisites to assess the visual layout, but found it to look nice and contemporary. I was, of course, pleased with her test—also because it showed the kind of commitment I value—and thanked her. On her way out of the office, she turned around and casually added that she'd noticed one tiny thing that had to be an error: next to the life expectancy box was a definitely out-of-place number that had no meaning and obviously shouldn't be there."

Ryan took a couple of big gulps of his cola, then continued.

"Before I left the office in the evening, I made several random checks in the database of rendered Lifeline documents. First, to see if the error existed in more documents, and then to see how far back the problem went. At first, I didn't think it was a big issue, but it still annoyed me—it looked sloppy with a random number like that. My samples showed that the bug first appeared in a document generated for a customer on March 29th, and that a total of 1,455 documents had been created with the bug, until the specific day when it was brought to my attention. Five days later, that is."

After a deep breath and another sip of cola, he continued his recap.

"I then talked to one of the coders—a nice guy who always sits there until late at night—about the bug. However, he couldn't locate where in the system the number was added; but he suggested we could do a quick hack by adding a function in the flow just before the calculated raw data gets translated into the Lifeline document. The function would remove the last part of the string after 'years' so that only '90 years' would remain, for example, and not '90 years', followed by the unexplained number. I thought it was a great idea and asked him to implement it immediately, which he did in less than five minutes. My plan was to involve some more experienced developers the following day and set them to work finding the bug so we could drop the temporary hack. And then I went home with a good feeling of closure and peace of mind."

"So, how long did it take to figure out that the weird number was the total number of days in the customer's life?" asked Dan. In the back of his mind, he was already visualizing where and how he'd look for the bug in the software.

"It wasn't me or the coder who figured it out, which, in retrospect, I regret," said Ryan. "When I got home later that night, I showed Gitte some of the documents where the error had occurred."

Ryan looked across the table at Gitte before he continued.

"Gitte looked at them and immediately suggested that the number might be the internally calculated value in days before being formatted as the number of years the field shows. And when I divided the number from the various documents by 365, it looked like years—but none matched our loose estimate. They were all five to ten years off—some even twenty and thirty years, or more."

He took another deep breath and continued. "I decided I wouldn't think about it anymore before talking to the developers the next day. But in the middle of the night, Gitte woke me up and said she had an idea of what the number could be."

Ryan shifted his gaze to Gitte—now referring to her in the second person as if he were retelling the story to her. "You said you felt certain that the number represented the person's exact lifetime."

Gitte nodded and proceeded with her summarization while looking at Dan.

"Well, I can't say how I got the idea, but I was one hundred percent sure that was the explanation," she said. "Ryan was annoyed at being woken up with the 'stupid' theory, as he put it, and I could also hear how crazy it must have sounded."

Dan also found it very difficult to see how the hypothesis about the number of days of life could have materialized out of practically nothing. Especially when the list of possible rational reasons was overwhelming. At the time, the strange number could have been anything from a random value to an insignificant intermediate calculation or something else entirely. There were plenty of potential explanations within the rational universe without resorting to looking for a supernatural reason. He didn't say it out loud, however.

"But Gitte persuaded me to spend a few hours looking through the faulty documents," continued Ryan—now addressing Dan again, "to see if any customers only had a short time left and died on the specified day; and conversely, whether any had died, even though the number suggested they would live for many years."

Dan nodded. "So, you didn't meet with the developers the next day?"

"Correct. I dropped it," replied Ryan affirmatively. "Solely to test Gitte's hypothesis, as I'd promised. But I told her honestly that I thought it was a waste of my precious time."

Dan looked at Gitte, who nodded as Ryan continued.

"The first thing I did the next day was to talk to the coder from the night before. I explained that I'd found out that the number was simply an ID of a transaction that was mistakenly included from one of the service providers that generates certain data for our system. He accepted that explanation completely, and I asked him not to implicate any of the other coders in the issue, but to add a comment in the source code documenting the hack we'd made, as if it was supposed to be there. Just in case another coder should stumble across it."

"And you're still sure that none of them have discovered the problem, and are talking to each other about it?" interrupted Gitte.

"Pretty sure," replied Ryan. "Most of them work primarily on interactive flows on the website, implementing new user experiences, and that sort of thing. Currently, no one is directly involved in the subsystems and services that provide input to the document content."

He nodded over at Dan. "Most code on that level are the systems you and Michael developed back in the day."

"So, what did you do after that?" asked Dan, curious to hear how Gitte and Ryan had arrived at the grotesque interpretation.

"I looked through the documents and found two, where the number showed that the customer would die within the next month—if Gitte's assumption was correct."

Ryan began to rise from the low sofa. Dan and Gitte also stood up, but neither offered to give Ryan a hand—they knew from experience that he didn't like that.

"But let's go down to the basement, Dan," he said. "Then you can see all the details. I look forward to showing you the relevant data and hearing what you say about the whole situation."

"Good idea," commented Gitte. "I'll go for a run in the hills."

They all walked along the lawn to the steps leading up to the terrace. Gitte had picked up all of Ryan's bottles from the grass and taken them with her. Dan took his bottle, from which he'd hardly been drinking.

"So, what happened to the documents you'd selected?" asked Dan when they reached the terrace and were heading for the open panoramic doors. "Did those people die?"

Ryan nodded seriously. "Yes. They did. They both died on the exact date that their respective numbers in the Lifeline document matched. That's when I started getting a little nervous."

Dan looked wonderingly at Gitte walking in front of him and Ryan, speculating about where she'd gotten the idea and why she'd been so sure it was right. If it was an example of female intuition, it was still far beyond anything else he'd experienced.

"Yes," added Gitte quietly, without turning around. "I really hope you can locate the problem so we can stop this. These things aren't something anyone should know about their own life."

They proceeded in silence through the living room and into the entrance hall, where Gitte continued into the kitchen, while Dan followed Ryan down the steep staircase to the basement.

SEVEN

The basement was a single large room, covering almost the entire ground plan of the house. Next to the stairwell in the corner was a bathroom, and after it was the big elevator used by Ryan to move his cars in and out of the basement. It was only in use when he acquired a new car for his collection or when he felt like driving another car—for example, when the seasons changed or on special occasions.

A dim reddish light lit up the room, but it was still bright enough to easily see the two rows of new and old cars lining the walls. The aisle between the two rows was wide enough to let Ryan quickly move the vehicles around. The room didn't feel like a basement but more like a large showroom.

On the walls were still the same pictures of cars, engines, and some large tourist posters from Greek islands—all lit up with small spotlights, so you almost had a similar sensation as real windows would have given.

At the far end of the room stood a series of sturdy worktables with various devices and machines that Ryan used when working on the cars. Here, bright white lamps lit up the work area, and large cabinets and shelves covered the end wall, containing everything from spare parts to different types of oil, tools, and old manuals. There was also a fridge where Ryan always kept an ample cola supply.

It was always an impressive experience to walk between the many cars. Dan counted nineteen in total—so the number hadn't changed since the last time he'd been there, more than a year earlier. He knew close to nothing about cars, so he couldn't tell whether there had been any changes in the collection. The only vehicles he recognized were a couple of Ferraris and a Lamborghini, but he couldn't really identify the rest.

The first time Ryan had taken him down to the basement, he'd presented every car, and Dan remembered him talking about different models from Bugatti, Bentley, and other brands. Still, he hadn't tried to remember every detail. Cars weren't one of his primary interests.

The only car in the collection that Dan knew a little about was an old, dark red Jaguar XJ220, which was Ryan's absolute favorite. It stood at the far end of the left-hand row, closest to the long tables. Ryan had enthusiastically explained all the details about the car and its previous owners—and it was evident that it had a special meaning for him. Although it wasn't the car Ryan drove most frequently, Dan had seen it in use a few times. And weather permitting, Ryan always moved it to the driveway for the annual summer party—so guests could admire his prized possession when they arrived.

They walked between the two rows of cars, around the large tables, and sat down on two office chairs at a table with no tools or parts on it. On the table was a large thirty-two-inch monitor and two prominent speakers. Dan knew that Ryan often listened to Verdi's operas when working in the basement. In front of the monitor stood Ryan's laptop with the display open. Ryan pressed the keyboard, and the laptop and the monitor lit up simultaneously. He quickly typed in a password, after which the screens switched to a blank desktop with no applications running, and then he double-clicked an icon for a PDF file.

"First, let's check out the strange number in one of the affected Lifeline documents that actually made it to customers," Ryan said as he scrolled down the open document. Dan watched the many paragraphs of text, charts, and numbers scroll by on the large screen until Ryan reached the paragraph with life expectancy near the end of the document. With his trackpad, Ryan pointed the cursor at the value, and Dan could see that the text showed '92 years15529'.

"15,529 days is roughly forty-two years," said Ryan before Dan could calculate it in his head. "And that's more than a hundred percent off our ballpark estimate of ninety-two years, calculated based on the customer's biometrics, lifestyle, education, various demographics, statistics, and more."

Dan glanced at the number. It was displayed without a comma or period as a thousand separator, but with the same font as the rest of the text. Based on the document itself, there wasn't much else to say about it. Ryan minimized the document and opened a spreadsheet before continuing the recapitulation.

"As I'd promised Gitte, I did a manual review of the 1,455 faulty Lifeline documents I'd found in our database, which took me all day and evening. First, I made this spreadsheet where I entered each document's ID, the customer's name and date of birth, and the mysterious number we now call the omega value. One row for each Lifeline document sent out. It was annoyingly time-consuming, although I could copy-paste the values from the individual documents."

Ryan took a quick gulp from his bottle. "It would have been nice having your skills with macros, automatic extractions, or whatever you would come up with to speed things up in a situation like this," he said, winking at Dan before he continued.

"In a new column, I then created a formula that showed a calculated date by adding the omega value to the customer's date of birth. The spreadsheet automatically adds leap years, which made things a bit easier. I then copied that formula to all the rows, and if Gitte's morbid theory was correct, the new column now showed each person's precise date of death. I sorted the list on the calculated column of dates and discovered that none of the dates was before the date when the customer had created the document. All the dates were in the future: either within the next few years or many years from now."

Dan nodded to show he understood what Ryan meant. If the omega value indeed showed the number of days in the person's life, measured from the day they were born, then it should never result in a date earlier than the day the customer had the document made. Because the customer had to be assumed alive at the time, they bought the Lifeline document.

"I hadn't expected to find any dates in the near future," continued Ryan. "But there was one already in late April and another in the middle of May. Using the document ID I'd entered for each row, I found the relevant documents in the database, including all our registered data for the two customers. The one with the calculated date in April was a customer from California, and the other—with the date in May—was a customer here in Denmark."

Ryan took the last sip from his bottle, set it down on the table, and rotated his chair so he could look more directly at Dan as he proceeded.

"The same evening, I showed the spreadsheet to Gitte, and we agreed not to do more about it here and now, but to keep an eye on whether the two people died around the date the document supposedly predicted. I still felt confident that nothing would happen to the two customers, so I was simply looking forward to the tests disproving Gitte's theory, so we could ask the coders to find and fix the bug and get on with our actual work."

Ryan slowly got up from the office chair and walked to the large fridge while he continued talking.

"A few days after the first, uh, test date, in late April, I contacted a lawyer I know in Los Angeles. I gave him the customer's name and address and asked him to get the most basic data on the person. The next day, the lawyer wrote back, with the little data he'd been able to find on such short notice."

Ryan had now returned to the table with a new cola. He unscrewed the cap from the bottle, but set it on the table without drinking from it, before sitting down on his chair again.

"And now comes the crazy part," he said in an incredulous voice. "Unfortunately, the man had passed away after a brief illness, as stated in the obituary the lawyer had found and attached as a quick scan. He died exactly on the date the omega value in the document showed—when added to his date of birth."

Dan didn't know what to say. He just sat staring at Ryan, his brain working in many directions, trying to find an acceptable explanation. Somehow, he expected Ryan to break down at any moment and confess it was all a joke. And even though he knew Ryan well enough to know that he'd never do such a thing, it was still the best reason he could think of. Another possible explanation was that the number had changed after the customer had died, but then Ryan wouldn't have been able to pick the specific document at the beginning of the process. A third possibility was that the Los Angeles lawyer was lying, and the customer was still alive. And finally, it could also be a rare coincidence—however unlikely—since it was still based only on a single test.

He was shocked, but far from convinced. Several things needed to be investigated, including every part of the Lifeline system, before he would be anywhere near accepting that a pile of software could precisely predict when certain people would die.

Ryan nodded. "Yeah, it's pretty hard to swallow," he said with a compassionate smile. "I've been through the same emotional spectrum that you're in right now—where you skeptically jump from one implausible explanation to the next, to avoid having to accept that the number actually predicts the customer's date of death. But believe me, it gets worse."

With a tap on the keyboard, he switched back to the Lifeline document he'd shown Dan a little earlier.

"This is actually the exact document we sent to the other person—the Danish customer—where the number showed he'd die on May 15th, this year," said Ryan.

"As we approached that date, I got the idea that I would have a man discreetly watch the customer in question, who lived down south in Køge. I made an appointment with a competent chap I know from the old days. He's in the security business and would be perfect for solving this kind of, uh, unusual assignment. And it was quite simple: he would check daily what the man was doing and observe whether he left his home during the day, and if so, where he went."

Dan watched Ryan speculatively as he went on, but he already had a nagging suspicion of where this was going.

"The plan was that he would discreetly follow our customer from three days before the calculated date to three days after. If nothing serious happened to him during that period, and he was still alive, then it was my opinion that Gitte's theory had been disproven. Although, of course, two samples aren't much to make statistics on. Theoretically, the first 'positive' test or the second 'negative' test, respectively, could both have been exceptions. But I would at least breathe a sigh of relief when the customer was still alive a few days after May 15th. Which was still what I expected at the time."

Ryan again paused briefly as he drank from his bottle. After setting it back on the table, he turned to look more directly at Dan.

"I can see in your face that you already know where the story ends," he said, before continuing with a grave voice.

"With his own eyes, my man saw him perish in a terrible traffic accident on the highway toward Copenhagen—exactly on the predicted day. He collided with a truck and was killed on the spot. The truck driver suffered severe bruising, but fortunately survived."

Hearing about the tragic incident shocked Dan, overshadowing, for a moment, the absurdities of the potential consequences of Ryan's story. He could see that Ryan was also affected by having to talk about the dreadful accident—even though the story was no longer new to him. Perhaps Ryan felt the Lifeline document, provided by his company, was somehow partly to blame for the tragic death, though, of course, that couldn't possibly be the case.

Without saying another word, Ryan got up and walked around the table and down the aisle between the two rows of cars. There was no need to explain where he was going: Dan knew he needed to use the basement bathroom. When Ryan wanted to go upstairs again, he would say so.

While Ryan was away, Dan rolled over to the laptop and scrolled to the top of the PDF file containing the deceased customer's Lifeline document. He read his name and address, as well as data on age, weight, family, and more; and he read what the man did for a living, for sports, and his interests and expectations, all the detailed information, he'd provided about his own life, that was used as input, directly and indirectly, to generate the document's recommendations and expectations. In addition, there were some results from the genetic analysis made from the submitted mouth swab. Everything looked fine, and there were no drastic recommendations for changes in diet or lifestyle. The man could easily have lived to be ninety-two years old, as their primitive calculation had predicted. Possibly even much longer. At forty-two, he was only ten years older than Dan, who still saw himself as a young man—despite the alcohol abuse that had taken its toll on him to the extent that it had almost cost him his life.

But life was risky, and everybody risked suffering an accident—especially in the traffic. There were no guarantees.

Dan forced himself not to spend any more energy imagining what the poor man's life had been like, and how it could have continued—in a better world. He resumed his frustrated attempts at finding an acceptable explanation for the events, still believing there had to be a rational causality within the bounds of science. He was sure it would be possible to find it, and whenever his thoughts began considering the prospect of a supernatural phenomenon, he dismissed it and blamed himself for even considering it.

Admittedly, the conversation with the Master Entity, which he'd told Gitte about, had fundamentally changed his view of existence and his place in the greater context. He no longer doubted that a higher power existed in or outside the observable physical universe. He still thought of the voice as the Master Entity—mainly because that was how it had referred to itself—but perhaps it was more accurate to simply start calling it God; although this would probably take some time.

Dan had never been religious—not even interested in the spiritual aspects of existence in the same way as, for example, Michael had. But the experience had been so fundamental and overwhelming—as if the voice had spoken directly to every cell in his body—that it had changed Dan forever. He was no longer afraid of what life would bring and knew that there was a deeper meaning to his existence that he had to devote all his willpower to realizing. The Master Entity had not only given him insight: it *was* the insight itself—something he knew he could rely upon without ever doubting.

But no matter if a transcendent and possibly omniscient God existed—and whether such a deity knew when every human being would die—it was still impossible for Dan to accept the conclusion that a computer system could have access to this supernatural insight. Particularly a system that he'd himself been a central part of developing.

At the other end of the basement, Dan could see the door to the bathroom open and Ryan come out. He pushed his office chair a little to the side so Ryan could get his seat at the laptop back. When Ryan reached the table, he sat down, gazing at Dan without saying anything. Dan didn't know what to say or how to rationally conclude anything based on the information he'd received. He looked pleadingly at Ryan—as if asking if there were any details he hadn't shared.

Ryan nodded thoughtfully while looking at Dan.

"I told you it would get worse," he said, smiling sympathetically. "I had some frustrating days and sleepless nights myself, repeatedly going over the events, trying to find a sane explanation—some weak link in the observations that I could investigate, hoping a palatable way out would appear."

Dan shook his head in disbelief. "What did Gitte say when you told her about the two incidents?"

"She was, not surprisingly, just as upset to hear about it as I was," replied Ryan. "But even though it was a terrible development, she was somehow relieved that the weeks of uncertainty were now behind us. She said we could now focus all our energy on finding the cause in the system and fixing the problem once and for all."

Dan nodded. He could feel himself homing in on the same conclusion: that the next step would be to look for the error in their software. Although he still wasn't ready to surrender and accept that their system could predict when people would die, he was slowly opening his mind to the possibility that it was a real risk. Another part of him still hoped that a reasonable explanation would emerge, and he was willing to give almost anything for that to happen.

With a deep breath, Ryan looked at Dan to make sure he had his attention. "I've now presented everything I know," he said and then paused briefly, holding his hands out, palms up. Dan intuitively sensed where the conversation was headed as Ryan continued. "The way I see it, the next step is for you to decide if you have the energy and courage to help solve the mystery."

With a slow nod, Dan showed he agreed with Ryan's assessment—not that he'd decided to be part of finding the solution.

"Obviously, you don't have to make a decision here and now," added Ryan. "Think about it for as long as you need, and then let me know—preferably within a few days, if that's enough."

Dan got to his feet and went to the fridge for a cola, feeling the need to stretch his legs. With the bottle in his hand, he walked slowly around the table, toward the other end of the basement, not thinking about anything in particular, but trying to get some distance from the shocking news and impressions Ryan had presented. When he reached the opposite end, standing in front of the large elevator, he opened the bottle and took a large gulp before slowly walking back to the table. Ryan followed him with his eyes but said nothing.

"I don't need more time to think about it," said Dan when he'd returned to his chair. "I feel like I have a responsibility to help solve this. In part because I'm fairly well suited to investigate our system—should it turn out that there's something inexplicable there—and also because I need to understand how all this is even possible."

He looked at the Lifeline document still filling the big screen. "I feel like someone has opened Pandora's box, and we're the only ones who can get it closed again."

Ryan looked as if he was relieved, maybe even touched, by Dan's decision. Relaxing a bit, his eyes were getting slightly shiny. Perhaps he was even a little surprised, too.

"I can't express how happy I am that you want to help with this, Dan," said Ryan, taking Dan's hand in both hands. "Now I feel like there's a chance we can locate the problem and probably even find a solution to this whole thing."

After a moment, he let go of Dan's hand and drank the last of his cola in one gulp before leaning back in his office chair with a sigh of relief.

"The alternative would have been to involve some of our other coders, which worried me," explained Ryan. "And even though they're talented, they've nothing like your background. Besides, both Gitte and I think it's important to involve as few people as possible."

They spent half an hour planning what they wanted to do. The first task was to make a list of all possible scenarios so that they could evaluate and prioritize each hypothesis separately. Included on the list were the things they'd already considered: the concurrences were mere coincidences; the collected observations about the two deaths were incorrect; and finally, the absurd prospect of their system actually having the capability to predict the dates.

Dan would delve into the Lifeline system and its many automated services, looking for an explanation from within the complex software. At the same time, Ryan would focus on the other hypotheses, trying to find more information to prove or disprove them.

"That's a brilliant plan," said Ryan, getting up. "But now I think we should call it a day, so you get a chance to process it all."

As they walked along the aisle between Ryan's cars, Dan had an idea. "I think we should try to persuade Michael to join the quest," he said, immediately sensing from Ryan that it wasn't a popular suggestion.

"Frankly, I would rather avoid it, if possible," Ryan said after they'd both stopped. "I don't like his attitude, and it's obvious he has a problem with me, though I don't have the slightest idea why. It was bad enough in the beginning after I bought your company—but it's only gotten worse since then."

Dan nodded. "Yes, I've noticed. I think Michael may have regretted that we sold Avaram and lost the control and advantages of being a small company in the process."

He didn't recap the other things Michael had said about his view of Ryan. "But I think it would be a tremendous advantage to have him onboard. It drastically increases our chances of locating the problem—if it's to be found in our software."

He could see that Ryan had picked up on his sentiment that it was important—even bordering on a condition—for Dan to participate himself, and after a few seconds of hesitation, Ryan consented.

"Okay, let's see if he has the time and inclination to help," he said resignedly. "Just make sure he doesn't talk to anyone else about it until we find the explanation."

"Absolutely. He'll definitely understand and respect that."

After they'd climbed the stairs to the entrance hall, they passed the door to the kitchen, where Dan waved goodbye to Gitte, who smiled back. Ryan followed Dan out the door and up the gravel driveway to the big gate, which he'd just opened with a control panel in the entrance hall. He shook Dan's hand for a long time, and when Dan drove down the road, he could see Ryan in his rear-view mirror, standing in front of the gate, waving at him.

Before returning to his summer house in the north of Zealand, he went into town to attend an AA meeting, but after the meeting, he couldn't remember a single detail of what had happened. He'd been unable to let go of the overwhelming impressions and information he'd received from Ryan and Gitte.

On the way to the summer house, Dan reflected on the day, trying to zero in on some ideas about how he would approach the task, but he felt his ruminations were taking him nowhere closer to a workable strategy. That would have to wait until the next day. But it would be nice to have someone to talk to about the whole thing—also on a more technical level—and he sincerely hoped Michael could help.

Again, he thought of Susan and what Gitte had said about trying to contact her. When he reached the summer house and parked the car, he sent her a text message asking if they could meet.

A few seconds after stepping through the door, he received a terse reply from Susan, saying she didn't want to meet him.

EIGHT

Dan and Michael ambled around the small forest lake, where Michael's cabin was located, while talking about the recent events.

The little cabin was painted dark red, typical of so many Swedish wooden houses. It lay a little out of the way, about twenty kilometers east of Malmö in southern Sweden, and Michael had bought it immediately after he and Dan sold their company to Ryan. He also had an apartment in Copenhagen—in the Nørrebro district, not far from where Dan lived in the Østerbro district—but typically spent most of the summer in his cabin, and had driven straight back there after the board meeting, three days earlier. There was quite a distance to the nearest town and other habitation, excluding a neighboring cabin—also on the lakeshore—which Michael said belonged to two brothers from Gothenburg. However, they didn't spend as much time there as he did in his cabin. No one seemed home, and they didn't encounter anyone on the narrow lakeshore path.

It wasn't an enormous lake—Dan estimated it to be the size of three football pitches. The water sparkled green from the many trees standing all the way down to the lakeshore, reflecting their crowns on the still surface. Walking under the canopy of old trees in the quiet forest felt pleasant on an otherwise warm summer morning. There was no traffic to be heard—only the mellow sound of the many birds.

The previous evening, Dan had pondered the situation unceasingly, trying to find a reasonable and realistic cause for the occurrences that Ryan had introduced him to, but hadn't succeeded. It was a frustrating feeling—and most of all, he'd felt like immediately diving right into the Lifeline system and the services and processes it comprised. Not because he expected to quickly find an explanation, but to at least feel like he was doing something to solve the matter.

Before he went to bed, he'd called Michael and told him that there was a problem he would like to discuss with him. And after assuring Michael that it was a technical problem they could probably solve—nothing critical about someone they knew being sick—Dan promised to give a full summary when they met. He preferred not to go into details on the phone: it would be easier to explain everything when they were together and could talk about it face-to-face—and about possible solutions.

He also hadn't told Michael that it involved Ryan and Lifeline, fearing that Michael would have immediately refused to hear anything about it. It would be easier to explain the whole situation, with all the details, when they were together before Michael decided whether he wanted to help.

Dan had visited Michael in his cabin several times and had found it again without problems after leaving the summer house in Liseleje at seven o'clock—knowing from experience that it would be a one-hour drive, depending on traffic.

He'd woken up early but still felt rested, and the many thoughts of the unexplainable predictions weren't preoccupying his mind as much as they had the night before. It had been helpful to get some sleep, distancing himself from yesterday's worrying talk. So, sitting in his car, he hadn't thought much about the problem per se, but more about how to explain it all to Michael. He tried to assess how he would react, but had no previous experience that was in any way comparable to this.

On the highway across the Amager island, he briefly thought of his mother, Anette. It had been a while since he'd heard from her, but he couldn't make up his mind if he should contact her—if for no other reason, then at least to make sure she wasn't dead. He deferred the decision, and as he drove over the bridge toward Sweden, his thoughts returned to the upcoming meeting with Michael.

The last stretch of the drive to Michael's cabin was along a narrow forest road, and when he'd reached the destination, he parked next to Michael's car—a big black Range Rover. He honked the horn once to signal his arrival, then walked around the small cabin to find Michael sitting on a small wooden bench with his eyes closed, enjoying the morning sun. On a small wooden box, which Michael used as a table, was an almost full water bottle.

Michael remained seated. "Do you mind taking a cola yourself? You know where they are," he said, pointing over his shoulder.

Dan nodded in reply, though Michael was still sitting with his eyes closed, and went into the little cabin. Apart from the fridge, where Dan took a bottle of cola, the room contained only a few things: a primitive kitchen table with a sink and a gas stove, a mattress with a gray blanket, a small wooden table with a three-legged stool, and a homemade bookshelf with twenty to twenty-five books and booklets, most of them—Dan knew from previous visits—about spiritual subjects. On the table stood Michael's laptop, with the screen closed.

The tiny room looked like the last time Dan had visited Michael. There was electricity, which Michael needed for the fridge and his laptop- and phone charger, as well as a single lamp hanging from the ceiling. But the cabin had no water or sewer hookups, so it was a bit of a hassle to use the toilet, which was just a tiny shed on the side of the cabin, with access only from the outside. You had to fill a bucket with water from the lake to flush it out. Although everything was more primitive than Dan's summer house in Liseleje, he knew Michael enjoyed the simplicity and that he often looked for new areas where he could cut down on 'luxury'.

Dan stepped out of the cabin with his cola and walked around to the small bench, where Michael opened his eyes and watched Dan as he sat down next to him.

For a while, neither of them said anything but just sat looking out over the small lake. After a minute, Dan took a sip of his cola before breaking the silence.

"It's as beautiful and peaceful as ever," he said without taking his eyes off the scenery.

Michael nodded. "Yes, it's nice here. It was such a stroke of luck that I found this place."

It seemed as if Michael wasn't eager to be updated on the problem Dan had come to talk about and that he was trying to postpone the time when it would be brought up. This was understandable, since the purpose of the cabin was also to provide a sanctuary where Michael could distance himself from the daily grind and the big and small problems that kept people busy in their everyday lives. It was a place where he could have a perfect setting for his personal studies and spiritual search.

Dan nodded but said nothing. After a short while, Michael reached for his water bottle and drank the remaining half of the contents before taking a deep breath and rising from the bench.

"Why don't we do like the other times you've been here, and walk around the lake while we talk?" he suggested.

"That sounds like a good idea," replied Dan as he followed Michael's example and stood up. They walked the short stretch to the lakeshore and turned right along the narrow path.

"I'm sorry I got so worked up about Ryan's plans at the board meeting," said Michael after they'd walked a few paces in silence. "I genuinely try to control my temper, but it's not always easy—especially when I have to listen to Ryan's ill-conceived ideas. But fortunately, I've gotten a little better at it in recent years."

Dan shook his head. "No need to apologize, Michael. And you certainly didn't get worked up, but argued calmly and logically. I totally agree that a subscription model for an app without a minimum of interactivity or news seems like a weird idea—at least from a technical and content perspective. And I would guess that some of the other board members feel the same way but might be afraid to stand up to Ryan—especially as long as everyone is making good money off his decisions and management style."

Michael nodded, but said nothing.

"If anything, I should have backed *you* up," continued Dan, "and not leave you hanging completely alone with your opinion—which I share, by the way. I can't quite assess the business arguments that Ryan presented, but my personal view of Ryan is that he usually thinks about things a lot. Maybe he's right, but there will certainly be much work for the developers."

Michael smiled. "Now you're the one apologizing—and it's completely unnecessary. I know Ryan listens to you—especially when you meet in private—so I'm sure you would bring it up with him when you thought it was optimal. For me, the problem is partly my temper and partly my poor relationship with Ryan."

Dan hoped to change the subject and address the problem he'd come to discuss with Michael, but he could feel that Michael needed to talk about his poor relationship with Ryan; and apart from that brief chat in Lifeline's new offices three days earlier, they hadn't spoken in over a year.

"I know you and Ryan never really got along," said Dan. "You were skeptical of Ryan even before we sold Avaram to him, and I guess it just went downhill from there."

"Yes, that's true," said Michael, nodding sadly. "I've often regretted selling the company. Not necessarily because it was Ryan, we sold it to—but because maybe in a way we also sold our soul."

Dan had never thought about it like that, but somehow it didn't surprise him that Michael felt that way.

They'd started their small company seven years before selling it to Ryan, including the system they developed. They were both in their early twenties but had already known each other for several years and had worked together on several major and minor programming projects.

The system they developed—which they named Avaram after their company—was essentially a platform that let customers work more meaningfully with vast amounts of data from many different sources. What set their system apart, compared to similar solutions from other vendors, was the capability to define and continuously adapt the schemas and indexes by which data were structured. This way, the customer's analysts and decision-makers could easily adjust the system to suit their needs and align with existing or planned data flows—without needing to involve internal or external system developers, such as those from Avaram.

They'd successfully implemented the system with a dozen private and public organizations, and Avaram had established itself as a flexible and generic solution for processing enormous data collections. Later, they'd started developing a range of AI systems—artificial intelligence, a technology spreading rapidly in the IT industry at the time. Besides the conventional methods of implementing and training AIs, they'd explored alternative in-house architectures that made adjusting the AI functions more flexible for customers—especially when defining or changing their data models and decision flows.

The Avaram system used the usual cloud platforms—from Amazon, Google, and Microsoft, for example—to store and process large volumes of data. Consequently, there was no need to purchase and maintain computers or other hardware at all—neither for the customers nor for Avaram itself in its development work.

One of Dan and Michael's key problems had been explaining the flexibility the users achieved with the Avaram system. Some found it simple and logical, while others couldn't visualize the connection between their current business needs and the abstract process of defining a system that could meet those needs. Unlike traditional development processes, it was a new discipline that didn't necessarily favor computer scientists and database designers, but anyone who could formulate an idea in an abstract yet structured way. This had been one of the reasons for accepting Ryan's offer to buy their company, since his investment would enable them to establish an organization that could scale the system to a much larger market than they could on their own.

Initially, however, Ryan had focused on using the Avaram system to optimize Lifeline's existing system, which had been an eminent way to develop the system further. But the plan was still to eventually market it as a standalone product—like Dan and Michael had aimed for in the system's earliest days.

"There was nothing wrong with the money we got from the deal," continued Michael. "It certainly gives you a certain security and some nice degrees of freedom—although I try not to let it run my life—but we must weigh all that against the things we lost: our absolute independence, the overview of the projects, and the speed with which we could turn ideas into reality. Life was simpler when it was just the two of us."

Dan could only agree, although the primary reason times had been simpler for him was that it was before he got caught up in his addiction. He'd lost control of his life, which overshadowed the experience of losing control of a company. He briefly contemplated whether there might be a connection between the two things—something he hadn't thought about before—but the process was too complex to be explained by a single cause.

"Nevertheless, we had some problems back then, too," said Dan. "But they were probably another kind of problems. Scaling and financing new initiatives became easier when we became part of Lifeline. In exchange for giving up absolute control, we got the opportunity to realize some of our plans on a completely different level."

He paused briefly as he reflected on their reasons for selling the company and becoming part of Ryan's universe.

"And the money we got for Avaram was undeniably a big part of the motivation. Of course, it was."

"Don't you think we were somehow swayed by Ryan's style and grand plans, too?" asked Michael. "And it overshadowed our reservations at the time, which perhaps we should have paid more attention to?"

"Yes. I think that's a fair analysis," admitted Dan. "Especially on my part. I should have listened more to your concerns. In the end, I think I was the one who convinced you we should sell."

"Not at all, Dan," Michael said firmly. "We were both convinced it was the right decision."

They'd now walked halfway around the small lake and paused at a clearing with a good view. On the opposite side of the lake, they could see Michael's cabin, and a few hundred meters to the right was the neighboring cabin, which looked bigger but was painted in the same dark red color. Apart from the two small cabins, there was nothing around the lake except the trees and the reeds along the lakeshore.

After standing for half a minute looking out over the lake—neither of them saying anything—Dan thought the time was right to update Michael on the problem, which was the main reason he'd come. He looked at Michael and nodded in the direction of the path on their right as an encouragement to continue their walk.

As they proceeded along the lake, he summarized the events for Michael in the order he'd planned in the car. He told how Ryan had briefly mentioned the problem to him after the board meeting on Friday and about the meeting with Ryan and Gitte at their villa the next day, where they'd elaborated on the situation. Then, he described how Ryan had shown him the spreadsheet he'd made with the individual customers and the inexplicable number, which Ryan and Gitte called the *omega value*, believing it showed how long each person would live. And finally, he told of the two customers who'd both passed away on the exact date the mysterious omega value indicated—when adding the number to the person's date of birth—and how a man Ryan knew had, in fact, witnessed one of them die in a traffic accident on the calculated date.

Michael said nothing as he listened to the lengthy account, but nodded thoughtfully several times to show that he understood. Undoubtedly, he was already trying to home in on weaknesses in the logic as well as arguments against the absurd conclusion, that their system was suddenly able to predict events in the future. Just like Dan himself had done when Ryan presented it all to him.

As he recounted the events, Dan felt a little disquieted again, despite having had twenty-four hours to process the shock. He was painfully aware that he'd come nowhere closer to a practical theory that would eliminate the frightening hypothesis that their system had gained a supernatural prescience about future events that no one could possibly know anything about.

After going through the complete story with all the relevant details, but without adding his own reflections and assessments, Dan heaved a long sigh. He looked regretfully at Michael, as if to apologize for involving him in a problem he probably would have preferred to steer clear of. It surprised him that, while he'd been explaining, they'd passed not only the neighboring cabin but Michael's cabin as well—without him noticing—and begun walking around the lake again.

They wandered along the path for a while, without either of them saying anything. Michael had the speculative look on his face, squinting his eyes and staring blankly ahead, and

Dan knew that the best he could do was give Michael the time he needed to grasp the surreal situation.

"Okay, I think I understand the problem," said Michael after thinking for a few minutes. "The simple and immediate theory—that our system can predict the future in the way you described—I think we can disregard completely for the time being. It clashes with every scientific principle, and I feel ridiculous just having to consider it. Although, on a spiritual level, I'm not opposed to the idea of God or some other transcendent power potentially possessing such knowledge. But either way, it would be a supernatural insight that could never ever be quantified or calculated within the rules and logic of science, and hence not by a computer program. As much as I would like to believe it's possible, it's simply not a sane hypothesis."

He glanced at Dan, who nodded apprehensively. Even if they started by rejecting the most unlikely hypothesis, it didn't mean the alternatives were much easier to accept. He was eager to hear if Michael could give a plausible proposal at an explanation.

"Right now, I'm assuming that what you're telling me—and what Ryan has told you—is correct," continued Michael. "But that's obviously the first thing we need to be sure of: whether the data and measurements are correct and that a date hasn't changed in a document after an event has occurred. But I get the impression that you don't think that's the case?"

Dan shook his head. "I don't see how Ryan could have known which dates to test and keep an eye on the persons, if the specified dates were not changed in the documents until after they died," he replied. "But it's certainly a gray area where something could have happened. I just don't know what it might be; but that's part of what Ryan will look into."

"Okay," said Michael skeptically. "But whatever Ryan finds out, you and I should check out his tests and documentation anyway—just to make sure."

Dan nodded but said nothing. He was grateful that Michael already seemed prepared to help solve the problem.

"But the statistical foundation is simply too weak, I think," continued Michael after a brief reflection. "Technically, there's only one sure test—that of the man from California—and although the probability of hitting a specific date is minuscule, it isn't zero."

Dan was about to protest and mention the other test with the man from Køge who lost his life in the fatal traffic accident—but simultaneously, he anticipated what Michael would say next.

"There's a detail in Ryan's recap of the traffic accident that we can't get around," said Michael, looking at Dan as he proceeded. "In my view, it's problematic that someone who expects a certain outcome is present in the scene where the incident occurs."

Dan nodded but said nothing. The same idea had occurred to him when retelling it all a few minutes earlier.

"It's impossible to observe a system without affecting what you observe," continued Michael. "This is a fundamental scientific principle."

"But Ryan felt sure that his man didn't have the slightest influence on the accident. Shouldn't we trust him on that?"

"Maybe. But the uncertainty still detracts from the value of the sample, I think. So, with only one measurement beyond doubt, the best hypothesis is that it's simply an astonishing coincidence. We need to get some more data: it'll make it easier to conclude categorically whether that isolated test was a coincidence."

They'd again reached the clearing, halfway around the lake. This time they didn't stop, but kept walking until they were back at Michael's cabin, where they sat down on the little bench and chilled.

Neither of them said anything, but Michael seemed satisfied to have pointed out the most likely explanation. And though Dan agreed with the arguments on the face of it, he still wasn't convinced.

NINE

A notification on his phone woke Dan a little before six the following morning. It was an email from Michael, who wrote that he was now driving from his cabin and would arrive a little over an hour later—depending on the morning traffic—and that he'd also discovered another problem with the observation of the deaths on the specific dates, which he would elaborate on when he arrived.

It had been a long time since Dan had spent the night in his apartment. Like Michael, he preferred to stay in his summer house whenever possible—especially in the summer months.

Before he'd said goodbye to Michael the night before, they'd chosen to use Dan's apartment in the Østerbro district as a base to work on finding the explanation for the inexplicable omega value in the Lifeline document. The location in Copenhagen made it easy for them both to get there—whether they stayed in their separate apartments in the city or preferred to return to their summer house or cabin in the evening. Consequently, Dan had opted not to drive back to the summer house in Liseleje, but had instead gone straight to his apartment. Fortunately, he'd brought his laptop with him on the trip to Sweden, so he didn't have to drive all the way to the summer house to pick it up.

The apartment also had the advantage of a good internet connection—especially compared to Michael's cabin, where he only used mobile data on his phone and didn't have much data on his plan. Dan was sure that Ryan would agree to the arrangement, although he could easily have offered them an office—either at the new address in the City Tower or one of the now empty rooms at the old office in central Copenhagen. But he and Michael preferred to work alone, without being surrounded by Lifeline colleagues, and in Michael's case, without the risk of bumping into Ryan.

Before Dan had left Michael to drive home, they'd tried to estimate how long it would likely take them to find and solve the problem—but it was too early to say precisely. They guessed it would take a couple of weeks at most, and since neither of them had any other obligations, they agreed to meet the next day to draw up a plan and then start locating the problem.

On the way home from Sweden, Dan had called Ryan, updating him on his meeting with Michael and their plan to begin the search the next day. Ryan was grateful for the update and that Michael wanted to take part; and he fully encouraged Dan's suggestion that the work could conveniently take place in Dan's apartment.

"After thinking about it, I'm glad you suggested asking Michael if he could help," Ryan had said. "And your apartment is fairly close to the City Tower so that you—or both of you if necessary—can get out here quickly. For example, if we need to talk about something too sensitive for us to do over the phone."

After a quick shower, Dan sat in his small living room with a mug of coffee, scrolling absentmindedly through the news sites and blogs that he used to stay updated.

It wasn't an enormous apartment. If anything, it was smaller than his summer house—but he'd loved it since he bought it at twenty-two. Before that, he'd lived in a rented apartment in the westernmost suburbs since he was seventeen and had moved out from the last of the many foster homes he'd lived with since he was a child.

The location was also good. It was on the fourth floor of a side street off Østerbrogade—the district's main street—and although he could hear some traffic noise, especially when the windows were open, it was still quiet enough for him to easily focus without being distracted. Besides the living room, there was a small bedroom and a narrow kitchen with barely enough space for him to cook. The bathroom was also a tiny room—with just enough space for the toilet and to stand and shower.

After they sold Avaram to Ryan, Dan had considered trying to find something bigger a few times. But the small apartment met his relatively simple needs, and after receiving the money from the deal, he'd bought the summer house, where he spent so much time.

Before his addiction had taken over, he'd lived for periods with Susan in her apartment in the Vesterbro district—in the western part of Copenhagen—which was considerably larger. But although he now knew that life with Susan was a closed chapter, he had no plans to find something more spacious. After his text message to her three days earlier and her short reply, he was determined not to contact her again—although there were still some things he'd hoped would have ended in a better way.

First of all, he felt a deep need to apologize to her for the mistakes he'd made while the alcohol abuse was gradually taking over. Additionally, he would have told her how his self-understanding had changed after the conversation with the Master Entity and during his addiction treatment, as well as at the AA meetings; and how it had given him an insight into his own mind, his thoughts, and feelings—his whole personality. He often thought about how important it had been for him to accept this self-knowledge and not be afraid of what he might discover in himself.

But on the other hand, maybe Susan didn't feel so comfortable receiving his text messages—even though he'd only sent her three after he got over his dependency.

At a quarter past seven, Michael rang the intercom and had only just climbed the stairs and entered the apartment before starting to explain what he'd discovered—while taking off his shoes.

"There's something we didn't talk about yesterday—which we should have thought of," said Michael as he walked across the room and put his bag on the dining table. After reading the email from Michael, Dan had tried to figure out what it was they'd missed—but to no avail. He said nothing, but waited for Michael to elaborate.

"Is it okay that I make tea while we're talking?" asked Michael, pointing toward Dan's tiny kitchen. Dan nodded and followed Michael out of the living room. Michael had been in the apartment many times and knew where to find the various things.

"We talked about how it was unfortunate for a given observation that someone with a particular expectation of the outcome was part of what was being observed," continued Michael as he filled the electric kettle with water, switched it on, and found a mug and a tea bag from the cupboard above the kitchen table. "But the gentleman Ryan had asked to watch the customer from Køge wasn't necessarily the only actor in the scene who expected that something catastrophic might happen that day."

Michael looked questioningly and with a mischievous smile at Dan, who still didn't know what he was referring to.

"It's obviously the Lifeline customer himself I'm thinking of, Dan!" revealed Michael vigorously. "What if he has been wondering about that out-of-place number at the end of the life expectancy field in the Lifeline document? And what if he's made a fluke guess that it might be the total number of days in his life? Then he can quickly do the same calculation Ryan did in a spreadsheet and calculate the date.

The time leading up to the ominous day becomes a nerve-wracking countdown. And on the day itself, you're filled with dread—depending on how much you believe your own absurd prediction."

Dan nodded contemplatively as he thought about Michael's reasoning. It was undoubtedly a scenario he should have considered himself. He didn't say anything, but listened as Michael continued.

"I can't estimate how likely it is—but I guess it just takes someone who is a bit technically inclined and happens to be a little superstitious and has a well-developed imagination, right?"

"But, from a customer making a wild guess that a random number should point to a date—plus expecting that date to mean something specific—to actually dying on that day? That's quite a stretch," interjected Dan. However, he agreed with Michael that some customers could hypothetically have had that idea, and that it could have impacted which day they died—even if it was probably very theoretical and had a minimal influence.

He remembered what he'd read about the man from the traffic accident when Ryan showed him the PDF file with his Lifeline document. "The man from Køge was a system developer," he said. "He might well be the type who would try finding an explanation for the number, and then come up with more or less imaginative theories about what it might mean. But whether he was the kind of person who would attach any greater significance to an arbitrary, self-made prophecy is hard to say."

Michael nodded thoughtfully as he poured boiling water into a mug and put the tea bag in. "Interesting. And the same mechanism could be applied to the customer from California. If he died while ill, even an irrational belief that he would die on a particular day might be a decisive factor in it actually happening that day. What do we know about him?"

"I haven't looked at his Lifeline document yet," replied Dan. "But we can easily retrieve it from the database."

Michael took the tea bag out of the mug and placed it on its paper envelope on the kitchen table so he could use it again. Dan considered making another mug of coffee, but instead grabbed a cola from the fridge and followed Michael back into the living room. They sat down on Dan's small sofa opposite his flat-screen TV on the wall.

"What we're talking about tastes a little like self-fulfilling prophecies," said Michael, sipping the hot tea. "We have no way of analyzing whether this was a contributing factor in the two cases—or if it's completely irrelevant. But we've all heard tales of people who attach so much validity to a prediction that they end up carrying it out—voluntarily or involuntarily. Our expectation of the future shapes the events and our interpretation of them—and if you strongly believe something is inevitable, you risk creating the conditions for it to happen."

"Good point—I think you're right," said Dan. "But it's complicated to assess how significant it might have been—and whether we can even use it as a probable cause."

"I absolutely agree. And for me, the key argument remains that there are only two incidents. From a statistical point of view, this is an insubstantial foundation. So even if the probability is tiny, the best hypothesis remains that they're random coincidences. I suggest we focus on looking for the location, in our system and all its various services, where the omega value is added, and in parallel, wait for some more cases."

"It sounds like a good plan," said Dan. He'd also thought of a feasible course of action, but wanted to give Michael a chance to share his thoughts first. "How do you think we should go about it?"

"What if we simply add some temporary log points in the code and track the creation of a customer's Lifeline document as it moves through the individual services, where each field is calculated and populated?" asked Michael, looking at Dan to see if he concurred.

A more traditional approach would have been to look for usable clues in the many pre-existing log lines from the individual services until they found the place where the omega value was added. Then they could identify the relevant function and dive into it to find the error. But that approach would require a lot of detective work, and there was no guarantee in advance that they would find a single log line that could bring them closer to an explanation.

Dan nodded to show he agreed with Michael's proposal. Independently, they'd thought of the same alternative procedure that had a better chance of bringing them faster to the finish line. It was an excellent example of how their cooperation had always worked. Usually, their ideas for models and solutions were overlapping—or even identical. Once in a while, their ideas were far apart. In those cases, they would typically quickly identify the best solution, which could be one of the two proposals or maybe even a completely different idea they discovered while discussing the options.

"First, the customer fills out the Lifeline questionnaire and submits their mouth swab by post," summarized Michael, mainly to recapitulate the workflow to them both. "Then our system waits for the mouth swab to be forwarded for gene sequencing by one of our service providers, who—once the sequencing is complete—sends back an automated message with a link to their web service, at which time our system can access the customer's genome in their database. And it's only at this point that our system has all the necessary data—including the user's original inputs plus access to the sequenced genome—and can generate the Lifeline document, which is then automatically sent as a PDF file to the customer with an email."

Michael looked at Dan, who picked up the thread and continued reviewing the plan they evidently agreed on, even if they hadn't fully outlined it yet.

"By adding our own temporary log points to the parent functions, we can more quickly locate the service where the error occurs and then fix it with a little luck. It's a super plan, I think. The advantage is that we're reasonably confident we can find the source of the problem, probably in less time. But there's a price for this shortcut. I can identify two problems we must deal with if we choose to go with that model."

"You're right," said Michael, continuing the train of thought. "Unlike the passive review of existing logs, this model requires us to tamper with an existing, live system. Even if we don't change a single existing line of code and only add a few log points, it's still an active intrusion. And if we make a mistake and a function crashes, it'll break the whole flow of creating new Lifeline documents for new customers. The question is, do we dare?"

They looked at each other for a moment and smiled.

"Of course, we dare," replied Dan. "As long as we double-check that there isn't a single syntax error in the log code we add, before we save the updated function. None of the other developers are directly changing the functions in the cloud, and I'm pretty sure they've never interacted directly with the online version."

"Exactly! All functions are edited and tested locally on an individual developer's computer, before being uploaded onto the server. But that introduces the risk that one of them executes a deployment and overwrites our modified version on the server?"

Dan nodded. "Yes, that risk exists; but it's not a risk to the flow of the system itself, only to the temporary log points we've added: they'll disappear because the function gets overwritten. We can live with that. And I'm pretty sure the scripts we want to tweak won't be updated regularly by the other developers. My best guess is that they haven't been changed since you and I wrote the code back in the day."

"You know that better than me—but you're probably right."

They drank from their tea and cola before proceeding with their deliberations.

"That was one problem," said Michael. "And I think I know what you think the other problem is. By bypassing the model where we review the existing log tables and instead write lines of code that add new log lines, we can't use the Lifeline documents that have already been created. We're forced to wait for new customers to have the document generated before any of our new log lines are added. And every time we adjust the code, we have to wait for a new Lifeline document to be generated and sent to a customer."

Dan nodded. "That's precisely what I identified as the other weakness of the simplified procedure, should we choose to go that route. But I'm sure we have similar ideas for a workaround?"

"Hmm, yes," replied Michael. "I guess you want to explicitly trigger the creation of a Lifeline document with data from existing customers as input. Then our new log lines will be added to the log tables immediately, after which we can review them. We only need to ensure that the last step in the process—where the generated document is sent to the customer—isn't executed."

Dan nodded. He wasn't surprised that Michael had the same idea for a solution to the problem as he did, and had also identified the only immediate weaknesses in the model.

"Yes, that was the flow I had in mind, too," said Dan. "We might work around the problem with the unwanted last step by setting a flag in the function that starts the flow, and then test on it before sending the email, so that step is bypassed. Then we can log whatever we want, using only existing data. Of course, the users' documents will be updated in the database, but that doesn't matter because none of them are sent."

They looked at each other to make sure there was nothing more they needed to consider before implementing their plan. Neither had anything to add, so they simultaneously got up and went to the dining table, where they sat down on the same side and opened their laptops. Both logged into the cloud platform's administration page, noticing that the password for the root account—which gave complete control over all parts of the Lifeline system—hadn't changed for over a year. They both smiled and shook their heads resignedly, and Dan made a mental note to remind Ryan to ask the developers to change it more frequently.

While coding and implementing the planned changes, they sat at one laptop, taking turns programming. They knew intuitively who was best suited to work with the different parts of the system, and while one typed, the other watched, pointing out when mistakes were made or if something could be done more elegantly. When they switched, the one who'd just been coding went to the kitchen to get fresh supplies: cola for Dan and water for Michael—although Dan noticed Michael changed to cola after a few hours of work.

For each call to the individual services that the system used to populate the Lifeline document, they added a line of code that logged the state of the document at that specific time in the flow.

The document was a JSON object—a simple text file with a formal description of a hierarchical data structure—containing individual fields for all the information to be calculated and populated by each service in the flow. Before the run, all fields in the document were empty, and after the run, all fields were filled out. Finally, the filled out JSON object was stored in the database and then used as input to generate the actual PDF file, which in the normal flow would be sent to the customer with an email. It was this last step that was now being bypassed in the test they were preparing.

Later in the afternoon, they ordered food from the local pizzeria, as they'd done many times before, and when it was delivered, they ate without either of them saying anything. Dan went through the whole flow in his mind, trying to see if they'd forgotten something in their code so it wouldn't work as intended or, in the worst case, would crash parts of the system. It looked like Michael was thinking the same, but neither of them could put their finger on anything they thought should have been done differently.

After eating, they carried the empty pizza boxes to the kitchen table and returned to their laptops. They spent half an hour making a complete backup of the systems and databases that would be affected, discussing what they thought could go wrong and what procedures they should prepare for the different scenarios.

When they both felt confident that everything was ready for the first test run of their adapted flow, all they had to do was execute a command in a Terminal window on Dan's laptop.

The Terminal was simply a neutral-looking window with white text on a black background, where you started a program by typing its name, followed by the information the program needed. This executed the program, and its output was written on the screen in the same simple way.

They looked at each other to make sure they were ready.

"Which customer should we use for the test run?" asked Michael.

"Although it may seem a bit morbid or even disrespectful, I think we should run the test using the customer from Køge as input. What do you think?"

"I agree. One customer can be just as good as another; and the poor man probably doesn't mind."

Dan found the man's email address in the database by searching for the part of his name and address that he remembered from the Lifeline document in Ryan's basement. He hadn't forgotten the email address, but he wanted to make sure it was correct. He copy-pasted the email address as an argument to the line in the Terminal window, looked at Michael—who nodded affirmatively—and then pressed Enter.

Dan's command did nothing more than call the function on the server that executed their test, creating a new Lifeline document for the customer that the email address identified.

After fourteen seconds, the program finished, writing a line of text indicating that the call to the server had been successful, and the prompt blinked again in the now idle Terminal window.

"It went faster than I remember," said Dan, relieved that the call hadn't returned an error.

"Yes, it was fast. I guess the cloud provider's computers have probably gotten more powerful since we last worked with the system."

At that point, it was just a matter of going through the log tables, inspecting what the JSON object with all the fields looked like—before and after each call to the individual services in the flow that filled out the empty fields with data.

Michael started from the top in the log tables used by the first services in the flow, and quickly reached the first log, where the life expectancy field had been filled out as expected by a simple function but without the mysterious omega value. Dan started from the other end, where all logs contained the expected field value, plus the added omega value. In the fourth log he examined, the omega value was missing, so they could easily identify which service had added the unwanted number.

"Here it is," said Dan, pointing. Michael moved closer to him and looked at his screen.

The log header showed that the omega value was added by an AI service they'd developed themselves at the beginning of the Avaram days.

"It's our old Primus AI adding the number," said Michael, shaking his head in disbelief. Dan nodded, finding it as hard to believe as Michael did.

"But that service shouldn't touch that field at all. Another service has already filled it out at the start," continued Michael.

"Yes, it makes no sense at all," agreed Dan. "And take a look at this." He pointed to the top of the list of log lines. "In the line showing what inputs the AI service used, there's only a reference to the customer's sequenced genome. Our Primus AI seems to have calculated the omega value based on the specific customer's DNA."

They looked puzzled at each other, and Dan could see that Michael was just as shocked as he was.

TEN

The next morning, Michael again arrived a little after seven, and like the day before, he started by making a mug of tea in Dan's tiny kitchen. While waiting for the water to boil, they attempted to find rational explanations for yesterday's discovery. Although they'd seemingly pinpointed the source of the problem, it hadn't become any easier to understand. The next step would be to dive into the Primus AI, trying to work out how it found the bizarre omega value.

The evening before, Dan had gone for a long walk along the Lakes—a long line of rectangular ponds separating the City Center from the districts to the north and west—after Michael had left and returned to his cabin in Sweden. They'd agreed to meet again the following morning and work on finding the explanation.

The sun had still been shining, and the pathways were full of people enjoying the warm summer evening.

Dan had tried to gain some distance from their discovery. Even though they now knew it was their own ancient AI they had to delve into, it was incomprehensible how it could possibly arrive at the omega value—regardless of whether the number was based on the customer's DNA, or was simply a random value it generated internally.

Walking along the pathway, Dan tried to get a clearer overview of how best to explain the AI's output. When he reached the far end of the Lakes at the Planetarium and was on his way back, he was surprised by an unexpected phone call. It was from Susan, and even before he answered it, he could feel his heart beat faster. Why would she call him unless something had happened—and whatever it was, it couldn't be anything good.

"Hi, Susan. Is there a problem?" he asked in a hesitant voice.

"Hi, Dan. No, no. Don't worry—everything's fine," she replied. "Listen—I've changed my mind about meeting you for a chat. So, I would like to get together sometime—if you're still interested?"

"Definitely—that would be great," Dan heard himself reply.

"Cool! We can text each other to find a time and place. I think it would be good for us to talk things over and get a proper, definitive end to the whole process."

Dan didn't know what to say and just stood on the pathway, nodding at Susan's suggestion. It was the first time he'd heard her voice in over a year.

"See you," said Susan, ending the call.

On the rest of his walk back to the apartment, he didn't think once about the problem with the Lifeline document and their AI, only about his brief conversation with Susan. He was looking forward to seeing her and getting the opportunity to apologize for all the problems his addiction had created in their relationship. And for all the anguish she'd had because of him. Having that talk with her would probably also be good for him and allow him to move on with his life.

After the water boiled and Michael had made the tea, they went into the living room and sat down at the dining table where their laptops were. Dan still had coffee, which he'd made shortly before Michael had arrived. After having drunk from their mugs, they looked at each other. Michael was the first to say anything—and he picked up the thread as if there had been no break in their conversation from the day before.

"I still think that the best hypothesis is that these events are coincidences, with the two people dying on the date that matches the omega value added to their date of birth—as if that might somehow indicate the number of days in their lives. Besides, there's obviously still the possibility that they had the same absurd idea as Gitte and that this may have 'calibrated' their demise to coincide with the 'predicted' date."

Dan nodded, but he no longer felt quite as confident in the hypothesis as it seemed Michael did.

"Plus, there's also the off chance," continued Michael, "that the numbers somehow, in some obscure manner, were altered at a point in time after the events. You and I didn't see the numbers in question before the two people died. But I agree that the likelihood of that theory is minimal—although it's all still based only on Ryan's information about the deaths of the two people. I honestly wouldn't be surprised if Ryan stumbles through the door any minute now, shouting 'April Fools' with one of his annoying grins."

Dan smiled as he imagined the scene. "Well, he knows where I live, so we can't completely write off that possibility. But I'm willing to bet that the probability is so close to zero that it doesn't exist in real life. Knowing Ryan, it would be totally unlike him to spend so much time and energy on a practical joke. What would he get out of staging that story, with all the preparation it would require? After all, I was with Ryan and Gitte when we talked about it—and I don't doubt their concerns were genuine."

"I agree," conceded Michael. "Obviously, I don't think that's the explanation either, and whatever one might think of Ryan, he's not the type who would come up with such an idea. He deserves that much credit, after all. I mention it solely as part of our list of potential causes."

"Maybe the next step should be to take a closer look at our Primus AI and see if we can deduce where it gets the number from," suggested Dan.

"That's a good idea! From a purely technical point of view, the AI is definitely doing something it shouldn't."

Dan thought back to when they made the Primus AI. At first, it was only meant to be a simple test. The cloud platform they were developing their system on had some exciting possibilities for implementing AI and Machine Learning into their systems in a generalized way.

In the first version of the AI, they'd taught it to find errors in the auto-generated Lifeline document and skip the sending of the email to the customer—until a manual review and edit of the document could be made. They trained it to detect documents where text sections were repeated by mistake, or the calculated values and recommendations didn't match. It was a form of automated pattern recognition—a typical utilization of AI.

Although the name AI sounded like something out of a science fiction movie, it was really just a program that could recognize pattern variations. After teaching it—using countless examples—it learned what output it should produce when presented with inputs that resembled the patterns it had been trained with.

The AIs differed from traditional programming by not being written as concrete instructions for the program to carry out but by letting it adjust millions of tiny 'weights' that, in combination, decided what output to give for different inputs—even if that input wasn't one hundred percent identical to anything the AI had seen before.

"I guess the first question is why the AI is adding a number to an already filled-out field," said Dan, "when it only needs to mark its own designated field to indicate whether the other values match, so they'll be experienced correctly by the customer."

"Exactly!" supplemented Michael. "And the next question is how it was given access to the customer's genome as input in the first place and whether it uses something from there to construct the omega value. After all, it's never been trained to find patterns in that data."

"I believe our cloud provider has an option for some extended logging, where you can have the AI dump its intermediate calculations," said Dan. "Maybe that can give us some clues that answer those questions." He pulled his laptop closer and logged into the administration page, the same page they used the day before, where they could see all the individual functions and databases that made up the Lifeline system.

Michael moved closer to Dan. "That's right; that should answer the questions. It would be nice if we could avoid tinkering with the code itself to get it to log more—at least for now. It could get confusing."

From the services menu, Dan selected the list of AI functions. The list contained twenty-two functions, of which only five were currently active in the Lifeline system. Their Primus AI appeared at the top when sorting the list on the last used AI function. Dan clicked on it, and the page switched to show all the details of the function. On a sub-menu, he found a checkbox to enable extended logging and clicked it. The page displayed a warning dialog, which said that this option could cause substantial amounts of logged data and, consequently, higher costs. Dan clicked OK, after which the page refreshed itself.

"Okay, let's see if it logs anything usable," he said, switching to the window with the Terminal program and pressing the arrow-up key to retrieve the command they'd used for testing the day before. "Have we forgotten anything?" He asked, hovering his finger over the Enter key.

"Nope," replied Michael. "Just fire it off."

Dan pressed Enter and leaned back. They waited the fourteen seconds it took for the program to run the test, which again generated a Lifeline document for the customer from Køge without emailing the PDF file. When the program ended—and the Terminal once again showed that there had been no error in the test—Dan switched back to the administration page window and updated the log of their Primus AI function. As expected, it showed a new log line at the top of the list.

"Let's see if there's any data in the log," said Dan, clicking on the line, after which the screen switched to show the entire logged text.

At the top of the page were the log time, log size in the table, and other statistical information. Below that was a line saying 'PHASE A STATE' followed by several pages of seemingly random byte values between 0 and 255, and Dan had to scroll way down to get to the end of the page. At the end of the log text were some additional lines:

```
PHASE B STATE
GGGAATGGTCCCTGGTCACCCAGGCTAATCACTGGTTCATTCCTAAGGATAATTACCAATCGGTCATCACAAATCTTAGGG
PHASE C STATE
15529
```

Dan and Michael studied the lines for a few seconds before turning on their chairs and looking at each other. Dan was the first to say anything, but he was sure they both had the same assessment of what the log showed.

"That last number is the inexplicable omega value the AI adds to the Lifeline document. It seems like the value is consistent over several runs. At least it's returned the same result in the three tests we executed today and yesterday—besides the first one done in the original Lifeline document sent to the customer from Køge. So surely we can rule out that it's a random number the AI is returning?"

"Yes," replied Michael. "And from what Ryan said, it was a different number for each of the customers who received a document with the error. So, unless the AI has a short array of values to choose from, we almost have to conclude that the number results from a calculation or lookup." He took a deep breath before proceeding.

"But I'm not crazy about venturing into speculations that the number should somehow be extracted from the string shown in the line above."

Dan shook his head. He was getting increasingly worried that things were moving in the direction he'd feared.

"No—that's a scary thought," he said. "That string can almost only be interpreted as a small slice of a DNA sequence from a full genome."

"I agree. It looks like a random distribution of the four bases—C, G, T, and A—that make up the human genome which codes for a person's inherited physical and psychological characteristics. How long is the string exactly?"

Dan looked again at the long string composed of the four letters.

"It's eighty-one characters," he replied after quickly counting the number of letters. "I have an eerie feeling that the string comes from the DNA file our Primus AI lists as its only input. That is, the customer's genome."

Michael nodded. "Yes, I'm afraid that it could look like that, too," he said after a brief hesitation.

Saying nothing, they got to their feet and went to the kitchen, where Dan opened the fridge and took out two colas. They unscrewed the lids of their bottles—and drank from them before returning to the dining table, where they put the bottles down.

"Let's just take a deep breath," said Michael, "before we even start to consider the possibility that the omega value was somehow calculated from the customer's DNA."

"Yes, that would be absolutely perplexing."

"Why don't we start by determining whether the logged DNA string indeed originates from the DNA file of the specific customer?"

"Excellent idea," replied Dan, moving back in front of his laptop. With his mouse, he marked the eighty-one letters in the long DNA string and pressed Control-C on the keyboard to copy it.

On the menu, he opened a new window with the cloud provider's administration page and switched to the service where all data files were stored. Here he selected a folder called 'customer-genomes' and scrolled down until he found a file whose name contained the email address of the man from Køge they were using for their tests.

"There are some ways you can search through the DNA file directly on the administration page," said Dan. "I know many use that option, but I haven't tried it myself."

"I've messed around with it a little," said Michael, "and it's actually brilliant. But the quickest thing right now is simply to download the entire file and then search for the string in it."

Dan nodded, then clicked on the filename and started downloading. The file was 250 megabytes and took about ten seconds to download.

"250 megabytes doesn't sound like much if it's supposed to contain an entire human genome," he commented, puzzled.

"That's right," replied Michael, leaning forward to explain. "The service provider who does the actual gene sequencing, based on the customer's submitted mouth swab, only sends us a so-called difference file. It contains the deviation between the sequenced genome of the person and the reference genome, which is identical for all humans and, therefore, doesn't need to be included in the file.

Additionally, they also keep a massive database of the whole sequenced genome and a ton of other information. I don't know how much storage space each genome takes up, but I'm sure it's several gigabytes. The Lifeline system then receives a link to that genome, which we can pass on to our other service providers—the ones that Lifeline increasingly uses to analyze various customer DNA characteristics. It's a reasonably standardized industry by now."

Michael drank from his cola before continuing.

"So, besides the link to the entire genome, we receive the copy of the difference file with the simplified genome. It comprises a long line with the genome itself—a string with all the letters, each showing one of the four bases—and after that a line showing the quality of the sequencing process for each of the bases in the file, that is, for each letter. We can also give other service providers access to that file if they only need the rudimentary data. It's also cheaper than if they have to pull the complete genome from the database."

"Okay, that makes sense," said Dan. He and Ryan had been in several negotiations with potential service providers who specialized in scanning the already-sequenced genome for information that might be relevant to include in the Lifeline document—especially if the service could be obtained for a reasonable price. With this knowledge, they could show customers whether they were predisposed to certain disorders, for example. But although prices for these services were generally going down, they'd initially only been used to a limited extent—mainly to legitimize the claim that the customer's actual DNA was used to produce the Lifeline document.

"Let's see if the file contains the string," said Dan, switching back to the Terminal program, where he jumped to the folder containing downloaded files.

First, he wrote a simple command to test that the selected DNA file had been completely downloaded. Then he wrote a new command, pasted the DNA string he'd copied from the AI's log, and finally typed the downloaded file's name. When he pressed Enter, the number 1 immediately appeared on a new line, which meant that the command had found a single instance of the eighty-one-letter DNA string in the file.

"It does," said Michael.

"Yes, but that was also what we expected. Right now, I'm more inclined to believe that the AI is somehow calculating the omega value based on the string of eighty-one characters from the customer's DNA."

"At least, that seems to be the case. Apparently, there's no other input it can use. But how it converts the eighty-one-letter text string into an integer—15,529 in this case—is anyone's guess. How do we determine if the number gets calculated from the string?"

"First, I suggest we run the test that generates the same Lifeline document for the same customer a few times—and then see if it's the same eighty-one characters the AI finds in the customer's genome. If it's not, we can almost assume that the omega value isn't calculated from the DNA."

"I agree—it'll give us a bit more information," said Michael.

Dan found the first command they'd tested in the Terminal program and pressed Enter. As with the previous calls, the program was active for fourteen seconds before ending with the message that there had been no error in the run. Dan then waited ten seconds and executed the command again. After fourteen seconds, the program ended in the same way—again without errors.

In the browser window showing the administration page, he updated the Primus AI's log list. They could now see a link for each of the three times they'd generated the same Lifeline document. The first was the one they'd already looked at, and the others were the new log lines created after the two latest test runs.

Dan clicked the first log line and scrolled down to the bottom, highlighting and copying the lines with the DNA string and the calculated number. He then pasted the copied text into an empty document in a code editor—a specialized text editor for programming.

After repeating this process for the other two log lines, the text file now contained the lines from the three test runs where the AI had been used—after they enabled the extended logging.

It was easy to see that both the DNA strand and the calculated omega value were identical across all three test runs.

"At least it seems to be consistent," said Michael. "But I don't have the slightest idea how the AI would calculate the number from the eighty-one characters in the DNA strand. That is, assuming that's what it's doing. It's somewhat problematic that we can't dive deeper into the AI and see how it finds or calculates the number."

"Yes, that would make everything a little easier. But I don't know if it's possible to trace from the many seemingly random byte values in the log. There are probably some developers somewhere who can use that output for something."

"I'm not enough of an AI expert to know how to do it, and if it's even possible. If we don't find another solution, the next step will be to ask the Lifeline developers if they understand this kind of thing."

"It's not my impression that any of them have that much experience with AI," said Dan. "And I've promised Ryan we won't involve more people than necessary. Preferably no one, apart from the two of us."

Michael was about to say something, but Dan cut him off. "What can we do to move forward?" he asked before Michael could start discussing his overall view of Ryan's assessments.

While considering their options, they rose and walked into Dan's kitchen to get fresh colas.

"I think we should take a step back," said Michael, "and try to get an overview across customers. So far, we've done a few test runs on the document for the man from Køge. But I think it might also provide useful knowledge to see the corresponding log lines for some other customers. Maybe even all customers in the database?"

"Good idea," replied Dan. "Let's make a script that performs the test run on all customers. I think we should limit it to the Danish customers; otherwise, it'll take forever."

After extracting a filtered list of the email addresses of all Danish customers from the database, they created a script that would run the test for each customer and add a line with the person's name, email and date of birth, and the omega value in a separate text file. There were 2,150 Danish customers and, subsequently, the same number of lines in their script.

If the test run took the same fourteen seconds for each customer, it would take about eight hours for the Lifeline document to be generated again for all the customers in the script. They would then have a lot more data that would hopefully prove helpful in their search.

They started the script and watched the screen as it did the test run on the first customers.

After agreeing to meet the following day, Michael again drove back to his cabin in Sweden. Dan went for a long walk down to the waterfront and continued along the harbor toward the city before returning home the same way.

Before going to bed, he set the alarm on his phone to wake him up at the time they'd calculated that the script would finish.

In the middle of the night, Dan was woken by the alarm and got up to see if the script was done and if there had been any problems with the execution.

It all looked fine. There hadn't been a single error, and on the AI's administration page, he could see that a new log line had appeared for each customer—created at fourteen-second intervals.

The new text file, with the output of the run for each customer, also seemed to be complete. In the code editor, he could see that there were 2,150 lines, as there should be—one line for each customer.

He opened the text file in a spreadsheet, which automatically converted the text into cells, with a row for each customer and individual columns for name, email, date of birth, and the omega value.

In the same way Ryan had done in his first analysis, Dan created a new column with a formula that added the omega value to the date of birth, which—according to Gitte's theory—should show the customer's date of death. He then sorted the list on the new column and got a shock.

In the top row, he saw the name Maya Luna—a popular media personality who'd been part of several entertainment shows and reality programs on TV.

Her calculated date, based on the omega value, was only three days away.

ELEVEN

Sitting in a cafe in the center of Copenhagen, Dan was waiting to meet Susan. He'd taken the metro—to avoid driving around the small streets to find a parking space for his car—and had arrived at the café ten minutes before the scheduled time. It was a nice place where he and Susan had met several times—especially at the beginning of their relationship.

Although the weather was nice and there were already several guests at the small tables in front of the café, Dan had chosen a small table inside, where he now sat and wondered about the latest discoveries in the Lifeline system and what they should do with that knowledge. After seeing the calculated dates, he'd been unable to fall asleep again but had spent the rest of the night and all morning looking at the spreadsheet and the top row with Maya Luna while waiting for Michael to arrive so they could discuss what to do.

Michael had arrived early in the morning and was as shocked to see the spreadsheet—calculating Maya Luna's date of death as three days away—as Dan had been when he'd seen the result the night before. After Maya Luna, the next customer's date was five months away. It felt eerie to be looking at a list of people, each with a calculated date possibly predicting when they would die.

As they sat looking at the list and talking about the different dates, Dan had received a text from Susan asking if he was free to meet her the same day at their old cafe. After having checked with Michael to see if being away for an hour was okay, Dan had suggested ten o'clock, which suited Susan fine. When Michael heard who Dan was going to meet, he asked Dan to give Susan a big hug from him.

At precisely ten o'clock, he saw Susan park her bicycle on the other side of the narrow street. After crossing the street, she entered the café through the open door. She looked chic but understated, only wearing denim shorts and a gray T-shirt. Dan stood up to show her where he was, but she'd already seen him. As she approached, Dan held out his hand to greet her, but instead of taking it, she gave him a short hug. It seemed primarily out of old habit, and she quickly let go of him, after which they both sat down.

The waiter—a young man Susan appeared to know—smilingly approached their table and asked if they would like anything to eat or drink. Susan ordered a cafe latte, and Dan asked for a cup of black coffee.

For a moment, they sat looking at each other, saying nothing. In his head, Dan went over the list of the things he wanted to say to Susan, but he couldn't find a good way to get started. Susan was the first to say anything.

"It's so unbelievable to see you," she said, looking at him appraisingly. "You look like yourself again—like before your alcohol problem."

"Thanks, Susan. I certainly feel much better than I have in many years, too."

"You can definitely see it! It's such a wild contrast to the last time I saw you when you were so caught up in the addiction that everyone feared you were dying."

He nodded, but chose not to tell her how close it had been. Evidently, she was already aware of it.

"It's amazing that a body so destroyed by alcohol can recover," continued Susan. "Almost like a miracle."

Dan nodded. "It is. More than you can imagine."

The waiter returned with the coffee they'd ordered. When he'd gone, Dan cleared his throat and looked at Susan.

"There are a few reasons I've wished to meet you for so long," he began, and then took a deep breath before proceeding.

"First and foremost, I owe you a huge apology for the way things turned out. You saw the problem long before I did and tried to convince me how bad it was, but I didn't believe you, and I dismissed it. Other people tried to make me aware of the problems, too—but not trusting *you* is what I regret most about the entire process."

Susan nodded slowly, with a distant look in her eyes as she bit her lower lip. He could see that she was contemplating the long process, and it was clear that it had been rough for her. No wonder she hadn't wanted to meet him and be reminded of that difficult time again. First with his gradual change and her unsuccessful attempts to get through to him, and then her ruminations about staying in a situation where she couldn't change anything. And finally, the tough decision to throw in the towel and end the relationship.

"The hardest thing was that you isolated yourself more and more the sicker you got," she said, still looking elsewhere in the room.

Dan nodded. Until he'd undergone treatment for his addiction, he'd never considered it a disease. His attitude had been that his dependency was entirely the result of his own choices and decisions and, consequently, his personal responsibility—not something he could explain away or justify with a disease or other causes beyond his control. He'd seen it as a lame excuse for a situation he'd gotten himself into.

But central to his treatment had been a slow acceptance that his alcoholism was indeed a disease. It was a physical condition he would never get rid of, but one he could live with just fine as long as he stayed away from alcohol.

This realization wasn't an attempt to excuse his long history of addiction. The responsibility for his actions still lay with him, even if the underlying cause was probably genetic and beyond his control.

It was harder to talk about than he'd expected. However, he still felt confident that it would benefit both of them—hopefully, at least Susan.

"You were completely unwilling to let anyone help you—even me," continued Susan, now looking directly at him again. "I felt I was letting you down, but at first, you shrugged it off and said you had it all under control—and then, gradually, you cut off all contact. Eventually, you didn't answer calls or messages, and even when Michael or I rang your door intercom, you didn't answer. Ryan and especially Gitte also tried everything—but nothing helped."

It surprised Dan that she'd felt that way, and he looked pleadingly at her. "Susan, listen to me: you've nothing to blame yourself for—not the slightest!" he said. "This may be the most important thing you take away from our meeting today. You all did everything you could to help me, you most of all. It was me who wouldn't—or maybe I couldn't—reach out for the outstretched hand."

He thought about the treatment process and the parts of himself he hadn't known before.

"In a way, I'm a completely different person today. Not only because I've escaped the addiction—in a way that's the least part of the change—but because I've gotten to know myself and my flaws in a completely different way than before. Now I understand that something in my body or mind makes me intolerant of alcohol and an involuntary slave to the abuse. I realize that I've been too confident in my own incorrect judgments and analyses and haven't trusted people around me enough. It was like a kind of pretentiousness—an arrogance—that I didn't accept that someone else might see and understand certain things in my behavior better than I did myself. In that way, it has, as a minimum, been a spiritual transformation for me."

This was the core of the insight he'd gained after his conversation with the Master Entity, which had fundamentally changed his perception of existence as something isolated to his individual personality and character traits.

"Now you almost sound like Michael," said Susan with a small smile, wiping her eyes quickly. "But I'm so glad you told me. Apparently, you found a solution to the problem before it killed you."

"Yes, but before I found the solution, I first got an explanation of what my problem was, and then it wasn't difficult to reach out and get help to solve it: primarily in the addiction treatment that I went through and after that at the AA meetings, where you meet other addicts who've also beaten their dependency—or are working on it."

"So you voluntarily attend meetings where you talk to strangers about personal things?" said Susan with a surprised look on her face. "I would never have thought that about you. That must have taken quite some courage if I know you correctly?"

"A little," admitted Dan. "But it probably does so for everyone."

"What did the treatment itself comprise?"

Dan smiled as he reflected on the process and how it had changed him.

"In my case, I became part of a group that met three times a week and talked about all sorts of topics related to the disease and how to live with it without problems or the risk of falling back into the destructive addiction—by really getting to know yourself."

"Are you never afraid of falling in again—for example, if you're at a party? Or if you're going through a crisis and feel a single glass might soothe things?"

"Not after I gained insight into myself and my disease and understood that there are certain things my body and, accordingly, my mind can't tolerate."

He briefly surveyed his mind again and felt confident that he would never be caught in the same addiction a second time—no matter what temptations and hardships he would face. But there was no guarantee—things that were impossible to predict could happen.

Susan nodded thoughtfully while inspecting her cup.

In his head, Dan went over the list of what he'd planned to say to her. He needed to explain everything now—there probably wouldn't be another opportunity.

But as far as he could tell, he'd said the things he wanted to say and could only hope that it would be helpful to Susan. The whole affair had evidently been complicated for her, which she'd also shown by repeatedly rejecting his proposals to meet.

"That was a short recap of the whole process and how it's changed me as a person," he said in an attempt to summarize. "But the most important part was for me to apologize in person for the things you've had to go through, because of me. Things you should never have been exposed to. I sincerely hope I succeeded in that."

Susan reached out and took his hand. "Thank you for your apology and for sharing your experiences with me. I'm sure it'll help me understand a lot of things and make it easier to put it all behind me. One day I might even be able to forgive you, but right now, I just need a little more time to contemplate the things we've talked about."

She let go of his hand and leaned back before she continued.

"I know you well enough to know how much courage it must have taken to talk openly about your disease like that. After all, you're a very introverted person, not to say shy."

Dan nodded. It wasn't easy to talk about, but it was much easier than it would have been in the old days—before he got to know himself better. It felt like a massive weight had been lifted from his shoulders by telling Susan about the process, and he just sat looking at her, feeling relieved, not knowing what to say.

"So, what else is going on in your life these days?" asked Susan. "Is it your plan to keep working with Ryan at Lifeline?"

"As a matter of fact, I'd made up my mind not to be a part of Lifeline—and the collaboration with Ryan—any longer," Dan said. "For several reasons, but mainly because I felt trapped in a lifestyle that wasn't healthy for me and that probably accelerated the development of my abuse. Today, I think I could cope without falling back into the abuse—but the growing dependency was probably also a symptom of feeling out of balance with that part of my life. It's something I've only realized here afterward, but I don't want to be part of that whole circus again, with the travel and the stress—and the parties and the nights on the town."

Susan nodded. "I definitely understand what you're saying. But you've always liked Ryan—unlike Michael, who can barely say his name without spitting."

"Yes, Ryan and I've had a good relationship since the day we met—when Michael and I considered selling Avaram."

Dan thought back to his conversation with Michael—about their first impressions of Ryan—a few days earlier, at Michael's cabin in Sweden.

"And it's true, Michael has never been fond of Ryan—but I never perceived how bad it was. Not until the other day, when Michael explicitly told me he regretted selling our small company to Ryan in the first place."

Susan nodded, showing that what he said about Michael's sentiments didn't surprise her.

"So, you've been talking to Michael, too? That's fantastic," she said.

"Yes, it was good to see him again. We met at a Lifeline board meeting last Friday and had a brief chat on that occasion. But since then, I've also visited him in his cabin in Sweden—and we're actually working together again these days. On a special task in the Lifeline system. He's in my apartment right now."

"That sounds nice. I hope it wasn't a bad time that I suggested meeting here, if it interrupted your work?"

"Not at all—it was perfect timing. By the way, Michael told me to say hi to you."

"Please say hi to him from me," she said with a smile. "I hope he's well, too. It's funny that the two of you are working together again. Is this a new project or something the other developers at Lifeline can't solve?"

"They could probably work it out, but Ryan asked me directly, and then I suggested asking Michael to help."

Dan wanted to tell her about the problem he and Michael were working on. It would have been nice to share it with her and hear her thoughts. Not because he expected her to find the explanation for the strange coincidences, but because they'd always been able to talk to each other about everything—including work considerations and problems.

Admittedly, Ryan had said they should involve as few people in the problem as possible, but Dan had always been comfortable discussing things with Susan because he knew she wouldn't dream of sharing it with anyone. It would also have been good to tell her about the prediction with Maya Luna and hear what she believed they should do—and what she thought of the strange prophecies.

But everything was different now. He couldn't tell Susan what he was working on because they were no longer together. Their relationship was over, and he was the one who'd ruined it. Somehow, it was only now, when he sat and talked directly to Susan—feeling that there was something they couldn't talk about—that he really understood how final their break-up was and that they would never have the same relationship again. It hurt thinking she might feel the same way—and had probably felt it for a long time. Hopefully, she could use this meeting with him to put it all behind her and move on with her life.

"Is everything else going well?" he asked. "Are there still enough challenges at work?"

"Yes, work-wise, everything is as it should be. As you know, I help define the projects I work on. So, in that sense, I'm very privileged."

Susan had studied to be a journalist when she was young and had worked at DR—the Danish national broadcaster—ever since, doing research for stories that were primarily used on their website but sometimes also on radio and TV. She'd started as a journalist, but after a few years, her responsibilities grew to include editorial elements, helping to identify relevant topics and people for the various stories.

"I'm excited to hear that," said Dan. "And it's not a problem that you're missing for an hour this morning?"

"No, it's fine. I'm working from home this week—so I'm in charge of that myself. Currently, I'm researching an article on some new urban plans in the westernmost suburbs. So all I need really is my laptop and an internet connection. Plus, my phone, of course."

Dan nodded. He would also have liked to ask her if she'd found a new boyfriend. Not to snoop in her private life, but because he hoped that part of her life was functioning as well as the work part. But he couldn't bring himself to ask. If she'd met someone and wanted to tell him about it, she would do it on her initiative.

For a moment, neither of them said anything.

"What about you?" asked Susan, breaking the brief silence. "Do you have any plans for what you want to spend your time and energy on once you and Michael have finished the task you're working on now?"

"I have an idea that maybe I can use my history with addiction—and how I got over it—to help others in the same situation. I just need to find the right way to do it first."

"Wow! That sounds like a great idea. Especially since you have the advantage of being financially well off and not having to spend your time on a regular full-time job. How did you come to think along those lines? It's quite far from your usual interests and areas of expertise."

"That's right. But it frustrates me to think that people are suffering and having their lives ruined—especially when there's a solution and a community that can help and has already helped countless people—myself, for example."

"It sounds like it's AA you're thinking of, but don't you think most addicts already know that offer exists?"

"Yes, but I sense many people are afraid to reach out for a helping hand and keep pretending they can solve the problems themselves—just like I deluded myself for too long. There's also a spiritual element that some people find a little strange—I sometimes experience this at meetings; and I probably would have felt that way myself in the past."

He didn't want to tell Susan about his conversation with the Master Entity and again wondered why he'd recounted it to Gitte at all.

"It's a new side of you I've never seen," said Susan. She seemed to mean it in a good way.

They sat for a while, saying nothing, looking at each other, before Susan broke the silence.

"Well, now I think I'll ride back home and get on with work," she said, getting up from her chair. "But it was good to see you and hear the things you said. It's going to take some time, but now I feel I have a better chance of processing the whole thing. It was nice to see how you've recovered. I'm glad I changed my mind and agreed to meet for a talk."

"I'm so relieved to hear that," said Dan after getting up as well. "What changed your mind, if you don't mind me asking?"

"It's actually a little bit odd. To be honest, I'd decided never to speak to you again. But then, last Sunday, Gitte called me and said that it would probably be good—for both of us—if we got together and had a chat, trying to find a better closure to our relationship. And now I'm inclined to agree with her. She also invited me to the summer party—but I said no thanks to that."

Dan nodded, and they hugged each other briefly again, after which Susan headed for the door. He watched her as she crossed the street and unlocked her bike. As she set off, she waved briefly through the large windows. He'd sat down again, and when he waved back, she was already out of sight.

Before Dan paid the bill and left the café, he noticed that neither of them had touched their coffee.

TWELVE

A little after eleven o'clock, Dan was back in his apartment, where Michael was still sitting at the dining table with his laptop in front of him. Dan went to the kitchen, took two colas from the fridge, and handed one to Michael, who'd got up and followed him.

"How was seeing Susan again?" asked Michael, after taking a sip from his bottle.

"I must admit it was special—a bit more emotional than I expected," replied Dan. "When I get the time, I'll have to process it more, but on the face of it, I think it went well. I got to apologize and explain what I wanted to share with her."

"Cool! That's great to hear. Did she understand what you were going through during that time—and what happened to you?"

"I think so—but it's going to take some time for her to come to terms with it all and put that whole chapter behind her."

Dan thought about how the meeting at the café had affected him. He'd felt how challenging the process and break-up had been for Susan—and it had surprised him. He knew it must have been hard for her, but it was only when he heard it directly from her, face to face, that he could feel how she must have experienced it all.

"She's a strong girl," said Michael. "She'll be all right; and so will you."

Dan nodded—he didn't doubt that. But he also knew that it would be long before he could think of her—and their time together—without feeling a twinge in his heart and that she might feel the same way.

"Does she have a new boyfriend?" asked Michael. "If I know you correctly, you wouldn't dare ask her about that."

"That's right—I didn't ask. But it's not because I somehow believe we can get back together—that's not going to happen."

Michael shook his head slowly. "No, that race is probably run; but it's still sad—I've always liked Susan."

They stood for a moment without saying anything, then returned to the living room and sat down at the table in front of their laptops.

"I'm still shocked to see the list of calculated dates you made after the run last night," said Michael. "I didn't anticipate we would have an opportunity to test another date so soon. But I still expect that nothing will happen with Maya Luna on Saturday."

Dan nodded as he tried to refocus his thoughts from meeting Susan and back to the uncanny occurrences.

"Yes, somehow, the situation has shifted. I think it can now aptly be described as a binary state with two possible outcomes: if Maya Luna dies on Saturday, then we have to acknowledge that our old Primus AI can predict something that shouldn't be possible, perhaps based on the customer's DNA. If she doesn't die—and I sincerely hope she does not—it'll be easier to rule out that the AI can't predict anything, at least not in all cases."

"Exactly!" said Michael. "The indicators are clearer if she dies than if she doesn't. Obviously, I hope she doesn't die, too—primarily because we're talking about a living human being, but also because it would push us beyond the realm of rational explanation. In case the AI has correctly predicted the date of death, in three out of three observed cases, our statistical arguments about coincidence start to falter—even if we factor in the diffuse uncertainty about whether the dead customers could have surmised the calculation, and that this may somehow have influenced their dying on the given dates—in other words, a kind of self-fulfilling prophecy like we were talking about."

For a long moment, they sat silently, looking thoughtfully at the spreadsheet on Dan's laptop.

Dan was the first to break the silence. "My best suggestion would be to continue looking for the reason why the Primus AI finds the mysterious omega value."

"I agree. We don't need to postpone it to see if anything happens with Maya Luna on Saturday."

"But first, I think we should discuss whether we should warn her."

"Warn Maya Luna?" asked Michael skeptically. "I sincerely think that's a bad idea."

"I thought you might say that. But since we possess the information—no matter how absurd we think it is—perhaps the correct thing to do would be to share it with the person it directly concerns. Surely it can't hurt our situation to call her and tell her to be careful, especially this weekend? She'll just think we're a couple of nutters."

"Yes, I'm sure she will. But if we warn her, we become part of the equation, and the warning itself can make all the difference. We can't tell her it's been predicted she'll die on Saturday—we don't even believe that ourselves, do we?—only that she should take extra care over the weekend. Whatever we say, I fear our input may do more harm than good. Something as mundane as her walking in her own thoughts and wondering about that weird phone call while crossing the street, and then getting hit by a bus, or something like that."

Dan nodded as he contemplated Michael's arguments. There had to be another angle from which to view their options.

"I think it's impossible to predict whether saying something will make a difference. However, our conscience will probably feel better if we've warned her—whether or not anything happens."

"That's a good point," admitted Michael. "If she dies, we'll either blame ourselves for doing nothing—or live with the uncertainty of not knowing if our warning may have been the cause."

"It's difficult because a key element in the equation is how much weight we assign to an unknown parameter: whether a supernatural force could predict or even plan a person's date of death. And while we would prefer to decide on a positivistic, scientific basis—there's something in us that prevents us from completely dismissing the alternative possibility."

"I vote to stick to the coincidence hypothesis and remove the supernatural element from our considerations. Nothing will happen to Maya Luna on Saturday—certainly not if we don't interfere."

They looked at each other to see if they agreed.

"That makes sense to me," said Dan. "We're not saying anything to her, and if—against all our expectations—she was to die on Saturday, we would certainly be in a new situation with a supernatural factor that we can't place. And then we still can't assess whether our warning would have made a difference."

Michael nodded, pointing at his screen.

"I looked through Maya Luna's Lifeline document while you were away. Apparently, she's our age and looks healthy. She doesn't seem to have any bad habits—and our internal calculation estimated that she would live to be ninety-five. It's been almost two years since she purchased the document, and her genome was sequenced, which was relatively new in our flow at the time."

"Yes, I also looked at her document this morning—everything looked fine. Actually, I've greeted her briefly a few times—including one time at a movie premiere. She always looked very healthy and fit."

"I've seen her on the town too—but never talked to her," said Michael. "There's not any current info when you search for her online. The most recent articles and photos are from a talent show last year, where she made a decent run but didn't make the finals."

They agreed not to think about Maya Luna and the date in the spreadsheet for the moment, but to focus on finding an explanation for the omega value calculated for each customer by their old Primus AI. But the notion that there might be something they could do to alert Maya Luna kept nagging just below the horizon in Dan's mind.

"My best guess is that the AI calculates the number from the DNA string of eighty-one characters," said Michael. "There seems to be no other input, and it returns the same number every time for the same customer—at least in the tests we did yesterday on the man from Køge."

"That's also what I've arrived at so far," said Dan. "That leaves us with two things we don't have an explanation for. First, why the AI extracts precisely that specific strand of eighty-one bases—and second, how it finds or calculates the omega value from that DNA strand. With the same result across multiple runs, mind you."

"Exactly! And I've absolutely no idea how it does either. Especially the first part might be hard to explain. But somehow, it should be possible to detect a pattern in how it finds the specific numerical value in the string."

"It could be anything it uses for the calculation," interjected Dan. "The number of A-bases multiplied by C-bases multiplied by G-bases, just to give an example."

"You're right; almost infinite combinations could be used to turn a string of eighty-one characters, comprising the letters A, C, G, and T, into a numerical value."

Dan thought of various options, most of which weren't straightforward to implement, and then tried to find a way to acquire more knowledge.

"Maybe the best thing we can do here and now is to compare the DNA strand extracted from different customers and see if there's a pattern we can use to figure out how the AI finds the number."

Michael nodded. "That sounds like a sensible place to start. Let's try it."

Dan changed to the administration page with the Primus AI log table and opened some of the log lines their test script had generated during the night. From each log line, he copied the individual customer's email, the eighty-one-character DNA string, and the calculated omega value into a new text file in the code editor. While Dan selected and copied the list of strings and numbers, Michael went to the kitchen to get two colas from the fridge.

Two minutes later, they were looking at the text file where—besides the five customers' email addresses and the calculated omega value—there were now five lines with the DNA string the AI had extracted for five customers.

```
GGGAATGGTCCCTGGTCACCCAGGCTAATCACTGGTTCATTCCTAAGGATAATTACCAATCGGTCATCACAAATCTTAGGG
GGGTCTGGTCATCGGCCTCCCCGGCTTCATTCCGGTAACTCTAATCGGATCCTCCTACCATGGCTCCCCATCCTTACAGGG
GGGAATGGACTTTGGACCAATCGGACCTAACTTGGTAATTCCACCAGGTACTCACCCCCTCGGTACATACATACATACGGG
GGGACAGGATATTGGAAACACAGGTCATTCATCGGTACAATACTCAGGAATACATTTCCCCGGTCCCCCCTCATCCAAGGG
GGGTACGGACTCAGGTATCTCTGGCTCCTTATAGGTAAAACCACCAGGATATTCAATCTTAGGCATCACAAATCTTAAGGG
```

They both drank from their cold colas while inspecting the lines—to see if they could see a pattern.

"There's something about the Gs," Dan said a moment later.

"Yes, each string starts and ends with three Gs."

"And as far as I can see, the Gs are similarly distributed in the rest of the string, too: in pairs at different positions."

"You're right—they are! Try replacing all Gs with another character—a dot, for example."

Dan nodded, and after doing a quick search-and-replace on the entire text, it was easy to see the pattern.

```
...AAT..TCCCT..TCACCCA..CTAATCACT..TTCATTCCTAA..ATAATTACCAATC..TCATCACAAATCTTA...
...TCT..TCATC..CCTCCCC..CTTCATTCC..TAACTCTAATC..ATCCTCCTACCAT..CTCCCCATCCTTACA...
...AAT..ACTTT..ACCAATC..ACCTAACTT..TAATTCCACCA..TACTCACCCCCTC..TACATACATACATAC...
...ACA..ATATT..AAACACA..TCATTCATC..TACAATACTCA..AATACATTTCCCC..TCCCCCCTCATCCAA...
...TAC..ACTCA..TATCTCT..CTCCTTATA..TAAAACCACCA..ATATTCAATCTTA..CATCACAAATCTTAA...
```

Neither of them said anything for almost a minute—they just sat staring at the pattern with the five lines, each showing the distinct strand extracted by the AI from five different people's DNA.

It was Michael who first commented on the strange pattern.

"That's the spookiest thing I've seen in a long time," he said, slightly shaking his head. "Ever, actually."

Dan didn't know what to say. At first glance, it seemed impossible to comprehend the implications.

"Just to cover every aspect—before we start commenting on the new pattern—why don't you try doing the same search-and-replace with the other three letters," suggested Michael, pointing to the screen in front of Dan to get his attention.

Dan said nothing, but did as Michael had suggested. First, he changed the dot characters back to Gs; then, he replaced all the As, Cs, and Ts with dots—one letter at a time. After each letter, he changed it back again before testing with the following letter. None of the experiments showed any pattern the same way as with the Gs.

"Okay, that's fine," said Michael. "It looks completely random with the other characters. There's a single column of Ts, but only the Gs have an identical pattern across the DNA strings for different customers."

Dan nodded and changed the lines to show the strings, with all the Gs replaced by dots again. After finishing the edits, he summarized what they'd discovered in the repeated pattern.

"For all five customers, we have a DNA strand where a distribution of pairs—consisting of two Gs—divides the string into seven blocks containing combinations of the other three characters, positioned in a way in which I can't see any pattern. At the beginning and end of each string, there's an extra G."

He paused briefly, trying to find the proper wording. Michael didn't comment, but just sat and nodded while Dan completed the summary.

"The seven blocks each comprise an odd number of characters: three in the first block, five in the next, then seven, nine, eleven, thirteen, and then fifteen characters in the last block—all the odd numbers from three to fifteen. It seems like a deliberately designed pattern—I can't quite calculate the probability that this exact pattern would emerge in more people's DNA. I simply don't have sufficient genetic knowledge to do that."

He looked questioningly at Michael.

"Me neither," Michael said without taking his eyes from the screen. "But it sure looks like the Gs function as some sort of delimiter—a divider that splits the sequence into seven blocks, as you said. One suggestion might be that the blocks have that specific size—covering all the odd numbers from three to fifteen—in order to construct a pattern that makes it unlikely to occur naturally. And, although it was an isolated test, we did only find a single instance of the string when we searched the entire genome of the customer from Køge."

"Yes, and such a unique pattern would also make it easy for a computer to locate the string of the eighty-one characters in the entire genome—no matter what the distribution of the other three characters in each block might be."

"Or for the biochemical system in the cell that parses the DNA molecule and makes new cells. Or for other processes in the body that haven't been discovered yet," added Michael in a low voice.

"This could also help explain how the Primus AI can locate the string if it knows precisely what pattern to look for."

Michael nodded. "I think you're right. It uses the unique pattern of Gs to find the string of the eighty-one characters in the DNA. But it's still absolutely incomprehensible how the AI would know that pattern and how it came up with the idea to look for it."

They pushed their chairs a little back from the table and looked at each other. It seemed to Dan that Michael was starting to yield a little, accepting the possibility that they were potentially dealing with a phenomenon that might lie outside a known scientific model of explanation.

Although it was a big pill to swallow, Dan was gradually accepting that this was the path they were being forced along. Each new piece of knowledge they uncovered, as they delved into the system, pushed the conclusion in a direction they didn't want to go—toward a cause that wasn't anchored in natural science. Maybe supernatural was the best word. They'd continually insisted that there was a tiny statistical possibility that the pattern in the increasing number of observations could result from chance. But the likelihood of that being the case grew smaller with every step they took and every discovery they made.

After ordering pizza and taking a break while eating, they discussed options to determine how the AI found the given DNA sequence for each customer. Neither of them could identify a satisfactory hypothesis.

While brainstorming ideas, they double-checked all data and extracts to ensure everything was correct. Among other things, Michael verified that the eighty-one-character DNA sequence found by the AI in the short version of the sequenced genome—the difference file—also existed in the customer's complete genome. He did this on an administration page belonging to the service provider conducting the gene sequencing—storing the complete genome in their database—for Lifeline.

All their tests and double-checks showed the data was correct, and that there were no errors in execution, logging, or anywhere else.

In the late afternoon, they decided to take a break—and continue working the next day—after which Michael drove back to his cabin in Sweden. The plan was to see if they could identify a system in the seven blocks of the DNA sequence and if it was possible to extract the omega value from one of the blocks.

After Michael left, Dan chose to go for a walk around the Lakes to get some perspective on the whole thing and maybe an overview of their latest discoveries. And to see if he could come up with an explanation of how the Primus AI found the specific sequence in the whole DNA and from where it knew what to look for. He had no clue how they should go about it and get the AI to log more data. Maybe some knowledge could be obtained from the thousands of bytes the AI logged with the extracted DNA sequence and omega value. Still, he hadn't the faintest idea how to make sense of all those numbers.

The weather was as good as it had been all week, and the paths along the Lakes were full of people enjoying the lovely summer evening. As he wandered, thoughts of Maya Luna gradually filled his mind again, eventually replacing the technical speculations altogether.

He found it hard to accept that they shouldn't try to warn her—even if they couldn't know if it would make a difference. However, he agreed with Michael that approaching Maya Luna directly risked becoming a decisive intervention in a complex system that they should ideally observe without influencing. But while this was certainly true from a scientific point of view, it still seemed very theoretical and uncaring—cynical even.

There were simply too many undefinable factors, some even outside the accepted scientific concepts. So, after fruitlessly considering the countless variables and their individual probabilities, Dan concluded that a better approach would be to give more weight to his intuitive feelings than he would usually do.

By the time he arrived back at his apartment, he'd made up his mind. He would call Maya Luna and warn her.

THIRTEEN

Dan called Maya Luna the next day, shortly after nine o'clock. She sounded a little tired and low on energy on the phone, but Dan guessed she'd just gotten up—maybe after a night on the town, a late night in the recording studio, or something like that. Besides, it was probably hard to muster up much enthusiasm when approached by a stranger who felt he had something important he wanted to share with her. This probably happened often to Maya Luna and other famous people.

He would have called her the night before, but couldn't find her phone number anywhere. There was an email address on her homepage, but the site looked like it hadn't been updated for a long time, and Dan wanted to be sure to speak to her straight away rather than risk her not seeing the message until a week later. Another option would have been for Dan to set up an account on one or more social media sites—where she would undoubtedly be more active—and write to her there, but there was no guarantee that she would see that message either.

The best solution he could think of had been to text Susan and ask if she could find Maya Luna's phone number—preferably as soon as possible.

Susan had responded immediately, writing that she would try to find the number—and send it to him when she got it. At the end of the reply, she'd written "you don't waste time", followed by two emojis: an ironic smiley face with a twinkle in its eye and a thumbs-up icon. Dan's cheeks had turned warm when he read it, although he was pretty sure Susan wouldn't suspect him of using her help to get a date with a celebrity—especially on the same day they'd met for a chat about the sad way he'd ruined their relationship. He'd only written to her because he couldn't find a better way to find Maya Luna's phone number, and he knew Susan would trust his intentions.

A little before nine, Dan had received two text messages: one from Susan, with Maya Luna's phone number—and one from Michael, who wrote that he was stuck in a queue on the highway and was delayed but that he had some ideas about how the DNA strand might be structured if it was meant to contain data.

So, Dan took the opportunity to call Maya Luna immediately, hoping it was the correct number. He'd prepared what he would say if he succeeded in getting in touch with her. While he waited, he went back and forth through the rooms of the small apartment, as he always did when talking to someone on his phone.

After half a minute, he heard a voice on the other end. "Maya," it said.

"Hi, Maya," Dan started, before telling her his name. "You probably don't remember me, but we've said hello a few times." He gave her a few seconds to think.

"Hmm, I don't think I—"

"I'm sorry to bother you—you're probably busy; so I'll be brief."

"It's okay," she said in a low voice after a short hesitation.

"I know this sounds silly, but I was thinking about you yesterday, and for some reason, I wanted to know if everything was okay?"

"Fair enough—that was sweet of you."

Dan gave her a moment, but she didn't elaborate on her answer, which he also hadn't expected.

"I won't take up any more of your time, and I promise I won't call again—but I would like to finish by reminding you to be careful, for example, in traffic. And especially this weekend."

He could hear that Maya Luna was laughing in a strained way, which was no wonder.

"Thanks for that. That sounds like good advice," she said in a sarcastic tone. "But why specifically the next few days?"

"I can't explain it—it was only a whim. I'm sorry to have disturbed you."

"No, that's fine," she said, sounding slightly more relaxed. "Can I ask you something?"

"Of course," replied Dan, expecting her to ask if he was a stalker or if the call was some sort of practical joke.

"Are you afraid to die?" she asked cautiously after a short pause.

The question surprised him—because it came out of the blue; but also because it was on the subject that had occupied him and Michael in recent days—and which touched on the real reason he'd called her.

"Uh, no. Not really," he replied after surveying his mind. "If you'd asked me a year ago, I probably would have said something else—but I've been through some experiences that have left me in no doubt that death isn't the end. Of life, yes—but not of the existence of the *self*. Those are two different things."

"How so?"

Dan had to think hard to find the correct wording.

"I think that we as individuals focus too much on our isolated personality and that the *self*—that is, the part of us that's aware of the body's experience of the world through the senses—consequently identifies with the physical body and its sensory apparatus and personality, which is an illusion."

He couldn't judge whether he should elaborate. It was all part of the insight he'd gained after his conversation with the Master Entity, and he had a clear picture of how it was all connected. It was just difficult to explain in common linguistic terms.

"I probably sound like a fool," he said hesitantly. "I didn't mean to, but I let myself get carried away."

"No, no. You don't have to apologize. It's rather interesting—so you think the soul lives on?"

"Yes, but not the soul in terms of the personality, with its thoughts, feelings, hopes, memories, and dreams. Only the *self* that's observed all these things as they took place in a given body and mind."

"So, you don't think there's anything to be afraid of? I mean, when you die?"

"I've no doubt that the transition, the end of biological life, can be tough—for the individual and certainly for the relatives. But it's only based in the attachment to the personality, and you aren't actually losing anything. That's the full essence of my understanding of life and existence."

He could hear for himself how speculative and pretentious it sounded. And just like after the conversation with Gitte, it surprised him he'd again told in such detail about his spiritual experiences and reflections—this time even to a stranger. But when he felt inside himself, he could see how much he'd changed in the process, starting with the conversation with the Master Entity—and how much that experience had helped to change the parts of his mind and personality that hadn't worked well or were even destructive. In addition, he could also thank the AA meetings for gradually enabling him to find the right words and descriptions when he felt it was relevant to share his experiences with others.

"Fortunately, it's not something we typically have to think about at our age—but for me, at least, all aspects of existence have become simpler with that insight," said Dan, breaking the silence.

Maya Luna said nothing, and he concluded he'd better round up.

"Thank you for taking the time to talk to me, Maya. I hope I haven't wasted too much of your time?"

"On the contrary," she replied warmly. "You've given me something to think about. Something I think I needed to hear. Thank you for that—you're an angel."

"That's good to hear," said Dan, relieved. "Take care."

"You too," she said and ended the call.

Dan put down his phone and went to the kitchen to get a cola. Although feeling like a clown after talking to Maya Luna, he was still glad he'd made the call. He'd done what he could—no matter what happened next. But it surprised him that he'd started talking about his views on life and death, even though she was the one who began by asking if he was afraid of dying. He could have limited himself to answering yes or no—without venturing into speculations that most likely made him sound like a religious oddball.

As he took the first sip from the bottle, Michael rang the intercom, and Dan let him in and went back to the kitchen. As Michael made his way up the stairs, Dan considered how to say that he'd called Maya Luna. The easiest thing would be not to mention it, but it would feel dishonest to keep it a secret. Another option was to wait a few days and tell him when they were sure Maya Luna hadn't died on Saturday.

Michael came through the door and entered the kitchen, where he said hi to Dan and took a cola from the fridge.

"I just talked to Maya Luna," said Dan, bracing himself for Michael's reaction, "warning her to be careful this weekend."

"Okay?" said Michael, surprised, as he opened his cola. "Didn't we agree that the proper thing would be not to contact her?"

"You're right—we did. But after much thought, I concluded I had to follow my conscience and weigh my intuition more than my rational analysis. I can't explain it any other way; I'm sorry I didn't talk to you about my decision before I called her."

"No need to apologize, Dan. First of all, when we talked about it yesterday, we had many doubts—especially because there are so many unresolved factors and parameters we don't know how much value we dare attach to."

Michael sipped his cola before continuing.

"And, as a matter of fact, I was just sitting in my car pondering the dilemma while queuing on the highway a little while ago—and I'm inclined to think you made the right decision. What did she say when you called?"

Dan recounted his conversation with Maya Luna—including the spiritual things they'd talked about—to Michael. He was glad that Michael thought it had been okay to contact her.

"Nice of her to talk to you," said Michael after Dan had finished. "She seems like a sweet person."

"That was also the impression I got while talking to her."

"I'm sure nothing will happen to her tomorrow—but I'm still looking forward to when we get into next week, and we haven't heard anything. Maybe you should call her again on Monday or Tuesday and check that everything is okay?"

"Yes, it's probably a good idea," replied Dan. "Or maybe you'd better call—otherwise, she'll think I'm a stalker for real."

Michael grinned. "Okay, I'll call. I'm sure it'll be nice to talk to her—and she might even be up for a date."

"Definitely a possibility," said Dan with a smile.

"Shall we look further into the DNA sequence and see if we can find out more?" asked Michael, pointing toward the living room. Dan nodded, and they sat down at their laptops at the dining table.

"Last night, I made a few walks around my little lake, thinking about different options," Michael began. "After all, we're still working from the expectation that our Primus AI finds the omega value in the extracted DNA sequence?"

Though the question was rhetorical, Dan nodded, agreeing this was the position they should proceed from.

"Yes, we concluded that the AI probably couldn't get it from anywhere else when it had no other input. Also, the only thing that differed between the customers was their individual DNA sequence."

"So, the hypothesis is that each of the seven blocks between the Gs contains data and that the omega value—returned by the AI—is somewhere in that data."

Dan nodded again and switched to the code editor on his laptop, where he marked the line with the man from Køge's DNA string as it looked after the Gs had been replaced with dots.

...AAT..TCCCT..TCACCCA..CTAATCACT..TTCATTCCTAA..ATAATTACCAATC..TCATCACAAATCTTA...

It was as strange to look at the string now as it had been the day before when they discovered the pattern. Seen on its own, it might have been a perfectly natural sequence from a single human's DNA. But it wasn't easy to explain why the same pattern—with a fixed placement of Gs, and a seemingly random distribution of the other three letters, A, C, and T—was identical for all the customers they'd tested.

"There are countless ways the three remaining characters could be used to contain numeric values," continued Michael. "But the logical one would be that each character corresponds to the value 0, 1, or 2 because there are only those three possibilities. I think the Gs are only used to create the fixed pattern, separating the seven blocks."

"Yes, it's a little redundant," interjected Dan, "but perhaps a fair price to pay for simplicity and robustness."

"Exactly! So if each letter in each block encodes one of the values 0, 1, or 2, that's a base-3 system, where each element can have one of three values. This contrasts with the binary principle we normally use in computers, where each element—each bit—can have one of only two values, 0 or 1. I did a little searching online last night and discovered that some computer systems—especially in the old days—were

THE KARMA SEQUENCE

based on the base-3 principle, that is, trinary and not binary. Each element isn't called a bit—but a trit."

Dan contemplated what Michael explained and understood where he was going. "It makes good sense—but how do we find out which letters go with which values?"

"There's no other way than to test all combinations until we hit the one that gives a workable result," replied Michael. "In this case, that means finding a solution where the omega value appears in one of the seven blocks. Though it may not be there explicitly—it may have to be calculated by combining several blocks. But it should be quick to test the possibilities."

"Yes, there are only six ways the letters C, T, and A can be combined," said Dan. "I'll make a quick script we can use to test."

"Good idea. We don't know if the most significant digits go from left to right or vice versa, but we'll have to test both possibilities. And we don't even know if it's a positional system. It's possible that other combinations of the letters—that is, trits—are used to form the values. But let's try."

Michael mentioned various other ways the blocks could contain numerical values—but Dan had already started writing a small program for the first simple test. He wrote it in the console in a browser window, which was how he usually tested quick ideas for new code.

A minute later, he'd written a simple line of code that took the DNA strand where the Gs were replaced with dots and removed the first three and last three dots, replacing all As with 0, all Cs with 1, and all Ts with 2. It then split the string into an array—a list of the seven blocks' contents—separated by the two dots; and finally, it converted the seven numbers from trinary—that is, base-3—to more readable decimal numbers using a simple integer function.

```
'...AAT..TCCCT..TCACCCA..CTAATCACT..TTCATTCCTAA..ATAATTACCAATC..TCATCACAAATCTTA...'
.slice(3, -3)
.replace(/A/g, '0') .replace(/C/g, '1') .replace(/T/g, '2')
.split('..')
.map(block => parseInt(block, 3))
```

When he pressed Enter, the little script turned the seven blocks in the DNA string into a list of numbers.

```
Array(7) [ 2, 203, 1740, 11129, 166095, 372121, 11580378 ]
```

"We're looking for the omega value—that is, 15,529—that the AI returned for the man from Køge," said Michael as they looked at the numbers. "Let's try the other combinations. If the number doesn't come up in any of them, then we've been too optimistic about how the string encodes the value—or my theory of trinary numbers as the most likely structure is wrong."

Dan nodded and ran the same script several times—switching the numbers with which A, C, and T were being replaced.

On their fifth attempt, they succeeded.

```
Array(7) [ 12, 78, 646, 14163, 15529, 611588, 3874204 ]
```

"There it is!" said Michael, pointing surprised at the screen. "In the fifth block, the one containing eleven letters—or trits."

Dan smiled. "Great! Somehow, it's still incredible that it wasn't harder encoded. But super with your hypothesis about the trinary numbers."

"Thanks. Although there are many possible combinations, this was probably the simplest, which is typically also the most robust."

"We now know that all the Ts represent 0, A is 1, and C is 2 in the DNA sequence," said Dan. "Fortunately, the order is left-to-right, so we hit it on the first try."

They both drank from their colas as they reflected on the discovery. It felt like a breakthrough, but it was also a step further away from the hope of finding an acceptable, rational explanation.

"So, the Primus AI finds the omega value in a weird sequence in the person's DNA," Dan continued the summary.

"And in both known cases, the number matched the person's date of death."

"Yes, it's getting harder and harder to explain it all as coincidences. We need to test more customers and see if the omega value is always found in the same way. But it's already quite inexplicable that all the customers we've tested so far seem to have the same pattern of eighty-one characters in their DNA. In my opinion, this is all taking a sinister turn—or maybe it's just me slowly accepting that we're looking at something that can't be rationally explained."

Dan nodded thoughtfully. He could sense that Michael was still struggling to accept that they might be dealing with something unexplainable—or even supernatural—but that he was reaching a point where he couldn't fight it any longer.

"What should we call the mysterious DNA sequence?" Dan asked, trying to get Michael to focus on an isolated part of the problem they could handle.

"I think we should call it the *karma sequence*," Michael replied after a moment's consideration.

FOURTEEN

Saturday afternoon, Dan was sitting in his car again, on his way to Michael's cabin in Sweden. The weather was still warm and sunny.

Actually, their plan had been to take a break for the weekend—and not meet again until Monday. Each would spend some days considering what they could do to get closer to explaining why the omega value was in the customer's genome—and why it seemed to match the number of days in the person's life.

In addition, every day that passed without their hearing about Maya Luna would make it easier to argue that the *karma sequence*—as they now called the eighty-one-character DNA strand—didn't predict the person's death and that the two cases Ryan had documented were most likely coincidences.

At least, that had been their hope and expectation the previous day—before the news that Maya Luna had died.

Her death had been another heavy step toward being forced to acknowledge that they had to incorporate a supernatural element in their search. And obviously, Dan was also saddened to learn that someone he'd spoken to just the day before had died—even though he hadn't known her personally.

Dan had received the news from Susan shortly after noon. He'd been at the local grocery store shopping when his phone rang.

"Hi, Dan," Susan had said. "I hope I'm not interrupting?"

"No, no—not at all," replied Dan, placing the shopping basket on the floor.

"This time, there's actually a sad reason I'm calling," continued Susan. Dan didn't say anything. From the moment he'd seen that it was Susan calling, he'd had a feeling what it was about.

"I've just seen a press release on our internal news page at DR, where Maya Luna's family says she has passed away after a long illness."

"I'm so sorry to hear that," said Dan after a short pause. He could tell he was shocked—even if the news didn't come as a total surprise. Deep down, he'd known there was a real possibility it could happen—even if he'd hoped it wouldn't.

"Yes, it's very sad," said Susan. "She was a brilliant musician and actor—but first and foremost, she was such a lovely and positive person. I've spoken to her several times and feel I knew her well, without us being close friends. Have you met her?"

"I've just said hi to her briefly a couple of times while out on the town—but it's true, she had such a positive and welcoming aura."

"But was it your intention to call her at some point since you asked me for her phone number? I don't want to pry into your private life—it just didn't seem like it was to get on a date with her. And then precisely the day before she dies."

Dan wondered how much he could tell Susan without mentioning that the Lifeline system had begun predicting when their customers would die. The easiest thing to do would be to say he hadn't called Maya Luna—but he didn't want to lie, even if it was only a white lie, and he would avoid having to explain.

"I actually called and spoke to her. Right after you sent me her phone number."

"May I ask why? Please say so if you want me to butt out, but it just seems a bit suspicious that it's exactly the day before she dies."

Dan looked around the almost empty shop before answering.

"I wanted to warn her and tell her to be careful—in traffic, for example. We didn't know she was sick."

He could hear how stupid it must have sounded in Susan's ears.

"It sounds like it has something to do with the project you told me you and Michael are working on with the Lifeline system," said Susan after a brief pause.

"That's true, but it's not easy to explain."

"How about coming to dinner—tomorrow night, perhaps? And then explain as much of it as you can and want to. Only if you feel like it, of course. Who knows—it might even help to talk to someone else about it."

Dan considered it briefly. It was only fair to share it with Susan, but it was also problematic to involve her—especially at a point when he had no rational explanation for why things were happening as they were.

"Thanks, Susan—that's sweet of you—but I don't know if it's a good idea."

"It's all right, Dan. I'm sure you have plenty to think about. Let me know if you change your mind. And at some point, it'll be nice if you get a chance to explain the strange coincidence to me, of course."

"Definitely—I'll remember that."

"Take care," said Susan and ended the call.

Dan picked up his shopping basket and went to the checkout. When he returned to his apartment, he called Michael and told him that Maya Luna had died. They'd agreed to meet the same day to process the sad news together and assess how much it had changed the whole situation and their chances of finding a logical explanation.

When Dan arrived at the little cabin by the lake, he found Michael inside, sitting at his little table, looking at his laptop. Michael stood up, gave Dan a long hug, and then pointed out the window. With a couple of colas from the fridge, they went outside and sat down on the little bench under the kitchen window. For a minute, they just sat looking out over the little lake, neither of them saying anything. As far as Dan could tell, there still didn't seem to be anyone at home in the neighboring cabin.

"It was awful to hear about Maya Luna," Michael said after taking a sip of his cola. "I'm surprised at how touched I am by this—I mean, none of us knew her personally."

Dan nodded—he felt the same way. On the way in the car, he'd tried to identify his different feelings and see why he was so affected.

"I think we're shocked that she died on the exact day our system predicted two years ago that she would die. And because it seems to dash our hopes of finding a rational and scientific cause for the omega value—as far as I can tell."

Michael nodded thoughtfully as Dan continued.

"Additionally, I think we also—on some level—feel complicit in Maya Luna's death: because we're responsible for the system that predicted it. Even if it's probably an irrational feeling."

"I hadn't thought of it that way, but it sounds right," said Michael. "It was bad enough with the other two customers, but we didn't know them and only heard about it after they died. And besides, back then, we didn't know about the omega value and the karma sequence like we do now; we were still pretty convinced that there had to be a more reasonable explanation for the coincidences."

Dan nodded. He felt the *karma sequence* was a suitable description of the mysterious DNA strand that the Primus

AI found in the customer's genome. When Michael suggested it the day before, he'd explained that karma was admittedly not a question of when you would die, but reflected all your life decisions and their consequences. However, he thought it could be argued that the term had an element of fate—and it had been clear to Dan that the suggestion also had an ironic element because they were still hoping for a rational explanation to emerge.

Neither of them said anything for half a minute. Dan thought about the entire process and his conversation with Maya Luna. It seemed they were both thinking the same thing.

"The more I sit and reflect on it," said Michael, "the happier I am that you called her and that you talked about the spiritual things. Maybe it even made her a little more comfortable with the situation."

Dan hadn't thought of it that way, but the possibility that it might be true gave him a warm feeling. "That would be nice," he said.

After they'd sat looking out over the lake for a few minutes, Michael put his bottle on the little table and turned to look at Dan.

"Shouldn't we try to get an overview of the situation with the new data?"

"Sounds like an excellent idea," replied Dan.

"I guess I've somewhat shifted my attitude about the whole thing," said Michael. "From insisting on the presumption that there had to be a natural explanation, I now have to say that I've accepted—albeit reluctantly—that we may be dealing with a supernatural phenomenon. And although that's also incomprehensible, I think we're now in a simpler situation—or at least a new one."

"I agree," said Dan. "From a purely technical point of view, it's a relief that we're less in doubt now—although it would have been easier to deal with emotionally if it had all gone in the direction we hoped for. But I believe it also changes the nature of our task?"

"Yes, definitely. We need to do more tests, maybe on some additional foreign customers, and see if there's a way we can check more omega values—and whether those people die on the specific date, their omega value predicts."

Dan nodded. "And we should also look into old backup files and make sure that the karma sequence—and thus the omega value—hasn't been manipulated after the gene sequencing was done."

"That's true. There are many things we can do to verify that the conclusion we're currently leaning toward is the most likely one."

They went on to talk about the different actions they could take to ensure that the current data was correct and hadn't been manipulated along the way.

After working out the options and how they would carry out the various tests, they shifted focus and started discussing the way forward.

"In a certain way, I've no problem accepting our discovery and the new situation it puts us in," said Michael. "It certainly doesn't contradict my personal convictions if there should exist such a prediction of when we'll die—and possibly for other things as well."

"It fits well in my universe, too," said Dan. "Although it's a chilling insight—and it's hard to fathom the consequences it'll bring. And probably opportunities, too."

"Yes, the prospects are completely crazy. And so, we shouldn't dismiss the chance that somewhere, there's some mundane detail we've overlooked or misinterpreted that provides a perfectly rational explanation for the whole thing. It's happened before."

Michael hesitated briefly while contemplating, before he continued.

"What's the chance that this is all something Ryan made up?" he asked. "Like an idea for a new product he wants to sell—and then he uses us as a test case to see if the idea holds up—after he fixes the data to match the observations."

Dan shook his head. "I'm quite sure we can safely rule that out. Ryan seemed shocked by the discovery—and he's not that good an actor. Besides, he's not technical enough to manipulate the data. He would have to come up with the principle of the blocks in the karma sequence and then change the genomes in our in-house database, plus in the fully sequenced genome in the service provider's database, where we've already checked that everything matched."

"And he would have to train the Primus AI to extract the omega value, which we still don't know how it does," admitted Michael. "But okay, you're probably right—he's certainly not that technical."

"There's still the possibility that it's simply a series of coincidences—it just seems completely improbable now, I think."

"Yes, in my best judgment, there are too many unlikely coincidences for us to reasonably write it off as coincidence."

"And even with the elusiveness of self-fulfilling prophecies, it's hard to believe in a rational explanation within a scientific realm."

Michael nodded. "But there's certainly a logical connection somewhere."

"I think so, too," said Dan. "But I'm afraid it's beyond our comprehension and anything we can possibly understand."

For a while, they sat without saying anything before Michael made an attempt to summarize.

"So that's the hypothesis we're working from now? That the omega value exists in the karma sequence in the person's DNA—and that it indicates how many days the person will live?"

"I suppose so," replied Dan. "We have three documented cases where the observations fit one hundred percent with that hypothesis."

"Okay, but then we can't avoid getting into a range of other fields where we're not at home—biochemistry, for example, and maybe also metaphysical topics: things that can't be explained within a scientific model."

"Exactly! And we should probably also be prepared for the risk that it'll not be possible to find a reasonable connection—and that we'll then have to accept that it's a supernatural phenomenon beyond our understanding."

"Yes, that will reduce our task to simply deciding what to do with that knowledge—which can prove difficult enough by itself," said Michael.

"But if we're still trying to find a scientific cause, then it primarily becomes a matter of biology and evolutionary theory—as far as I can tell?"

"That's my assessment, too," replied Michael. "It's just hard figuring out an evolutionary reason why our genome should contain data about events in the future. How would such a mutation provide an advantage in natural selection?"

Dan shook his head. "It's not easy to see—with thousands of factors influencing how and when we die. And even if the omega value might be hardcoded as a somewhat random number in the genome, it would still require an incomprehensible degree of control over external circumstances for the person to die on the precise date."

"The way I see it, there are two options," said Michael. "Either there's a kind of determinism, where the exact course of life and thus the day of death is predestined and known in advance, down to the smallest detail—like a movie being shown in a cinema. Or the omega value is only a target for when the person should die—and it's then up to nature or the universe to guide the person through events and choices that produce the planned outcome."

"Nature, cosmos, providence, fate—or God, if you like," added Dan. "But whether it's a plan for an undetermined future or an exact knowledge of an already determined future, surely it'll end up in some form of determinism?"

"Yes, but maybe there are different degrees of determinism," said Michael. "There's a wide stretch from a rigorous plan where every detail is known or determined in advance, to a reality where only a few key events are forecast."

"Do we have any way of finding out whether the karma sequence results from one model or the other?"

"No, I don't think so. Both are deep in the metaphysical—or even religious—sphere. And the explanation may also be a combination, or lie somewhere between the two extremes."

Dan gazed speculatively out over the lake and the perfect reflection of the trees in the still water. He could feel that it would take some time to get used to the idea that someone, or something, knew—or perhaps even decided—how long each person would live. Maybe all living organisms had such an expiration date in their DNA.

"But if everything is planned in detail in advance, then every human being doesn't have to carry around information about when they're going to die?"

"That's what I think, too," replied Michael. "The information is linked to each individual—as a kind of metadata—because it has to be accessible in specific situations, either continuously or at crucial events or choices. But that's pure speculation and projection—I don't think we'll ever understand that part."

"It would certainly change all aspects of life if everyone knew when they would die. Some wouldn't care about life, and others would get super busy."

"But isn't that how it is now?" asked Michael, with a twinkle in his eye. "We know we're going to die, and most people have a statistical expectation of approximately when it'll occur. If it happens before the average lifespan, we feel we've been cheated—and if it happens after, we think that's a gift in itself—if you're reasonably healthy, that is."

They both took a sip of their cola.

"Would you like to know exactly how old you'll be?" Michael asked. "Then it seems you have the opportunity to find out now. But you never had a Lifeline document created, I believe?"

"That's correct—and I'm not sure I'll do it to get that information," replied Dan. "You never had the document made either?"

"No," answered Michael, shaking his head. "I always felt that the Lifeline document wouldn't give me anything of value. After all, we both knew how little factual information was originally in that document. However, from a purely objective and technical point of view, knowing the date of one's death could certainly be interesting. Also, to study how that knowledge would affect daily life. I'm not afraid of the future, so maybe I'll send my mouth swab to a sequencing company and find the karma sequence myself to see how old I'll be. But I need to think about it some more before I decide."

Michael got up from the bench and went into the cabin to get two cold colas. When he returned and sat down, Dan felt it would be a good time to discuss a sensitive issue.

"There's something else we need to find out. We have to decide what we're going to tell Ryan."

Michael nodded contemplatively. "Yes, that's a good question. I don't think we should tell him about the karma sequence and how the Primus AI finds the omega value."

"I think we need to tell him about it," said Dan. "It's something that's going on in his system."

"That you and I developed, Dan! I think we're justified in making an overall decision—especially if there are ethical aspects outweighing the technical and economic potential."

Dan sensed that Michael's dislike of Ryan was affecting his stance on the issue. "Why do you think updating Ryan is such a bad idea?"

Michael looked at the lake for a moment, shaking his head in resignation before answering.

"You know how Ryan is. He'll inevitably end up abusing that insight—one way or another. You forget Ryan has no morals!"

FIFTEEN

On his way home from Michael's cabin, Dan spontaneously decided to visit his mother—now that he was passing Amager island, where she lived, anyway.

Thinking about it, he knew that this couldn't be the real reason for his decision. He was just as close to Anette's address when he stayed in his apartment in the Østerbro district. The best explanation for why the idea had popped up—while he was crossing the bridge over the Sound between Sweden and Denmark and could see Amager to the west—was the past few days' events and the thoughts and feelings they'd set in motion in him.

Not least, the news of Maja Luna's death had made him speculate even more about his own life and future, and—for some reason he didn't quite understand—his mother's too, even though they had no actual contact. It wasn't like he had any formal responsibility for her, but even so, there was a sense that he might be able to help her, and that he had a duty to make a difference where he could.

Overall, he'd become good at identifying his feelings—and being aware of them—both in the situation when they surfaced and afterward as part of his reflection. Following the conversation with the Master Entity, the self-knowledge he'd gained had also enabled him to observe the feelings as separate from his actual *self*—and categorize them as part of the body's physical functions.

This ability to externalize his emotions—to observe them disjunct from his innermost consciousness—had also been a central point in the treatment he'd received for his addiction and, subsequently, in many AA meetings. He'd learned how important it was to know and accept his feelings, and how they were easier to deal with when you could put them into words, and understood where and why they arose. It had been a tremendous realization to discover that he wasn't identical with his feelings, although they were a concrete, physical condition he had to deal with—even if they weren't actually part of his innermost *self*.

Although the Master Entity hadn't spoken directly to him since the experience when he'd been deep in the torments of addiction—at least not verbally or in the same overwhelming way—he was convinced it was still there and that he was somehow connected to it in a way he couldn't explain. Consequently, he also imagined it listening to his thoughts and reflections and that he could speak to it—and that what he said and thought might be heard. When he meditated and reflected on his existence, an essential exercise was always trying to understand this connection.

Additionally, he worked on identifying and putting into words the different areas in the landscape of his emotions to better understand where there were white spots on the map: parts of his personality he didn't know well enough and which he would prefer to change or remove altogether—with the help of the Master Entity, if possible.

After crossing the bridge, he turned off the highway at the airport, drove along the coast, and then through the residential areas of eastern Amager. He didn't need the GPS to find Anette's address and only used it to locate a flower shop on the way, where he bought a ready-made bouquet that he thought looked good.

He found a parking space near the old hospital and walked to the street where Anette lived and where he'd visited her twice before. Walking the last bit, he again went over what he would like to talk to her about—once he'd seen how she was.

When he reached her apartment building, he stood for a moment at the street door, wondering if he was doing the right thing, before he rang the intercom. A few seconds passed before there was an answer.

"Yes?" it came from the little speaker. Dan recognized his mother's voice from the previous times he'd spoken to her.

"Hi, Anette, it's me—Dan," he said. "Is this a bad time?"

A few seconds passed again before Anette answered.

"No, no—come in," she said, and the lock buzzed, allowing Dan to open the door and enter the stairwell. There were six steps up to the ground floor, where Anette had her apartment—and her door was already open when Dan reached it. Anette wasn't standing in the doorway, so Dan stepped into the small entrance and found her sitting on the sofa. She waved him over, and he closed the door and went into the small living room. The TV on the wall opposite the sofa was on, showing a talk show with some people Dan didn't know.

"Sorry, I just sat back on the sofa," she said with a small smile while reaching for the remote on the coffee table and turning off the TV. "I get dizzy easily if I stand up too long at a time. But please come and sit down." She gestured to a seat on the corner sofa, diagonally opposite from where she sat.

"I know that feeling," said Dan, thinking back to the days during his addiction when he could barely get up from his bed or sofa, and even going to the bathroom had seemed an insurmountable struggle.

He went to the sofa and bent down, squeezing Anette's hand.

"What a beautiful bouquet—is it for me?" she asked and continued after Dan nodded. "Can't I ask you to take a vase in the kitchen—in the cupboard to the left of the sink? And then fill it with some water from the tap?"

Dan nodded and went into the kitchen. When he returned to the living room, he placed the vase of flowers on the coffee table, where a bottle of red wine and a half-full glass already stood—along with several magazines, local newspapers, and various stuff.

Anette leaned forward, took a cigarette pack from the table, lit a cigarette, and then leaned back on the sofa again. She kept looking at the vase of flowers on the table and looked a little uncomfortable with the situation. Maybe she'd also been like that the other two times Dan had visited her, but he had no recollection of that.

She didn't seem to have changed much since his previous visit—just over two years earlier—either in appearance or habits. She still had that slightly too slim build and looked a good deal older and more timeworn than the fifty-five years Dan knew her to be. Her jeans hung a little too loosely from her skinny legs, and the worn, gray-green sweater looked several sizes too big.

"Your place looks like itself," said Dan, for lack of anything better to say—mostly to break the silence.

Anette moved her gaze from the vase and looked around her own living room.

"Yes. Once in a while, I feel like painting some new pictures, but I can never find the energy; and I actually like the old ones as they are."

Dan nodded and looked at the two paintings Anette had created herself. The style might have been Impressionism, but it wasn't an area he knew much about. She'd told him about the paintings on the other occasions he'd been there, so he chose not to ask about the same things again. But he knew she was interested in art and had painted a lot in her younger days.

Anette had trained as a primary school teacher at a very young age—before she had Dan—and had, among other subjects, taught Danish and visual arts at several schools in the Copenhagen area. She'd also overseen several art courses at evening schools—with classes on both art history and painting on canvas. But already at their first meeting, she'd told Dan that she was no longer teaching and only managed to make ends meet with various unskilled jobs from time to time—doing cleaning, for example. Dan guessed that her growing abuse had gradually made her unable to hold on to a steady job, and supporting herself with casual jobs at different workplaces had also slowly come to an end.

Six years ago, she'd been validated for early retirement—Dan knew because she'd written it to him in one of her text messages—and since then, she'd just been hanging around at home and around the local area without doing anything specific. Dan knew she wasn't bored—at least she said she wasn't—and that she spent much time on her computer, following her different areas of interest on the internet.

Dan moved his gaze to the bottle on the table and judged that Anette's alcohol dependency hadn't changed either. He decided he would try to talk to her about it—which, in a sense, was also why he'd come. But he didn't know how to approach the subject, and he feared she would be angry or upset if she felt he interfered in her personal life.

"I haven't offered you anything at all. I'm so sorry," said Anette self-reproachfully. It was obvious that she'd noticed him looking at the bottle. "Do you mind getting a glass yourself from the kitchen? That bottle has just been opened—it's an okay red wine, even if it's cheap."

Dan sent her a thankful smile. "That's sweet of you, Anette. But I really don't need anything," he said. "And, as a matter of fact, I don't drink alcohol anymore—it's been a year since I quit."

He was glad he'd gotten an opportunity to bring up the subject, but feared that she might take it as a criticism of her and her habits.

"That's terrific, Dan," Anette said in surprise with a cheerful voice. For a moment, she said nothing, and Dan could see that she was getting teary-eyed.

"I did have the impression that you were struggling with alcohol too—just like I always have," she continued. "I've seen you in the magazines from time to time—and in some of those photos, it looked like you'd had a few drinks. But now you mention it; there have been no articles with you for a long time."

She paused briefly and gazed in front of her before she proceeded.

"Besides, I couldn't help noticing that you were pretty drunk the last time you came to see me—even though I'd been drinking myself. But it's certainly good for you—and your health—if you can take a break. I wish I could do the same, but I've given up now—I'm afraid it's impossible."

"Don't say that," interjected Dan. He'd noticed a box of paper napkins on the table and handed it to her. Smiling through her tears, she thanked him, took out a napkin, and wiped her eyes.

"But it's definitely hard if you don't get the right help," he continued, looking at Anette, who sat looking at the bottle of red wine, biting her lower lip and shaking her head slowly. It seemed she had to concentrate not to start crying.

"Anette," he said, looking at her compassionately. "You certainly shouldn't refrain from enjoying your red wine just because I'm here—even if that's the subject we're currently discussing."

She looked at him hesitantly, but after sensing he was sincere, she nodded, leaned forward, and took her glass, drinking its last half.

When she'd emptied the glass and set it back on the table, Dan reached for the bottle and refilled her glass. He was aware of the irony: he had come to see if he could help

Anette with her drinking problem, and now he was helping her to more alcohol. But it wasn't his job to make her stop here and now. He just wanted to give her the incentive to consider it. It wouldn't get any easier if she suffered because of a decision she herself hadn't had time to reflect on.

"It's totally fine with me; and I'm not tempted because you have a drink," he said. "The key thing in my life is that I'm not having a temporary break from alcohol. I've stopped permanently—and will never consume a drop of alcohol again. Not so much as a single drink."

He could see that Anette got a skeptical look on her face.

"That's so amazing, Dan—and I don't want to discourage you—but isn't there always a risk of falling in again? I've tried to quit too—several times, actually—but on every occasion, it was only a matter of time before I had to give up and slipped back into the old abuse."

"You're right. I've no guarantee that I'll never fall into the same addiction again—or any other type of dependency, for that matter," said Dan. "And even if I'm one hundred percent sure that something won't happen, I could be wrong—or something can occur that I didn't see coming."

He took a deep breath before continuing.

"But for me, it's no longer a question of willpower. I've received invaluable help, so I don't have to constantly struggle to control my thoughts and the urge to drink. I'm still an alcoholic—I always will be—but now I can live my normal life as I want to. Because I don't drink anymore—and, mind you, I don't want to, either."

Anette sat and nodded thoughtfully. Apparently, his conviction had made an impression on her.

"That's the most wonderful thing I've heard in a long, long time," she said after a few seconds. "I must confess that I felt bad for a long time, fearing that you might be an alcoholic—and that it was something you could only have inherited from me."

She started to get teary-eyed again, but kept talking before Dan could say anything.

"Maybe that's all I've ever really given you in life," she said, smiling wryly as she wiped her eyes.

Dan shook his head dismissively.

"Whether I was genetically predisposed to my alcoholism or not, it's entirely my personal responsibility what I do with my life," he said as urgently as he could. "You simply mustn't go around blaming yourself for that—on top of whatever problems you might have already. That would be so unfair."

He could see she brightened up a little, smiling through her tears—although she didn't seem entirely convinced.

"That's sweet of you, Dan," she said, before taking another sip of her red wine.

They talked for nearly fifteen minutes, and Dan tried in various ways to convince Anette that the treatment which had helped him beat the addiction could also make a difference for her—and that he would help her through the entire process. But she didn't seem to believe that her life could be changed in the same way, saying it was too late to do anything about it.

Dan could sense that she was getting exhausted. She was nodding her head from time to time, and he guessed the red wine was probably making it worse, too.

At one point, Dan asked if he could use the bathroom. Although he was only out there for two minutes, Anette was sitting with her eyes closed—leaning back and with her mouth open—when he came back into the living room.

He looked around and found a piece of paper in a bookcase and a pen on the coffee table and wrote a quick note, which he put on the sofa next to her.

"I'm leaving now—it was good to see you," he said in a hushed voice, giving her thin forearm a gentle squeeze before adding, "Mom."

Anette didn't open her eyes, but he thought he saw the hint of a smile on her lips.

He found a blanket and put it over her before leaving the apartment and walking back to his car.

SIXTEEN

On Sunday morning, Dan drove out to Ryan and Gitte to update them on the latest developments, with the discovery of the karma sequence in the genome and the sad story of Maya Luna's death on the exact date the omega value had predicted.

He'd gotten up early and gone for a long walk by the harbor to think the whole situation through and see if he could figure out the right thing to do—and how much of it to tell Ryan.

In recent days, he'd become more affected by Michael's animosity toward Ryan and he could easily understand his fear that he would find a somewhat immoral way to use—or abuse, in Michael's words—the momentous insight they'd gained. On a personal level, his sympathy for Ryan, and the joy of their friendship, hadn't changed. But he couldn't help thinking about Michael's conviction that Ryan might potentially do much harm with this new knowledge.

On the way back to his apartment, he'd made up his mind about what to do. Despite his doubts, he would give Ryan and Gitte a complete and accurate update.

He'd instantly called Michael to tell him of his decision and to give him one last chance to convince him it wasn't the right thing to do. Maybe Michael had some new arguments and ways of looking at it—perhaps something that could persuade Dan to change his decision.

"Hi, Dan," Michael's voice sounded on the phone. "I anticipated you would call me this morning after you'd had time to think about it all. Have you decided what you want to tell Ryan about the astonishing things we've discovered with the karma sequence?"

Michael answered his own question before Dan had a chance to say anything. "I guess you're going to update Ryan on everything—despite my disagreement?"

"That's right," said Dan after pausing a few seconds. "But it wasn't an easy decision, and I still very much agree with you—on many of your points, at least."

Michael said nothing, giving Dan a chance to elaborate.

"I've tried to list all the pros and cons, but it hasn't given me a simple, unambiguous answer. So basically, I've based the decision on the reflection that I would feel bad about lying to Ryan and Gitte. We're doing this job for Lifeline, and it's the company's systems generating the ominous predictions, so I think it's our duty to share all the knowledge that comes into our possession with Ryan."

Michael started objecting, but Dan already knew what he was going to say, and cut him off. "Yes, I think it would be lying—if we hide what we now know from them."

He paused briefly before sharing his second reflection.

"And wouldn't keeping it a secret from Ryan actually be the same as saying we don't want to share our discovery with anyone at all? After all, if we decide to tell others about the karma sequence, Ryan is bound to hear about it sooner or later, and then he'll—justifiably—blame us for not updating him first, right after we discovered it."

"You're right," conceded Michael. "Maybe we shouldn't base our decision primarily on our fear of what Ryan might do—but more on whether it's something we should keep hidden in the first place and never share with anyone, whatsoever."

"Exactly. And I think that's too big a decision, and too heavy a responsibility, to hold. It's certainly not something I would feel comfortable carrying on my shoulders."

"That's a good point. Whatever we choose to do and with whom we get involved will have immeasurable consequences, one way or another. That's probably how we should look at it."

There was a brief pause, during which neither of them said anything—until Michael broke the silence.

"Fair enough, Dan—good on you for following your conscience. And I completely understand the argument about not lying. I'm just afraid of the consequences and what Ryan might come up with when he gets access to the knowledge of where the omega value comes from."

"Yeah, I'm a little worried about that, too," admitted Dan. "But maybe our role will be to advise and influence him—so that he doesn't get ideas that are too wild and bordering on what we think is morally acceptable. I believe there are several examples where we've been able to influence his decisions and turn them in a better direction."

"You're right—although it's mostly you, he has included in his deliberations and strategies."

Dan said nothing, but gave Michael a chance to reflect further.

"You know," said Michael after a few seconds. "I back your decision, even though I still have many doubts—but it's certainly not impossible that I'll change my mind at some point. And I can't help thinking about the other day when you opted to call Maya Luna—even though I didn't agree with that either—where I realized afterward that you'd done the right thing. Sometimes you're right, even if you decide something different than I do."

Dan could tell that Michael had said the last part with a twinkle in his eye. It was positive that he hadn't tried to veto the plan to update Ryan and Gitte—but Dan also knew that he probably would have stuck to his decision, no matter what Michael had argued.

After confirming their plan to meet the following day again—to continue work on the karma sequence and perhaps decide what to do with the new knowledge—they ended the call.

A couple of minutes later, Dan began preparing to meet with Ryan and Gitte. He called Ryan and said he had some important things he wanted to share with them—and asked if it would be okay if he stopped by later that day or if Ryan would rather postpone the meeting until the next day at the City Tower office. Ryan had said that he and Gitte were both at home—and it would be perfect if he came by straight away.

Half an hour later, Dan was in his car on his way to Ryan and Gitte's villa in the Strandvejen district.

When Dan arrived, Ryan and Gitte were sitting at the end of the long dining table in the enormous living room—both with a laptop in front of them. Ryan sat on one side of the table, facing the large panoramic windows, overlooking the garden and the Sound, and Gitte sat opposite him, with her back to the windows, facing the bar between the living room and the kitchen and above it, the first-floor landing. The landing ran the width of the house and had an excellent overview of the living room and the garden.

Dan got the impression that he interrupted them in an argument as he entered the living room from the entrance hall, as they both suddenly went silent. Gitte smiled and waved him over to the table where they were sitting—at the end wall at the far end of the living room.

"Hi, Dan—good to see you," said Gitte. "Grab yourself a cola in the kitchen if you fancy one; and one for Ryan, too, please."

Dan was about to ask if he should bring Gitte a bottle of water, but she preemptively shook her head, pointing to an almost full bottle on the table in front of her. He nodded and went into the kitchen, retrieving two colas from the fridge.

When he returned to the living room, Gitte was moving a chair to the end of the table for Dan. He put both colas on the table and sat down—and Gitte sat back on her own chair again.

"Thank you, Dan," said Ryan as he closed his laptop and unscrewed his bottle cap. "Yeah, Gitte's right—it's good to see you again."

Ryan took a sip from the bottle before he continued.

"We're both very excited to hear what you've found out. I didn't expect much to happen so soon after our talk out here last weekend."

Both Ryan and Gitte looked expectantly at Dan, who nodded and began the presentation of the points he'd prepared.

"Let me start by saying that it's not just me who has figured all this out—it's at least as much Michael's effort. But I dare say it's some incredible things we've discovered."

In the next ten minutes, Dan gave a complete and detailed account of what he and Michael had found in their investigation and logging of the individual services that made up the Lifeline system.

He explained how they'd discovered that it was their old Primus AI—trained initially only to find errors and repetitions in the generated Lifeline document—that had spontaneously started extracting a short sequence of eighty-one base pairs from the customer's genome and that it found the omega value in this string. He also noted that they'd not yet found an explanation of how the AI had found out where in the genome to find that strand.

While Dan narrated, Ryan had pushed a squared A4 pad and a pen toward him.

"Please draw a schematic of the sequence—so we understand it better," he said, pointing to the pad.

"I don't think that's necessary," said Gitte in a worried tone. "We don't need all the technical details that Ryan and I don't understand, anyway."

"Yes, please draw it, Dan," repeated Ryan in a casual voice. "It's very interesting!"

Dan was already drawing an overview of the composition of the string and the distribution of the ACGT base pairs, where the Gs were used in a fixed pattern separating seven blocks—composed of As, Cs, and Ts—one of which contained the ominous omega value that had started it all.

When Dan mentioned that Michael had suggested referring to the unexplained string as the karma sequence, Gitte snorted in surprise.

"Typical Michael, to make up such a term just because he's interested in eastern mysticism," she said, a little wryly.

"I think that's a fine term until we know more," interjected Ryan. "Not that I believe in karma—but because it refers to something fundamental that we don't understand. Not yet, anyway. Creative thinking on Michael's part, I'll give him that."

Ryan took the last sip of his cola and placed the empty bottle on the table. "That was a super walkthrough, Dan. You're good at explaining—even when it gets slightly technical," he said, winking at Gitte with a mock sympathetic smile. Gitte just smiled back sarcastically, shaking her head in resignation.

Dan nodded as he reviewed the list in his head—to see if he'd missed anything in the technical review. He didn't think so and decided to continue his recount of the sad developments of the past few days.

"The pattern of the karma sequence and the omega value that I've outlined here is confirmed by all the tests Michael and I have done. We've run a test script on all the 2,150 Danish Lifeline customers—including those who'd their document created before the Primus AI started finding and appending the omega value to the document. Without exception, they all have the karma sequence in their genome, and all have an omega value within a normal distribution of the number of days a person can be expected to live."

Both Ryan and Gitte nodded contemplatively as Dan proceeded.

"Now I've explained what the pattern looks like, in all the customers' sequenced genomes. But even after we found the pattern in all the customers we tested, it was still our rational assessment that there had to be a coincidence in the observations of the two customers who died—as you originally told us about, Ryan."

"Yes, that would be the easiest to grasp on all levels," added Ryan. "But as you know, Gitte and I have had a hard time buying that hypothesis from the beginning—precisely because it's so statistically implausible—even if the alternatives are so inconceivable. And I guess what you're saying about the DNA makes it even harder to attribute it all to coincidence?"

"At least that's the assessment Michael and I have arrived at," replied Dan. "Especially now that we know the omega value comes from a well-defined pattern in the person's genome."

"The karma sequence," added Ryan solemnly, as if repeating the term to himself.

"Exactly," said Dan. "And, on top of that, something happened this weekend that, in our opinion, makes it impossible to keep insisting on explaining it all away as mere coincidences."

"Another person died on the predicted date?" said Gitte spontaneously, before Dan had said so. Although it was a question, it sounded more like a statement. Dan nodded somberly while recalling the latest events.

"Yes, unfortunately, that is the case," he replied and then described the whole process, with the extraction and calculation of all Danish customers, followed by sorting them all on the expected date of death—and how the calculated date for Maya Luna was the previous day, and that she had indeed passed away on Saturday, as predicted by the omega value from her own genome.

Both Ryan and Gitte looked sad as they quietly listened to Dan's retelling of the last few days' events. Gitte got a tight-lipped look on her face and, at one point, stood up and started walking around the dining table while listening.

Dan told how he'd called Maya Luna and talked to her on Friday—the day before she died—and he recounted the entire conversation, including the spiritual reflections on what happens after death.

When he'd finished, he took a deep breath and remembered his still unopened cola on the table in front of him. He opened it and took a sip, his throat dry after describing the incident with Maya Luna. Although he'd talked about it before—first with Susan and then Michael—it hadn't been easier this time. He looked back and forth between Ryan and Gitte to see how they reacted. Primarily, of course, to the sad news of Maya Luna's untimely death but also to the incident as possibly providing definitive proof that the events could no longer be explained away as mere statistical coincidences.

Ryan sat quietly, staring speculatively out the large windows, seemingly not focusing on anything in particular. It seemed as if his brain was running at full speed, trying to process all the information and the new situation—even though the latest development confirmed what he and Gitte had long expected and feared.

Gitte said nothing either, but instead took Ryan's empty bottle and her own, which was half-empty, and walked slowly into the kitchen. Less than a minute later, she returned with two fresh bottles—cola for Ryan and water for herself—and sat back in her chair.

"It's shocking to hear that Maya Luna is dead," she said, blinking her eyes several times. It looked like she was trying not to get tears in her eyes. "I knew her somewhat and had actually invited her to this year's summer party—but she wrote back that she unfortunately couldn't attend. I didn't know she was ill—she kept that very secret. But I'm somewhat surprised she let herself be lured into buying such an insignificant product as the stupid Lifeline document—which doesn't tell anyone anything that they're not already, in some way, aware of."

The negative comments on his product and company didn't seem to provoke Ryan, who instead looked compassionately at Gitte.

"Yes, I was well aware that you knew Maya Luna and liked her," he said quietly. "And that's completely understandable. She has always come across as a creative person prepared to help others."

None of them said anything for a minute. Ryan gazed absentmindedly out over the Sound again, and Gitte looked worriedly at the A4 pad with Dan's detailed outline of the composition of the karma sequence.

The first to speak was Ryan.

"My immediate assessment is that we now have no choice but to conclude that we're dealing with something unexplainable—perhaps even something supernatural," he said, looking alternately at Dan and Gitte. "This also seems to be the conclusion Dan and Michael have arrived at after careful analysis and long deliberation."

Dan nodded. "Yes, I think that must be our starting point now: something supernatural or some advanced form of engineering and control beyond our understanding—which might be the same thing. Michael and I still have a long list of tests we want to run, so we're one hundred percent sure that the data is consistent, and that there isn't some tiny obscure thing we've missed. But at this stage, it's probably a waste of time to keep hoping or expecting something new to emerge that will fundamentally change the situation."

Gitte straightened up in her chair and cleared her throat.

"I just don't think it's satisfactory simply to conclude that there must be something supernatural going on," she said reluctantly, looking alternately at Dan and Ryan. "Surely there must be something we can do. Some sort of plan for how to move forward?"

"I think there is, too, Gitte," replied Ryan gently. "But at this point, I don't believe there's much we can do other than reflect on the new situation—and then later try to establish what the next step should be."

"We'll probably never be able to explain why that karma sequence is in the genome—not in any rational way," continued Gitte, unaffectedly. "But regarding the other incomprehensible thing—that the Primus AI has taught itself to find this sequence and extract the omega value from it—there's a simple solution: we simply have to stop it! That is, turn off that function and delete it, or whatever it's called technically."

Ryan looked thoughtful as he contemplated Gitte's proposal.

"It's not the AI as such that's the game changer," he said. "It's our newfound knowledge that every human's genome apparently contains the omega value."

"Yes, but surely we wouldn't have had that knowledge if the AI hadn't found it first—and pointed out to Dan and Michael where in the genome to find it?"

She looked questioningly at Dan.

"That's correct," said Dan. "We only detected the karma sequence because the AI logged it as an intermediate calculation. From there, finding it in the full genome was fairly easy. Now, Michael and I can find the karma sequence in a complete, sequenced genome at any time—because we know the pattern and precisely what to look for." He pointed to the sketch on the paper in front of him.

"But if you don't know that the karma sequence is there—and if the AI doesn't exist to point it out—then we have one less problem, right?" argued Gitte with a pleading look in her eyes. "I'm not so worried about our genome containing the omega value—but more about how the AI found it. That's what I find scary."

Dan couldn't figure out where Gitte was going with her argument. He didn't think it changed their situation or the eerie insight they'd gained—with the ability to predict every person's death. But he agreed it was technically incomprehensible how the Primus AI had discovered the pattern and found the sequence of its own accord.

"Don't you think we have a moral obligation to share our knowledge of the karma sequence with other people?" asked Dan.

"No, I certainly do not!" replied Gitte indignantly. "It's not knowledge that anybody needs or will make anyone happier. No person should know that about their own life."

Ryan strained to rise from his chair, making a calming motion with his hands.

"Let's not make any hasty and emotional decisions now—but sleep on it, and then meet again in a few days and look at it with fresh eyes. I think the most important thing is to keep our feelings out of it and focus on what all this gives us in terms of opportunities."

With a resolute movement, he tore the top page—with Dan's schematic of the karma sequence—off the A4 pad, folded it, and put it in his pocket.

SEVENTEEN

Dan visited Susan in her apartment in the Vesterbro district later the same evening.

On the way home from his meeting with Ryan and Gitte, he'd called Susan and asked if it was okay if he changed his mind about her offer to meet—and if she still thought it was a good idea. Susan had replied that she would love to see him and that the same evening was fine. She was looking forward to talking to him and hearing what he and Michael were up to—or as much of it as he could share with her and felt like talking about.

Dan took the metro to Copenhagen Central Station and walked from there along Vesterbrogade—the central street of the district—until he reached Susan's side street and her door.

It felt strange to ring the intercom and wait for her to let him in. He'd instinctively taken out the key, which he still carried around in his pocket, along with his other keys. He made a mental note that he would give it back to her, now that they were meeting, anyway. It surprised him he hadn't thought of it at their meeting in the café on Thursday, but he guessed it was because he'd been too nervous to think of that specific detail.

There was no elevator in Susan's building, so he climbed the stairs to the fourth floor, just like he'd done hundreds of times in the old days: first, after they'd become lovers, and he went to see her as often as he could—when she wasn't visiting him in his apartment in the Østerbro district. And later, when they got to know each other better, they almost lived permanently in her roomy apartment for extended periods.

Susan had already opened the apartment door for him, so he went directly into her long hallway, where he took off his shoes and placed them in their former fixed place by the doormat.

"Hi, Susan," he said loudly as he closed the door behind him.

"Hi, Dan," Susan's voice rang out. He could hear that she was in the kitchen at the end of the hallway—across from the spacy bathroom—and walked out to her.

There was the lovely smell of a stew—obviously with chili, which they both loved—and Susan stood with her back to the door, washing her hands at the sink. After drying her hands, she came over to Dan, standing in the kitchen doorway, and gave him a long hug. They held each other for a long moment—without either of them saying anything—until Dan reluctantly forced himself to let her go. He could see from her face that she, too, had found it a little awkward—and both smiled sheepishly.

Once again, her scent reminded him of their many times together and how relaxed and content he'd felt in those situations.

"Sorry—old habit," said Susan, but Dan knew her well enough to judge that it was a hastily thought up excuse—and that neither of them had wanted to let the other go. He was starting to regret that he'd changed his mind about meeting her if it made it harder—maybe for both—to put their relationship behind them.

Worst of all, he was also beginning to question whether his desire to meet her again was really based on a wish to update her as he'd promised—getting a chance to discuss the complex situation of the karma sequence with her—or whether it was all just a rationalization, and that the real reason might stem from a subconscious wish to spend a little more time in her company.

And if her motivation for inviting him had some of the same elements, it risked making the process of finally cutting the ties harder for both.

He pondered if it was something he should bring up at dinner—or if it would be too difficult to talk about. Perhaps the most straightforward solution would be not to meet each other more than necessary in the future.

"I guess you took the metro to get here?" asked Susan casually as she turned around and walked back to the kitchen table.

"That's right," replied Dan, glancing around the kitchen. Everything looked the same, though it seemed the wooden floor throughout the apartment had been resanded and waxed in a lighter shade. "It's a quick way to get across town."

"I figured as much," she said with a smile. "Even though you have a nice car, you still think it's easier to get around without it."

"That's true. At least in the city. The car is nice when I go to the summer house and, of course, when I visit Michael in Sweden. Or Ryan and Gitte north of Copenhagen."

Susan didn't have a car and typically took the bike to her job at DR, which was located in the southern end of Copenhagen on the Amager island. But she did have a driving license and booked a car online from time to time—when she had to go on a more extended trip that didn't fit in well with public transport.

"Could you take the rice and pour the water from the pot, please?" she asked, pointing to the stove. "Then I think we're ready to eat."

They each took a pot and carried them into the living room, on the other side of the hallway, where they placed them on the large dining table. Susan had already set the table and prepared salad, baguettes, and chips. She'd also set out a jug of water and a large bottle of cola, which she pointed to as they both sat down in their old places: Susan facing the windows to the courtyard and Dan on the opposite side, looking out over Susan's large living room. Dan nodded and leaned forward to pour water in her glass.

"You know what?" said Susan, holding her hand over her glass. "I think I'll go for the cola today."

Dan nodded and poured cola into both glasses. Usually, Susan would drink water, but she also liked wine with her food on festive occasions. If she'd been eating with one of her friends, they probably would have opened a bottle of wine, but Dan guessed it was because of him she hadn't done so now—though it wouldn't have bothered him or tempted him in the least if she had.

They started eating, and Dan told Susan how delightful the food tasted. She smiled and nodded a thanks, but neither of them said anything for a few minutes.

Even when Dan wasn't looking directly at her, he could feel Susan watching him with a speculative demeanor—but he had no clue what she was thinking. He looked around the room, noticing how major and minor things had changed since he'd last been there. At the opposite end of the room was still the gray corner sofa where they'd been sitting—and lying—together many times, but the old glass coffee table had been replaced with a new wooden one. Perhaps the old had shattered. The TV on the wall opposite the sofa was also the same, as was the bookshelf, although he could see that several new books had been added. Next to the bookshelf and on the end wall by the door to the hallway were the same framed posters showing a rocky stream in a forest and a large lake surrounded by snow-capped mountains.

Dan hadn't wanted to dive directly into explaining the events of the past week, which was the real reason he'd come. But when they'd finished eating—and had carried plates, cutlery and pots back to the kitchen and washed everything up—he felt it was a good time.

They'd sat down on the sofa—in their old places, where they could see each other as they talked—each with a mug of hot coffee. Dan was getting ready to tell Susan the complete story, including the explanation of why he'd called Maya Luna the day before she died; but Susan cut him off the moment he started talking.

"It's so weird to be sitting in this room with you again," said Susan. "In a way, it's as if a year and a half hasn't passed, and all the sad events are just something that happened in a dream. I'm still startled by how much you look like yourself again—from before you got sick."

Dan nodded. It all seemed like one long, horrible dream—an embarrassing memory he was now sitting in Susan's living room looking back on.

"Well, if I hadn't ruined everything, we would probably still be together—maybe sitting here enjoying a movie," he said in a low voice. He was sad—and a little annoyed—that the subject had come up again. But he was also perfectly aware that this would inevitably happen for years to come—in different situations and with other people—and that there was no one to blame but himself.

"What's done is done," said Susan. "I don't think you're doing anyone a favor by continuing to go around blaming yourself. The important thing is that you've escaped your addiction and gotten well again. The rest we can only take note of and learn as much as possible from—without forgetting it, of course."

Dan nodded, grateful for her compassion—but also a little wistful.

He knew he would always have to carry around the awareness of his disease and that it would only take one wrong decision to risk it all again. And while he was looking forward to putting it all behind him, he was aware that there were still some people, besides Susan, who'd suffered during his addiction—either through his behavior or his absence.

Although he'd already spoken to Michael, Ryan, and Gitte about other things, he knew that he also needed to talk to them, one at a time, about the process and what he could do to make amends. The same was true for Anette, his mother. He was sure he would have acted differently toward her, too, if he hadn't been caught up in his abuse.

"Isn't that the kind of thing you talk about at AA meetings?" asked Susan.

"Yes, that's a big part of it," he replied.

"It's always good to be able to talk to others about things. I often miss our conversations and time together," Susan said with a nostalgic smile. "Although you weren't exactly the most romantic person I've ever met."

Dan put up a face of mock surprise and pretended to be hurt by her statement—but he knew that what she said was true. He'd always tried to take things and processes apart, to see their individual parts, so he could better understand how everything worked; which sometimes made for a somewhat too objective and cynical approach to things.

Susan laughed at his fake indignant reaction. "For example, when you said that love is the less-disgusting cousin of intercourse. I thought that was rather unromantic. But somewhere, I also knew you were joking, or hiding your shyness, when you said stuff like that."

Dan nodded and concluded that this wasn't the best time to list various scientific arguments for his statement.

"And when we talked about having kids someday," proceeded Susan, "you were quite dismissive and said you certainly didn't want that. But now I know that was probably also based on your experiences in your childhood and how your mother placed you for adoption."

Dan nodded, thinking back to his visit with Anette the day before. He was curious if she'd seen the note he'd written before he left.

Susan had never met Anette, and Dan hadn't talked much about her—only briefly when Susan, out of interest, had asked him about his family and upbringing. Susan knew

Anette lived on Amager and that she had a drinking problem, something both Dan and Susan—even in the early days—had begun to fear that he might have inherited. After the treatment for his addiction, Dan was less worried about the hereditary component of the disease and no longer felt people were necessarily subject to a genetic determinism that controlled or limited their options. On the other hand, his realization of his addiction had also shaken his confidence in his notion of free will.

But between the two extremes—genetically determined traits and free will—there were, after all, comprehensive options for navigating one's life and always trying to make sensible and healthy decisions.

Dan didn't know what to say. It sounded as if Susan had come a long way in putting their problems behind them—which he was, in many ways, pleased with. At the same time, he couldn't help but wonder if there was an element of repression, perhaps accompanied by a hope that they could still have a relationship of some kind. This feeling was further reinforced as Susan proceeded.

"I've been thinking about it a lot since we met the other day," she said, "or actually since Gitte called me, and she and I had a good talk, in which she suggested I take up your suggestion to meet and talk about everything. And I've concluded that, in a way, I want to maintain our friendship—but without it developing into an outright relationship again. Do you think that could be a possibility?"

Dan thought about it for a moment. Although it sounded appealing, he felt sure it wouldn't be realistic. Not after they'd been together in the intimate way they had been—while they were each other's partners in every way. With Michael, it had been perfectly smooth to pick up the thread and continue their friendship—even after the long time they hadn't spoken. But it was probably also more straightforward when they weren't simultaneously trying to change the nature of the relation. He and Michael weren't in a situation where they had to build a new kind of relationship that was manifestly different from what it had been before Dan had cut ties and put their friendship on indefinite hold.

"I wish such a model were possible," replied Dan regretfully. "I miss our time together too, but I'm afraid it'll be difficult—at least for me—to keep things separate; the friendship and the romantic element. The two have always been part of the same inseparable whole that made up our relationship."

Susan nodded, biting her lower lip speculatively.

"Hmm. You're probably right," she said resignedly. "In a way, I'm also well aware that it's probably either-or. Either we don't see each other at all, or we're lovers again, like in the old days. And I have to say frankly that I wouldn't dare that. I couldn't bear to see the person I love going through that change—both physically and psychologically—and see our relationship destroyed in the same grueling way. Not again. I would rather do without the whole thing—including the friendship element—than live with the constant fear."

Dan nodded. He was glad that she'd come to the same assessment of their future relationship as he had. However, he wondered why she'd changed her mind, from refusing to meet or talk to him to speculating about the possibility of resuming the friendship part of their relationship. It seemed like a significant change in less than a week—but he had no idea what could have caused the change. Nor was it certain that she herself had an explanation for it, so he chose not to ask.

After a deep breath, Susan got up from the sofa and grabbed her own and Dan's coffee mug.

"I'll just put some hot coffee in," she said as she walked through the room.

While Susan was in the kitchen, Dan tried to get an overview of their situation and assess what the decision would mean for their future. It seemed they both felt they shouldn't see each other again. It was sad to think that this might be the last time they were together in private—even though that had been his expectation all along, especially since Susan had been so dismissive of his request to meet. The possibility of holding on to their relationship as friends hadn't entered his considerations and had come as a surprise. But he was glad they agreed it wasn't realistic.

When Susan returned from the kitchen with the two full coffee mugs, she seemed serene and utterly unaffected by their conversation. Dan couldn't help thinking that maybe she'd decided to put on a brave face.

"It was a good talk," she said after putting the mugs on the coffee table and sitting down on the sofa. "But maybe we should change the focus to the weird story with Maya Luna—which I think was also the real reason I invited you?"

Dan nodded as he drank some of his coffee and began his summary of the entire process.

The review took a little longer than it had taken in the afternoon with Ryan and Gitte because he first had to tell the backstory—with Ryan's discovery of the omega value and Gitte's speculation that it showed how many days the customer would have in his life. Then he explained about the California customer and the man from Køge, who'd died on the day predicted by the omega value.

Susan listened intently though with a skeptical look on her face, as if waiting for him to reveal a reasonable and acceptable explanation for the mystery—the same reaction Dan had when Ryan presented him with the problem and the tentative conclusion he and Gitte had reached. She said nothing but, at one point, gestured to Dan's mug to remind him to enjoy his coffee while it was hot. Dan nodded and drank some of his coffee.

Then Dan told her about his and Michael's search and logging in the Lifeline system and how they'd discovered that their own Primus AI had begun to find the karma sequence and extract the omega value from each customer's genome. Unlike earlier in the afternoon with Ryan and Gitte, he didn't go into detail about the composition of the karma sequence and the location of the omega value—but simply explained that it was apparently beyond doubt that the omega value came from the genome and that all humans had to be assumed to have an accurate indication of the duration of their lifespan encoded in their DNA.

"That's crazy!" said Susan. "I'm sorry to interrupt, but if what you say is true—and I know you wouldn't lie—then it changes everything; our entire outlook on life and what being human means. Not to mention the philosophical and religious aspects."

"Yes, it's a big mouthful," said Dan. "I've wondered about it for days—and nights—and I'm still shocked. The final gut punch came when you called yesterday to tell me that Maya Luna had died—which was exactly on the predicted date. Until then, Michael and I were clinging to a tenuous hope that, despite the unlikely coincidences, there was some slight possibility of finding a reasonable explanation for it all."

Susan got a sad look on her face when Dan mentioned Maya Luna.

"I'd completely forgotten about poor Maya Luna while you were telling me about your crazy discovery," she said. "But your system had actually predicted that she would die yesterday?"

"That's right," replied Dan. "She'd created a Lifeline document two years ago—and the karma sequence in her genome predicted that she was the next to die."

"And that's why you wanted to give her a call? To warn her?"

"Yes. I was hesitant about whether it was the right thing to do—and whether it would make any difference. Michael also pointed out that there was a risk that contacting her might itself influence what happened."

Dan could see that Susan was also surprised by that aspect of the prediction. She said nothing but just sat staring incredulously at her coffee mug.

"What did you say to her?" she asked after a moment.

Dan recounted his entire conversation with Maya Luna—like he'd done, first for Michael and then for Ryan and Gitte. When he'd told her everything, Susan had tears in her eyes but still managed to produce a small smile as she looked at him.

"Wow, Dan," she said, shaking her head a little. "I'm so happy you talked to her about those things—I mean, the spiritual things you mention. Not many people would have done that. I feel confident it may have helped her—and maybe mitigated some of her fear of dying."

Dan nodded. He knew he would never forget the conversation with Maya Luna.

"When you and I spoke the other day, you said you knew her," said Dan. "It would be nice if you could tell me a little more about her—if you're up to it?"

"Of course," Susan said and smiled, wiping her eyes, adding "You bet I am," before she began vividly describing the times she'd met Maya Luna, her work in music and theater—her welcoming personality and interest in other people.

It was almost midnight when Dan thanked Susan for a lovely evening. After he put on his shoes in the hallway, they gave each other a long hug, and Susan said she was grateful that Dan had shared the recent developments with her—even though she was expecting a hard time processing it all. Dan promised to update her as soon as anything new happened and then headed down the stairs.

When he'd descended all the way and was standing on the sidewalk, he realized he'd forgotten to give her the apartment key. For a moment, he wondered if he should ring the buzzer again and jump up with it—or drop it in her mailbox—but chose to keep it until the next time they met. Even if he wasn't sure they would meet again.

EIGHTEEN

Early Tuesday morning, Michael arrived again at Dan's apartment in the Østerbro district, so they could continue working on the problem together, brainstorming what to do with their discovery of the karma sequence in the human genome.

Dan was sitting at the dining table with his laptop when Michael rang the intercom. After he'd climbed the stairs and taken off his shoes, he went into the kitchen where Dan was waiting.

"Hi, Dan. Everything okay?" asked Michael.

"Hi, Michael—yes, I think so," replied Dan. "Except for some confusion on an existential level, but nothing serious."

They both smiled at the sarcasm—a little strained.

"Cola or tea?" asked Dan.

Michael thought about it for a few seconds.

"You know, I've been drinking so much tea and cola this past week while we've been nerding with the system. Now it would be nice to have a cup of coffee."

Dan nodded and filled the electric kettle with water.

As they waited for the water to boil, Dan recapped his meeting with Ryan and Gitte the day before. He told how they'd reacted to the news that it was Lifeline's own Primus

AI that—apparently of its own accord—had found the pattern of the karma sequence in the customer's genome and extracted the omega value. And he told how shocked and saddened they'd been by Maya Luna's death and how it had seemingly removed any possibility of attributing the first deaths to coincidence.

Finally, he told how Gitte had suggested that they turn off the Primus AI and never tell anyone about their discovery of the karma sequence, which apparently existed in everyone's genome. Michael listened with interest and didn't say anything until half a minute after Dan had finished his summary.

"I'm inclined to agree with Gitte," he said, squinting his eyes and scratching the back of his neck. "It'll save us a lot of rumination and trouble. And it'll certainly spare many people worldwide from dealing with an insight with immeasurable consequences for the individual; knowledge that might shatter their worldview and self-understanding. We have no way of assessing the effect that knowing the karma sequence will have on people and their beliefs, including their understanding of their place in the cosmos."

"Yes, I also understand the argument that it's the simplest decision with the least unpredictable consequences," said Dan. "And I think I could live with that decision too—especially if that's the way you're leaning. It's mainly the philosophical and religious implications of sharing this knowledge that I can't fathom. But I'm sure you've given that side much thought."

"I don't know if I think more about the spiritual aspects of life than other people do—but it's certainly something I spend a lot of time and energy on. However, that doesn't make me an authority in any way. Besides, there's also an element of playing devil's advocate in my agreement with Gitte's suggestion. I certainly haven't made up my mind if this is the right way to go; I only concede it's a temptingly simple and manageable solution, here and now."

Dan nodded as he reflected on the argument again.

"Simplicity is certainly a super argument in itself," he said hesitantly. "But there's also the big issue of responsibility. We don't know whether our new insight into the genome would have a predominantly positive or negative effect on people. But maybe this is exactly the question we need to investigate to see if it'll give us an answer or a direction. Maybe there's no simple answer to this question; maybe there will be tremendous benefits, for example, in health and medicine; and maybe the information could be an invaluable guideline in many people's lives? It's very complex, and we don't know if it's possible to arrive at a definitive decision that will be best for most people—and result in the least suffering."

"I agree," said Michael, "Meanwhile, the argument of least suffering may not be the right objective. Maybe other considerations carry more weight."

Dan nodded, though he didn't quite understand what could be more important than minimizing suffering for as many people as possible—given an opportunity to do so. He'd come to see suffering as a fundamental condition and as an inevitable side-effect of the biological process that is life. On top of this came the existential uncertainty many people suffer in their search for meaning and purpose in life and the things that happen around them.

"Any decision should probably also be judged by its intent," Dan said after a minute. "I mean, whether the choice is founded in good and compassionate judgment—or intended for personal gain or to harm someone. In that way, it's no different from any other decision we make. We can't be expected to take responsibility for all unexpected consequences—if we felt confident it was the right thing to do in the situation. On an informed basis, of course."

Michael nodded and looked out of the kitchen window at the blue sky for a few seconds before he said anything.

"Whatever the right decision may be—and whether such a decision even exists—the knowledge of the date of death of individual people and how to find it in their genome is too heavy a responsibility to carry. At least for me."

"Yes, I feel the same way," said Dan. "One option might be to share the discovery with experts from the scientific community, involving biologists, sociologists, philosophers, theologians—people generally considered to have different approaches to relevant aspects of the issue. We could frame it as a purely hypothetical problem—as if it were a thought experiment—without having to publish any part of our discovery. And depending on their considerations and conclusions, we could then decide to publish our findings in relevant journals."

"It's certainly a possibility," Michael said hesitantly. "But isn't that just a way of postponing the decision—waiting for some hopefully convincing arguments for a choice that we should already have all the prerequisites to make ourselves? Even if it's a difficult decision."

Dan nodded as he considered Michael's argument.

"We'll certainly have to think about it a lot—maybe for a long time," said Dan after a few seconds. "But as you say, perhaps a good approach is to look at how the knowledge of the karma sequence and its prediction of lifespan has affected the two of us—as humans—and not just deal with the problem from a technical point of view? And then base our decision on the assumption that other people's reaction will be comparable to ours?"

"Yes, I think that sounds like a reasonable approach," replied Michael and continued after a brief pause. "For myself, it's been a terrible journey, with the whole transition from frantically trying to hold on to a hope that the explanation could positively be found in a known, scientific framework—to being forced into a new realization that while there's a straightforward cause behind the coincidences, it lies beyond any rational experience. I feel I've been dragged, howling and screaming, into accepting what I now know. But although the process has been hard, I'm happy to have gone—or rather, been forced—through it."

During his summarization, Michael pointed to the kettle, which had boiled. Dan nodded and poured hot water into two mugs, making the coffee—while still listening.

"Now I see our discovery as a kind of revelation," continued Michael. "Something that reinforces my belief that there's an overarching meaning to existence—maybe even a plan or purpose to our individual lives. Even if I don't understand the plan, where it comes from, or how it all started. But if the insight into the karma sequence has changed one thing in me, it has given me the determination to spend even more energy searching behind the scenes and trying to reach an understanding. To seek our creator—or God, if you will."

Dan needed a few seconds to consider whether he'd understood everything.

"That was a great description of the progression," he said after comparing it to his own thoughts. "The process you describe covers the stages I went through myself very well—and the assessment I arrived at. But you're better at putting many of the spiritual elements into words."

"Don't say that, Dan. You've been through a difficult phase in your life and have come out on the other side with an insight into yourself and a spiritual interest that I haven't previously observed in you."

"Thanks, Michael. That's also how I see the changes I've gone through—but it means a lot to me if you've noticed it, too."

Each with a mug in his hand, they went into the living room and sat down on Dan's sofa. They sat contemplating their thoughts for a minute, sipping the hot coffee.

"Who or what do you think is behind it all?" asked Dan as he leaned forward and placed his mug on the coffee table.

Michael shook his head in resignation.

"Well, that's the big question—and the same question people have been asking for thousands of years," he said. "Maybe the only difference is that we're now in a situation where we know there may be a rational answer to the question—even if that rational explanation may well be beyond anything we're able to discover or understand."

Michael took a sip of his coffee and smiled absentmindedly as he proceeded.

"I think I've walked around my little lake a hundred times in the recent days—trying to figure out who might have encoded the karma sequence in our genome and how they make sure the expiration date is met—if I may say so."

Dan was just about to calculate how long it would have taken Michael to walk a hundred times around the lake, but stopped himself. He guessed Michael had exaggerated to make his point clearer.

"I've thought of several models," continued Michael. "Everything from aliens from other planets or universes to superhumans living secretly in our midst. However, it often ends up sounding like bad science fiction or fantasy. How about you? Have you come up with a theory or theories about who might be behind the karma sequence?"

Expectantly, Michael leaned back on the sofa while Dan quickly reviewed his thoughts before presenting them.

"We were talking earlier about the possibility that everything was predetermined in detail—absolute determinism, as you called it—and why we didn't think that was the best theory."

"That's right," interjected Michael. "Because in that scenario, each human would hardly need to have the metadata—as the karma sequence appears to be—directly in their individual object instance."

He gestured to Dan to continue.

Dan nodded. "Another possibility is that the entire universe is a simulation running on some kind of computer outside the universe being simulated."

"Which is also a theory many recent philosophers argue for," said Michael. "There's a lot to suggest that it could be a plausible model."

"And that would fit nicely with our analogy of comparing humans to objects in programming, each with a specific set of fields or metadata. But we're probably limited because we can only think as humans—and developers—and because we, accordingly, try to find explanations similar to technologies we know or can imagine."

Michael nodded. "That's true. The possible theories easily end up sounding like science fiction. But that doesn't change the basic hypothesis that the cosmos is somehow an illusion. Which is fine with my fundamental outlook—also on the spiritual level."

Dan briefly thought about his conversation with the Master Entity and how the experience had changed him into a more spiritual person.

"The problem is," said Michael, "that there's an almost infinite number of potential causes and that we probably don't have—at least this is my conviction—the possibilities or the physical prerequisites to fathom the whole thing. It isn't something we'll be able to see with our own eyes. We may be able to get an explanation, but then we'll still be in the same situation where it's a matter of personal conviction whether or not we choose to believe that explanation."

Dan nodded eagerly. "Exactly! So perhaps we can do nothing but relate to the fact that there seems to exist manifest evidence of control or predetermination beyond our control or understanding. And surely, all things being equal, this must be some form of non-human intelligence?"

"It almost has to be," said Michael speculatively. "Unless we're talking about time travel, where people or computers from the same universe travel back from the future, set the karma sequence, and ensure it's followed. But that's really just a variation on the transcendent intelligence—the only difference being that it's not from a different space, but from another time."

"Now it's getting very speculative," said Dan, smiling resignedly.

"Of course—but that's the only starting point we have: to hypothesize about who or where this intelligence is. The key point is that it's planning and controlling key elements of human life at a level we can't imagine."

As they both sipped their coffee, Dan decided to canvass something with Michael that he'd begun to think about a lot.

"Now that we know that this intelligence exists, at least in the sense that we've found it—or something resembling proof of its existence—can we in any way get in touch with it?"

"I doubt it," replied Michael. "Not unless it wants to contact us. But it's hardly interested in a dialogue with anyone within the physical universe. It's probably not even interested in anyone discovering the karma sequence. Otherwise, surely it would have shared it with someone at an earlier stage?"

"Yes, but detailed knowledge of our genome is relatively recent, so knowledge of the existence of the karma sequence wouldn't have been of much value until we were able to sequence a complete genome for individual humans. It's only in recent years that it's become possible at an affordable price."

"But if it's not interested in us knowing about the karma sequence—isn't it conceivable that it could contact us to prevent us from sharing our knowledge with anyone? One way or another?"

"Yes, I think so, too. Put a little speculatively: one might fear that it'll do everything to stop us if it anticipates that we'll make our discovery public. That's super hypothetical, but perhaps the best argument for doing as Gitte suggests—turning off the Primus AI and forgetting everything about the karma sequence."

After drinking their coffee and putting the mugs back in the kitchen, they took a couple of colas from the fridge and sat down at the dining table to continue working. The goal was to attempt to find an explanation for the Primus AI's output, but also to ensure that the data they'd gathered so far was consistent.

They ran numerous tests on the running Lifeline system to ensure their findings matched the other customers' data. They tested on all foreign customers in parallel runs and saw that the karma sequence was found the same way it had been for all Danish customers who'd purchased a Lifeline document. The same pattern, with the eighty-one base pairs, was found in all the tens of thousands of tests they did—and their own script, calculating the omega value, gave the same result as the Primus AI found.

By late afternoon, they had a complete list of all customers, and the estimated date of death, for every one of them. Some dates were only a few weeks and months ahead, but most lay years in the future.

After seeing the complete list—sorted by closest date of death—they discussed whether they should contact the individual persons, regardless of where they lived, and warn them, just as Dan had done with Maya Luna. But they concluded that the question was linked to their undecided position on what to do with their knowledge of the karma sequence—and that it probably wouldn't make any real difference to the individual. Plus, it would also be an unwieldy task.

They updated Ryan and sent him the complete list of customers and their dates, leaving it up to him—probably in consultation with Gitte—to decide whether further action was needed for each Lifeline customer. Ryan said he would spend some time keeping an eye on the top rows in the list—as their time approached—and see if he could verify whether they died on the predicted dates, the same way he'd done with the two customers from California and Køge.

It was early evening when Dan and Michael chose to call it a day—and Michael drove back to his cabin in Sweden. They agreed not to meet the next couple of days, but that they would each continue thinking about what they could do to find a reason behind the Primus AI's altered behavior; and whether it would be necessary to involve one or more AI experts, thereby inevitably revealing the existence of the karma sequence. This question was also related to the outcome of their deliberations on what to do with their new knowledge—both about the Primus AI and the karma sequence, which was perhaps the most crucial issue to try to find a plan for.

Dan decided to go back to his summer house in Liseleje and take some long walks in the woods and by the beach while pondering the tough questions.

While driving on the highway—halfway to the summer house—he received a text message from Anette, who wrote that she was deeply touched by the note he'd written before he left her apartment on Saturday, and that she would like to accept his offer.

Dan took the first off-ramp, crossed the bridge, and returned back on the highway again—now in the opposite direction—heading for his mother's apartment on Amager.

NINETEEN

Crossing the Langebro Bridge in the car, Dan and Anette were on their way back to her apartment on Amager.

It was Wednesday, a little after noon, and Anette had attended her first meeting in a treatment program for her alcohol dependency, planned to last two months, with three weekly sessions. Together they'd left Anette's apartment shortly after eight in the morning for a treatment center in the heart of Copenhagen. When they'd arrived, Dan had asked the secretary—a young woman he remembered from his own time in treatment—if his mother could start treatment immediately and if there was room in the current group, which was scheduled to meet the same day, from 9:00 a.m. to 1:00 p.m.

The secretary was surprised and happy to see Dan again, and after checking her computer screen, she said there was room in the group so Anette could start immediately. Typically, a new participant would have to attend an introductory meeting—before treatment started—but the secretary was confident that Dan had prepared Anette with all the knowledge and support she needed based on his own treatment history.

THE KARMA SEQUENCE

For the four hours that Anette's first meeting with the treatment group had lasted, Dan had waited in the reception—thinking back to the many times he himself had been to the center and how much of an impact it had on him and his recovery from addiction. An addiction that had taken not only control of his life but also the joy out of it. He felt convinced it could also help Anette beat her abuse—especially after their conversation the night before when he'd arrived at her apartment on Amager.

Anette had opened the door, with tears in her eyes—and told him how much his recent visit, and especially the message he'd written, had touched her. While returning to the sofa, she'd explained how she discovered his note Sunday morning and had then immediately made up her mind to stop drinking. But it had only been a few hours before she was trembling all over and had no choice but to give in to her body's merciless demand for alcohol. She'd drunk far too much the rest of the day and had been a mess both Monday and Tuesday, at which point she'd chosen to write the text message Dan had read in his car half an hour earlier.

After they'd sat down on the sofa, Anette had kept crying—no longer just because of Dan's offer of help, but probably also because she was ashamed of her helpless situation and had perhaps even given up hope of ever escaping her addiction. Her resigned and dejected appearance reminded Dan of the time when he'd been at the very bottom of his disease.

Talking calmly to Anette, he'd tried to appear in control, explaining why he was sure everything would be all right and that her decision to accept help was a giant step in the right direction.

At one point, Dan had picked up two pizzas from the nearest pizzeria. As they sat at the coffee table eating, Dan talked about his experience with the treatment process, what happened at the meetings, and what it was like to discuss the dependency with other people in the same situation. After they'd eaten—Anette had only eaten a single slice of her pizza and a few chips—Dan suggested that they go to the treatment center the following day and that, with any luck, Anette could immediately start the same course that had helped him get over his addiction.

When she heard his proposal, she'd hesitated at first but then gritted her teeth and, with a determined look in her eyes, declared that she was ready and hoped there would be a place so that she could start at once.

As they talked, Dan had said he didn't mind if Anette had a glass of wine to calm her nerves. She'd said yes, with a relieved but apologetic look—and Dan had poured the last of a bottle of red wine into her empty glass. They talked for over an hour—with Anette occasionally taking a sip from her glass—before Dan suggested they go to bed so they would be rested for the next day. He could easily sleep on the sofa, with one of the blankets already there, and Anette found a fresh toothbrush for him. Before she said goodnight and went into her little bedroom, Dan got up from the sofa and gave her a long hug, promising her in a comforting voice that everything would be all right.

In the morning, he'd woken Anette early, so she had plenty of time to shower and get ready at her own pace. A little before eight, Dan had picked up his car—which he'd parked a few hundred meters from Anette's building the evening before—and supported her as she walked the few steps down to the street and got into the car. She'd said nothing in the fifteen minutes it took to drive into the city center and find a parking space. Still, Dan could sense that she was unsure what would happen next—and whether it would make any difference—even though he'd explained a lot, trying to prepare her as best he could and make her as comfortable with the unfamiliar situation as he possibly could.

While waiting in the reception during Anette's meeting, Dan had also had the opportunity to speak to the secretary and a few of the therapists he remembered—and once again expressed his gratitude for their invaluable help in his effort to put the addiction permanently behind him.

When Anette's session with the first treatment was over, and she came out in the reception, she looked physically exhausted—but still had a confident look in her eyes. After she'd given Dan a big hug and they'd said goodbye to the secretary, they left the center together and walked to Dan's car so they could drive back to Anette's apartment.

Throughout the drive back to Amager, Anette talked passionately about her meeting and what the treatment comprised. She mentioned how emotional and inspiring it had been to meet with the eight people in the group she'd joined—and hear them speak about the same problems she knew all too well from herself and how they were replacing their addiction with different and better life interests and activities. She recounted how the therapist had explained some of the mechanisms—both physical and psychological—that kept people addicted and how the insight into these mechanisms, and consequently your own personality, made it easier to distance yourself from the need to get into a particular mood, using alcohol or other artificial means.

Anette also explained the treatment center's concept of not having fixed start and end dates for the treatment course but that you could join a group—like she'd done the same day—no matter if the other members of the group had been in their program for a shorter or longer time. Everyone would receive the same amount of valuable knowledge and self-insight—but in a different order, depending on when they'd started.

Dan smiled as Anette narrated—also because it reminded him of his own experience with his first treatment session. It was nice that the meeting affected her positively and strengthened her belief that she could successfully get over her addiction. She described in detail the things that had happened at the meeting and seemed to momentarily forget that Dan had gone through the same treatment process, which he thought back on with warm feelings.

"What did the therapist and the other group members say to you when the meeting started?" asked Dan as they drove south along the busy main street.

"They were all super nice, introduced themselves, and explained how many weeks they'd each been in the treatment. And after that, I was asked to tell them a little about myself, my addiction background—and what had persuaded me to accept treatment."

"And you weren't too shy to talk about yourself in front of the other people?"

"Not at all. It felt like we already knew each other a little—even after that short time—because we shared a similar background," replied Anette. "And remember, I'm a teacher, so I've gotten used to speaking to large and small crowds. Of course, not about such personal things as this—but still."

She paused as she pulled a piece of paper from her pocket and unfolded it.

"I also showed them the note you wrote when you visited me on Saturday—and read it to them."

After taking a deep breath, she read Dan's short message aloud. "Hi, Mom. I'm sure you can escape the dependency as I did. Just let me know, and I'll give you all the help you need. I love you. Your Dan."

She mumbled the last part indistinctly and got tears in her eyes. Dan was about to ask why she'd brought the note, but she beat him to it.

"You won't believe how much those words mean to me," she said quietly, wiping her eyes with one hand. "It was your visit on Saturday—and then this letter—that made me believe that I can have a normal life again and maybe even be a little part of your life too, Dan."

Now it was Dan's turn to be touched. He could feel the emotions welling up in his chest, but he couldn't find a good way to express them. Although he shared his mother's joy at the prospect of a better life, he was ashamed of not having done something earlier when he'd known she had a problem, too.

"This is a new beginning—for both you and me," he said after a few seconds. "We'll be part of each other's lives—and not just a small part. I promise."

After stopping at a red light, Dan let go of the steering wheel with his right hand and reached out for Anette. He just wanted to squeeze her arm, but she took his hand and held on to it with a gentle grip. When the traffic light changed to green, they continued along the street until they came to the intersection, where they had to turn for Anette's side street.

As they approached her house number and Dan was looking for an available parking space, Anette said she had an idea.

"Why don't we take a walk on the beach before returning to the apartment?" she suggested. "The weather is so nice, and it's been a long time since I've seen the Sound."

"Good idea," replied Dan, although he didn't think Anette would have the energy for a long walk. However, it was a good sign that she wanted to do something active—instead of just hanging around in her little apartment.

He drove on, past the old hospital and through the residential area—until, after a few minutes, they reached the large beach park by the Sound. There were lots of people going to and from the beach, but he still found a free parking space quickly. He parked and let go of Anette's hand before getting out of the car and walking around to the other side to help her out. When she'd got out, she stood for a moment looking out over the beach and the water, which was perfectly blue on the cloudless day. The recreational area was full of people swimming, sunbathing, or playing beach volleyball—enjoying life and relaxing, one way or another. Then she closed her eyes and stood still, letting the sun warm her face.

As they stood by the car, Dan took a look around. He didn't understand why it was so popular to take off most of your clothes and lay down among a lot of strangers, but everyone seemed to be having a good time—and he was well aware that he was the one who was a little unusual.

After standing by the car for a moment, Anette opened her eyes and looked expectantly at Dan.

"Let's walk some of the way across the bridge," she suggested. "Unless there's something you need to do? I don't want to take up your time—so you're putting off important things."

Dan smiled at her and shook his head as they started walking toward the bridge that led to the other side of the beach park, where there were even more people.

"I don't have anything on my calendar," he said. "And even if I did, there's nothing more important than what you and I are doing now."

The bridge was full of people heading to and from the beach park—but not so crowded that Dan and Anette couldn't walk undisturbed at their own leisurely pace. When they were halfway across, they stopped for a rest—looking out over the large lagoon between the original beach and the artificial isthmus the bridge connected to. Anette watched in fascination children bathing close to the shore, youngsters on paddleboards, and trained athletes swimming long distances in the middle of the lagoon. Dan knew there were often kite surfers in the lagoon too, but not on this day—probably because there was no wind of significance.

After standing for a few minutes watching the many people playing, having fun, or exercising in the water and on the beach, Dan looked at Anette, trying to assess whether she had enough energy to walk a little further or whether they should turn around.

"Just let me know if you think we should go back to the car," he said.

Anette thought about it for a moment, then shook her head decisively.

"I think I can go all the way around. That is, out to the isthmus and then over to the next bridge, and from there back to the car," she said, pointing out the route with her finger.

Dan nodded in surprise, and they continued their slow walk. He could see Anette's forehead and arms were sweaty, but it was hard to tell if it was from the heat or the physical exertion.

"Now it would be nice to have something to drink," said Anette after they'd crossed the bridge and were walking on the long sandy isthmus. "Water, of course," she added a few seconds later when Dan hadn't responded.

"That's a very sensible idea," said Dan with relief, pointing to a building further along the concrete pathway. "There's a little kiosk over there. I'll buy us some water."

When they reached the kiosk, Dan bought two bottles of water. He'd forgotten to ask Anette whether her water should be sparkling or still—so he bought one of each. A little further along the pathway, they found an empty bench where they sat down. Anette chose the sparkling water, and they both took a big sip of the cool liquid.

They sat on the bench for almost fifteen minutes, and Dan could tell that his mother enjoyed being surrounded by so many people. She smiled at children and adults passing by on the broad pathway—and occasionally closed her eyes, seemingly soaking up the sounds of the many happy and active people. Part of the time, she just sat looking out over the Sound and at the many ships sailing in different directions.

A few minutes after they'd sat down on the bench, Dan received a notification on his phone and took it out of his pocket. It was an email from Ryan asking if Dan could stop by the office—preferably the following day, if that was convenient. He wrote that he now had a super plan he would like to review with Dan.

Before answering, Dan looked at Anette to get an overview of what was on the agenda for the following days. Her next treatment wasn't for another two days, so he wrote back to Ryan, telling him that Thursday morning was fine and that he was very much looking forward to hearing about his plan. After sending the reply, Dan sat and pondered what decision Ryan might have reached with the karma sequence. Somehow, he hoped that Gitte could have persuaded Ryan to turn off the Primus AI and never share their knowledge with anyone. On the other hand, he could also sense that it might be too easy a decision and that much time would still be needed to weigh the potential benefits of making their discovery public.

Dan's thoughts all day had been about Anette and her treatment, but after reading Ryan's email, he felt the karma sequence starting to occupy his thoughts again. Until now, he hadn't paid much attention to the many people on the pathway and beach, but now he began looking at them individually, imagining a small label on each of them, showing their omega value and the date they were going to die. It was an uncomfortable and frightening thought. In a way, he had the power to point at each of them, one by one, and tell them how old they would live to be—using a simple mouth swab or a blood test. He closed his eyes and tried to think of something else, hoping that Ryan—with Gitte's help—had reached a good decision.

Sitting with his eyes closed, he felt Anette move closer and rest her head on his shoulder. It was a nice feeling because it helped shift his thoughts from the karma sequence—a responsibility he couldn't find out how to handle—to the responsibility for himself, his family, and people around him. This responsibility was in many ways just as great—perhaps greater—yet he felt better suited to bear it because it was so manifest and present. It was somehow easier to relate to, even though it involved real people, too.

He thought about how much had happened in the past twenty-four hours—how his mother had accepted his extended hand and started the addiction treatment he hoped would give her back a normal life as it had done for him. He also thought about Susan and the attempt to help her put their relationship behind them—in a good way. Maybe it hadn't gone as well as he'd hoped, and he would have to try to find a solution.

At one point, he felt Anette's hand on his arm and opened his eyes. She sat looking at him with a tender and caring expression.

"Did you fall asleep?" she asked quietly.

"No, no," he replied, looking around to remind himself where he was and what they were doing. "Or yes—maybe I did doze off for a moment."

"How about it—should we walk on?"

Dan nodded and stood up from the bench, offering Anette his hand and helping her get up. After throwing their empty water bottles into the nearest trash can, they continued their walk toward the next bridge and back to Dan's car. Anette held Dan's arm, and he could feel that she was getting tired and that their active day and the many impressions were starting to have an effect.

They found a parking space near Anette's building, and after returning to her apartment, they stood for a moment and talked about the plan for the next few days. Dan said he would at least stay for dinner in the evening and planned to go to the nearest grocery store and buy groceries immediately.

Anette nodded and asked if she should come, but Dan encouraged her to take a well-deserved rest instead. He could see that she was relieved not having to walk anymore, and when she gave him a hug, he could feel her body trembling a little. Then she went into the bedroom and lay down on the bed. Dan quietly closed the bedroom door, took her door keys, and went out shopping.

In the evening, they cooked together in Anette's small kitchen. Dan had bought ingredients for the rice casserole he always made for special occasions—but without the hot chili pepper, which he only added when he made the dish for himself—or when he'd made it with Susan. Standing at the kitchen table, preparing the food with Anette while they chatted about anything and everything, felt nice.

As they enjoyed the food they'd prepared—drinking nothing but tap water—Dan talked about his own experiences with the same treatment Anette had now started. He described the mechanisms that, to his best estimation, made the treatment so effective.

Anette asked whether it hadn't been challenging to stay away from alcohol altogether after the treatment had ended and it had become everyday life again—no longer having the support that the therapists and the rest of the group had provided. Dan replied that he'd never wanted to drink again, even though he was often in the same situations where he would have fallen for the temptation in the old days. That was part of the effect of the treatment: you became more aware of your psychological patterns and learned to look at your feelings more objectively, recognizing the situations where in the past you would have tried to use alcohol to establish a certain mood where you knew you would feel good—at least for a few hours.

Dan also talked about how the AA meetings had the same aims as the treatment and how helpful it was to speak with other people in the same situation regularly—hearing about their experiences and even being encouraged to put your own feelings and needs into words.

Anette listened attentively, often asking questions, and it seemed to Dan that she was still confident she'd made a good decision. He made a mental note to himself to transfer the payment for the treatment the following day.

After they finished eating and doing the dishes, Anette came up with the idea that they throw out all the alcohol she had in her apartment. They found all her red wine and spirits bottles, emptied them into the toilet, and deposited them in the glass container in the courtyard.

Before Anette went to bed, she gave Dan a long hug.

"Thank you for a lovely day, Dan," she said as they held each other close. "It's been the best day of my life. Not only because of the treatment, which I've so much faith in—but also our closeness and all the things we talk about."

"I think it's been a fantastic day, too, Mom," said Dan. "And this is only the beginning. If it's okay, I would like to come and stay here with you—just for a week or two?"

"That's sweet of you, Dan—but I don't think it's necessary," Anette replied hesitantly. "I would rather not be an inconvenience more than I have to."

"It's no inconvenience," said Dan assuredly. "On the contrary, it'll mean a lot to me to spend some time with my mother—as a real family."

Anette nodded silently, and Dan could feel her body slightly trembling—probably both from fatigue and emotion.

TWENTY

Dan woke up at six o'clock on Thursday morning after sleeping on Anette's sofa and got his laptop out of his backpack. He sat for a couple of hours looking at the Lifeline system—including the extracts of Danish and foreign customers he and Michael had made two days earlier and sent to Ryan.

A little after eight, Anette came out of her bedroom, wearing a blue T-shirt and gray sweatpants.

"Good morning, Dan," she said and sat down on the sofa, diagonally opposite Dan.

"Good morning, Mom," Dan greeted back, looking up from his laptop. "How are you after the big upheaval yesterday?"

Anette smiled thoughtfully as she looked ahead, unfocused. Her hands were trembling slightly, and her face occasionally twitched.

"I can feel my body struggling somewhat to adjust to the new situation without alcohol," she replied. "The first thing I always do in the morning is to drink some red wine to stop shaking and to calm my nerves so I can relax."

Dan nodded. He remembered the phase when his body rebelled against the decision not to start drinking again.

Fortunately, it didn't need many days to adjust to the new reality, after which the urge to drink was primarily a psychological dynamic that could be just as difficult to overcome—until you gained the tools and self-awareness to solve the problem.

He placed the laptop on the coffee table, got to his feet, and went into the kitchen, where he poured cold tap water into two glasses. When he returned to the living room, he gave one to Anette and sat back on the sofa. Anette drank most of the water in one go and set the glass back on the table while Dan shared his own experiences from the first phase of the addiction treatment. He felt convinced that Anette could use it and that the things he told would make the situation a little less confusing than it might seem when you were in the middle of it.

Anette listened attentively, silently nodding her head in a slow rhythm.

"Would you've succumbed to the temptation to drink if I hadn't been here?" asked Dan gently. He could tell she needed to survey herself before answering.

"Frankly, I don't think I would," she answered after a few seconds. "But it's all still so new, so I don't know if I'll feel the same way tomorrow or the next day. That's what I might be a little afraid of. But I'm happy you're here, and the things you share about your own experience are a tremendous help."

"Your treatment has only just begun," Dan said encouragingly. "You'll feel the need many times until your body has forgotten the bad habit, and you've got to know yourself so well that you can handle the psychological dynamics without problems."

Anette nodded thoughtfully. "Yes, I'm expecting it to be a struggle—especially here in the beginning," she said. "But I'm also confident that it'll get easier, eventually."

After assessing the situation and Anette's condition, Dan told her he was meeting Ryan at Lifeline's new offices in the Nordhavn district, but that he would be back in a few hours.

Anette assured him she wouldn't succumb to the temptation to go out and buy red wine—but that it was also a relief to know that there was no alcohol in the apartment. She would spend the time reflecting on what she'd learned at the treatment meeting the day before and on what the other group members had shared about their individual situations and experiences.

It was a little before nine when Dan arrived at the City Tower. Outside the large glass doors, he met Vibs on her way to work, and they accompanied each other into the building. Vibs pointed around, updating Dan on the status of various parts of the site and the interior. Although he was prepared to take the stairs up to the seventh floor again, he was pleasantly surprised when Vibs told him that the elevator was now activated and could be used—something Ryan had been exceptionally pleased about.

On the ride up—and after they'd exited the elevator and were walking around the curved corridor—Vibs continued speaking about the new premises and how few colleagues still needed to be relocated from the old premises in central Copenhagen.

Although they'd only met once—before the board meeting two weeks earlier—it felt as if they'd known each other for a long time, and Vibs's optimism and joy in conversing about the building and the plans rubbed off on him, giving him a warm feeling inside.

He hadn't thought about her since they'd first met: primarily, because of the problem with the karma sequence, and recently, the attempt to help his mother get over her dependency—but now he was reminded of how charming Vibs had appeared to him at their first meeting. He listened with interest to the things she explained—and completely forgot his usual shyness. It annoyed him a little that he hadn't taken the detour around his apartment—when driving from Anette to the Nordhavn district—to shower and get some clean clothes. Fortunately, Vibs didn't seem to notice.

When they reached the reception door, they could see that Ryan had also arrived and was standing in the conference room, in his favorite position by the large panoramic windows, with a view of the Sound, the harbor, and the southern districts of Copenhagen.

"Please go ahead into the reception and to Ryan's office," said Vibs, opening the door for Dan. "I typically go round to the various departments and say good morning to those who've met already. And especially to some of the coders who've often been here all night. They often need some encouraging words or a fresh cola." She sent Dan a warm smile, then continued down the corridor. After a few meters, she turned around.

"I almost forgot to ask you. Are you coming to Ryan and Gitte's summer party tomorrow?" she asked interestedly, lighting up in a big smile when Dan nodded affirmatively.

"Super! I can't wait to see you out there," she said, winking at Dan before turning again and walking toward the door to the developers' office.

Dan stood for a moment, speculatively looking at her, before going into the reception and along the glass wall to the door leading into the conference room. When he knocked, Ryan turned his head, gesturing for Dan to come in—even though he was still busy with his conversation on the phone. When Dan entered and approached the large conference table, Ryan pointed to the small fridge and then to Dan. Dan nodded and took a cold cola for himself—after checking that there was still some in the bottle at Ryan's seat at the end of the table.

Half a minute later, Ryan finished his conversation and smilingly approached the table, where he sat down and took a sip of his cola before saying anything.

"Hi, Dan," he said after a deep breath. "Glad you could make it. I have some exciting things I would like to discuss with you. I hope everything is fine?"

Dan nodded. He wanted to tell Ryan about the latest developments with his mother, but chose to postpone it for another time—perhaps when Anette was a little further along in her treatment.

"Great," continued Ryan, "I'm glad to hear. It can't help but weigh on you, with all the responsibilities—and opportunities—that have opened up for us."

They sat without saying anything for a moment before Ryan cleared his throat and leaned forward in the chair.

"First, thank you for the complete list of Lifeline customers and their omega values. It was mind-boggling to see the list—especially when sorted on the day of death. To be honest, I started by looking for my own record in the list, to see when my date was set for. I was a little bit anxious until I found the row and saw that, fortunately, I'm going to be an old man. That is, according to the karma sequence. Our internally calculated value says I don't have quite so many years—but that's probably understandable, given my size, eating habits, and lack of physical activity. But I'm very relieved. Now I have the opportunity to better plan ahead."

Dan looked at Ryan in surprise while he was telling him about his omega value. Earlier, he'd quickly looked through the list of Danish customers to see if it contained anyone he knew. At first, he'd been unsure whether he should, but it was hard not to look when you had the list right in front of you. But he didn't remember seeing Ryan, or anyone else he knew, on the list.

"I know what you're thinking, Dan," said Ryan with a smile. "You've looked at the list and haven't come across my name."

Dan nodded, and Ryan proceeded to explain.

"I've created my Lifeline document under a pseudonym. To prevent people with access to the database from seeing my private data. Most people share all kinds of private information, trusting the systems to be secure—but professionals like you and me know that's an illusion. And with the discovery of the karma sequence, I'm even more relieved I did it that way."

"Good point," admitted Dan with a smile. "Glad to hear you're going to live a long life—I'm happy for you."

"Thanks, Dan. You have to remember, of course, that the omega value doesn't tell you anything about how life will turn out or whether you'll always be healthy—but maybe that's some of the information hidden in the other six blocks of the karma sequence."

Dan nodded. He and Michael had already spent some time wondering what the other blocks might contain.

The first block contained three letters, the following five letters, then seven, nine, eleven, thirteen, and finally fifteen letters in the last of the sequence's seven blocks. Each letter represented the base pairs T, A, or C—covering the values 0, 1, and 2. At least, this was the case with the fifth block—the one with eleven letters, or trits, as Michael had called them—where they'd located the omega value.

They'd found only one additional correlation between the values in the blocks and the known data for the individual customer. The first letter in the first block looked like it covered the person's gender—at least, there was a consistent pattern where customers who'd stated their gender as female had the letter T in this field of the karma sequence, and males had an A.

Apart from that, they'd wondered whether the karma sequence might contain data about the person's health history, intelligence, personality traits, and several other possibilities—but they'd agreed that this was pure guesswork. Michael had suggested that one block might contain a count of the person's incarnations. However, admitted that this idea was only based on his interest in eastern religion and mysticism. And while the theory wasn't unthinkable, verifying it would be incredibly complicated, most likely impossible.

"I can see you're already thinking of solutions," said Ryan approvingly. "No doubt it'll require a lot of database- and computing power, but I expect it'll be worth the investment. After all, there could be all kinds of interesting and useful information about the individual customers in the sequence; and in combination with the knowledge we already have about the omega value, this could turn into a gigantic business."

"I wasn't thinking about solutions," said Dan, "but about the unsurmountable problems of extracting that knowledge from the karma sequence."

He hesitated, searching for the best argument. Ryan said nothing, but gave him the time he needed.

"With the omega value, it was quite simple," continued Dan after a moment. "We already had specific knowledge of what we were looking for. The Primus AI had shown us that it extracted the omega value from somewhere in the karma sequence, and after some experimentation—and testing various assumptions—we located its position in the sequence. What we're talking about now is going in the opposite direction: we know the values of the karma sequence, and then we have to find a pattern in what they code for in the real world—for each individual person."

"You're absolutely right, Dan," conceded Ryan in an accommodating voice. "It's going to be an enormous task. We'll need all the knowledge we can get about each customer—in addition to what they've already filled out on the questionnaire—from social media and observations, plus whatever we can persuade them to contribute on their own. Then we need to store all that knowledge in a structured way in databases many times larger than those used in the Lifeline system today. And finally, we'll need a group of experts in big data who can dynamically structure all the information—using our Avaram system, which can also be used for training new AIs in finding patterns in the vast amount of data and correlate them with fields and patterns in the karma sequence."

Dan could feel himself becoming infected by Ryan's enthusiasm for the technical challenges and the fascinating considerations of defining and organizing it all using the Avaram platform. At the same time, he also felt a growing concern that Ryan had seemingly not tried to find a solution to the ethical question of what to do with their knowledge of the karma sequence. Apparently, he'd instead focused on the gigantic technical and business opportunities that their discovery presented. But if the enormous amounts of data about each customer actually expanded their understanding of the karma sequence—wouldn't this added insight make their responsibility even more significant and harder to carry—pushing the right decision even further away?

While Dan was caught up in his own contemplations, trying to balance the technical challenges and the ethical and human responsibilities, Ryan got to his feet and walked to the other end of the big table, where he bent down and took a cola from the small fridge. When he returned, he stood for a moment, looking out the large glass windows, as he took a sip from his bottle—before turning and sitting down in his chair again.

"Did you consider our situation's more philosophical and ethical aspects?" Dan asked hesitantly, after taking a sip of his cola. "I can't help thinking about what Gitte said last time—and her suggestion to shut down the Primus AI completely and not share our discovery with anyone."

"Yeah, I sure did," said Ryan, putting his hands on the table as he leaned forward. "And I've also concluded that we shouldn't share our discovery with anyone."

"So you want to keep the insight secret while turning it into a business? That's not how I perceived Gitte's concern and the solution she suggested."

"You're right," said Ryan, holding out his arms in resignation. "My new vision isn't exactly what Gitte was hoping for—and it's not like I don't understand her arguments; in a certain way, everything she says is true. But I just think the business aspect—and the gigantic market, I'm sure there is—overshadows any unanswered questions we might have. And think of the impact our product will have on people's lives and decision-making! Surely that has value in the big picture, too?"

Ryan had a pleading look in his eyes, as if hoping for Dan to support him and agree with his assessment, approving the grand plans.

"I think it's a tough decision," said Dan after a few seconds. "But I can easily see the enormous business opportunities that will surely disappear if we choose to make our knowledge of the karma sequence public."

"Then our incredible knowledge would be pretty worthless," interjected Ryan, gesturing for Dan to continue. "Sorry, Dan. I didn't mean to interrupt you."

Dan shook his head disarmingly as he proceeded.

"Perhaps the time has come when we should shift our focus from the purely technical and business-oriented prospects to a consideration that's one hundred percent ethically based. And once we've made the right decision, we can assess the economic opportunities with a clear conscience. Even if it might turn out to be less profitable than the model you present here."

Ryan nodded thoughtfully while at the same time getting an adamant look on his face.

"Yes, that's pretty much what Gitte has been saying—repeatedly—in recent days. You know her—she can be quite stubborn when she's made up her mind about something. And she hasn't talked to me all week, except when we're coordinating practical details for tomorrow's summer party. Almost every time we've talked about the plans for the karma sequence, it's escalated into a regular quarrel."

Ryan paused, drinking from his bottle. Dan didn't know what to say and felt sad that Ryan hadn't been more forthcoming toward Gitte's sentiments.

"But this is the worst mood I have ever seen her in," continued Ryan after setting his bottle back on the table. "She has alternately tried to appeal to me calmly and deliberately, and at other times begged me fervently—as if it were a matter of life and death—to drop the plans and do the right thing, as she calls it. To make matters worse, she has also threatened to leave me. I simply don't understand why this matters so much to her."

"But isn't Gitte's concern about the plans a good reason to reconsider?" asked Dan.

"There's nothing I would rather do than remove all obstacles from Gitte's way," replied Ryan sincerely, but with a regretful undertone. "But it's just hard to change who you are. It's my whole identity and purpose in life, and it's so deep in my nature to identify technical opportunities and create a good business—almost at any cost—for myself and the other owners. And preferably a positive experience for the customers, too—otherwise the word would get out and it would risk affecting revenue."

Ryan looked expectantly at Dan as if hoping he could formulate a new proposal for a solution that was palatable to all.

"Although attempting to change yourself and your priorities is challenging, it's not impossible," said Dan after evaluating the situation for a few seconds. He tried to sound encouraging as he reflected on the significant change he'd himself undergone. "Especially if you get help."

"You're right about that," conceded Ryan, while simultaneously shaking his head doubtfully. "But sometimes it's tough for an old dog like me to learn new tricks—it's how I'm created, after all."

Ryan placed both hands heavily on the conference table, leaned forward in the chair, and stood up. Again, he walked to the large panoramic windows and paused with his back to Dan.

After half a minute, Dan got up and walked over to Ryan. They both stood silently, looking out over the harbor and the Sound sparkling in the light from the morning sun. Neither of them said anything until, after a minute, Ryan hesitantly broke the silence.

"And I can't imagine how Gitte will react when I tell her about my latest idea," he said with a wistful smile. "I'm afraid she'll have a heart attack."

Dan said nothing—he knew Ryan would update him on his idea when he was ready. As he waited, he briefly thought back to Ryan's plan to keep the karma sequence secret and spend resources finding the meaning of all its blocks and selling that unique insight to people worldwide. It wasn't the decision he'd hoped Ryan would have arrived at.

After a brief pause, Ryan cleared his throat and took a deep breath before talking passionately about his latest idea.

Dan hadn't expected that it could get much worse than the plans Ryan had already presented.

But it could.

TWENTY-ONE

On the way back to Anette on Amager, Dan drove around his apartment in the Østerbro district to pick up some clothes, his hair trimmer, and his toiletries. He wanted to avoid going back and forth too often after he'd moved in with his mother and was staying with her for a week or two—or however long it might be necessary.

He was still in shock after the meeting in Lifeline's office, where Ryan had filled him in on his latest ideas and plans. Part of the reason was the disappointing realization that Ryan wasn't going to prioritize the moral responsibility that came with their discovery of the karma sequence.

But that was nothing compared to the new plans Ryan had shared with Dan as the last item on the meeting agenda. It had come like a bolt from the blue, and Dan could feel he needed to talk to someone about it, and there wasn't a better candidate than Michael—though he worried about his reaction when he got the news. But together, they might be able to find a way out—or some arguments—that could put a stop to Ryan's ominous plans.

When Ryan had told him about his idea, Dan had said that it sounded exciting but that he would need some time to understand it and fully get into the necessary disciplines.

He hadn't told Ryan how crazy he thought the plan was—which maybe he should have done. Not because he believed it would change Ryan's agenda—it seemed like the idea had been almost a revelation to him—but at least to make it clear that he didn't want to be part of Ryan's insane circus anymore.

He'd said goodbye to Ryan and had left the City Tower. While he was walking through the reception, Vibs had sent him a big smile and said something to him—but he couldn't remember what she'd said or if he'd replied.

In retrospect, he was glad he hadn't slammed the door and told Ryan he didn't want to be involved any longer. That would have deprived him of any chance to influence Ryan in the future—even after he might have found a better way to stop him.

After packing a sports bag with the things he thought he would need, he checked that everything was okay in the apartment and all the windows were closed—before leaving and driving back toward Amager. While driving through the city, he called Michael, asking if he had time to meet and if he was either in Copenhagen or at his cabin in Sweden. Michael said he was in his cabin and that Dan—as always—was more than welcome to drop by. He asked if there was anything specific they needed to talk about. Dan apologized and said he'd just been to a meeting with Ryan, but would prefer to wait to talk about it until they met—which was fine with Michael.

Since he'd left Anette's apartment earlier in the day, she'd been on his mind most of the time—until Ryan told him about his latest idea. But now that he was on his way back to her, and the initial shock of Ryan's elaborate plans was wearing off, he was once again aware of how much he was looking forward to seeing his mother again and making sure she was all right.

There were plenty of free parking spaces near Anette's apartment, so he didn't have to walk far after parking the car. The door opened seconds after he pressed the intercom. After walking up the few steps and entering the apartment, he was welcomed by Anette with a big hug. She then resumed the restless wandering—back and forth in the small rooms—that she'd apparently been engaged in before Dan arrived.

"How's it going, Mom?" asked Dan as he filled two glasses with water in the kitchen and carried them into the living room, where he sat down on the sofa. Anette followed him and sat in her usual place—diagonally opposite him.

"It's okay," replied Anette after sipping her glass. "But it's hard. I don't know what to do with myself, and I'm trying to tidy up some of my stuff a little and see if there are other practical tasks—so I can focus my energy on that. Sometimes, I lie down and close my eyes to see if I can sleep away from it all—but I can't. I'm constantly aware of my body's craving for alcohol. And of my mind and the old habits that try to lure me back to drinking. It almost feels like a poison that my system slowly tries to dissolve and excrete."

Dan nodded sympathetically as he listened to Anette's description—he remembered all too clearly the first difficult days of his own process.

"It's precisely a poison that your body needs time to break down," he said with conviction. "Fortunately, it won't be many days before that part is over. After all, the body has an amazing ability to heal itself. And from there, it merely becomes a mental task of preventing yourself from giving in to the desire to take that first drink—which is what the addiction treatment gives you the tools to do: because you learn to understand your mind and your needs better and understand how to put words to your feelings and identify where they come from and why they arise."

Anette nodded as she listened, but it seemed she was still intimidated by the project and perhaps even doubtful that it would all succeed.

"I understand what you're saying," she said, a little worried. "I'm just afraid I won't be able to understand all the things I have to learn. It seems overwhelming."

"It's only normal for things to look a bit unmanageable at the beginning," said Dan, putting his hand on Anette's arm. He could feel that she was still trembling a little. "But you'll be surprised how quickly you'll feel better. Besides, you don't have to learn a lot of new stuff; on the contrary, you have to unlearn and clear out the things that get in the way of understanding yourself and your life."

She nodded, but Dan could see that she wasn't convinced, and he also clearly remembered how difficult it had all seemed at first. But somehow, he felt reassured he could use his experience to support his mother through her journey. Although he'd made mistakes—and still did—he'd become better at recognizing and admitting them so that he could correct them more quickly, and he hoped to share that skill with her.

"Believe me, Mom," Dan said urgently, but in a cheerful voice. "I'm sure you'll be more optimistic after the next treatment session tomorrow. Everything is progressing as it should, and it won't be long before you're as healthy as I am!"

Anette looked at him and smiled; it seemed she was getting over some of her doubts. Dan contemplated taking her to an AA meeting that evening but decided to wait until she'd been to a few more therapy meetings; he didn't want to risk presenting her with too many impressions—and new people—too quickly. He suggested that she spend some time preparing what she would say about her first days in the program when she met with her group for the subsequent treatment the next day. Anette thought that was a good idea.

After they'd sat and talked for a while, Dan stood up.

"Mom, I have to go talk to Michael in Sweden—just across the Bridge—but I'll be back in two or three hours.

Remember, you can always call me if you feel bad or can't resist the temptation of a glass of red wine."

"Sounds good, Dan," she said, standing up as well. "And don't worry—even though I'm not feeling so great right now, I'm not tempted to try to make myself feel better by drinking."

She took a key from the kitchen table and handed it to him.

"I can tell by your sports bag that you're serious about moving in with me for a few days," she said with a smile. "So, here's an extra key: it fits both the front door and my apartment door, so you can come and go as you please."

"Thanks, Mom," said Dan, hugging her before walking out the apartment door. "I'll see you in a couple of hours."

Dan again spent the time in the car—on the way to Michael's cabin—thinking about how best to convey Ryan's latest idea to him. On the one hand, he was looking forward to the opportunity to talk about the new situation, which radically changed their considerations about ethics—and on the other hand, he feared that Michael would overreact and do something stupid when he heard about the plans. But that risk was impossible to dodge unless he chose not to update Michael—an option it took him only seconds to reject. He needed to hash it out with someone, and Michael was so involved that he had a right to know about the latest developments, too.

When Dan reached the cabin, Michael wasn't there—neither on the tiny lawn in front of the cabin nor inside. His car stood parked in its place, so Dan guessed he wasn't far away. He grabbed a cola from the fridge and sat down on the bench outside the cabin, looking out over the small lake. While enjoying the silence and the cold cola, Dan again pondered Ryan's latest plan, trying to anticipate how Michael would react when he heard about it. He feared there was a real risk that Michael might be tempted to do something drastic, but had no idea what it might be.

After sitting there for five minutes, Dan heard footsteps on the narrow path by the lakeshore and, shortly after, saw Michael approaching.

"Hi, Dan," Michael said in a loud voice, still fifty meters away. "I'm sorry; I thought I would be able to make it back before you got here."

When he reached Dan, he sat down beside him on the bench and patted him on the back.

"I was just over saying hello to the neighbors who arrived at their cabin this afternoon. It was nice to see them again. It's the first time this year they've been here."

Michael paused briefly, taking a deep breath before continuing.

"So? Have you made any progress contemplating what you think should happen to the karma sequence? And what's Ryan come up with?"

Dan nodded, considering whether to recount the entire conversation with Ryan, but chose to skip straight to the primary reason he'd come. The rest seemed less relevant, given Ryan's latest visions.

"Gene therapy," Dan answered without further explanation.

Michael turned his whole body, looking at him quizzically, but Dan didn't answer his unspoken question and watched him while he figured out the sinister meaning himself. After a few seconds, Michael's expression changed from puzzled to understanding, and finally, a horrified look came over his face.

"Are you telling me that Ryan will offer Lifeline customers the option of changing the omega value in their genome so they can live longer?" He asked incredulously, the color draining from his cheeks.

Dan nodded sadly, but said nothing.

Michael rose and started walking back and forth the short distance between the bench and the path by the lakeshore. It was apparent he was trying to wrap his head around the implications, the same way Dan had tried when

Ryan told him about it earlier in the day. After half a minute, he stopped in front of Dan.

"This is crazy! How serious is this on Ryan's part? How many resources and energy does he plan to pour into this insane project?"

"Whatever it takes and whatever it costs," replied Dan quietly.

Michael scrutinized Dan for a few seconds—perhaps to make sure he wasn't joking—then turned and walked the few meters to the path. Here he stopped, took a deep breath, and then screamed a long "fuuuuuuck" at the top of his lungs. All around the lake, ducks and other birds took off in fright, flying randomly over the water, then disappearing over the woods.

"Sorry, Dan," he said as he returned to the bench. "It was simply too much for me. I didn't think Ryan could keep surprising me negatively, but he's certainly done it again."

Michael was about to sit down when they heard running footsteps, and seconds later, two young men—with worried and aggressive expressions—stood on the path next to the cabin. They were both completely blond, with short haircuts and tattoos covering their arms, necks, and legs, visible under their white T-shirts and black shorts. Clearly in good shape, they looked like they'd spent plenty of time in the gym.

"Has something happened?" one of them asked in Swedish.

Michael waved them over and shrugged apologetically.

"I'm sorry, boys," he said. "I've just had some bad news. I didn't mean to frighten you guys. Everything's fine here."

Dan could see that they both breathed a sigh of relief and relaxed a little as they stepped closer.

"We thought someone might have been hurt," said the other, also in Swedish—as his expression changed from concern to relief.

"No, fortunately not," said Michael in a reconciling voice. "Not yet, anyway."

His face changed to a smiling expression.

"This is my old friend, Dan—whom I think I've mentioned to you," he continued, pointing to Dan, who'd stood up.

They both lit up when they heard Dan's name—and as he shook hands with them, they introduced themselves. Michael offered them something cold to drink and began walking toward the cabin door, but they both shook their heads and insisted that they didn't need anything.

After ensuring everything was in order, they smilingly said goodbye and started walking back to their cabin. Dan and Michael stood for a moment, looking after the two men as they disappeared among the trees on the narrow path.

"Super nice brothers," said Michael. "They remind me of myself when I was their age."

Dan smiled. He could definitely see the resemblance.

"What do you say—should we take a walk around the lake?" Michael asked before Dan could sit down on the bench again. "Then you can tell me everything you and Ryan talked about."

"Sure—good idea," said Dan and followed Michael to the lakeshore, where they headed left along the path.

As they walked, Dan presented all the elements of Ryan's idea for Michael. He spoke of Ryan's plans to hire a range of experts in cell biology and biotech from around the world and, simultaneously, integrate much of the technology and processes—required for manipulating the genome of living humans—in the form of subcontracted services. In the same way, they currently did with the gene sequencing and analysis flows.

As they passed the neighboring cabin, they waved to the two brothers, now sitting in a pair of garden chairs in front of their place, bare-chested and wearing sunglasses—each with a beer in their hand, looking out over the lake. Both waved back enthusiastically, as Dan and Michael continued their walk along the path under the canopy of trees by the lakeshore.

Dan went on to explain Ryan's new plans and how he was already researching the technology of altering specific strands of the human genome and getting an overview of how far science had come in this field. From time to time, Michael asked additional questions about the plans, and Dan tried to answer them as best he could. Some of the questions were too technical for Dan and showed that Michael had been interested in genetic technology for a longer time than Dan had.

By the time they reached the clearing—halfway around the lake—Dan had recounted his entire conversation with Ryan. Michael had commented, asked for details, and updated Dan on various aspects of gene therapy and techniques for cutting and pasting strands in the genome, explaining what the technical capabilities were. They stood in silence, looking out over the lake and toward the two cabins on the opposite side. The ducks and other birds had returned, some of them swimming around in the reeds along the lakeshore.

After standing there for a few minutes without either of them saying anything, Michael suggested they move on—and they again started walking along the path between the trees.

"But there's no guarantee that such an intervention in the genome will work and consequently prolong life," said Dan, picking up the thread where they'd left off. "Even though we now know there is a correlation between the omega value and the day the person dies, we still don't know if it's the actual value in the karma sequence that triggers the events—or if it's just some kind of label that the unknown intelligence or power uses for something else entirely. Monitoring, or something like that."

"You're right," said Michael.

Dan tried to think of a helpful parallel. "For example, if I hack into the municipality's database and change my zip code to 8,000, my apartment won't magically teleport to Aarhus overnight."

Michael smiled at Dan's example and made a comparison with the second possible option.

"But if it's your tax rate you're changing—now that you're messing with the system anyway—there's a good chance you'll actually pay less in taxes next year."

"Exactly," said Dan. "And we don't know which of the two mechanisms we're dealing with in the karma sequence. Ryan knows this too—he estimates that the probability is fifty-fifty whether it's one model or the other. If it's the passive model, some of his investment is lost. However, if it works, he becomes the most powerful man in the world—and that's big in Ryan's universe."

They'd gone all the way around the lake but proceeded along the path, passing Michael's cabin as they continued talking.

"It's just so typical for Ryan," said Michael. "He comes into possession of an incredible insight like the karma sequence, and immediately identifies the most sinister and unethical way he can exploit it. An idea that's so horrific that it would never have occurred to you or me. But I'm not surprised for a second. Ryan couldn't care less about the ethical and philosophical implications of all this. That man only cares about money and power."

Dan could feel that Michael was getting agitated, but didn't know what to say.

"Our responsibility—and the dilemma we face—has grown, Dan," proceeded Michael in an emphatic tone. "It's no longer only an abstract question of what the right thing to do with the karma sequence is. Now, we also have to deal with stopping Ryan and his plans. We've passed the point where it would be solved simply by shutting down the Primus AI and deleting it. Ryan knows what the karma sequence looks like—so he can find it, and at some point, he might be able to change it, too. That is, if his plans succeed, of course."

"What Ryan uses his knowledge of the karma sequence for isn't something we can change," said Dan in a neutral voice, trying to slow down Michael in his musings, which Dan had a feeling where were heading.

"Believe me, Dan," said Michael with a bleak smile. "I'll find a way to put a stop to Ryan! I don't want him getting away with this without consequences."

They passed the neighboring cabin again, where the two brothers were still sitting in their deckchairs. One had apparently fallen asleep, lying with his head to one side, but the other smiled at Dan and Michael and gave them a thumbs-up.

Although Dan had tried to brace himself for Michael's reaction to Ryan's latest plans, he was still a little shaken by his aggressive response. However, he guessed it was just an example of Michael's hot temper and a way of dealing with the overwhelming news.

He felt confident he knew Michael well enough to be sure he wouldn't follow through on his vague threats.

TWENTY-TWO

Friday evening at eight o'clock, Dan arrived in his car at Ryan and Gitte's villa to attend the big summer party. The weather had been perfect all day, and it was still bright and warm. He'd had to drive around his apartment in the Østerbro district because he'd forgotten to bring some more formal clothes when he packed his sports bag the day before.

In the morning, he'd accompanied Anette to her second treatment session at the addiction center and again waited the four hours in the reception. He'd spent the time reading various online articles on gene therapy and the biochemical techniques that made it possible to alter the specific genome of a living human being. The technical explanations, and especially the chemical reviews, were far from Dan's field of knowledge and expertise and didn't seem like something he could master in a reasonable amount of time. He was glad Michael had been interested in the subject for a longer time and felt sure it would be an invaluable help.

When Anette's meeting was over, they went to the beach park again, taking an even longer walk than they'd done on Wednesday. Anette passionately recounted what she'd learned in the day's meeting and what they'd talked about. It was clear that she'd become good friends with both the therapist and the other members of the group. Dan had bought water for them both at the same place, but this time Anette hadn't required sitting down, so they'd continued their walk to the farthest bridge and all the way back to the car.

From the beach, they'd driven to a large shopping center near the airport, where they walked around, browsing through the many shops and buying groceries for the coming days. After a few hours, Dan could sense that Anette was getting tired, so they returned to her apartment. Here they'd both taken a long nap after eating a sandwich.

After making sure his mother was okay and not feeling tempted to drink, Dan drove home to his apartment to get ready for the party. He'd arranged with Anette to spend the night there as well and not return until the following day, avoiding waking her if he came back late from the party.

Cars were parked on both sides of the street outside the white wall, and Dan had to drive a little further up the road to find a place to park. In previous years, he and Susan had taken a taxi—both when arriving and leaving—because he'd typically been a little drunk even before departing for the party.

The large wrought-iron gate was open, allowing guests to wander in and out unhindered. When Dan entered the backyard, he saw that Ryan had lined up six of his cars from the basement along the gravel driveway that led down to the house. In front was his beloved Jaguar, and after that, his Lamborghini, a Bugatti, the Ferrari, and two cars Dan couldn't immediately identify.

In front of the garage door were a row of portable toilets and two trailers from the catering company that provided the food.

Walking down the driveway, he passed a small group of people looking admiringly at Ryan's various cars and talking excitedly about his fine collection, which some of them had also seen in the basement. Several had cocktail glasses in their hands, raising them in greeting as Dan passed and said hello. He continued along the path to the front door, which was open, and walked directly through the entrance hall and into the large living room.

About thirty guests were standing and sitting in large and small groups, talking excitedly to each other. Everyone was dressed in festive attire—some women in long gowns and several men in suits or other formal wear. The many voices blended with the live music, which could be heard through the open panoramic doors. It came from a jazz quintet playing on the left side of the large terrace. Dan knew the tune they were playing—it was one of the classics—but he couldn't remember the title. Three couples were dancing while others stood scattered around the expansive terrace and on the different levels of the garden, enjoying their drinks, the music, and the company of other guests. Small masts had been erected everywhere, with lamps of different colors, but it was still too early for them to compete with the evening sun, which gave everything in the garden a warm, reddish glow.

Dan walked through the living room, nodding and saying hello to people as he passed them. As he stepped onto the terrace, he spotted Gitte walking toward him with a long-stemmed glass in each hand.

"Hi, Dan," she said with a big smile, handing him one of the glasses. "Welcome to the summer party."

She looked dazzling in an all-white, tight-fitting evening dress and matching high-heeled shoes, making her appear taller than usual. Her hair was down to almost her shoulders, and she wore more makeup than she typically would—but as always, it was tasteful and suited her marvelously.

Dan hesitantly accepted the glass and was about to recite the excuse he typically used in such situations, but Gitte beat him to it.

"Cola—straight up," she said. "You didn't think I would give you anything with alcohol, did you?"

"Thanks. No, I couldn't imagine that either," replied Dan with relief.

"As you can see, many guests already had a lot to drink—but that's all part of the summer party. The most important thing is that everyone has a good time."

Dan nodded and looked around.

"Ryan just went down to the basement with a handful of car nerds," said Gitte with feigned annoyance.

"Yeah, I've been with him down there myself at a couple of summer parties," said Dan. "So, it's not only car nerds—it's all kinds of nerds."

Gitte smiled and winked at him before turning and pointing to the other end of the terrace—opposite the jazz quintet—where three chefs were preparing various dishes at an extensive buffet.

"Remember to enjoy some of the lovely food!" she urged him. "I'll leave you for now and mingle and talk to the other guests—while they're still reasonably intelligible. I'll see you in a little while."

Dan watched her as she walked toward the panoramic doors and into the living room, nodding and smiling to each person as she passed them. The quintet finished the song, and applause, along with cheers, was heard from the dancing couples on the terrace, from inside the living room, and from across the vast garden.

The musicians thanked, looked at their papers, and began playing another jazz classic. Dan had never been particularly musical—but he couldn't help nodding his head to the rhythm and humming along to the catchy tune.

As far as he could tell, the same musicians had played the last time he'd attended the summer party—two years ago. He had no clear recollection of most of that party—but did remember that he and Susan had enjoyed themselves with the other guests until, at one point, Susan had suggested that they go home. Dan had protested a little, saying it was still early in the evening—but he now understood it was because she'd judged that he'd had as much alcohol as he could handle. Again, he felt his cheeks flush at the memory. Although he'd considered his life wonderful—especially his relationship with Susan—there was a part of him that hadn't been healthy and well. It was too late to change now, but if he'd known, he would have dealt with his abuse sooner, and then maybe Susan might still have been part of his life.

He smiled at his nostalgic self-pity while simultaneously analyzing how that feeling would, in the past, have served as a pretext for a drink. And though he felt how he missed Susan as he stood there thinking about her, it wasn't an emotion that would make him so much as consider taking a single drop. He knew the feeling was an authentic condition, whereas the mood the alcohol would put him in wasn't part of himself and his personality.

While reflecting on his feelings, he'd registered that he felt a bit hungry and decided to follow Gitte's recommendation to check out some of the food. As he approached the buffet, he was greeted by the smell of delicious dishes and felt the hunger even more distinctly. He said hi to the three chefs, all wearing white aprons and tall chef's hats. Two of them stood with their backs to him, working at the portable stoves, but turned briefly and nodded. The third came up to Dan and asked if there was anything he could serve him.

"A cheeseburger would be nice," Dan replied. "Or something simple like that."

"You bet," said the cook. "I'll make you a special one. Any requests?"

"Well done and very strong, please," replied Dan.

A few minutes later, he was eating the best burger he'd ever tasted. The well-fried meat, and the sharp spices, gave him a warm feeling throughout his body—and he felt a sense of optimism and excitement about the future. As he looked out over the Sound, shining golden in the last rays of the setting sun, he thought of all the latitude he had in his life—now that he was no longer a slave to the addiction. There were still some problems from the past to deal with—

and people he needed to talk to about the problems he'd created and how they could be solved. But for the first time in a long time, he felt the old energy and zest for life flowing through him. Perhaps the time had come to focus on looking forward—without forgetting what had happened, but not letting it overshadow his spontaneity and sense of freedom.

After thanking the chefs for the lovely food, Dan put down his slim cocktail glass, found a large beer mug on one of the many tables with drinks, and filled it with cold cola.

The terrace and garden had darkened a little, and the many lamps were starting to have significantly more effect. Several of the guests began moving down to the lower levels of the garden to enjoy the view and the warm evening after eating—and perhaps to talk to each other more undisturbed.

From the outside, he also had a better view of the many people in the living room—and not just the reflection of himself in the windows that had dominated when it was lighter.

Dan noticed Ryan had returned from the basement and was now sitting at the big dining table—in his usual chair, overlooking the garden—talking to four board members. The same place as the previous Sunday, when Dan had told Ryan and Gitte about the structure of the karma sequence and Maya Luna's death.

Although he couldn't hear what they were talking about, it was clear that Ryan was entertaining and the others were listening. It looked like Ryan had already had a lot to drink, and Dan hoped he wasn't explaining about the discovery of the karma sequence and the big plans he had for it. Besides the people sitting at the table, a smaller group stood listening at the far end, under the large TV screen on the wall—but from their facial expressions and reactions, it didn't look as if Ryan was sharing anything serious. Dan guessed it must be some of Ryan's many anecdotes that he enjoyed telling—

especially after he'd had a drink—or maybe he was talking about his cars or his watches.

At the far end of the room, Dan spotted the older board member who always sat on Ryan's left, opposite Gitte, at board meetings. She was sitting alone on a two-seater sofa, seemingly enjoying the jazz music pouring in through the open doors from the terrace. Without giving it a second thought, Dan decided to go into the living room and join her.

She noticed Dan as he entered the panoramic doors and waved him over, pointing to the empty seat to her right.

When Dan reached the sofa, she smiled in surprise and acknowledgment at his large mug of cola, which he placed on the low coffee table before sitting down.

Dan asked if he could get her something to drink, but she shook her head, saying that one of the many glasses on the table was hers.

Several people sat on the three sofas on the other sides of the table, talking together or listening to the quintet. Dan smiled and nodded to them as he leaned forward to take his mug. Above the stairs, on the long first-floor landing, several guests stood by the parapet looking out over the large living room or into the garden and toward the Sound. From time-to-time laughter sounded from the open sitting room, which was part of the wide landing.

The quintet finished another song, and everyone applauded. The left part of the terrace was now almost full of couples dancing.

"Fabulous!" said the older board member to Dan. "To be honest, the live music is the primary reason I attend these summer parties. The music reminds me of another, perhaps better, time, and the musicians are so skillful and precise."

Dan nodded. "Yeah, it somehow feels more real. And a lot of the classics certainly touch something deep inside you."

As they continued listening to the quintet, who'd started playing another song, she told Dan about the many bands and artists from the genre's heyday. Dan recognized some of the names, but far from all. Then they talked a little about the plans Ryan had presented at the board meeting, and she said she thought it was all a bit too ambitious and overblown. Dan nodded, thinking if only she knew Ryan's latest visions. But at some point, Ryan would have to share his plans with the rest of the board, and then she would find out.

"Hi, Dan," a cheerful voice suddenly sounded from the door to the entrance hall. Dan turned his head and spotted Vibs, who'd just entered the living room, and was headed straight over to the sofa where he was sitting. She was dressed in light jeans and a short-sleeved pink shirt that went down a little over her trousers. Although she wasn't as festively dressed as many other guests, she looked at least as lovely and stylish as the few times he'd spoken to her at the City Tower. Several people around the coffee table looked up from their conversations and followed her with their eyes as she approached.

"Hi, everyone," she greeted energetically, waving around as she maneuvered herself down on the sofa next to Dan, forcing him to move to the left. There was plenty of room on the sofa, but Dan felt somewhat squeezed between Vibs and the older woman—who didn't seem to notice, though. Apparently, she'd shifted her attention back to the music.

Vibs turned ninety degrees and pulled her legs up on the sofa, sitting with her bent knees right up against Dan's legs, her back against the sofa's armrest.

"I'd hoped to be here from the start," she said, now addressing Dan only. "I came straight from the office; there was so much I wanted to finish before the weekend—even though Ryan said it could easily wait until next week. Did I miss anything exciting?"

"I don't think so," replied Dan, trying to turn slightly so he could speak more directly to her. "But then, I've almost just arrived, too. There might well have been face painting and gladiator fights before I arrived."

Vibs leaned back with a loud laugh and looked around the large living room. "I've been here to Gitte and Ryan's lovely villa a couple of times," she said. "But this is my first time at the fabled summer party. I suppose you've attended many times?"

"Not many," replied Dan. "Only three times before tonight; but it's always been lavish and, at the same time, enjoyable."

She nodded in fascination, looking at him as if he'd climbed Mount Everest.

"I'll get us something to drink," she said, rising in a simple, supple movement. "Which glass is yours?" She smiled when she spotted Dan's colossal mug, still containing a little cola. "Okay, stupid question."

Dan intended to get up too, to go with her, but she put a hand on his shoulder, holding him back on the sofa.

"Stay put, Dan. But make sure no one takes my place."

Dan looked after her as she gracefully maneuvered between several guests and disappeared into the kitchen.

A minute later, she returned with Dan's mug and a smaller glass for herself—both filled with cold cola—and sat down on the sofa again.

They sat for a while and talked about the party and the music, which Vibs also found fascinating—and about the celebrities present. Vibs identified several people that Dan didn't recognize, and she tried to point them out as discreetly as possible.

The more they talked, the more Dan relaxed and enjoyed her company. It was as if he was being sucked into her presence and infectious energy.

At one point, the quintet began playing 'What a Wonderful World' and, as in the original, the trumpet player switched to the role of singer.

"I love that song," Vibs said enthusiastically after hearing only a few notes. "Come, let's dance."

She took Dan's hand and pulled him to his feet, and then they walked behind the sofa and out onto the terrace, which was still crowded with dancing couples. When they found a good spot, Dan placed himself half a meter from her—but she pulled him close and put one arm around his back while still holding his hand.

They stood close and danced throughout the song, and Dan could feel himself enjoying their closeness and her warmth. He no longer doubted that she'd long since crossed the border from purely being friendly and was heading into the romantic realm. The question was whether the same was about to happen to him. It would require nothing more of him than to dismiss—once and for all—the possibility that he and Susan might eventually get together again. He assessed that he had come a long way toward not thinking about Susan with romantic feelings. But he was also aware that it had primarily happened on the intellectual level. He'd intentionally forced himself to think that way because it was objectively best for all parties. On the emotional level, he wasn't sure that the clarification was as final as he would like to think.

But if ever there was a good time to reach a decision, it was probably here and now. Vibs wasn't Susan—but she didn't have to be. Vibs was Vibs and fabulous in her own right. The question was whether he should simply close his eyes and let fate decide for him.

Dan was interrupted in his deliberations when, out of the corner of his eye, he saw that Michael and the two Swedish brothers had entered from the entrance hall and now stood surveying the living room. All three were nicely dressed but had clearly not come to enjoy themselves. Michael had evidently spotted Ryan at the dining table at the far end of the living room and started walking directly toward him—with the two brothers following right behind.

"Sorry, Vibs," said Dan as he let go of her, looking into her surprised eyes. "I'm afraid there's trouble brewing."

He could hear her starting to ask him something, but he was already at the big panoramic doors and on his way into the living room. Here he walked briskly toward the dining table, moving through the passage between people who'd instinctively stepped aside as Michael and the two brothers marched through the living room. By the time he got there, Michael was already blasting Ryan, calling him the worst things he could think of. Ryan had gotten up from his chair, and the guests standing around the table had cautiously taken a few steps back.

"Michael!" said Dan quietly. "You won't solve anything by violence or threats—you know that."

Michael glanced over at Dan, who could see the anger in his eyes. The two brothers smiled in surprise when they saw Dan and said hello.

"Listen," said Ryan in a calm and authoritative tone. "Let's go down to the basement where it's more quiet—and then you can explain what you're so angry about. I'm sure it must be a misunderstanding."

Dan could see that Michael was about to say something, but stopped him by shaking his head while pointing firmly toward the entrance hall and the staircase to the basement.

"Alright," Michael said disarmingly and began walking across the room, with Dan and Ryan following close behind him. The brothers wanted to tag along, but Dan discreetly shook his head at them, which they understood and respected.

After they'd descended the stairs, they walked to the far end of the basement and stood between the large tables. The empty spots where the six cars, now exhibited along the driveway, normally stood made the room feel even larger than usual.

"Michael," Ryan said. "I assume it's something important when you show up like this and try to ruin the party Gitte and I prepared?"

Michael nodded, then spent five minutes going over Ryan's idea to use gene therapy to alter people's karma sequence so they could potentially extend their lives—while emphasizing how unethical and nefarious he thought the plan was. Ryan listened attentively, without interrupting, until Michael had finished. Then he stood for a few seconds, considering Michael's arguments—before saying anything himself.

"That's an understandable and sympathetic attitude, Michael," Ryan said. "But there's nothing new in what you are saying. It's pretty much the same thing Gitte has been telling me over the past few days. I can't say more than I'll take your well-intentioned recommendation on board and consider it. But I'm pretty sure it won't change my plan: it's simply too good an idea—provided it works, of course—we can't know that at this stage. But time will tell; and if we don't do it, someone else will."

Ryan turned his head, looking questioningly at Dan. "Do you agree with the things Michael says?"

"Yes," replied Dan after a few seconds of hesitation. "I must confess that I share Michael's concerns. Which I believe is also in line with what Gitte is thinking."

"I'm a little surprised," said Ryan after a short pause. He sounded disappointed. "I was hoping you would think it was a brilliant plan."

"Maybe it is," admitted Dan as gently as he could. "But the problem is that it lacks a moral dimension. The temptation is strong—but the repercussions are impossible to fully grasp."

For half a minute, none of them said anything. Dan could see that Michael was still angry and perhaps frustrated at not being able to reverse Ryan's decision, one way or the other. Ryan looked tired and barely had the energy to wipe the sweat from his brow. He suggested they go back to the party and that they could continue the discussion at a later—more appropriate—time.

They followed each other and slowly climbed the steep stairs to the entrance hall. Ryan and Michael walked into the living room, where the party sounded like there had been no interruption. The jazz quintet was playing, and the sounds of the guests' chatter and laughter mingled with the music, spilling out into the entrance hall.

Dan went to the kitchen, hoping to be alone there for a moment and get some distance from the confrontation between Ryan and Michael—and himself. He also wanted to try to find out what to do about Vibs. But most of all, he needed something to drink—preferably a cold cola.

The kitchen was empty, except for a familiar-looking person standing with her back to him at the near end of the enormous kitchen island. When Dan entered, she turned and lit up upon seeing it was him.

"Hi," she said quietly and with a shy smile. "I'm Susan."

TWENTY-THREE

Dan stood completely nonplussed and needed a few seconds to convince himself that it was indeed Susan.

"Hi, Susan," he said, dumbfounded. "I didn't think I would meet you here tonight, too."

He stood in the doorway looking at her, trying to guess why she'd chosen to come to the summer party, and why so late. Perhaps she'd accompanied Michael and the two Swedish brothers, but he couldn't see what role she might be expected to play in that plan. She didn't seem to have intended to go to the party, either. Her clothes looked like what she would typically wear to work—and she wasn't wearing the more pronounced makeup that Dan remembered her using when they'd taken part in festive events together.

"I wasn't planning on coming either," replied Susan as she slowly walked toward him. She looked like she was about to cry.

When she reached Dan, she put her arms around him and held him in a long hug. Dan instinctively put his arms around her.

"Did something happen?" he asked cautiously.

"No, no," said Susan, her voice muffled against his shoulder. "Well, yes—but nothing bad."

Susan let go of him and took a step back, looking deep into his eyes.

"Do you want to be my boyfriend again?" she asked, obviously having to work up the courage.

"Yes!" Dan heard himself say in surprise before he'd had time to consider the implications. He wasn't sure he understood why she was asking. On top of an already strange evening, with entirely unexpected situations and impressions, this moment in the kitchen with Susan was the last thing he would have imagined.

Now Susan was visibly teary-eyed as she looked warily at him to make sure he meant it. She smiled as she wiped the tears from her eyes.

Dan took a step forward and gently held her face in his hands as she wrapped her arms around his waist, and they shared a long kiss. Her body was trembling as they stood holding each other, and he could also feel tears welling up in his eyes. It was the same feeling as when entering a warm room and only then becoming aware that you'd been freezing for a long time.

"I love you—and I'll never let you go again," whispered Susan. "No matter what happens!"

Dan could barely say a word, but nodded and pulled her closer. He was sure he didn't have to say it and that she already knew, but he still managed to say that he loved her too, just so there would be no doubt—for either of them. Everything suddenly seemed much simpler and better.

They stood holding and kissing each other for several minutes. From time to time, other guests came into the kitchen—either to refill their glasses or on their way to the bathroom. At one point, Susan asked if they should find somewhere better to talk, and Dan suggested they go for a walk in the garden. Still holding hands, they went through the living room toward the panoramic doors to the terrace and garden.

As before, the guests in the living room stood talking to each other in large and small groups. Dan could see that Ryan was again sitting in his chair at the big dining table with a big glass of whisky in his hand, entertaining even more people—including Vibs—grouped around him, listening attentively with smiles on their faces. Dan noticed that Ryan looked more pale and tired than before Michael had arrived, and they'd had their intense exchange in the basement.

In the large sofa group at the opposite end of the room, one of the Swedish brothers sat next to the older board member—in the same place Dan had been talking to Vibs less than half an hour earlier. Fewer people were sitting on the other three sofas, and those who'd remained looked nervously at the young man with the many tattoos. The older woman was still enjoying the music—seemingly unaffected by the man beside her or the tense atmosphere around the coffee table.

As Dan and Susan stepped out onto the terrace, they paused to listen to the quintet play the final bars of a ballad and clapped along with everyone else when the song ended. The musicians bowed and smiled at the crowd, thanking them all for a lovely evening—and after a long round of applause, some of the guests began moving back toward the living room. Behind the band, a DJ was setting up to keep the music going far into the night.

It had darkened a little more, and the many lamps on the terrace and in the garden covered everything in a romantic and fairytale-like glow. But it was still warm enough for people to stay outside in the garden without freezing in their light dresses and party clothes.

Dan stood for a moment, watching the musicians—busy turning off their amplifiers and packing away their instruments—when Susan squeezed his hand and pulled him along down the stairs to the top level of the garden. They first walked past the garden sofas, where guests enjoyed themselves, and continued down to the far end of the garden. Dan knew they were thinking the same thing. They would find their old bench and talk some more while they sat looking out over the Sound.

As they got further down the sloping lawn, they could see that their little bench was already occupied. They were about to look for another place to sit when both people on the bench got to their feet and started walking up through the garden. It was Gitte and Michael, and for a moment, Dan thought it looked as if they'd held hands before getting up and going their separate ways around the bench. But it wasn't easy to tell for sure in the semi-darkness.

Gitte waved Dan and Susan over to her and Michael and asked them to sit down. Michael looked pleased to see Dan with Susan—especially how she held Dan's hand—but it didn't seem as if the sight had surprised him.

Dan sent Michael a quizzical look, but Michael pretended not to notice, looking around the garden as if something had caught his interest.

Susan let go of Dan's hand and walked over to Gitte, hugging her while at the same time saying something that Dan couldn't quite make out. Gitte looked a little taken aback and apparently couldn't think of anything else to do but pat Susan gently on the head.

After standing for a moment looking after Gitte and Michael as they slowly walked back toward the terrace—between the colored patches of light—Dan and Susan sat down on the small wooden bench. Although it had grown dark, there was still a clear view of the water and the lights from the towns on the other side of the Sound. Susan still held onto Dan's right hand with her left, as they both turned their heads to look more directly at each other. From the terrace, the DJ's dance music began sending its solid rhythms out over the garden.

Neither of them said anything for a minute. Dan was still overwhelmed by the recent development and still couldn't quite get used to the idea that he was now back with the most wonderful person he'd ever met. Nevertheless, he sensed how the analytical part of himself had a hard time understanding why it had happened and was hoping for an explanation. But it wasn't urgent—and he was sure Susan would reveal it to him when she believed it was a good time.

"I'm more in love with you now than the first time we sat on this bench," said Susan, surprised at her own feelings.

Dan smiled but said nothing.

"When we first met, I didn't know you as I do now," continued Susan. "Back then, I felt an attraction, but now there's also a connection—a history that binds us together. I know I'll never find another person like you."

Dan could see tears in her eyes, and emotions were overwhelming him, too. He leaned toward her, and they put their arms around each other.

After a minute, with neither of them saying anything, they let go, and Susan took Dan's hand in both of hers, taking a deep breath.

"I think it's time I told you what made me change my mind," she said, smiling apologetically. "I'm sure the analytical part of you is speculating about it right now, trying to find a reason for it all."

Dan nodded and was about to say that she didn't need to explain anything, but stopped himself. On the one hand, he would like to understand the background of what had happened, and on the other, he suspected Susan might actually need to share it with him.

"For a long time, I've been having doubts about my decision not to be together anymore," Susan began. "When you lost control of your life to addiction, I felt like I'd lost the Dan I knew and loved—and it hurt so much that I promised myself I would never risk finding myself in that situation again."

She took another deep breath as she searched for the words before continuing.

"But even with all these reservations, I still missed you—and all the things we had together—so much. That companionship was one of the things I hoped to get back if we became friends again—without engaging with each other in the old emotional way. That way, I wouldn't risk losing a part of myself if you got sick again. And that's what frightened me the most: to lose you again if we were together."

Dan felt her squeeze his hand tighter, and he squeezed hers back.

"I've been so unsure about what to do and say," she said. "Yet constantly afraid of again placing myself in a situation where something could happen to the one I loved."

She paused briefly, then lit up in a small smile.

"And then, like a bolt from the blue, Gitte called me tonight—just an hour ago," she said, glancing at her watch in disbelief. "She said something that forced me to make a definitive decision, here and now, which set my feelings dazzlingly straight for me."

Dan briefly tried to think back and figure out what might have prompted Gitte to call Susan—in the middle of the big summer party she was busy hosting. And as Susan proceeded, he realized it had probably been while he was dancing with Vibs, where they were holding each other. Gitte must have judged that there was an imminent risk that Dan was falling for Vibs; and that a future with Susan would consequently be out of the question. But while that might explain the timing, it was still a little incomprehensible why Gitte was so committed to his and Susan's relationship—especially after he'd told her he'd given up on the possibility of him and Susan getting back together.

"Gitte started by saying that she sympathized with my reasoning for not being with you, not daring to take the chance and risk going through the same pain and loss—something I couldn't be sure would never happen again. However, even though she understood my feelings, she felt compelled to say that it was the wrong way to think. She said it was irrational to deliberately inflict a loss on oneself—here and now—to avoid the risk of experiencing the same loss at some unpredictable point in the future. You're throwing away something valuable now to safeguard yourself from the potential suffering of losing it at some later time, she said."

Dan nodded thoughtfully, thinking it was an excellent argument.

"When you have something you love, you also have to live with the risk of losing it and the pain that comes with that," said Susan. Dan couldn't tell whether those were still Gitte's words or Susan's own conclusion.

"Finally, Gitte asked me to choose whether you and I should be part of each other's lives—or whether it should be over completely. She said I had to make that decision on the spot and take a taxi out to the party, right there and then. Otherwise, it would be too late, she said. I didn't understand the urgency—but I'm glad I did what she told me. The conversation took less than two minutes, but I was so unbelievably relieved afterward—even though I couldn't know what you would say when I got out here."

Susan leaned forward, and they hugged each other again.

Dan was pleased to learn what had happened and what considerations had led Susan to change her mind. Although it had all happened in a short space of time, she seemed pretty clear about her choice, and he knew he would do anything not to disappoint her.

"I think I know why Gitte called you at that exact moment," Dan said quietly. "But it's not important right now—I promise to explain later."

He could feel her nodding as they held each other—and he felt her slow breathing and the warmth of her body.

It was hard not to wonder how close he'd come to falling for Vibs and how close they'd come to kissing while dancing. If he hadn't seen Michael arrive, Vibs probably would have kissed him—and if he had to be honest with himself, he wasn't sure how he would have reacted. It wouldn't be easy to explain to Susan, but he knew she would understand and that it wouldn't affect their rekindled relationship. Now they were both out of the ambiguous emotional gray area where they couldn't predict what would happen—and how they would react.

"Why don't we go home?" asked Susan a little later. Dan didn't have to ask her if she meant his or her home—they were already back to their old habit of thinking of her apartment as their home.

"Yes," replied Dan. "Good idea. I came here in my car, so we won't have to wait for a cab this time."

They both rose from the bench and kissed again, then wandered up through the garden, holding hands.

"You don't want to stay and watch the fireworks?" asked Dan as they approached the terrace, the sound of the DJ's dance music getting louder.

"I would like that," replied Susan with a big smile. "It's always really beautiful. But there's something I want even more. We'll make our own fireworks when we get home."

They smiled as they climbed the steps to the terrace, zigzagged between the dancing couples, and continued into the living room.

In the large sofa group, Michael now sat in the seat where the older board member had sat earlier. Dan guessed she'd left the party shortly after the jazz quintet had stopped playing. One of the Swedish brothers was still sitting on the same sofa—next to Michael—and the other was sitting alone on the sofa on the opposite side of the coffee table. The longer sofas on the two other sides were again filled with guests, who sat talking to each other and, from time to time, glancing nervously at Michael and the two other men.

Dan and Susan walked over to Michael, and Dan squatted down and told him he and Susan were leaving. Although Michael nodded and smiled, Dan could see that he was still tense, and he didn't quite understand why he was still there after he'd had a chance to let Ryan in on his frustration with his plans. Dan knew that he would have to talk to Michael about how he'd tried to solve the problem—but that would have to wait for another time. They agreed to meet on Sunday, two days later, at Michael's cabin and talk some more.

After getting back up, Dan waved goodbye to everyone in the large sofa group, and those who saw him waved back. Both brothers sent him a big smile and nodded many times.

As he and Susan walked to the other end of the room to say goodbye to Ryan, Dan spotted Gitte standing by the parapet on the wide landing, talking to two guests. Both he and Susan waved up at her.

"Thank you for an unforgettable evening," said Dan, hoping Gitte could hear him over the dance music coming in from the terrace through the panoramic doors. Gitte waved back, looking alternately at Dan and Susan with an appreciative smile before she turned and continued her conversation with the two guests.

Ryan was sitting in the same place as before, but was no longer explaining and entertaining. He had an empty glass in his hand, looking possibly more tired and weak than when Dan and Michael had talked to him in the basement. The group of guests, still sitting around the large dining table, were engaged in other conversations or watching the dancing couples on the terrace.

Dan and Susan walked to the far end of the table, and when Ryan spotted them, he lit up with a big smile.

"Hi, Dan. And Susan!" he said, pleased to see them holding hands. "What a lovely surprise. I hope you're enjoying the party?"

"It's a fabulous party, Ryan," said Susan with a caring smile. "And it's so nice to see your beautiful home and the magnificent garden again."

Ryan nodded and sent Susan a grateful twinkle. He lifted his glass but immediately put it back on the table when he saw it was empty.

"Would you like me to get you a refill?" asked Susan obligingly, taking the empty glass. "Whisky?"

"Thank you, Susan," replied Ryan, surprised, and then pointed through the panoramic windows at one of the tables on the terrace, where there was an extensive collection of bottles. "That's sweet of you."

"Then you can say a proper goodbye to Ryan," Susan softly urged Dan and walked along the dining table, holding Ryan's glass.

"Are you on your way home?" asked Ryan, with a disappointed look on his face. "I was hoping you would stay and watch the fireworks."

"It's been a long day," said Dan. "And right now, I'm mainly looking forward to being alone with Susan. I still can't quite believe we're back together."

"That's great, Dan—and you certainly deserve it. Although Vibs is an amazing girl, too."

Dan felt his cheeks getting warm as Ryan reminded him of Vibs. Ryan must have seen them when they danced. In a way, Dan felt ashamed that he'd completely forgotten about a woman whose company he'd enjoyed so much and who, to be honest, he'd felt attracted to.

"It's all right, Dan," said Ryan compassionately. "She was a little distressed, but she's fine now."

Dan nodded thoughtfully, looking around the living room and onto the terrace to see if he could spot her.

"She's gone home," said Ryan, as if reading Dan's thoughts. "You don't need to agonize about it."

They both looked at Susan, who was now heading back to the table.

"Take good care of Susan. Promise me you'll behave yourself, so you don't lose her again. And remember to go to your AA meetings!"

"I promise," said Dan, smiling gratefully at Ryan.

When Susan reached them, she placed Ryan's glass—now filled almost to the brim—in front of him. Ryan smiled and took three big gulps from the glass before setting it down on the table.

"Thank you, Susan," said Ryan, a little invigorated. "That's just what I needed. And will you two get moving already!"

Dan mumbled a quiet "thank you", then moved closer and put his arms around Ryan's neck. Ryan put his right arm on Dan's shoulder. When Dan let go of him a moment later, Susan smiled and kissed Ryan on the cheek, then followed Dan across the living room and toward the door to the entrance hall.

Late at night, Dan woke up and, at first, didn't know where he was—until he remembered that he and Susan had left the summer party and gone to her apartment in the Vesterbro district.

The room was dark, but he could discern a faint streak of light along the edge of the large curtains. Susan lay on her side, facing him, with one arm across his chest. He could tell by her slow breathing that she was asleep.

It was still hard to comprehend everything that had happened the night before and how wonderful and incredible it was to be with Susan again. He had to give her forearm a soft squeeze to convince himself that it wasn't just a dream.

For a while, he lay there, reflecting on his life. If it hadn't been for the unresolved issue with the karma sequence and what to do with their knowledge about it, everything would be almost perfect. He knew he would have to find something to use his energy and skills on—once they'd found a solution to the problem—but he wasn't anxious about that prospect. He already had various ideas. Among other things, he would try to find a way to communicate with the Master Entity, if possible. If it was everywhere—and perhaps even was everything—it would also know his thoughts and hear his requests for help and guidance. The mere awareness of its existence gave him the clarity and strength to do what he needed to do—when he eventually got an idea about what those things might be. Perhaps the Master Entity could even explain the existence of the karma sequence and how it worked. Dan smiled as he compared his plan to the technical challenge of figuring out how a system worked, even though he accepted it might not be something a human would ever be able to understand.

He was jolted out of his thoughts when his phone rang. He hurriedly reached for it on the small table next to the bed so that the noise didn't wake Susan. The clock on his phone showed a quarter past four, and he could see it was Gitte calling.

"Hi, Gitte," Dan said in a hushed voice. "Has something happened?"

"Yes," answered Gitte. She sounded tired, but also anxious. "I'm at the hospital. Ryan's been admitted—he's in a coma. I think he's had a stroke!"

TWENTY-FOUR

As carefully as he could, Dan moved Susan's arm and sat up on the bedside. He tried to remember where he'd put his clothes when they'd come home late Saturday night—and then remembered the sequence of events. He slowly got up from the bed, walked into the hallway, toward the living room. Even without turning on the light, it was just bright enough for him to make out his and Susan's clothes, spread across the sofa and the floor beside it.

Once he'd dressed and made sure he had his keys in his pocket—he tiptoed into the bedroom and around the bed, where he sat down next to Susan. Even in the dim light, he could see her and again felt how his heart beat faster and how happy he was that they were together again.

He put his hand on her arm and shook it lightly, whispering her name. Susan mumbled something, turned, and opened her eyes. In the semi-darkness, she had to focus her eyes before she saw Dan sitting on the edge of the bed.

"Hi, Dan," she said in surprise, smiling as she stretched.

"Hi, Susan," said Dan, and leaned over to give her a short kiss. "I'm sorry to wake you—but I just wanted to let you know that I'll be gone for a few hours."

"Why?" asked Susan warily.

"Ryan's not doing so well—he's been hospitalized. I'll drive up to the hospital and ask Gitte if there's anything I can do. I told her I would come, even though she insisted it wasn't necessary."

Dan could feel that Susan was instantly wide awake, and after a few seconds, she sat up in the bed and moved so that she was sitting on the edge of the bed next to him.

"Give me a minute—I'm coming with you," she said.

"You don't have to, Susan. I only woke you up so you wouldn't be nervous when you saw I wasn't here."

"Of course I'll come, you clown," she said, kissing him on the cheek. "I want to see how poor Ryan is doing and be there for him and Gitte if they need it."

Resolutely, she got up from the bed and switched on the light, then opened a cupboard and found some clothes, which she quickly put on. They were in the car three minutes later, heading for the hospital.

Gitte had briefed Dan that Ryan had been admitted to a private hospital in the northern end of Copenhagen, and after Dan had informed the GPS of the name, they followed its proposed route through the city to the hospital. It was only half past four in the early morning, and there was virtually no traffic, apart from taxis bringing happy and tired people home from the city nightlife.

While on their way in the car, Dan briefly told Susan about the hospital and Ryan's association with it. One of Lifeline's board members was the CEO and chief surgeon at the hospital, and if Dan remembered correctly, he'd actually attended the summer party the night before. Susan said she'd heard about the hospital and knew some people who'd been helped there. To her knowledge, there wasn't the slightest compromise in its professional and technical capacity, so Ryan presumably was in the best possible hands. Hearing this had an encouraging effect on Dan.

"I never saw Ryan so pale and haggard as at the party last night," Susan said as they passed the Lakes in central Copenhagen. "He's usually always on top of the world—full of energy—and the center of the party. A little drunk, obviously—but not significantly more than so many other guests."

Dan nodded as he thought back again to his own abuse.

"Sorry, Dan," added Susan regretfully. "I didn't mean to remind you of your disease."

Dan shook his head. "No problem. We shouldn't be afraid to talk about anything. I know my addiction and disease will be brought up—one way or another—many times in the future. It's part of me and my story, not something I intend to forget."

He could see Susan nodding.

"But you're right," Dan immediately added. "Ryan definitely didn't look good—especially at the time we left; but I'm sure he'll be fine."

He smiled nostalgically as he continued reminiscing about Ryan.

"The man is strong as an ox. In all the years I've known him, I've seen how he can overload his body—with nonstop work, lack of sleep, poor diet, and drinking—and he's bounced back every time: always optimistic and focused on his goals and the possibilities the future might hold. And until recently, I've never seen him stressed or worried."

"Was that when he discovered the omega value, and Gitte feared it predicted when people would die?"

"Exactly," replied Dan, contemplating how the entire process of discovering the omega value and, later, the whole karma sequence in the human genome must have affected Ryan. "That discovery has forced us into some tough considerations about ethics and consequences for all humans; questioning whether we should share the insight or keep it secret. Ryan has undoubtedly tried to process it all, by focusing on what he does best: seeing opportunities, combining technologies in new ways, and turning it all into a business. Maybe sometimes at the expense of some ethical reflections that the rest of us tried to address before we started thinking about possibilities and money."

"I think that sounds like a good analysis," interjected Susan. "I imagine it's also led to some discussions between Ryan and Gitte?"

"Yes, very much so," replied Dan, describing what Ryan had told him about his and Gitte's disagreement and her attempt to appeal to Ryan to forget about the karma sequence and turn off the AI that had detected it. Finally, he told how Gitte had threatened to leave Ryan if he chose not to listen to her concerns.

"Okay, it sounds like she's taking it pretty seriously," Susan said thoughtfully. "I get that it's a big question, but isn't it a little odd that she's reacting so violently—before Ryan has even implemented any of the ideas he's talking about?"

"Yes, especially considering how calm and deliberate she usually is."

The GPS announced they'd arrived at their destination, and Dan turned into the long parking lot near what looked like the entrance.

The front door was locked, but there was a button they could press to get in. A few seconds later, the lock buzzed, and they pushed the door open and stepped inside.

In the small reception area was a counter, but no one was sitting behind it. Dan and Susan looked around and noticed two large red doors, one on each side of the reception. After unsuccessfully trying to open each of the doors, they sat down next to each other on a couple of chairs in a small area that was intended for people waiting—either to be helped at the reception or to visit friends or family members. Susan reached out and took Dan's hand in hers.

"I don't understand why Gitte called you in the middle of the night," said Susan speculatively, "if it wasn't because she wanted you to come out here? She could have waited until morning—and then she would probably know more about Ryan's condition and when he would be able to come home."

Dan nodded as he thought about it.

"Don't you think she needed to talk to someone, but at the same time, didn't want to disturb more than necessary?"

"Maybe you're right," replied Susan, a little skeptically. "It just seems a bit odd to me. Especially considering how controlled Gitte normally is."

Their conversation was interrupted when one of the two large doors opened, and Gitte entered the reception. She looked around, and when she spotted Dan and Susan, she walked quickly toward them as the red door closed automatically behind her. Dan and Susan both got to their feet and met Gitte in the middle of the room. She was no longer wearing the elegant dress from the party—only a white tracksuit—and all makeup was gone from her face, and she'd gathered her hair in a bun at the nape of her neck.

"Hi, Dan," she said, hugging Dan. "How sweet of you to come!"

They held each other for a few seconds, then she turned to Susan and gave her a hug as well. "And you too, Susan? You really shouldn't have."

"How is he—is it possible that we can see him?" asked Dan, looking toward the door Gitte had come out of.

She sent him a regretful smile.

"I'm afraid that's not possible right now," replied Gitte, gesturing at the chairs Dan and Susan had got up from when she entered the reception. "He's still in a coma, and the doctors watching him say they don't dare wake him right away."

The three of them walked to the chairs, and Gitte moved a chair and sat down opposite Dan and Susan.

"Maybe you could take Dan in to see him—just for a minute?" asked Susan cautiously.

Gitte shook her head. "Let's wait and see if he gets a little better. Frankly, I'm afraid he won't make it." She bowed her head and put her face in her hands. Susan leaned forward and placed her hand on Gitte's knee.

"On our way here, Dan reminded me of how strong Ryan has always been," Susan said encouragingly. "I'm sure he'll make it through this challenge, too."

Gitte looked up and smiled at them both, then took Susan's hand from her knee, giving it a quick squeeze before letting it go.

"What about you, Gitte? How are you coping with it all?" asked Susan compassionately. "It can't have been easy for you, either?"

"It's been a tough night," replied Gitte, forcing a thankful smile as she looked out the windows behind the other two. "I wasn't prepared for this to happen."

"What actually happened?" asked Dan. "When did Ryan get sick? Do you think it was from overexertion?"

Gitte looked at Dan hesitantly for a few seconds without saying anything.

"Gitte," said Susan. "If it's too hard to talk about now, that's fine. It's not important now."

For a moment, all of them sat in silence. Gitte looked unfocused ahead of her, as if trying to collect her thoughts and remember the details of what had happened.

"The fireworks started exactly midnight—and it was even more magnificent than I remember from previous years. It's a shame you didn't stay to see it. Everyone stood on the terrace and spread around the garden, enjoying the impressive spectacle. I think it lasted almost fifteen minutes—it was absolutely intense."

Gitte paused briefly, trying to recall the events before she proceeded.

"After the fireworks ended, the party continued; many danced on the terrace, and everyone seemed to be in a good mood. There was no shortage of anything. Ryan and I were sitting on the sofa at the end of the living room, and it was obvious that Ryan was enjoying the spectacle of all the cheerful people, even though he did seem exhausted. I have to say I was a little worried about all his drinking, too—it was worse than usual, in my opinion."

She paused again for a short moment.

"After the fireworks, a few guests were starting to break up. They typically came by Ryan and me and said thank you for a lovely evening. Several praised the beautiful fireworks display, which livened Ryan up a bit—as if he was the one who'd created it. Around three o'clock, the last guests left, and Ryan and I were alone. We talked about how the evening had gone, and a little about you guys, too," she continued, smiling warmly at them both. "After filling Ryan's glass again, I decided to go for a run in the hills—to clear my head and enjoy some fresh air. When I got back, I was standing on the gravel driveway in the back garden, doing some stretches, when I noticed something terrible. Ryan's old Jaguar was completely marred by deep scratches all over: on the doors, hood, windows, hubcaps, lamps—everywhere. Even on the roof."

Dan felt how simply hearing about it hurt him. He knew how much that car meant to Ryan and how much money and energy he'd invested in it. Susan seemed surprised but not shocked—probably because she didn't know the background. To her, it was merely a car, just like it would have been to Dan if he hadn't known its backstory.

"I was deeply shocked," Gitte proceeded. "And when I got closer to the car, I could see that—besides all the other deep scratches—the words 'fuck you' were scratched on the hood in giant letters."

"Who on earth would do such a heinous thing?" asked Susan incredulously, shaking her head.

Dan thought the same, but said nothing. He had a nagging sense of who it might be, and the fear only got worse the more he thought about it.

"After standing and looking at the wrecked car for a minute, I went into the living room and told Ryan. He was dozing on the sofa, and I had to shake his arm a little to get his attention. Even though he was exhausted, he practically jumped up from the sofa and staggered to the backyard and the car. I followed him back there, of course."

Gitte took a deep breath before continuing.

"When he saw his beloved Jaguar so mutilated, he first seemed resigned and sad. He had tears in his eyes and stood with his mouth open, shaking his head. Then he slowly circled the car, feeling the many deep scratches with his fingertips, becoming increasingly agitated. At first, he cursed loudly at every touch; then it escalated to shouting and screaming. I was terrified. I've never seen him so furious. By the time he'd walked all the way around the car, his face was red with rage, and he kept screaming that Michael and his gangster thugs had done it. I tried to calm him down and tell him that, even though it looked bad, it could probably all be fixed. But he didn't listen and kept shouting curses and threats at Michael. I won't repeat what he shouted—but some of it was downright insane. Finally, he became completely unintelligible and just made incoherent noises."

She paused for a short moment, slowly shaking her head. "And then he collapsed—right there in the gravel—like a giant marionette doll with its strings cut."

For a little while, none of them said anything. Gitte's face had taken on a sad and distant expression, and she seemed almost on the verge of tears.

With a resentful expression, Susan got up from her chair and bent down, putting her arms around Gitte.

"Poor Ryan," she said as she patted Gitte gently on the back. "And what an ugly experience it must have been for you to witness."

Gitte said nothing and just sat staring ahead. A moment later, she began to stand up, prompting Susan to let go of her.

"I better go back and check on Ryan," she said in a steady voice, a determined look on her face. "It was sweet of you to come—especially here in the middle of the night—it has touched me deeply. But I really think you should go home now. I promise to call if Ryan gets better and is able to recognize his surroundings and communicate again."

Both Dan and Susan shook their heads dismissively, insisting that they would stay until there hopefully was an improvement in Ryan's condition. Dan got up and stood next to Susan while Gitte expressed how grateful she was for their support and promised she would return to the reception and update them as soon as there was any news. Then she turned around, walked to the big red door, and opened it by swiping a key card over a keypad.

As the door closed behind Gitte, Dan thought he would have liked to ask her how Ryan got to the hospital. He guessed Gitte had called 911—and then directed the paramedics to drive Ryan and herself to the specific hospital where they were now sitting. It occurred to him that she might also have called the hospital's CEO and chief surgeon—the one on Lifeline's board—and that he might have arranged what was necessary. After some speculation, Dan concluded that it wasn't important how Ryan had got there—only that it was good to know that he was now in caring and professional hands.

"Let's sit down again while we wait," said Susan, and went back to her chair. Dan followed her example. After they sat down, they held hands, and it struck Dan what an invaluable support it was, having Susan there. Even in a situation as sad as the one they were going through now, it was nice to know there was someone he could share the moment and his feelings with.

They sat for a while, saying nothing. Dan's thoughts kept reverting to what Gitte had told him about the broken car and how Ryan had reacted. He tried to find a reason why someone would do such a despicable thing and who it could be. He still had an all-too-clear suspicion of the latter, though he struggled to accept it. Even if Ryan couldn't know, he'd probably been right about Michael being the best candidate: unfortunately, the hypothesis fit nicely with Michael's temper and dislike of Ryan. And for Michael, it had probably only been an expression of his frustration and an attempt to annoy Ryan, to send him a warning. Of course, he hadn't planned for it to inflict a stroke on Ryan, sending him to the hospital.

Dan had hoped and believed their talk with Ryan in the basement had taken the top off Michael's fury. He knew that Ryan's plans to manipulate the human genome, hoping to postpone death, had shaken Michael. So much so that he'd shown up at the party with the Swedish brothers and threatened Ryan in front of his guests. From there, it wasn't far to also suspect him of planning vandalism, perhaps even before they arrived—as a manifest and unambiguous warning.

He couldn't help feeling disappointed in Michael—even though he was his best friend—and decided to have a serious talk with him about it when they met on Sunday.

The many unresolved issues with the karma sequence, along with Ryan's plans to exploit it, drained the last of Dan's energy, leaving him feeling suddenly very tired. Also, because he didn't know what to do—or if there was anything at all he could do. He thought about getting a couple of blankets he always kept in the back of his car, but the temperature in reception was comfortable, so he opted to stay where he was.

A little later, Susan leaned to the side, resting her head on his shoulder. Dan also closed his eyes, trying to distance himself from his many thoughts. One part of him kept thinking about Ryan, who was lying in a critical condition close to where they were sitting—but another part couldn't let go of the thoughts about the karma sequence. Something in the overlap between the two concerns was important, but he couldn't quite establish what it was. He was about to fall asleep—or maybe he'd even dozed off a little—when it hit him. Ryan's Lifeline document!

"Susan," he said quietly—so as not to wake her if she was sleeping.

"Mmmh," she said. "I'm not asleep."

"Ryan told me the other day that he'd checked a list of extracted karma sequences for all customers Michael and I had made and sent to him."

Susan sat up and turned her head.

"You sound somewhat invigorated, Dan," she said expectantly. "Did Ryan find out anything important?"

"Yes, he did," replied Dan, feeling how the sudden hope had made him wide awake. "Ryan had found himself on the list and told me how the omega value revealed he'd live to be an old man."

"That sounds absolutely marvelous, Dan! Finally, some good news from your toils with that karma sequence."

Dan's relief rubbed off on Susan, and they decided to drive home. They felt sure that the next update on Ryan would be that he was awake and that they could visit him—but it wasn't something they needed to stay in the hospital waiting for.

Dan started texting Gitte about Ryan's omega value and his and Susan's decision to leave. Before he could press the send button, the red door opened, and Gitte returned to the reception. She slowly walked over to them, and Dan could see the tears on her cheeks as she approached.

"What happened, Gitte?" asked Susan softly, looking at her sympathetically. Before answering, Gitte took a deep breath.

"He's dead," she said in disbelief, looking out the windows behind Dan and Susan. It sounded like she didn't quite understand the words coming out of her mouth.

TWENTY-FIVE

On Wednesday evening, Dan dined with his mother and Susan at a Chinese restaurant on the Amager island—within walking distance of Anette's apartment. They were celebrating the one-week anniversary of her sobriety, and although it had been a long day, Anette didn't seem particularly tired.

The day had started with the treatment meeting at the addiction center, where Dan had again driven Anette back and forth. This time, however, he'd gone for a walk in central Copenhagen until her meeting ended. When they met again, Anette had said that from now on, she could easily take the bike or the metro to the three weekly meetings on her own, so Dan didn't have to plan around it.

In the afternoon, they'd gone for a long walk on the southern shore of Amager, and in the evening, Dan had accompanied Anette to her first AA meeting. Here she'd experienced the company of other people in her and Dan's situation and seen how everyone supported each other and talked about self-insight and ways to break the addiction habits. After the meeting, they'd walked to the nearby Chinese restaurant where they'd arranged to meet Susan.

Dan and Susan sat next to each other on one side of the small table in the restaurant, and Anette sat on the other. As they enjoyed the excellent food from the buffet, Susan interestedly asked Anette about various things from the addiction treatment and told her how happy and impressed she was about the significant anniversary. Dan was delighted at how good friends his mother and Susan had become in the short time they'd known each other. From Saturday morning, when Dan and Susan had arrived at Anette's apartment, she and Susan had got on well, talking about all sorts of things—as if they'd known each other forever.

After Gitte had returned to the reception early Saturday morning at the hospital and told Dan and Susan that Ryan had died, they'd sat with her for a long time, trying to process the shock and grief they all felt. Around eight o'clock, they'd driven Gitte home and made sure she was all right. The cleaners were already busy tidying up the villa and garden and packing away lamps and other equipment. Susan had asked Gitte if she and Dan should stay with her, but she'd insisted that they go home and that she could manage. Susan had been a little worried about Gitte because she didn't seem to have any family or close friends she could spend time with—but Dan felt he knew Gitte well enough to be comfortable with the situation. Especially after they'd instructed Gitte that she should just call them—and they would be out there straight away. Every day, either Dan or Susan had talked to her on the phone to see how she was doing.

While they were eating, Anette told Dan and Susan how nice it was to be with them, simply enjoying their company and the food without feeling the need for wine or beer to stimulate the experience. All three had a large glass of cola in front of them and toasted warmly every time they tasted it.

"So, how was your first AA meeting?" asked Susan after Anette had talked about the treatment at the addiction center. "I guess it must have been easier for you because you're not as shy as your son?" She turned her head and sent Dan a big smile and then made a kissy face at him. Dan smiled and pretended not to notice.

"It was very similar to the meetings at the addiction center," replied Anette while smiling at Susan's and Dan's nonverbal communication. "There were a few more people at the AA meeting, but the concept was more or less the same: everyone could share their experiences and development, and there was a positive and embracing atmosphere—I really felt welcome and that I was part of the group, even though I didn't know anyone."

"Wow, that's fantastic, Anette," said Susan, smiling. "It sounds almost like a kind of evening school."

At first, Dan smiled at her comparison, but on reflection, it wasn't entirely off the mark: you learned something at every meeting, often about yourself, and it was nice to have some regular events to look forward to.

"Sometimes there will inevitably be some sad stories as well," said Dan, trying not to sound like a know-it-all—even though he'd been attending AA meetings for almost a year. "The process of staying sober and getting to know yourself better can feel harder for some people than for others. Everyone lives with the risk of a relapse—and if that happens, it's sometimes tough to motivate yourself to go to the next meeting. Although it definitely helps to show up and talk about it."

"Having a setback like that must be awful," said Susan, looking at Dan worriedly. "Does it happen often?"

Dan reflected on his AA meetings and the many people he'd met.

"Obviously, the risk is there for all of us," he replied after a few seconds, looking briefly at Anette. "So the very purpose of the meetings is to minimize that risk and help each person distance themselves from the danger zone. But suppose something violent or unexpected happens in a person's life. In that situation, it can seem tempting to try to escape it all with a single drink—which you're convinced you can keep to just one; but inevitably, you get caught up in the addiction again."

Cautiously, Dan placed his cutlery on his plate and turned in his chair to get a better look at Susan.

"Susan," he said reassuringly and put his hand on her arm, trying to counter the concern he had sensed in her question. "You don't have to be afraid of that happening to me. I would like to ask you to put that fear completely out of your mind. There are so many other things you can worry about: traffic accidents, disease, terrorism, and whatnot. But I feel confident I won't get caught in that particular dependency again."

By now, Susan had also put down her cutlery and placed her hand on Dan's, looking at him uncertainly.

"I'm not afraid, Dan," she said quietly. "But can you really say it so confidently? Especially after you've witnessed other people in the same situation falling back into the old abuse or having a hard time fighting the urge to drink."

Dan nodded and took a deep breath before sharing the most crucial element of his own journey toward healing and self-awareness.

"At the core of the invaluable help I've received in my healing process—including the insight into my personality and the processes that create my emotions—has been the spiritual element."

Pausing briefly, he looked at Anette to gauge her reaction to the subject of spirituality being brought up, while at the same time trying to find an analogy that might describe the change his worldview and self-conception had undergone.

"I'm no longer like a small, unprotected rowboat on a stormy ocean. I'm part of the ocean, and I try to take care of the rowboat, which is also part of me—my consciousness or personality."

"That was a beautiful metaphor, Dan," said Anette, fascinated. "But I simply don't understand it. Does it have anything to do with God?"

"I think so," replied Dan. "At least with the acceptance that there's something bigger and more important than oneself. Or rather, your *self* is part of a cosmic entity—something conscious with a purpose and the ability to communicate it to us. Calling it God is undoubtedly a suitable term, though the word itself has a different meaning for many people."

It seemed to Dan that both Susan and Anette understood the comparison, but perhaps found it difficult to see themselves in the context he was describing.

"Yes, you did mention the spiritual element when we met at the café two weeks ago," Susan said. "I've wondered about it a bit since, especially after our dinner last Sunday—when you told me about your conversation with Maya Luna and the problem with the weird karma sequence you and Michael are working on."

They both looked briefly at Anette, who seemed lost in her own thoughts before Susan continued.

"But are you saying that your spiritual insight and sensation of being part of a greater cosmic whole is an insurance against taking so much as a single drink?"

Dan nodded. "Yes, because I know that I'm neither my body nor my mind and that a single glass of alcohol will be the first step in my personality falling back into addiction, ultimately ending with my physical death."

"But doesn't what you say also imply that the poor people who relapse aren't as far advanced in their spiritual self-understanding as you are?"

"Yes, that's my conviction. Although many explanations and ways of perceiving the spiritual interconnection may exist. And the profoundness of the impact will vary from person to person. I'm not quite there with my personal quest either—and don't know if I ever will be."

"It sounds very abstract," said Anette hesitantly. "But also very exciting. I hope you'll spend a little time and energy explaining it to me at some point?"

"Sure, Mom," replied Dan readily. "Whatever it takes. But I'm convinced you'll realize much of it on your own as part of your treatment and recovery process. I can hardly express how much this has helped me to set things straight in my life—and I'm sure it can make a huge difference in yours, too."

"You also mentioned that you wanted to see if you could find a way to help other people escape their addiction," said Susan. "Is what you're describing now the insight you want to try to share?"

"Yes. It is," replied Dan. "To the best of my ability and with all my resources. I just need to find the right platform to communicate it well."

He contemplated whether it was the right time to tell his mother and Susan about his conversation with the Master Entity, but decided to do so another day—in quieter surroundings. Perhaps on a relaxed walk in the countryside or at the summer house.

"Isn't the simplest thing just to write a book about it?" Anette spontaneously suggested.

"Good idea," Susan chimed in, looking at Dan. "And maybe it could be relevant to people other than addicts—people struggling with other problems."

"I haven't thought of that at all," Dan said in surprise, though he didn't know if he could write a book or what kind of book it should be. "But yes, maybe a book is a good place to start."

Anette nodded, looking more optimistic. She raised her glass and smiled alternately from Dan to Susan, who also raised their glasses, and they all toasted. For a minute, all three enjoyed their food, with none of them saying anything. At one point, the waiter came to their table and asked if everything was okay. They commended the food, and all three asked for refills of their glasses.

"So, are you guys recovering from the horrible incident last Saturday?" asked Anette after the waiter had brought their cola.

"I believe Dan is the one who is most affected by Ryan's death," replied Susan, glancing at Dan, who nodded. They'd talked about it many times—not least when they called Gitte to check everything was okay and offered to drop by.

"Yes, I still find it hard to believe he's no longer with us," said Dan. "It's probably going to take a while for everything to fall into place."

They'd told Anette the complete story, with the party and Ryan's hospitalization, and how they were both in the hospital when Gitte had come out and told them Ryan was dead. But they hadn't mentioned the vandalism to his favorite car and that it might have been that incident that had pushed Ryan over the edge and given him the brutal stroke.

Nor had Dan told Anette anything about the karma sequence and the responsibility their insight had brought—and how the matter had caused division and dissent among the small group of people involved. And he still wasn't sure if it was something he wanted to share with her—even though she was his mother. It depended on what conclusion he would reach after discussing it with Susan and probably also Michael and Gitte.

Not that he doubted his mother's ability to keep a secret, but to avoid placing her in an awkward position if they chose not to make their knowledge public. So she wouldn't have to carry the same unresolved sense of responsibility for deciding what to do with the profound knowledge.

However, he'd shared all his contemplations with Susan. Although she, too, was overwhelmed by the implications of the discovery of the karma sequence—how every person apparently had the number of days in their life encoded in their genome—their conversations had been a great help. It made it easier to deal with the immense responsibility. That aspect of their friendship meant as much to him as the physical intimacy.

On their way to Anette, after dropping Gitte off on Saturday morning, Dan had also shared his nagging suspicion that Michael could very well be behind the mutilation of

Ryan's dearest possession—just as Ryan had shouted before collapsing. Even though Susan also viewed Michael as her friend, she shared Dan's concern. She, too, could imagine that, unfortunately, it was something he might be able to do if he felt sufficiently provoked.

But to Dan's surprise, Michael had adamantly denied any knowledge of the vandalism.

Dan had called Michael later that same Saturday to tell him that Ryan had died—and Michael had sounded as shocked and saddened by the news as Dan and Susan had been when Gitte told them what had happened. They'd agreed to stick to the plan of meeting at Michael's cabin on Sunday where they could review the new situation and whether it had changed their options on deciding what to do about the insight into the karma sequence.

When Dan had arrived, Michael was sitting on the bench in front of the cabin. He asked Dan to grab a couple of colas from the fridge before sitting down.

They sat in silence for a while, looking out over the lake. Dan felt the need to ask Michael if he was responsible for the vandalism seemingly instrumental in causing Ryan's death. And he also wanted to talk to him about his temper problems and whether he'd reverted to some of the old aggressive tendencies. But he didn't know how to put it. It wasn't easy talking to your best friend about such things.

It was Michael who broke the silence.

"Has this been the craziest summer or what?" he asked rhetorically after gazing at a duck take off from the lake.

Dan nodded, thinking back on all the things that had happened the recent weeks.

"First, there was the board meeting, where I met the old Dan again—which still overshadows everything else," proceeded Michael, sending Dan a warm smile. "But then the shocking news started coming in quick succession: first, Ryan's discovery of the omega value; then our discovery of the karma sequence; and then Maya Luna's death. Most recently, it was Ryan's grotesque plans of offering gene therapy to people who'll pay for—possibly—prolonging their lives. And now the terrible news about his death! It's simply too much for one person to bear."

While they both sipped their colas, Dan thought Michael could also have added his threatening confrontation with Ryan at the summer party to his list. And maybe the distasteful vandalism that had led to such fatal consequences—if it was him, obviously. He chose to jump right into it and ask him directly.

"Did you have anything to do with the vandalism of Ryan's favorite car?" he asked directly, looking at Michael to see his reaction.

"Did someone wreck one of Ryan's cars?" replied Michael in surprise. "Damn, that's a bitch!" He turned to Dan in shock. "And you think I was somehow part of that?"

"You did behave rather threatening at the party—along with the two brothers," Dan replied quietly.

"You're right. It was probably wrong to bring them along," admitted Michael—clearly annoyed by his decision. "But they came with me, and they left with me again. So, they certainly didn't do it. I didn't know one of the cars was Ryan's favorite—which one is it?"

"The old Jaguar," replied Dan and then recounted the complete story: what Gitte had said about the discovery of the vandalism, Ryan's reaction, the wait in the hospital, and finally, the news of Ryan's death.

After listening to Dan's summary, Michael was infuriated. "Then it's not just vandalism—it's downright murder!" he said, outraged. "But you have to believe me, Dan—I wouldn't think of doing something like that. In the old days, perhaps—but not anymore."

"It's all right, Michael," Dan said accommodatingly. "I'm sorry that I suspected you."

"No, no, it's understandable—with my background and the aggressive way I showed up at the party. But ultimately, I only wanted to deter Ryan from his twisted plans."

They talked briefly about who might have done the vandalism, but neither had any candidates. It could have been anyone—potentially someone who hadn't even been a guest at the party in the first place. The choice of the Jaguar could also be a coincidence, or simply because it was the first in the line of cars exhibited.

Then they discussed what Ryan's death would mean for the karma sequence and whether it affected their dilemma about publicizing their insights. They were both still in doubt and chose to wait until Gitte had recovered so they could all meet and talk it over.

"By the way, did you check yesterday's date with our list of Lifeline customers and their omega values?" asked Michael a little later.

Dan nodded. "Sure—I checked that as soon as I got over the first shock of Ryan's death," replied Dan. "There was no match for Saturday. And I know Ryan was on the list—under a pseudonym—he told me so himself."

"Right," said Michael. "I would also be surprised if he hadn't had a Lifeline document made up himself. But then there should be a row on the list for the date yesterday—and there isn't."

"No, it's weird. Either Ryan lied when he said he'd created a Lifeline document—or his omega value was incorrect. Also, none of the rows on the surrounding dates seem to match Ryan's profile."

"Okay, so maybe the karma sequence isn't as accurate as we thought. That would be nice—it would all seem a little less deterministic," said Michael optimistically. Dan hoped he was right, but didn't quite believe it.

Before Dan returned to Copenhagen, they agreed to talk about their options with Gitte at a later point—and promised each other that they would each work to reach a conclusion on what they thought should happen with their knowledge of the karma sequence.

After having finished dinner at the restaurant, all three walked back to Anette's apartment, where they sat talking on her sofa for almost an hour before Dan and Susan drove back to the apartment in the Vesterbro district. Dan had tried to stick to his decision to stay with his mother for a while, but Anette had insisted that he at least spend the night with his girlfriend. Subsequently, he'd started commuting between Susan's and Anette's apartments—either in his car or by metro—and every day, Susan had come by Anette's apartment after work and spent the evening before she and Dan had said goodnight and gone home.

In the middle of the night, Dan suddenly woke up with a jolt. Susan lay close to him, sleeping peacefully—he could feel her arm on his chest and her breath on his cheek.

He'd had an idea that he was surprised he hadn't thought of before. It was as if the subconscious part of his mind had opened a door he'd so far avoided going through. The thought was so obvious that he wondered why he hadn't at least considered the possibility earlier—no matter how unlikely it might be.

When he and Michael had speculated about who might have vandalized Ryan's Jaguar, neither of them had considered the one person with the best chance of doing it without being discovered—Gitte, who knew all the guests had left and certainly knew which car was Ryan's favorite.

On the rational level, Dan could suddenly find no better hypothesis than it must have been Gitte who'd done it. And when examining his own mind, he also understood the feelings that had prevented him from contemplating that terrible thought: primarily his respect and admiration for Gitte but also his gratitude for the things she'd done to allow him to share his life with Susan—who was right now lying next to him—not once, but twice.

At first, he wondered if Gitte might have done it as a warning to Ryan, but now that the genie was out of the bottle—and after thinking it over several times—it occurred to him that no person would benefit more financially from

Ryan's death than Gitte and that her intention might have been to kill Ryan all along.

Dan lay awake for the rest of the night, searching in vain for arguments dispelling his suspicion of Gitte and pointing to a better theory.

TWENTY-SIX

Dan, Susan, and Anette arrived at Ryan's funeral in the big villa in the Strandvejen district north of Copenhagen a good twenty minutes before the formal part of the ceremony was due to start at two o'clock on Thursday afternoon.

After driving to Anette's apartment early in the morning, Dan and Susan had joined Anette in a long walk on Amager Common—a large, green, undeveloped park area on the western side of the island—enjoying the beautiful summer weather.

On their walk, they'd talked about various things, primarily related to Ryan, because of his funeral later that day. Dan had told them about the old days when Ryan had bought Avaram—Dan's and Michael's company. And he'd shared stories from his travels with Ryan and how he got to know Ryan on a more personal level—and how he'd tried to advise and guide him as best he could.

It hadn't been difficult for Dan to talk about Ryan. However, he still felt his heart sink whenever he was reminded that the person he was talking about wasn't alive anymore.

Dan parked in the gravel near the wrought-iron gate in front of Ryan and Gitte's villa. There was plenty of parking space, so they didn't have to walk as far as he'd had to when arriving for the summer party. They were a little early, and there would probably be fewer guests than the previous week.

The gate was open, and they walked straight into the backyard and along the long gravel driveway down to the house. Ryan's cars were no longer on display along the driveway. In one of their phone conversations, Gitte had told Dan that all the vehicles had been moved back to the basement—except for the battered Jaguar, which she'd asked a garage to pick up and try to restore.

The portable toilets along the garage door had also been removed, and the catering trucks and fireworks trailers were already gone the morning after the party when Dan and Susan had accompanied Gitte back from the hospital. Everything looked normal again. Even the marks on the beautiful lawn had been patched and smoothed over.

They walked through the open front door and waited in the entrance hall for a moment. Voices were coming from the kitchen, so Dan headed for the kitchen door, with Susan and Anette following right behind him. At the kitchen table, Gitte and Vibs were busy preparing coffee and dishes with food and biscuits. They both looked toward the door as the three entered the kitchen.

"Hi, Gitte—and hi, Vibs," said Dan.

Gitte looked up and smiled, wiped her hands with a tea towel, and walked over to them. Vibs stayed at the table but nodded and sent them a smile. She winked briefly at Dan, who interpreted it as her way of saying everything was okay and that he wasn't expected to explain what had happened at the party.

"Hi, Dan and Susan," said Gitte as she approached them. "Good to see you! And thanks for your kind support all week. It means a lot to me."

"It was the least we could do, Gitte," said Susan, about to hug her, but stopped in her tracks when she saw Gitte had already shifted her focus and was now looking at Anette, somewhat puzzled.

"Hi, Gitte," said Anette, maneuvering between Dan and Susan. "My name is Anette, and I'm Dan's mother." She held out her hand and waited until Gitte took it. "I want to offer my condolences for your loss and say how sorry I am for your husband's death. Even though I never met Ryan, I feel like I know him—from all Dan has been sharing lately."

"Thank you, Anette—that's sweet of you," said Gitte as Anette energetically shook her hand up and down. "I'm glad to finally meet you. You've no idea how much Dan has meant to Ryan—to both of us. I'm happy and grateful you're able to take part today, too."

Dan could see that Gitte—both her appearance and the reception she'd given them—made a big impression on his mother. Anette hadn't wanted to go to Ryan's funeral, but Dan had pushed her a bit, and she'd assented after Susan said she also thought it was a good idea. Although it was a sad occasion, Dan and Susan wanted to show Anette the magnificent villa that meant so much to them—because they'd met and fallen in love there.

When Gitte had gotten her hand back, she gestured toward the entrance hall behind them. "The ceremony will take place in the basement. You're a little early, but feel free to go down there now if you like. Dan, you know where Ryan's fridge is—and there are water bottles now, too. Plus, everyone's invited up here for coffee and cookies after the funeral."

After descending the stairs, they entered the large basement, where a surprise awaited them. Although the enormous room didn't usually seem cold and basement-like, there was now a completely different ambiance. All the cars—except the Jaguar—were in their regular places, in two long rows along the sides of the room. Leaning against the bumpers in front of all the cars were large wreaths of flowers—with ribbons displaying a final greeting—from Ryan's many contacts in business, Lifeline's board, and others who knew him. Susan discreetly pointed to one of the wreaths as they passed it, and Dan could see that it was the one they'd bought at a flower shop the day before and which the shop had delivered to the address given. There were also large and small bouquets on the hoods of all the cars.

The large worktables at the far end of the room had been moved to the side and covered with red cloths that hung almost to the floor. On the midmost of the large cabinets that filled the entire end wall hung a large picture of Ryan, showing him with a big smile, apparently from a vacation in the Mediterranean, with what looked like ancient excavations in the background.

Under the picture—almost at the end wall stood Ryan's bier: a casket raised a meter above the ground on an extended base on small wheels. It was a simple, white, closed casket, and on top of it were three wreaths and a large bouquet.

To the left of the casket—where the Jaguar would normally have been parked—were four rows of black folding chairs facing the casket, five chairs in each row.

The lights throughout the basement were dimmed, giving the entire room a solemn glow. Dan had the sensation of being in a cathedral—or perhaps more accurately, in a large crypt beneath a cathedral.

As they slowly walked through the room toward Ryan's casket, Dan could feel how he was affected by the thought that he would never be able to talk to him again—despite their physical proximity. When they reached the casket, they all stood thoughtfully looking at it for a minute before Dan pointed to the chairs and suggested that Susan and Anette sit down. He asked if they would like something to drink while they waited—to which they both declined—and then told them he would go back up to the entrance hall and help Gitte guide people down to the basement as they arrived. Susan squeezed his hand before she and Anette sat down in the back row of folding chairs.

When he'd climbed the staircase to the entrance hall, he saw Gitte was already standing at the front door—ready to receive the mourners.

"The basement looks amazing," said Dan as he got closer to her. "What a beautiful idea, using Ryan's beloved workshop, with the cars as the setting—he would have appreciated that."

"Thank you," said Gitte, smiling sadly. "Yes, it's really lovely. The undertakers have been a tremendous help, and Vibs has helped a lot with the practical stuff, too."

Gitte moved her gaze from the backyard, watching him speculatively. "I've wanted to ask how you're handling it all, Dan?"

"It's not easy," admitted Dan, shaking his head resignedly. "I know I'm going to miss Ryan a lot."

Gitte nodded. "Don't you think it would be comforting to remind yourself what you shared with Maya Luna the day before she died? The things about life and death you've been speculating about since your conversation with the Master Entity—as you recounted to me in the kitchen almost three weeks ago," said Gitte. "It's certainly been a good support for me to have that understanding and way of looking at life."

For a short moment, Dan was a little astounded, but then smiled at her. "I think you're right, Gitte. Reflecting on those things will probably make it easier."

While they'd been talking, they could see cars arriving and parking by the gate—and soon after, the first guests began approaching on the long gravel driveway.

"I'll stay and welcome people," suggested Dan. "You don't have to be here if you would rather be near Ryan in the basement."

"Thanks, Dan," said Gitte quietly and started walking toward the staircase, but turned around after a few meters. "On a practical note: I would be happy if you and Susan would join me as pallbearers and help carry the bier. It only needs to be rolled on its base to the elevator."

"Thank you, Gitte—we would be honored to," said Dan, moved by her request. Gitte nodded and continued to the staircase and descended to the basement.

Over the next fifteen minutes, all the mourners—fourteen people in all—arrived. Most were dressed in black, many visibly affected by Ryan's death. Dan recognized most of them from Lifeline's board, including the older board member he'd talked to at the summer party. After greeting the guests, he explained the funeral was in the basement, pointing them to the staircase.

One of the people to arrive was Michael, which slightly surprised Dan. They stood for a moment, looking approvingly at each other's formal, dark attire before Michael answered Dan's unspoken question.

"It wasn't my plan to take part today," he explained, "but Gitte said she would appreciate it, so I didn't really have a choice. She also wants me to be a pallbearer, and I've accepted that, too. A little reluctantly, admittedly—mostly because Ryan probably wouldn't like the idea."

"I'm glad you came, Michael," said Dan, hugging Michael. "And I think Ryan cared for you more than you might think. Despite your dislike of each other."

Michael nodded, but still looked skeptical before he followed Dan's instructions and disappeared down the basement stairs.

At five minutes to two o'clock, a black hearse arrived and carefully backed from the gate down the gravel driveway before stopping with its rear end aligned to the garage door. Two undertakers got out and walked to the front door, greeting Dan. One of them encouraged Dan to join the other mourners in the basement—and said they would stay and welcome any participants who might be late.

Back in the basement, Dan was again struck by the solemn atmosphere of the decorations and the dimmed lighting as he walked between the two rows of flower-adorned cars.

As he approached the far end of the room, he saw that most of the folding chairs were now filled with the black-clad guests. A few were conversing in hushed voices, but most sat in silence, looking contemplatively at Ryan's casket. In the front row, Gitte sat in the middle, with the older board member on one side and Vibs on the other. In the flanking chairs were two other board members from Ryan's company, one of whom was the CEO from the hospital where Ryan had died. Michael sat two rows back, with two board members on one side and two people Dan didn't know on the other.

After walking along the rows of chairs, Dan sat down on the empty seat between Susan and Anette. Both smiled compassionately at him, and Susan took his hand, holding it firmly as he leaned to her and whispered what Gitte had asked of them. Susan looked a little surprised and said nothing, but nodded after thinking about it for a few seconds.

After the congregation had waited in silence for a few minutes, the older board member stood up and walked over to Ryan's casket, where she turned and glanced out over the small gathering. After introducing herself, she thanked everyone for attending.

"Gitte has asked me if I would say a few words at Ryan's bier," she said, smiling sympathetically at Gitte. "And I'm honored and grateful for that. Thank you, Gitte."

Across the people in front of him, Dan could see Gitte nodding briefly.

The older board member turned again and looked at the large image of Ryan for a moment before proceeding. She told of her first meeting with Ryan—many years before Lifeline—and how she knew from the start that he was an extraordinary man with some remarkable abilities. She then depicted some of her experiences with him that reflected his character and unique approach to life and problem-solving. Her anecdotes brought smiles to the faces of the participants, sometimes followed by a tear. Most nodded, agreeing to her description of Ryan's life—either because they'd been part of the events she described or if they simply recognized Ryan's personality in her depiction.

"But I can't give an honest and complete description of Ryan, the man, without mentioning his great handicap," she continued with a regretful look before placing her hand on the casket. "I'm so sorry, dear Ryan—but I think most people here already know what I'm talking about."

Many of the guests nodded while she turned back to face the group of mourners.

"Ryan's disability was that he sometimes had trouble identifying what was right and what was wrong. Especially when he got caught up in an idea for a specific new technology or business opportunity. This was never the result of bad intentions as such—but sometimes his eagerness to solve a problem and complete a task made it difficult for him to see the implications it might have for others. Sometimes, he forgot to ask if a fascinating technical thing he could do was actually something he should do. Fortunately, there were people around him he could consult, who could point out certain aspects of his plans that he might not have taken the proper time to consider—because they didn't directly affect the technical part of his vision."

She took a deep breath and looked warmly at Gitte.

"And here I have to mention you, dear Gitte. You've been an invaluable support to Ryan since that day long ago in Glasgow, when he met you. In a way, you became his conscience, and he was always happiest when he thought of you or when the two of you were together. He adored you, and we who know you understand why. You're special too, Gitte—and undoubtedly the best thing that ever happened to Ryan in his life."

Dan noticed how everyone was nodding, and several leaned over and squeezed Gitte's shoulder. She tried to turn and smile at everyone as best she could, and Dan could see that she had tears in her eyes.

"I would also like to mention Dan and Michael, who—each in their own way—have influenced Ryan's decisions," continued the older board member, smiling at both of them after quickly locating where they were seated. "Dan—I don't think you fully realize how much Ryan appreciated you: your company on the many trips to distant places, your sense of humor, observations, and feedback. You were an essential pillar in Ryan's life, too."

Her words surprised and touched Dan and he completely forgot his shyness, as most of the assembly—including Gitte and Michael—turned and sent him appreciative and encouraging smiles. He felt tears coming to his eyes, and because Anette was now holding his other hand, he couldn't even wipe his eyes, so he settled for nodding and smiling back at everyone.

The elder board member concluded her eulogy, expressing how much Ryan would be missed. After a moment's silence, she asked if anyone else in the assembly wanted to say something, which no one did. She added that there would also be an opportunity to do so after the funeral service—at the commemoration in the living room—which she should say on Gitte's behalf that everyone was welcome to attend.

Then she sat down, and solemn and atmospheric music began playing from the speakers of Ryan's stereo. Dan had heard the music before—it was a slow march from one of Ryan's favorite operas, but he couldn't remember which. Everyone sat still, contemplating the white casket in the dim light, listening intently to the beautiful and emotional music.

After five minutes, the music faded out, and the elderly board member and Gitte got to their feet and walked to opposite sides of the casket, a cue to the other four pallbearers to follow. Dan and Susan rose from their seats and walked to the casket, where they found a place behind the other two. They were followed by Michael and Vibs, who took the last two positions. All the other guests were also standing up.

All six pallbearers standing around the casket grabbed a handle and pulled the bier forward. Slowly they rolled it on its base across the room, between the two rows of cars, to the opposite end of the basement, and into the big elevator where one of the two undertakers received them. The other mourners had quietly followed the casket and now spread out in the elevator. When everyone had entered, the undertaker pressed a button, after which the large door closed, and the elevator slowly began its ascent.

When the elevator had reached its top and stopped, the big garage door opened. As it slowly rolled up, the room was gradually filled with sunlight coming from the outside, much brighter than the glow from the tiny lamps in the garage. Dan noticed the sound of a small electrical motor starting inside the base under the casket, which then slowly rotated ninety degrees on its axis. When it stopped, they pulled it the last stretch to the hearse, where the rear door was now open. The height was perfectly aligned, and it was easy to push the casket from the base into the back of the hearse, where a mechanism pulled the casket the remaining distance into the vehicle.

Gitte stayed by the hearse while Dan, Susan, and the other pallbearers stepped back a few paces and mixed with the rest of the mourners.

"It was Ryan's wish to be burned after his death," said Gitte in a steady voice, audible to everyone, "and for his ashes to be scattered over the Aegean Sea. And so it shall be. I'll fly down there myself in two weeks and make sure it all happens, just like Ryan wanted."

She turned and looked at the casket. "Thanks for everything, Ryan. I'm sure we'll meet again in another dimension."

After she'd stepped back a few steps, the hearse's back door began closing, and when it was completely shut, the vehicle silently set in motion and started its slow drive up the gravel driveway toward the open gate.

An hour and a half later, Dan and Susan sat with Anette and Gitte on the garden sofas below the terrace and relaxed.

After the hearse had left with Ryan's casket, Gitte had invited everyone present to stay for the memorial gathering in the living room. Everyone had accepted and followed Gitte through the entrance hall into the living room, where there were platters of sandwiches and bottles of beer, soft drinks, and water. There were also biscuits and thermoses with coffee and tea.

They hadn't been more people than all could be seated in the large sofa arrangement, with the addition of a couple of folding chairs.

After starting in a somber atmosphere, the mood slowly improved—especially after the older board member had encouraged everyone to share the experiences they'd had with Ryan over the years.

An hour later, the first guests started to say goodbye, and when they were only the four of them left, Gitte had suggested they go outside and sit on the garden sofas. It was evident that she was tired, but relieved that the ceremony was over.

Anette sat next to Gitte on one sofa, and Dan and Susan sat on the opposite side of the coffee table. They said nothing for the first few minutes, enjoying the warm afternoon sun and the bottles of water and cola they'd taken along.

"How beautiful it all was," said Anette a little later. She turned on the sofa so she could talk more directly to Gitte, but still see Dan and Susan on the other sofa. "Thank you for allowing me to take part—I'll never forget it. But it must have been hard for you to say goodbye to Ryan—especially here in your own home?"

"Yes, it was quite exhausting," confessed Gitte. "But I'm relieved it all went as well as it apparently did."

The other three nodded in agreement.

"Gitte, can I ask if you've given any thought to what's going to happen to Lifeline and Ryan's fine collection of cars, or is it too soon?" asked Susan gently. "Please let me know if it's bad form to talk about such mundane things on a solemn day like today."

"That's fine, Susan," Gitte replied graciously. "In fact, it would be nice to share my thoughts with you and hear what you think."

She took a sip of water, put the bottle on the table, and presented her plan.

"The short version is that I'm going to sell everything: this house, Ryan's cars—and both Ryan's and my shares in the Lifeline company. I probably could have closed the company if I wanted to—but I would feel bad for all the people who would then lose their jobs. Maybe new management and a couple of new board members can come up with some better products than the Lifeline document. Although, if you look at it generously, you might consider it a kind of harmless entertainment that doesn't necessarily have to give the customer anything of lasting value."

It was evident that she was slowly getting weary after a long day with many tasks and emotions. For a moment, she sat silent, watching the view over the Sound, and then she looked at Dan.

"I'll also try to find a way for Dan and Michael to get back the rights to their Avaram system—so it can be applied for something useful and be further developed—if you would like that?"

The generous offer came as a complete surprise to Dan, who'd never imagined such a prospect. Speechless, he looked quizzically at Gitte to see if she was serious. She smiled and nodded affirmatively.

"I'm sure no one will take better care of it than you guys—and use it wisely and constructively."

Although completely overwhelmed, Dan managed to express his deep gratitude, saying that he knew Michael would be as happy with the proposal as he was. For a moment, he almost forgot what a sad day it was.

"On a personal level, I plan to keep up my consulting work," said Gitte after a few seconds, "and at the same time, look for a new mission I can commit myself to with life and soul."

She smiled knowingly at Dan as she continued.

"First, though, we need to make some simplifications to the Lifeline system so that the output isn't quite as, uh, detailed as it is now. Dan, would you be able to meet me at the City Tower tomorrow morning and help me with some of the necessary steps?"

Dan glanced at Anette and was about to suggest another time—because Friday was one of Anette's treatment days—but Anette beat him to it.

"I'm taking the metro to my meeting at the addiction center tomorrow, Dan," she said, smiling but firm. "And I can do that—or use my bike—for the rest of my meetings."

"Great!" said Dan after briefly assessing Anette's proposal. "Well, then I'll drop by the City Tower tomorrow morning."

After an emotional goodbye, Dan, Susan, and Anette left Gitte and headed back to Anette's apartment on Amager.

During the drive, Susan and Anette talked about Gitte and how exceptionally she'd handled the whole arrangement. Dan was caught up in his own thoughts. There were several things he wanted to discuss with Gitte in private when they met the next day. Among other things, there were some strange incidents that he'd recently begun to piece together.

During the ceremony in the basement, he hadn't thought about it, but while all the mourners had been gathered for the memorial in the living room—and while the four had talked in the garden—he hadn't been able to look at Gitte without being reminded of his suspicion that she might intentionally have killed Ryan.

Moreover, he was surprised that Gitte had explicitly referred to the Master Entity when they'd spoken in the entrance hall.

He knew he'd never mentioned it by name—neither to Gitte nor Susan, who were the only people he'd spoken to about his spiritual experience.

TWENTY-SEVEN

Friday morning, Dan took the metro from the Vesterbro district to the Nordhavn district and walked the last stretch to the City Tower.

After using the elevator to get to the seventh floor, Dan walked into Lifeline's reception. Here he briefly glanced at the two white sofas where he'd sat and talked with Ryan three weeks earlier—the first time he'd come to the new building—and thought about how many strange and unexplainable things had happened since then. He had an uneasy feeling that it wasn't over and that there still remained problems waiting to be solved, as well as questions that might stay unanswered.

At the large desk with the Lifeline logo, Gitte sat and smiled at Dan as he walked across the room.

"Hi, Dan," she said cheerfully as he reached the desk. Dan almost expected her to go on and welcome him to Lifeline, just as Vibs had done the first time he'd been there.

"Hi, Gitte. Thanks for making yesterday so special—it was a beautiful farewell to Ryan."

"Thanks. That's sweet of you—and I'm glad your mom and Susan were there, too. It was an invaluable support to have you guys around me."

For a moment, neither of them said anything, and Gitte seemed to have her mind elsewhere.

"Have you been promoted to receptionist?" asked Dan with an approving smile.

"Yes, it's more convenient that I sit here, so I don't have to step out from the conference room whenever there's a guest or a parcel—or an employee who needs to discuss something with me."

She stood up and pointed toward the glass door to the conference room. "But let's sit down and have a chat. I think there are some important issues we would both be happy to get settled."

Gitte sat down on Ryan's chair at the end of the big conference table, and Dan chose the first chair on her right, moving one place—from where he usually sat at board meetings—to Gitte's old seat. For a few seconds, she just sat and looked appraisingly at Dan.

"I know you suspect me of having killed Ryan," she said out of the blue. Dan was too shocked to say anything.

"I could see that in your eyes yesterday at the memorial," she continued, without taking her eyes off him. "The analytical way you kept looking at me. You'd deduced it had to be me who made the scratches in Ryan's Jaguar."

And wrote the subtle message, Dan thought to himself. It surprised him she brought up the horrible events the day after the funeral. Especially since she apparently didn't try to hide that she was the one who'd done it.

"And I openly admit that I'm complicit in Ryan's death. But there was no other option, no other path we could take."

He could see Gitte watching him, waiting to see how he would react.

"I suppose I ought to report you to the police for this?" asked Dan rhetorically. Her admission had shocked him, mainly because it seemed utterly uncalled for. What interest might she have in confirming his unspoken suspicions about something he would never be able to prove and perhaps had no interest in revealing? With the confession, she could, at a minimum, be convicted of vandalism and possibly even manslaughter.

However, he sensed that Gitte's revelation was only the first step toward a conversation on another and even more far-reaching subject, which he himself wouldn't have dared to bring up.

"Yes, but you won't do that," replied Gitte, ascertaining but accommodating, "because you also suspect that the incident is part of something greater. Something infinitely greater."

He couldn't help feeling hurt that she now referred to Ryan's death as merely an incident. Still, he tried to ignore his feelings because she was apparently signaling that he could safely ask her about the other suspicion that had been growing for some time. He'd speculated about it whenever he was with Gitte or talking to her on the phone, as well as in quiet moments when he tried to correlate his experience with the Master Entity and their new insight into the karma sequence—how it controlled, or at the very least predicted, the length of any human's life.

"I think you're in contact with the Master Entity," he said tentatively. It wasn't a question, although he couldn't be sure of the preliminary conclusion he'd reached. Over the past few weeks, some indications, small and large, had made him consider that scenario. In the beginning, as an unlikely possibility, but recently, more and more as a likely explanation. First, there had been her reaction when he told her about his conversation with the Master Entity, and the most recent example was the day before when she'd mentioned the Master Entity by name, even though Dan was certain he hadn't used that term once in any of their conversations.

The look on Gitte's face hadn't changed when he presented his theory—she just sat and nodded speculatively.

"Yes," she said after a long moment. "That's correct. But so are you, Dan—all humans are part of the Master Entity. It is the *self* within you that consciously observes your body and mind, your feelings and thoughts. You think the *self* is isolated to you and your person—your consciousness—and separate from other people's similar experiences. But there's only one *self* in the cosmos. The identification with your own person is an illusion created by your mind. Not an illusion for the *self*—only for your own personality, which sees itself as an independent individual, separate from the surrounding world and other people."

Gitte paused to give him a chance to let it all sink in. It was clear that she was aware of how big a leap it was for him to take. He could feel the analytical part of his mind working at full speed, looking for a more rational and scientific alternative. Like when Ryan had introduced him to his and Gitte's theory that the Lifeline system had started predicting when people would die and the many succeeding events while working with the karma sequence.

At the same time, he also felt a more profound sense and awareness that it had to be right—and that he had no choice but to give in and accept it. Even though his mind was still trying to keep up a desperate resistance to the understanding, a resistance it already knew would be futile.

"You've known this for a long time," said Gitte quietly. "But you simply weren't sure you dared to believe it."

He looked at her and nodded, even though he could feel there was still some way to go before reaching the full realization.

"On a deeper level, you haven't been in doubt since your first conversation with the Master Entity. This was also the insight you shared with Maya Luna when you spoke to her the day before she died. What's happening in you right now is that, on the analytical level, you're slowly accepting a truth that you've long understood on the emotional level. It's a real paradigm shift—an understanding that will influence all your considerations and decisions from now on."

"That pretty much describes how I feel right now, Gitte," said Dan after surveying his feelings. "But I actually think I can say that I'm almost at the point of rationally understanding what you're describing. Many things, big and small, have happened recently that make it easy for me to adjust my analytical outlook on life to the new situation. After all, the discovery of the karma sequence is incontrovertible evidence of something supernatural. What you're now telling me about the Master Entity is probably the simplest model for explaining that phenomenon. I still need to understand a lot, technically, about how the karma sequence is created and monitored. But that's somewhat insignificant compared to the simple but all-encompassing explanation you've just put into words."

Gitte smiled at him. "There's still a lot I don't understand, too—but I think the technical details are slightly less important once you understand the general elements of the system."

"That's probably true," said Dan. "But even though it's new and overwhelming, one part of me wants to understand all the elements in detail, while another feels satisfied just knowing the overall context. You said before that everyone's *self* is part of the Master Entity. Why aren't more people reaching that realization?"

Dan immediately saw the irony of the question, given how new the revelation was to him—and how many changes he'd had to go through before he understood it himself.

"There are probably more people aware of the shared *self* in the Master Entity than you think," replied Gitte. "But only some of them have a direct dialogue with it. Often they may have a dialogue, but without knowing who or what they're talking to—or they attribute it to hallucinations and other local effects in the mind. A few have *realized* that they can have a dialogue with the Master Entity and consult with it for help. The bottom line is that a central piece of themselves is already part of the Master Entity."

"May I ask how you found out about all this yourself?" asked Dan interestedly.

"Of course," replied Gitte. "And I would be more than happy to explain, even if it's a somewhat different story in my case."

She took a deep breath, reached for her bottle, and took a sip. It seemed she was searching for the best way to explain it.

"Most people who gain this insight do so through long study and meditation, typically based on a desire to understand how and why the cosmos works—in a more comprehensive way than is possible with the natural sciences, which can explain many things but not everything. But additionally, there are a few who have the insight from birth—or rather long before birth—and I belong to that special group. I guess a neurological defect or mutation in a specific part of the brain causes the illusion of ego—the *self* as something separate from the rest of the world—to malfunction."

Gitte smiled as she continued.

"You could say that my challenge, from a very young age, has been the reverse. I had to learn that people around me didn't have this knowledge and that they each saw themselves—and each other—as small, isolated islands of consciousness, in an empirical and shared external reality."

Although Dan didn't fully understand Gitte's explanation of what had happened to her, he believed he could imagine what the process must have been like. At the same time, he wondered how many people had the insight and whether it was something everyone could achieve.

"All this, with the shared *self* in the Master Entity, is that something that, for example, Michael would be able to understand?"

"Absolutely," replied Gitte matter-of-factly. "Intellectually, he's already closer than he thinks—but it's always hard for the conscious mind to let go of the illusion that it's the main and deciding thing and not only a limited part of the specific person and personality. And the last stretch is almost impossible to walk by oneself, without the help of the Master Entity—directly or indirectly."

"Am I allowed to talk to Susan about it?"

"Sure—you can share it with anyone you want. Thousands of people already do. The shared *self* in the Master Entity isn't a secret—it's just difficult for most people to understand."

She smiled at him and shook her head resignedly. "Just be prepared for people to think you're either a religious fanatic or a nutcase when you try to explain it. The ego doesn't let go of the illusion of an individual and autonomous personality that easily."

Dan decided that he would try to explain it to both Susan and his mother. They probably wouldn't question his seriousness—besides, he'd shared a lot with them already. Maybe he could even talk to the Master Entity and ask for its help.

As he considered how to share his knowledge with those closest to him—and perhaps even with more people who could potentially use the insight to help solve their problems—the expression on Gitte's face changed, and she got a severe look in her eyes.

"But you can never tell anyone about the karma sequence and its structure in the human genome! It's a central part of the overall cosmic governance and evolution, with information on how to realize the potential and purpose of all biological beings. Every human depends on the notion of free will. And although most people are reasonably aware of their own physical limitations, few would be able to live normal lives if they also knew the precise time limitation—besides the other values encoded in the karma sequence. They would lose the illusion of free will."

Gitte smiled and lifted her hand preemptively, knowing what Dan was about to ask. "Perhaps you'll get an understanding of the other blocks in the sequence at a later point in time. Some of it is much more advanced than the omega value and the indication of the person's gender that you and Michael have so far identified in the sequence."

Dan nodded, accepting Gitte's arguments against sharing their knowledge of the karma sequence with anyone—although he thought there could probably be good reasons for doing so. This was precisely the dilemma they'd faced since the discovery of the karma sequence, but he was glad that a clear and unambiguous decision had now been made about its fate. A decision he couldn't dream of questioning or challenging—partly because he now had a sense of what he risked if he tried.

He chose not to mention that he'd already told Susan about the karma sequence, but made a mental note to tell her she could never talk about it with anyone but him.

"But isn't there a risk that someone else will find the pattern and guess, or figure out, the meaning of the karma sequence?" asked Dan.

"Yes," answered Gitte. "But in the long history of life, it's only now—with the sequencing of the human genome—that this risk has arisen. That's why I and many others are constantly working to ensure no one discovers and shares the pattern. Maybe it'll be necessary to move the information out of the genome. It's just a super convenient place to store it—along with all the other data that codes for the individual's traits and characteristics."

"We found the sequence by pure chance because our Primus AI showed us where it was and how the omega value could be extracted from it. So, I think it's pretty safe, many years into the future," said Dan.

"That's my assessment, too," said Gitte, nodding thoughtfully. "And that's why it's important that we turn off that AI as soon as possible—and delete all the setup and source code. We need to make sure there are no backup files and prints and whatever else could be used to recreate the AI or parts of it."

Dan nodded. Though they didn't know how the AI had located the karma sequence—and would never be able to find out once it was deleted—it felt like the right solution in every way except for the satisfaction of his technical curiosity. But that seemed like an insignificant detail—not least compared to the understanding of the way the universe worked which he might be facing.

"Do you think we can get Michael in on it too?" asked Gitte cautiously.

"No doubt about it," replied Dan optimistically. "After all, he's been hoping for the same decision as you've recommended ever since we discovered that the omega value came from the sequence in the genome. His dislike of Ryan has only increased throughout the period where no decision was made that he felt we could vouch for ethically."

"Yes, we—and our guests—experienced that last Friday at the summer party," said Gitte with a wry smile. "I really worried that, in his rage, he was going to blurt out the karma sequence to everyone—so it was great that you got him and Ryan down in the basement."

"Thanks. Yes, unfortunately, Michael sometimes tends to overreact if he feels something isn't right."

"It'll help when he gets better at viewing his emotions as something separate from himself," said Gitte. "And that will happen. In fact, that's what I was talking to him about when you and Susan found us at the party—on the tiny bench at the end of the garden."

Dan nodded, thinking back on how it had looked like they were holding hands on the bench. However, it wasn't the right time to ask Gitte if she and Michael were having an affair. The question reminded him of Ryan, whom he hadn't thought about after Gitte had started explaining about the Master Entity.

"Did you try to explain the Master Entity to Ryan?" he asked. "Don't you think that insight would have caused him to drop his plans with the karma sequence?"

"I've spent a lot of energy trying to get him to understand the Master Entity and how we're all part of it," replied Gitte resignedly as she sank back into her chair. "But he never budged an inch. He couldn't believe in something so abstract—something he couldn't measure and weigh or test and prove in other ways. If he'd only been flexible on that point, he would have had an easier time understanding why no one must know about the karma sequence, too."

"But couldn't it have been solved more humanely than by him dying?"

"Maybe. But I couldn't see any other way out, even though it was the hardest thing I've ever had to do."

Dan reflected on his many experiences with Ryan and his zest for life, his energy and ability to solve technical problems, and, not least, his optimism about the future.

"Why didn't the omega value in Ryan's karma sequence match the day he died?" he asked after remembering the difference.

Gitte nodded slowly while contemplating how to answer the question.

"Put simply," she explained after a few seconds, "nothing in the karma sequence is one hundred percent static—not even the omega value. Most people have no major upheavals or decisions in life—they follow the impulses and motives they're genetically endowed with. But occasionally, someone does something so radically unusual and unexpected that it requires an adjustment in one or more values of their karma sequence. And when someone is on the verge of discovering the meaning of the karma sequence, for example, the Master Entity may decide to override one of these values. As a system developer, you'll probably understand this better by comparing it to a computer's operating system."

Dan nodded. "Each process follows its individual instructions, but if it becomes a threat to the core, it'll be terminated?"

"Exactly," replied Gitte appreciatively. "And the analogy is actually much closer to the real-life system than you can imagine. Only the Master Entity can end a person's life, but it can ask any of us to deliver a message."

For example, by scratching it all over an expensive car, Dan thought, but chose not to say it out loud. He didn't know what to say and still had a hard time accepting that a human being had to die in order to prevent the knowledge from being shared. Even if Ryan was about to tamper with something he absolutely shouldn't touch.

"I loved Ryan too and will miss him," said Gitte a moment later, probably because she could feel Dan's frustration over Ryan's death.

"But I'll tell you something I'm probably not supposed to share with you; now that it's all resolved in another manner. You must prepare to be shocked."

Gitte looked expectantly at Dan before continuing. He nodded, although he didn't know if he could handle more surprises in one day.

"You would have died a year ago at the rock bottom of the dark hole from your alcohol abuse if the Master Entity hadn't talked to you."

Dan said nothing. It didn't seem like a big revelation; he'd reached the same conclusion himself. But suddenly, he understood what she was implying.

"You were the one who asked the Master Entity to step in and help me!" he said in surprise. Now that he knew the meaning of the Master Entity and Gitte's connection to it, it surprised him he hadn't thought of it earlier in their conversation. Suddenly, the complete overview became much more personal to him and his understanding of his way out of the addiction.

Gitte had intervened and saved his life.

He took her hand and squeezed it, but didn't know what to say. Tears welled up in his eyes, but he couldn't help smiling.

Empathically, Gitte smiled back as she gently tried to pull her hand back. "I only mention it to show that the problem wouldn't have existed if I hadn't intervened, and you'd died back then. Ryan certainly wouldn't have contacted Michael about the omega value, but instead, some other developer who wouldn't know the system and who I don't think would have found and understood the karma sequence like you two did. And Ryan would never have gained the detailed understanding of the structure of the karma sequence that you gave him after you and Michael had discovered it."

"I'm afraid you're right," said Dan, trying to wipe his eyes with his free hand. "The whole thing would have been simpler for everyone; and poor Ryan would still be alive."

It suddenly occurred to him he might be the one who—directly or indirectly—had given Ryan all the knowledge and ideas he needed to come up with his ominous plans.

"Maybe, maybe not," said Gitte. "I only mention it as an example of the omega value being actively circumvented by the Master Entity. If you have your genome sequenced one day, you'll see your omega value confirms that you would have died that day last year. Unless your karma sequence has already been updated."

On the way home to Susan's apartment in the Vesterbro district, Dan sat on the metro and thought about the overload of impressions he'd received during his meeting with Gitte. He was oblivious to what was happening around him and almost forgot to get off at the right station.

His mind was full of different thoughts, attempting to understand all the new information he'd received—and he knew it would take some time before it all fell into place and became a natural part of his self-understanding and outlook on life. He looked forward to sharing it all with Susan.

And at some point, he might learn to understand the Master Entity and perhaps even communicate with it. Reluctantly, he promised himself not to be disappointed if it never happened. Gitte had said that she didn't doubt that he had high morals and human understanding and was capable of good analysis and sound decision-making. She was convinced there was a good chance he would hear from the Master Entity. And even if that didn't happen, it was essential to remember that the Master Entity always listened when he consciously addressed it.

Late at night, Dan suddenly woke up to find that Susan had turned on the light and was gently squeezing his arm.

"Are you okay, Dan?" she asked. "You don't usually talk in your sleep, but I woke up because you were lying there mumbling some weird words."

"All is well," he replied, and turned to kiss her. "I just had an amazing conversation."

EPILOGUE

On a sunny Saturday in late August, Dan and Susan got married.

Dan had put his apartment in the Østerbro district up for sale after first offering it to his mother, who'd been grateful for the proposition but preferred to stay in her apartment on the Amager island. However, he'd kept the summer house, where he and Susan—and often Anette too—typically spent their weekends and where they'd been during most of Susan's summer holiday.

On days when he wasn't working at home—sitting in his and Susan's living room, working on his book—he took the bike or metro to Michael's apartment in the Nørrebro district. They were updating their Avaram system, which—with Gitte's generous help—they'd been able to buy back from Lifeline at a reasonable price. Working on discovering the karma sequence had reminded them how effective they could be and how much they enjoyed their collaboration.

The Primus AI had also been taken out of the Lifeline system, and all source code and other evidence of its existence had been found and deleted. At least they were sure of that.

Their family and friends were present at the town hall where the wedding took place, and afterward, everyone went home to Susan and Dan's apartment in the Vesterbro district to celebrate. Susan's parents and her sister had come from Jutland—the peninsula in the western part of Denmark—to attend, and in addition to Dan's mother, Michael and Gitte also took part; along with a handful of Susan's colleagues and friends.

When the guests arrived back at the apartment, after the official part of the ceremony, they gathered in the living room, where Anette unveiled a large painting she'd made as a wedding gift. Dan and Susan had seen the picture the day before when they all had hung it on the wall—but Susan had insisted they do a proper unveiling, with Anette pulling a bed sheet away from the painting.

Everyone applauded and praised the picture, comprising many large and small abstract symbols and figures but kept in a color tone that gradually changed from blue at the top to green at the bottom. Dan and Susan were delighted with the picture, which fit perfectly in their living room.

Anette, who'd now fully recovered and didn't miss the alcohol—and certainly not the years of addiction—had found an art workshop on Amager where she could work on her pieces. A few galleries had already shown an interest in her work.

Before they all sat down at the dining table, which had been extended with two picnic tables, Susan tapped a glass to get everyone's attention. When the conversations had died down, Susan and Dan took each other's hand and told Anette that she was going to be a grandmother. Anette had tears in her eyes and didn't know what to say, but crossed the room and hugged both of them simultaneously. After everyone had congratulated and shared their joy with Dan and Susan, Dan noticed Gitte standing close to Michael, looking at him as she removed a thread or something that had apparently been on his shirt.

When Anette had recovered from the big news, she asked Dan and Susan if it was a boy or a girl. Susan smilingly replied that they'd decided not to know in advance—and that it was actually Dan's suggestion to wait until the baby was born to find out. Whatever it was, they knew they would be happy with the baby.

Several guests wondered why they didn't accept the offer to know something specific about the future event so they could prepare in advance—but Dan could tell from Michael and Gitte's smiles that they understood their decision.

* * *

AUTHOR NOTE

Dear Reader,

Thank you for choosing to read my book. As a writer, there is nothing more rewarding than knowing that my words have reached a reader.

I've been writing software for most of my life but decided to focus on writing books at the beginning of 2022. While I had previously tried to write alongside my work, I found it challenging. As a result, I made the decision to redefine myself and my life by becoming a full-time writer.

This novel aims to tell an exciting and captivating story while also sharing my personal experience with addiction. I hope it shows that there is a realistic and tangible way out of addiction, allowing people to regain a sense of meaning and purpose in life. I believe books have the power to change lives, and it's my mission to share this message with as many people as possible.

If you enjoyed reading my book, I would be honored if you could take a few minutes to write a review on the book's

Amazon page. Reviews are vital for independent authors like me. They help attract new readers and ensure that my work reaches a wider audience. Your honest opinion can make a meaningful difference and help others decide whether this book is right for them.

Lastly, I want to emphasize that I read and appreciate every review. Your feedback not only helps me improve my writing but also encourages me to keep creating stories that connect with readers like you.

Thank you again for taking the time to read my book.

Sincerely,

A. O. Wagner

Printed in Poland
by Amazon Fulfillment
Poland Sp. z o.o., Wrocław